Praise for Leonard B. Scott's other novels

Charlie Mike

"One of the finest novels yet written about the war in Vietnam."
The Washington Post

"Enthralling from first page to last... Scott combines romance, humor, tragedy to make this a first-class reading experience."
Military Review

The Last Run

"It's more *Charlie Mike*, but better.... The kind of book that leaves you wanting more."
Atlanta Journal & Constitution

Also by Leonard B. Scott
Published by Ballantine Books:

CHARLIE MIKE
THE LAST RUN

THE
HILL

Leonard B. Scott

BALLANTINE BOOKS • NEW YORK

Grateful acknowledgment is made to Random House, Inc., for
permission to reprint a map from *The Eyewitness History of the
Vietnam War 1961–1975* by George Esper and the Associated Press.
Maps copyright © 1983 by Random House, Inc. Reprinted by
permission of the publisher. Map by Alex Jay.

Library of Congress Catalog Card Number: 88-61367

ISBN 0-345-37347-2

Manufactured in the United States of America

First Trade Edition: March 1989
First Mass Market Edition: September 1991

The battle of Dak To, June–December 1967, happened as told within these pages. Information on United States Army and North Vietnamese units—as well as dates, times, locations, tactics, and casualty figures—is based on U. S. Army declassified technical reports, unit histories, diaries, letters, and personal interviews with survivors.

The names, main characters, and dialogue in this work are fiction. Any resemblance of the fictional characters to real persons living or dead is entirely coincidental.

The single most costly battle of the Vietnam War for U.S. servicemen was the battle of Dak To: they paid dearly.
296 Killed 1,188 Wounded 18 Missing in Action

The Hill is dedicated
to the men who were there

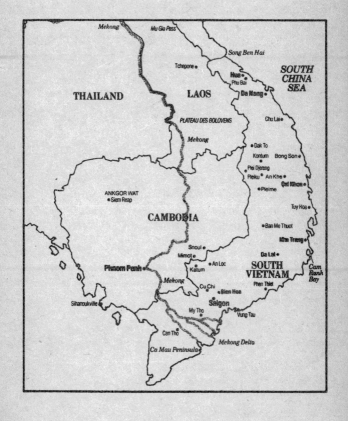

... held his ground without ... a toe and spoke with the same ...

PROLOGUE

It was February 2, 1954, in the Central Highlands of Vietnam. Death was in the wind. The stink of impending destruction was as real as the sudden silence and the clouds of cordite smoke that floated over the small earthen fort. The artillery barrage had been pounding the fort for eight hours. It was only a matter of time before the Vietminh made their final assault. The reinforcement column from Kontum had already been ambushed. They had been the lucky ones—they had died quickly. Those in the fort were not so fortunate. Most of them had suffered agonizingly slow deaths, losing life bit by bit, part by part, lying on bloody bunker floors, wounded and screaming.

Now, only 51 men of the original 206 who had defended the outpost were huddled in earth-covered bunkers on the fort's perimeter, waiting for the inevitable. Among them were French, Vietnamese, Cambodians, Laotians, and Senegalese. They knew they were abandoned. The Southern Plateaux Montagnards force had crumbled. Two other forts along the border had already fallen. Groupement Mobile 100, the battle-hardened elite troops who had fought with the UN forces in Korea, were too far away to help. The fighter-bombers that had kept the enemy at bay had returned to their fields in Nha Trang and Seno to re-arm and refuel. The defenders, lying with their dead comrades, could only sweat and wait. Death was coming.

Major Binh Ty Duc, observing from a hilltop that overlooked the smoking fort one kilometer distant, rose to his full six feet and raised his hand. Slowly he lowered his arm to signal the last barrage. The sound of rounds sliding down mortar tubes sent chills up his spine. After so many years and so much blood, victory was at hand. He watched the compound erupt in flashes of red and orange

1

and in blinding black smoke. The pack-75 howitzers joined in with direct fire from the opposite slope, adding to the din. Major Duc began a slow run down the trail to join his men. He would lead them as always.

Twenty minutes later, Major Duc rose up from the front trench as the mortar rounds slowly crept toward the center of the fort, until it seemed there was a constant geyser of earth and fire at its center. An explosion shook the ground beneath his feet. The last of the wire entanglements was blown to bits by the bamboo bangalore torpedoes. Raising one arm, he yelled to his assault battalion, "FORWARD!"

Over the last echoes of the barrage the defenders in the bunkers could hear a blood-chilling sound—men screaming, hundreds and hundreds of men screaming, "Tien len! Tien len!"

The garrison survivors moved silently to their positions. To die fighting was all that remained. A soldier in the bunker closest to the attack began whistling. Lieutenant Le Bleu, the only remaining officer, heard the sweet sound over the chatter of gunfire and slowly stood up from his covered position. The soldier was whistling "The Marseillaise," the French national anthem. The lieutenant walked through the gunsmoke toward the charging Vietminh with tears in his eyes as he fired his pistol.

Major Binh Ty Duc completed his tour of the battlefield and stopped at the front gate. He lowered his head, sickened by the grisly scene behind him. He had hungered four years for a victory, but not at such a cost. His beloved soldiers of the 108th Battalion had left over ninety men in the lingering, eerie mist of death. Their bodies were strewn over the ground in every conceivable gruesome position. There was no time to bury and honor them. The planes would return soon. Their blood, as well as that of the brave defenders who had exacted the toll, would stain the ground forever.

Eight wounded French lay to his right. By his orders they were not taken prisoner or harmed. Their battle was over. To take them would be to kill them. His battalion would soon force march the forty kilometers to Kontum and finish the remaining outpost there.

When the major turned to join his battalion, he saw one of the wounded Frenchmen staring at him with a look of defiance. The man's wounds were such that he would be scarred forever. Duc took the canteen from his belt and tossed it toward the proud soldier. Someone from this fort had to live and tell of the bravery of the others . . . someone had to remember the battle of Dak To.

1

16 August, 1965, Meyers, Oklahoma

Jason Johnson pushed open the door of the John Deere store and stepped out into the dry Oklahoma heat. The stagnant, hot air smelled of baking dust. He strolled down the sizzling sidewalk, passing the stores and people he knew he would soon be missing. Meyers wasn't much to look at, but it was his hometown. He knew all of the store owners and their families, right down to the names of their dogs. The center of town comprised only two blocks of stores and a stoplight, but it was a place big in heart, where everybody cared about everybody and nothing could stay secret for very long.

"Hiya, Jay."

Jason smiled and turned around, recognizing the unmistakable gravelly voice.

Coach Lambert walked out of the drugstore and extended his hand toward him. Buzz Lambert was a town legend. He had a real talent for organizing scrawny farmers' sons into winning football teams for Meyers High School. He was getting on in years now, but the fire was still in his eyes. "Jay, I wanted ta wish ya the best before ya left for college. I'm headin' upstate for a few weeks and won't be seein' ya before ya go."

Jason shook his hand warmly. Buzz was responsible for getting him the football scholarship to Central State College. "Thanks, Coach. You made it all happen."

Buzz looked the 190-pounder over from head to foot. "Ya been pumping the weights this summer. How much ya put on, ten pounds?"

Jason dipped his head shyly. "Yeah, Coach, I think I'm ready for them." His face came up with a grin. "Wait till you see Ty. We worked out together. He put at least an inch on his chest, and he's even faster than last year."

3

"Did ya work on his damn temper? Your stepbrother could be an all-stater if he wasn't so damn hard-headed. He can't be gettin' thrown out of four games for fightin' like he did last year, or he'll be out of the running."

Jason smiled and put his arm around his coach. "That's why you're the best. You'll work it out of him."

"Ty is the best damn natural hitter I've ever seen. He loves knocking people on their ass. He won't have ya throwing passes to him, so it ain't gonna be the same on offense, but on defense he'll make it. I've already contacted Oklahoma State and Central to come and take a look at him. Hell, he might even be joining you next year." Buzz wiped sweat from his forehead and put out his hand again. "Jay, ya take care of ya'self and watch out for Coach Duggin. He's been at Central for eight years now, and I hear he's turned into a real bastard. Just do what he says, no matter what. The first year is always the toughest."

"I'll make it, Coach. I was taught by the best."

Buzz thumped him on the back. "Me and Meyers will be countin' on ya."

Jimbo Akers shook his head in disgust at the old man and his hound dog sitting on the porch. Cecil Waters, standing beside Jimbo, wasn't going to give up so easily. He put his hands on his flabby hips. "Look, old man, we've been hired by the government for the eradication. You can't stop us from our job!"

George Many Moons rocked in his chair, not looking at the two red-faced men. He raised a gnarled hand and pointed toward the front gate. "Y'all ain't nothin' but bounty hunters. Git off my land."

"Come on, Cecil," Akers said, turning around to leave. "We're wastin' our time with this old bastard. We'll talk to the county game warden."

Cecil pointed a fat finger at the silver-haired Indian. "You should listen to your son-in-law and take the money."

Many Moons kept his stoic expression and continued rocking. The two men strode through the gate toward a bright red pickup. In seconds the Chevy was speeding down the dirt road.

Many Moons smiled and began to get up, but suddenly froze. In the distance he saw the long-awaited vision. It was time. The Chosen Warrior was coming for him at last.

The old man blinked and his eyes began to moisten. His eyes had betrayed him. The shimmering heatwaves distorted the approaching horse and rider's image. The red powdered dust disturbed by the Appaloosa's slow gait swirled upward as if the horse were approaching in a vermillion cloud. It wasn't the vision Many Moons had been waiting for, but he was not disappointed. The bare-chested rider was his own blood. Many Moons felt pride and sadness. The years were passing by too quickly. It seemed like only yesterday that his grandson had been a small boy and had had to climb a fence to mount Sa Tonkee. The young man riding the old gelding was no longer a boy. Raven-haired and broad-shouldered, he looked like a warrior ready for the hunt. His body was lean, exposing rippling muscles and bulging veins that ran up his arm and across his shoulders like thick chords. His Indian blood was evident in his black hair, brown skin, and high cheekbones. But there the influence stopped. He had his father's square jaw and deep-clefted chin and his mother's brown eyes. John Nance would have been proud of him.

Ty Nance swung off the saddle and tossed the reins over the fence. He bent over to pet his grandfather's old, nearly blind coon dog, Rowdy, and looked up the road where the dust of the red pickup was just settling. "Who was that, Granddad? They sure were in a hurry to leave."

Many Moons motioned for a beer from the rusted Coca-Cola icebox across the porch. "Bounty hunters. They want ta hunt coyotes on our land."

Ty took a Coors and a Dr Pepper from the ice water and opened them with a bottle opener hanging from the side of the icebox. "Screw 'em. The coyotes don't bother anything except rabbits, and we got too many of them." He handed the old man the beer and sat down on the wooden porch.

Many Moons shook his head. "They talked to your stepdad and he told 'em they could hunt. They was gonna give me ten dollars for the ones they kilt."

"He can't do that! This is your land. If they paid a hundred dollars it wouldn't make any difference."

Many Moons felt pride at the anger in the boy's eyes. Ty understood. Red Hill was a final sanctuary, the last of the lands that used to be. It was a haven for trees and animals, the only place for miles around unspoiled by man's greedy hands and machines.

"Don't worry none. I told 'em it weren't for Duane to say if they could hunt on my land. I told 'em ta git."

Ty gave his grandfather a reassuring nod. "I'll watch out for 'em."

Many Moons weakly raised his beer as if in a toast. "The Coon Dog and me gonna protect our hill together."

Ty smiled as he lifted his bottle and took a drink. His grandfather had called him "Coon Dog" since he was five, after he'd gone on his first coon hunt. He didn't remember the hunt, but Many Moons had told him he'd cried most of the night, wanting to run with the dogs.

Ty took another drink and motioned with the bottle down the road.

"The big split paw was in your watermelons again. I checked the field and found some half-eaten melons with his tracks all around."

Many Moons's brown, wrinkled face seem to sadden as he gazed down the dusty road. "The old cuss is gettin' along in years, like Rowdy and me. He can't hunt anymore. He eats them melons to live out the summer." The old man's voice trailed off as he lowered his head and stared at his hands. He knew he was like his dog and the old coyote—he wouldn't live to see the winter.

Ty sensed his grandfather's depression. The old man's worn, faded overalls were stained from dribbled chewing tobacco. He was looking weaker than Ty had ever seen him.

He stood up. "Come on, Granddad, let's go up to the meadow. We'll visit the family, then see the sunset."

Many Moons lifted his head, brightening. "It'd be good to see our place again . . . Come on, Dawg." He took Ty's hand and pulled himself up.

Ty held his grandfather's arm to support him as they walked around the shack and followed a path that wound its way through the majestic trees and up the hill. Rowdy followed as they walked the five hundred or so yards out onto a small, grassy field, which covered the hilltop. In the center of the field were three headstones, and near them, a log bench Ty had made a few years before. Ty stopped between the first two markers and squatted down to pull out a few weeds. Beneath the red soil was his grandmother, his uncle Richard, and the father he had hardly known. Sergeant John Nance had been killed in Korea in 1952, leaving behind his five-year-old son. Next to his father was Corporal Richard Many Moons, George's own son, who died in Italy during World War II. The three resting souls, and the stories his grandfather told about them, were part of this hill Ty loved.

Standing over Richard's grave, Many Moons stole a glance at Ty. The young man was like Richard in so many ways that he often thought of the boy as his lost son.

The old man's eyes shifted to the middle grave, and he knelt down to pull out a milkweed by his wife's headstone. Mea, his daughter and Ty's mother, was his wife's favorite. He had often thought how proud his wife would have been of Mea when the telegram had come with the news about John. Mea had found love again and had gotten married again ten years ago to Duane Johnson, a widower like herself. His boy, Jason, was a year older than Ty. Duane was good to Mea, but for some reason he'd never taken to Ty.

He pulled another weed and stood up. Deep inside he knew he had needed Ty as much as the boy had needed him.

Tossing the weeds into the wind, Many Moons turned around to take in the view that had given his heart strength for so many years. He stood on the highest elevation in the county. He'd been given the land in the early twenties by his father, who first settled Red Hill's 1,280 acres. To the north were the rich Canadian Valley bottomlands, and five miles distant, the small town of Meyers. To the south, beyond the trees, was the hidden ravine, and stretching for miles beyond that was the Washita Valley. To the east stood a thick hardwood forest that covered a descending ridge for three-quarters of a mile down to U.S. Highway 81. The road was the eastern boundary of his land and ran due north and south like a magnetic arrow. To the west, on another gentle ridge, was the old cedar grove.

The bare lands around Red Hill were cultivated by their neighbors with cotton, wheat, and alfalfa, so the hill bore the only trees for miles around. Like his ancestors, Many Moons had kept only a garden and a few small fields cleared, enough to grow a little food to live on.

Many Moons had given Mea five acres for a wedding present in 1946, and later he and John had built her and his new son a house before John left for Korea. Duane, her new husband, had since expanded the home, which was situated three-quarters of a mile away at the northern base of the hill. Many Moons had lived in the house with them for the past year because of his age. He couldn't get around with his arthritis and couldn't cook for himself in the shack. Mea or Ty drove him every day to the shack his father had built. The shack wasn't much, but it was on his hill and was the home that held his memories.

Ty joined his granddad and walked him to the log bench. They sat down with Rowdy at their feet and looked to the west, where the sinking sun painted the horizon in brilliant orange and red.

Ty put his arm around the old man's shoulder. Many Moons's frailness made Ty want to cry. Just a year ago he had weighed thirty pounds more and was as spry as a fifty-year-old. He had built barns and sheds for neighbors and had taught Ty all his skills as a master carpenter. But in just the last two months, his grandfather's eighty-four years of living had caught up to him.

Ty gave him a gentle hug and motioned toward the magnificent view. "Have the sunsets always been like this?"

Many Moons nodded. "It depends on who ya share 'em with. Your grandma and me saw the most wonderful sunsets the sun ever painted. Later it was Richard and me who sat on this hill. Now, over these past years, me and you have had some fine sunsets."

Ty kept his eyes on the horizon. "Granddad, what kind of woman was Grandma?"

Many Moons looked up at the darkening sky. "She was a white flower so purtay I couldn't take my eyes off her. We met at Fort Reno, where I was workin', trainin' the Army's horses. She brought some of her students from the Indian school where she was teachin', and I took her ridin'. The magic happened that no one can explain. The magic was strong enough for a young white woman to give up everything for me. She was like your mom, one hell'va woman."

Ty looked at his grandfather with questioning eyes. "But you gave up a lot, too?"

Many Moons smiled, reflecting. "Yep. The tribe and my folks didn't understand, and there was some problems, but the magic was too strong to separate us."

"Why didn't you remarry like Mom? Grandma has been gone twenty years."

The old man patted Ty's leg affectionately and looked back at the sunset. "Because the magic is still in me. She still rides with me in my heart and my dreams."

Ty knew his grandmother only by her grave and the single picture that sat on a shelf in his mother's living room. The woman was small and plain but had a smile that always made him feel sad for not having known her. She stood by a young man wearing an Army uniform who looked like Ty himself. The young man was her son, Richard.

Ty's thoughts turned to his father. From his dad he had only a picture and a few Army papers. John Nance had been a member of a platoon that was protecting a pass. The Chinese had attacked their position in human waves and had been beaten back three times. Sergeant Nance took command of the few survivors who had run out of ammunition and had led his men in a desperate bayonet charge when the weakened Chinese unit had tried a final assault. The charge had been successful, but John Nance had died in the attempt, never knowing a relief force had arrived and saved the rest of his men.

Ty knew his father had wanted to come home to him, just as his uncle Richard had wanted to come home to George, but they were Chosen. His grandfather had once explained, years before, that those who were taken before their time were the spirit world's children. The Chosen remained in the hearts and minds of their loved ones just as they were in life. They would always be remembered as young and in their prime, never growing old and wrinkled. The Chosen's spirits were the strongest of the spirit world and were the most cherished by the living.

Ty knew his dad didn't feel the cold of Korea or the pain of his wounds. He was happy on the hill he had loved.

Ty looked at his grandfather, knowing the old man wouldn't come home tonight. He would want to stay in the old shack. Many Moons was drawing strength from his hill and needed to be with his wife and son again in his dreams.

"I'll walk you back to the shack and fix you somethin' to eat," he said. "I'll explain to Mom why you're stayin'."

Many Moons eyed his grandson. "How'd ya know I wanted ta stay?"

Ty glanced at the headstones, then at the magnificent view before him. He rose slowly and held out his hand for his grandfather. "I just knew."

Ty put his arm around his grandfather. Many Moons felt his eyes moisten. Ty was the last of his blood, his last connection with youth. Many Moons could see the boy growing and coming to understand the world. His only regret was that he knew his own time was short and there were still so many things he wanted to say and teach to his grandson.

Ty opened the door of the shack and set the rocking chair down beside the small bed. He lit the kerosene lamp as his grandfather sat down and reached under the bed for something. Ty opened the valve of the butane tank and lit the stove. "You sure this spaghetti will be enough?"

"Plenty," his grandfather said, then held up the yellowed cigar box he'd retrieved from under the bed. "By the way, I thought you might like to have this, Coon Dog."

Ty sat on the bed and, almost shyly, took the box from his grandfather's hands. He stared at it for several seconds. He knew what it was—a treasure chest of his grandfather's memories. Many Moons had often talked about how this little container was his only link to the past. Finally, he opened it.

Lying on top of the contents was a picture like the one his mother had of his grandmother and Richard. Beneath it was a picture Ty had never seen before. It was a close-up photo of Richard in his uniform. The resemblance to himself was uncanny. The young soldier was smiling proudly. On his shirt was a parachute badge. Beneath the picture were some medals, patches, three opened letters from Italy, and, on a silver chain, the silver parachute wings.

Ty felt a tingle run up his spine. He looked at the picture again, feeling closer to Richard than ever before. He glanced at the contents and thought how simple his grandfather's treasures were, but they somehow were what he had expected. Many Moons always thought of his family and the land as the real wealth of his life.

Many Moons nodded toward the box. "Your daddy wore that parachute badge. I gave your dad Richard's wings when he went to parachute school before going to Korea. They were a living part of my own son."

Ty ran his fingers over the silver badge in reverence. He had seen pictures of his dad in uniform but hadn't realized the meaning of the wings on his chest. Neither his mother nor his granddad had ever mentioned both men resting on Red Hill were paratroopers.

He now understood why his grandfather wanted to give him his treasure box. Tears trickled down Ty's face as he closed the lid.

2

Mea Johnson set the plate of fried pork chops on the kitchen table and took her seat. Duane, her husband, looked at the two empty chairs beside her and angrily stabbed a piece of the meat with his fork. "They could at least get to dinner on time!"

Mea didn't respond. It would be of no use. She passed a bowl of mashed potatoes across the table to Jason, who gave her a look of support.

Duane shook his head as he cut the chop. "This is it. You talk to your dad again. He's too old to be up at the shack all day. He's getting senile. Today some bounty hunters came by the store asking permission to hunt coyotes on the hill. They offered ten dollars a hide. But they called me again before I closed. Said George threw them off the land." He took a bite. "He needs to be in a home where he can get some professional care."

Mea's brow furrowed. "Dad couldn't live in a rest home. It'd kill him. He's having a hard enough time adjusting to staying with us. Just leave him be, Duane. He's happy on his hill."

Duane sighed and put down his fork. "What about that son of yours? He's turning into a bum staying around George. He needs a real job instead of mooching off our neighbors. The kid needs responsibility. He's been around your father too long."

Mea winced at the sting in his words. "Ty isn't mooching, he's working hard and making good money."

She didn't answer his comment about Ty being like her father because it was true . . . and she was secretly proud of it.

"Yeah, he's making a few dollars," Duane persisted, "but he's spendin' it on that old car George gave him. He hasn't saved one dime for college. And *you* always let him do whatever he wants to do."

Mea didn't speak. Maybe he would drop the subject if she didn't argue. She knew Ty could never live up to Duane's expectations the way Jason had. It was impossible for Duane to understand that the boys were different. Jason had responded positively to her husband's unmerciful pushing and browbeating. Ty had rebelled. He wanted no part of the sort of life Duane wanted him to live.

She looked across the table at Jason. "Gravy, honey?" As Jason took the bowl and set it down, she studied his handsome face. He resembled his father: six feet tall and muscular with fair skin and sandy blond hair. And he was everything his father had wanted him to be: smart, athletic, and a natural leader.

Mea broke her gaze from her stepson as footsteps sounded on the back porch. The screen door opened and Ty stepped into the kitchen.

" 'Bout time," Duane grunted.

Mea looked at Ty with concern. "Where's Dad?"

Ty winked at Jason and walked to the sink to wash his hands. "He stayed up at the cabin. I fed him and I'll go up later and stay with him."

Mea nodded in understanding, but Duane shook his head. "The hell you will! You've been bumming around up there too much as it is. Let him stay on his hill; maybe he'll get hungry enough to appreciate what we've done for him by lettin' him stay here."

Ty's eyes narrowed, but the looks his mother and Jason gave him warned him not to say anything. He sat down by his mother, speaking to her softly. "He's looking weaker, Mom. He had a run-in with some bounty hunters."

"Yeah, and he ran them off and wouldn't let 'em hunt," Duane said. "That was stupid. He could have made some money and helped pay his keep."

Ty clenched his teeth and gave his stepfather a cutting glare. "He built this house and it's on *his* land!" Ty said. "Granddad has more than paid you for his keep."

Duane's face reddened at Ty's defiance. "This house is mine! If you don't like it, get out! See if you make it on what George has taught you. Maybe you'll learn that doing nothing doesn't pay the bills."

"Stop it, both of you!" Mea tossed down her napkin. "The dinner table is not the place to argue, and I won't have it. Ty, you eat some dinner, and Duane, you let him eat in peace and don't say another word about Dad. He's sick, and you know it."

Ty and Duane stared at each other like boxers before a bout. Only when a car horn honked outside did they finally break their glares.

Jason smiled uncomfortably and scooted back his chair. "It's Becky."

Ty noticed his mother's lips tighten and patted her leg under the table in consolation. She didn't like Jason's girlfriend, who always seemed too poised and expressive, as if she were on stage. Her father owned all the granaries in Meyers and spoiled his only daughter by giving her everything she wanted. Mea thought everything about her was insincere. She didn't believe Rebecca Sodder was capable of loving anyone—except herself.

When Becky opened the screen door and filled the kitchen with her effervescent smile, Mea forced one in return. As always, the girl looked as if she had stepped out of the pages of a teen magazine. "Sit down, Becky, and join us. I'll set a plate."

Becky's green eyes widened and she spoke in a rush. "Thanks, Mea, but I really can't. Jason and I are running late. We're going to see *The Sound of Music*."

Duane, who always seemed completely taken with the girl, smiled indulgently. "We understand. Y'all have a good time."

Becky glanced at Ty. "Everybody in town is talking about you making the all-state football team this year. They say we'll win district easy."

Feeling uncomfortable, Ty lifted a fork full of potatoes to his mouth and took a bite before nodding.

"Yeah, Ty," Jason said, patting Ty's back, "the whole town is excited. I talked to Coach Lambert, and he says you'll be an all-stater for sure."

Becky, already bored with the subject, took Jason's arm and tugged him toward the door. "Come on, good-lookin', we have to go. 'Bye everybody!"

Ty couldn't help but notice his mother's look of relief.

Twenty minutes later, Duane sat in the living room watching "Kraft Theatre" as Mea and Ty cleaned up the kitchen. Mea spoke softly as she washed the dishes. "Don't mind Duane. He gets angry because he only wants the best for you. He doesn't think you care about your future."

Ty dried a plate and put it on the counter. "I don't, Mom. I don't know what I want yet, but I know I don't want Duane pushing me and talkin' bad about Granddad."

Mea dried her hands on her apron. "Duane has always been embarrassed by Dad. Maybe because Dad's Indian or because he never conformed to what Duane thought a father-in-law should be, but it's always been there. You being with Dad so much bothers him."

"Are you telling me not to spend so much time with Granddad?"

Mea took her son's hand and squeezed it tightly. "No, you need each other. I just want you to understand."

Ty grinned. "I guess I could get me a girlfriend like Becky who was rich and would take me to movies."

Mea glared at him then broke into a smile. "If you do, I'll wring your neck. What in the world does Jason see in her?"

"He sees a future."

Mea laughed and hit Ty's chest with the dishrag. "Get some of those bones for Rowdy and check on Daddy. Duane is right—you are impossible."

Many Moons was awakened by a loud noise and Rowdy's barking. He bolted upright in his bed and stiffened at what he saw. In trying to get to the half-eaten spaghetti on the small table, Rowdy had knocked the plate and kerosene lamp to the floor. The glass lamp now lay in front of the door, leaking kerosene over the wooden planks, while the blue flame of the lamp wick still flickered.

Holding his breath, Many Moons got up to douse the wick before the kerosene ignited, but he had taken only a step when the cabin suddenly lit up in a red-orange burst of light and heat. The flames spread along the floor, engulfing old newspapers stacked by the door and igniting the window curtains. Many Moons quickly looked around. He needed something with which to smother the fire. He grabbed the blankets off the bed, but the blaze had already spread up the wall. The thick smoke and heat quickly became too much for him as he tried desperately to beat out the flames. It was no use. He gave up and hurried to the back window, where he smashed the pane with a cooking pot. He began to crawl but stopped. Turning around, he went back for his yelping dog and the treasure box that Ty had left on the table.

As Ty rode toward the hill, he leaned back in the saddle looking at the twinkling stars far above. The warm summer nights always made him feel good and brought back memories. It was on nights like this that Many Moons had taken him and Jason to gig frogs on Crystal Pond and run trout lines. There were also the nights they had gone coon hunting, and his grandfather had taught them how to read the stars. Making ice cream on the front porch and catching june bugs were for nights such as this.

He ducked a branch and leaned forward in the saddle as Sa Tonkee climbed a rise that overlooked the road just fifty yards from the shack. It was only then that he saw flames licking skyward from the burning shack. His body tightened and he reigned Sa Tonkee's head toward the fire, kicking the gelding's flanks. The horse bolted onto the dirt road as Ty screamed, "Granddaaaaad!"

Ty's heart raced as Sa Tonkee galloped toward the flames. Approaching the gate, he swung off the saddle and jumped, clearing the fence. He landed on his feet, tumbled over, jumped up, and ran straight for the steps. Slowing only to lower his head and shoulders, he ran into the crackling flames and threw himself at the burning door. He fell into the smoke-filled cabin and rolled off the smoldering, shattered door. His eyes stung as if pins were sticking them as he raised up to look for his grandfather. He fell back to the floor gagging, feeling as if his whole body were on fire. His singed hair stank like burning feathers, and his exposed skin felt as if he were in scalding water. Rowdy was yelping somewhere against the far wall as Ty fought the pain and screamed out in desperation, "GRANDDAD!"

He crawled away from the flames licking at his feet toward the bed and felt the empty mattress before dropping to the floor. "Granddad?"

As he crawled through the smoke toward the back window, he felt his grandfather's leg. Many Moons was balled up on the floor, clutching the old cigar box to his chest. Jumping to his feet, Ty grabbed the old man's shoulders to drag him toward the window, but the smoke overcame him. He fell to the floor, gasping and choking. Feeling as if his chest were about to explode, he opened his mouth, sucking in the trapped air along the floor. Taking one more breath, he grabbed Many Moons under his neck and legs and picked him up. He felt along the wall until he found the window and spun around. Holding his grandfather in a death grip, he flung himself backward through the window. A piece of jagged glass slashed Ty's cheek open from ear to chin as he smashed through the frame and fell six feet onto his back.

Ty lay stunned, with the breath knocked out of him. He had to listen helplessly to the sounds of Rowdy's last, pathetic yelps amidst the popping and crackling of the flames devouring the cabin. Sparks fell on Ty's face and jolted him from his dizziness. He jerked upright, gagging. His grandfather lay sprawled on the ground, his hair smoldering in the eerie orange light. Ty patted the sparks out and grabbed the overall shoulder straps. He began crawling backward, dragging his grandfather away from the intense heat that was sucking all the air from him. He felt he was going nowhere, he was so weak, but he kept digging his feet into the red soil and forced himself to push.

Twenty yards from the flames, he reached a small depression and pulled his grandfather into it. He leaned over him to see if he was alive. Many Moons still clutched the cigar box and was wheezing in air through his blackened nose. His eyes were open in a fixed stare. Suddenly, dark spots appeared on his face and spread. Ty reached out to wipe them away but felt a coolness on the back of his hand. The spots were drops of blood dripping from his own slashed face. He patted his grandfather's forehead, ignoring the wound. Many Moons's eyes rolled to the side. He looked at his grandson and tried to speak. Ty leaned closer to him and spoke in a painful whisper. "Don't try to talk. Save your energy, Granddad."

Many Moons lifted the cigar box toward Ty and whispered in a sickening gurgle, "I . . . I love . . . you . . . my son." His hands trembled and released the box that fell to his chest. The old man's eyes began to close as Ty leaned over and kissed his grandfather's cheek. "I love you, too, Granddaddy."

The wheezing stopped. Ty looked at his grandfather's still face and lay down beside him to hug him one final time. He felt a blissful peace spreading through his body. The horrible pain was gone as he closed his heavy eyelids, knowing his grandfather would soon be riding with his wife and son.

3

Mea wiped her eyes with a Kleenex and held Ty's arm tightly as they walked away from the flower-draped casket. Duane walked behind them with Jason and Becky. Mea felt devastated and empty, yet she was also relieved—at least her father had not lingered on to life in a burn ward.

At the church service there had been standing room only, and she'd been pleased so many old friends had come to pay their final respects. She had requested that only immediate family be present at the burial on the hill because her father had never shared his hill with anyone but family.

Mea squeezed Ty's arm closely to her side wishing she could say or do something to ease his hidden pain. He hadn't cried or showed any emotion since the fire. Doc Riddle had added to his loss by telling him he wouldn't be able to play football. His hands would need several months to heal, then require extensive rehabilitative exercises to regain full function. His hands and the top part of his face were still covered in bandages. The rest of his face was splotched with new pink skin. His right cheek was still partially swollen from the thirty-eight stitches that held the wound together. Doc Riddle had said he would have a bad scar because the tissue around the cut had died and had to be removed. Mea knew her son's hands and face would recover long before his heart. His brooding silence worried her.

Duane stepped in front of her. "You'd better thank the pallbearers again; they had quite a time getting up the hill. And don't forget the appointment with Charlie. We've got to be there in thirty minutes.''

Mea had forgotten about the appointment with Charlie Doss, the town's only lawyer. Duane had wanted to settle the affairs of her father as soon as possible to get it behind them. She nodded to him and patted Ty's back. "Honey, you go on to the car, and I'll be there in a few minutes.''

Ty turned around and looked at the grave. He spoke quietly but forcefully. "I'm staying here awhile.''

Duane began to protest, but Mea raised her hand and gave her husband a warning glare that was unmistakable. Duane threw up his hands and spun around. Mea put her arm around her son and hugged him tightly. "I'm going to miss him so much''

Ty returned the hug and kissed his mother's cheek. "It's all right, Mom, he'll always be with us.'' Ty gently pushed away from his mother and looked into her teary eyes. "I want to be alone with him awhile. You go on and pick me up later.''

Tears trickled down Mea's face as she nodded in understanding. She wanted to be with her son but knew of his need to be alone. She wiped her eyes and joined her husband as Ty began walking back up the hill.

Ty sat on the log bench, looking at the fertile valley, lost in thoughts of his grandfather. Fifty feet away, directly below him, a large coyote walked out of the underbrush. The movement caught Ty's eye, and he instinctively held his breath. Many Moons had taught him how to track the animals years ago and he had snuck up on quite a few, but never this one. The coyote took several more cautious steps and froze. He swung his head in Ty's direction and lifted his nose, sniffing. Ty smiled to himself. It was Split Paw. The old boy was almost blind, but there was nothing wrong with his nose. Ty stood up, taking in a deep breath of the fresh air, and noticed a red-tailed hawk making lazy circles far above him. He looked around at the trees scattered over his grandfather's hill. Before he hadn't wanted to leave his grandfather alone, but now he understood that George Many Moons would never be alone. He was with his family and the countless animals, birds, and trees of the unspoiled hill. They would always be with him.

Duane listened to the reading of the will, trying to contain his anger. The old bastard had given everything that mattered to Ty. Mea only received three thousand dollars and ten acres adjoining the house, while Ty had gotten the whole damn hill and a thousand bucks to waste. That irresponsible kid had it all!

Ty walked back to the blackened remains of the shack and saw Jason sitting on the wooden fence, waiting for him.

Jason hopped to the ground. "I couldn't leave my little brother here alone . . . thought you might want some company."

Ty nodded in silence and walked to the shade of a nearby oak and sat down. Jason sat down beside him and put his arm over his brother's shoulder. "It all seems so unfair. I wish I could do something."

"It was Granddaddy's turn."

"What about you, Ty, are you gonna be all right?"

Ty nodded and looked up with a sad smile. "Remember when Granddaddy took us to Fort Sill to hunt the buffalo? He was the happiest I ever saw him. He really got a kick out of telling us about when the big buffs ruled the plains."

Jason grinned. "Yeah, but he was happy because his grandson got up close enough to almost touch one of the big bastards. I was with him watching you sneak in close to the herd. I thought I was going to have to hold him down, he was so excited. You really made him proud that day."

Ty shut his eyes and could hear his grandfather telling him he was a true Kiowa hunter. He had surpassed the test of stealth and cunning of the best of the hunters and had proven he was blessed with the gift. He hadn't killed the protected buffalo but had done even better by sneaking up so close. His grandfather had said he had taken the big bull's spirit. He'd had the gift to become the buffalo, to feel the animal's fear when he had surprised him that day. The bull had meekly walked away, knowing he was no longer the master.

Jason patted his brother's back, seeing tears trickle down his cheeks. "George gave you a lot of memories, didn't he?"

Ty fought back his tears and stood up. "The best . . . I'm going to remember him by that day we went on the hunt. Granddaddy always said remember the dead when they were the happiest. Thanks, brother, for being here . . . you've always been there for me. . . . Things are gonna work out."

Jason walked through the showroom where a new tractor sat and entered the large work bay. Two tractors were parked on one side, with various parts scattered between them. On the other side was a partially disassembled combine. Jason stepped over an oil puddle and looked around the garage where he'd worked since he was fourteen. After today the smell of grease and oil would be nothing but a memory.

Duane tossed his wrench into a toolbox and picked up a grease rag. He noticed his son standing to his right and broke into a smile. "How's it feel knowing you're through with this place?"

Jason grinned. "Great!"

Duane laughed and walked toward the office showroom, still wiping his hands. "It's a big day, all right. Mea and I are taking you out tonight for a celebration dinner. It's not too often I get to send my boy off to college."

Jason followed him into the office. "Hey, thanks for the new clothes; you didn't have to do that."

Duane tossed the rag on top of a pile of others in the corner. "Don't thank me. Mea picked the stuff out with Becky. By the way, Becky is coming with us tonight. I didn't figure you'd mind." He gave his son a wink. "Come on, let's get out of here."

Jason took a few steps and turned around. "Dad, I'm worried about Ty. It's been a week since the funeral and he's still really down."

"Don't worry about him. He doesn't have any real problems but himself."

Jason stiffened. "How can you say that? His hands are burned so bad he can't feed himself, can't dress himself, he can't even wipe his butt himself. He knows he's not going to college because no school gives scholarships on a junior year's performance. And when he goes back to school he won't be able to carry his books or take notes. Damn, Dad . . . aren't those problems?"

Duane sighed and nodded with reluctance. Knowing his son was upset, he softened his voice. "There's nothing I can say that will change things. He doesn't listen to me; you know that better than I do. He's working things out in his mind. He'll bounce back once he starts school."

Jason lowered his head dejectedly, knowing he wasn't getting through. "I wish you'd try and be a little more understanding . . . he's been through a lot."

Duane put his arm around Jason's shoulder and walked him toward the door. "I'll keep an eye on him. Now, quit worrying about Ty and start worrying about making the team."

"But . . ."

Duane interrupted by opening the door. "Doc Riddle is lettin' him start school tomorrow. Being with the other kids will bring him out of the blues. Come on, we gotta get going. Mea is waiting for us.''

Mea stood in front of Ty as he rocked in her father's chair. "Honey, you sure you don't want to change your mind and go with us? We're going to the Cattlemen's Cafe in Oklahoma City."

Ty raised his bandaged hands. "Mom, I'd be a freak show. You couldn't enjoy yourself, having to feed me and yourself, too. Go on and have a good time. I'll be fine."

Mea patted her son's arm. "I set the channel on four so you can watch "The Virginian," and after that is "Red Skelton." There's a milkshake in the refrigerator for you with the straw already in it, and I'll bring you something from dinner." She leaned over and kissed his forehead. "I'm going to change my shoes. Tell Duane I'll be ready in just a minute."

When Ty walked into the kitchen, Duane was standing by the door, waiting with Jason. He rolled his eyes when Ty had delivered the message. "Women. I swear they were born late. I'm gonna get the car and bring it up to the walkway. We'll be back around ten."

Duane pushed open the screen door and started for the car.

"I wish you'd come with us," Jason said.

Ty smiled faintly. "I'm not quite ready for the stares just yet. You have a good time with Becky. You won't be seeing her for a while. Bring me a doggy bag, huh?"

"Are you sure?" Jason did not like leaving his brother alone.

Ty playfully kicked at Jason's behind. "Get outta here, will ya!"

An hour later, Ty lay in bed thinking how empty the house was going to be without Jason. Their morning freeweight workouts would come to an end, and there would be no one to push him to his limit. Jason was more than a brother; he was a best friend and protector. When Ty was young, it had been Jason he had run to in the schoolyard for protection from Indian haters. They had called him half-breed and brown trash and had made fun of him and his granddad. The insults had hurt more than the rocks and fists. As the only Indian-blooded boy in Meyers, he had been the obvious target for people who loved to hate, and they had delighted in making a little boy cry. It had been the start of a new life when Jason had become his big brother. Jason had always been there for him to wipe away his tears and to pay back insults for him with bloody noses and bruises. As the years passed, Ty had grown strong enough to fight his own battles, but still Jay had always been there to back him up. Jason had been more like Ty's real father, a man about whom Ty could remember only gentleness and kindness.

The one person Jason couldn't protect him from was Duane. The punishment the young boy had taken from his stepfather had hurt much more than Duane ever realized. Ty had never understood why a man who loved his mother so much had so wanted to hurt her son.

Ty closed his eyes and thought about his real father. If only his father had come home from Korea, things would have been different.

The shrill sound of bugles and screaming men shattered the morning calm. The wave of charging Chinese soldiers came into view as they crested a ridge opposite the Americans.

Sergeant John Nance spoke calmly to his men. "Steady. . . . Let the machine gun fire first. Pick your targets and make every shot count." He lowered himself back into his foxhole and brought up his M-1 rifle.

The screaming Chinese platoon ran through the snow as they charged down the ridge, jumping over frozen bodies left from previous failed assaults. They fired from the hip. The first of their numbers were mowed down by machine-gun fire, but the bugle blared on, and they continued their suicidal charge.

The machine gun quit its deadly chatter, and the wounded gunner yelled, "I'm out of ammo!"

Nance cussed under his breath and gently squeezed the M-1's trigger. The lead Chinese soldier pitched over into the snow. Nance fired at his next target, knocking him down. He quickly aimed and squeezed the trigger again, but the ping sound of the clip ejecting after releasing its last bullet sent a tremor up his spine. He knew he was going to die. He had no more ammunition. Five more Chinese went down with the last rounds fired from his squad. Nance stood up, ignoring the bullets popping over his head, and raised his bayoneted rifle. "Come on, let's make the bastards pay!"

Nance and his men faced the charging enemy and broke into a slow run. Screaming in defiance, he swung his rifle butt at the first charging soldier, knocking him down, and thrust his bayonet into another. Withdrawing the bloody knife, he spun around but suddenly jerked with the tremendous impact of bullets tearing through his legs.

Ty bolted upright in his bed, his body drenched with sweat. His father had died again in his dream. Ty shivered, feeling Korea's deadly cold. This time he had heard the crunching snow beneath his father's boots and seen the vapor cloud blowing from his nostrils as he ran toward his death. The first bullets tore through his numb legs and he fell to the frozen ground. Blood from his wounds smoked in the frigid air as he raised up, only to be shot again in the neck and face. His head snapped back and then the emptiness . . . floating, helpless emptiness. There was no feeling, nothing to grab onto and hold. There was no up, down, sight, sound, or smell. There was nothing but the black emptiness.

Ty lay back down in the darkness as he had done for so many years and fought back the tears. He hated the dreams and yet he loved them. They were all he had left of a father he hardly remembered.

Years ago in the dreams his father had come home. It had all been a mistake. He wasn't dead like they said. He had come back from Korea and stood in the doorway in his uniform with the same smile as in the picture on the dresser. Later, his father would laugh and wrestle with him on the floor and play ball in the lazy summer afternoon. His dad was so strong and yet so gentle. He had never hit him or had to raise his voice. His eye expression was always enough.

Those were the young years when every day a little boy would stand by the front door and wait for the dream to come true. Later, the dream became cruel. The small boy grew up and learned the truth about death, Dad, and Santa. The dream changed. Sergeant John Nance became a hero, a man who would have been a wonderful father. Instead, he had been a great soldier who had died too far away.

Ty Nance shut his eyes knowing in the morning he would glance toward the doorway and still hope.

Ty woke up early and walked down the hall to Jason's room. Suitcases were lined up at the door, but Jason was still in bed, asleep. Ty sat down at the foot of the bed and nudged him with his elbow. Jason raised his head groggily. Ty smiled. "Wake up, college boy. You don't want to miss your first day."

Jason sat up, rubbed his eyes, then playfully cuffed Ty on the shoulder. "I'm going to miss ya, brother."

Ty kept his grin. "You'd better make the team and send us tickets. We wanna see you get smeared like ya did playing at Meyers."

Jason pushed Ty back with mock anger. "Smeared? Me? Come on, Ty, you know I never get smeared. I'm almost as fast as you."

"What about the Tuttle game?" Ty asked with a smirk.

Jason blushed and lowered his eyes. "That was a smear."

Both boys laughed, and Ty got up to let his brother dress. Mea walked in to see what the commotion was. To see her boys laughing and joking with each other for the first time since the accident pleased her.

She tried, with difficulty, to put on a stern face. "You two have managed to wake up the whole house. Do you realize it's only six o'clock?"

"Mom, I'm starved," Ty said, patting his stomach. "I gotta have a full tank to make the long drive to see Jay's school."

Mea put her hands on her hips. "You're going to school today yourself, remember?"

Ty winked at Jason, then looked at his mother with a sad frown. "Yeah, but I was hopin' *you* wouldn't remember. Come on, Mom, I wanna see some highfalutin college girls."

Mea shook her head. "Forget it. School started two days ago, you're behind already. Get dressed, both of you. Jason, help your brother dress, then come to breakfast. I'll fix y'all's favorite— biscuits and sausage gravy."

Ty let out a whoop and elbowed Jason in the ribs. "You heard her, hurry up and help me get dressed!"

Jason smiled smugly. "I'm going to shave you, so be nice to me."

Ty swung his head to his mother in desperation, but she had already turned around and headed toward the kitchen. "Mom, Jason will cut my face to ribbons!"

Mea wiped a tear from her eyes and kept walking. One of her boys was leaving her, and home would never be the same.

4

Central State College,
Edmond, Oklahoma

The quarterback took the snap, spun around, and faked a hand-off to the fullback. He ran down the line looking as if to run but suddenly pitched out to the freshman halfback. Jason caught the ball but was immediately hit by the defensive end and driven to the ground.

The offensive back coach blew his whistle and leaned over Jason. "Johnson, that was sorry. You're too damn slow. You have to be three yards farther out to get by the end."

Jason picked himself off the ground, his head still ringing from the blow. "Yes, sir."

The coach slapped his helmet. "Stand behind me and watch Simmons do it . . . Simmons, get in there for Johnson!"

Jason watched as a stout young black man ran onto the field and joined the huddle. Jerome Simmons was five inches shorter than Jason, but he was twenty pounds heavier and three seconds faster in the hundred. Though he was just a freshman, he had already been given the nickname "Cannonball Express" by his coaches and fellow team members.

Jason lowered his head as Simmons took the pitched ball and streaked untouched around the end. Today was just one more day to add to the most miserable three weeks of his life. College football was not what he thought it would be. The glamour, success, and fun of playing in high school were fond memories of another world. College ball was the big league and most assuredly not fun. The two-a-day, two- and three-hour practice schedule had reduced his body to nothing but aching bones and bruised muscles. His sense of success was derived from just getting up in the morning and putting on his cleats for practice.

The coach blew his whistle and pointed to the goal line. "That's it for the day. Running backs and ends, four hundred-yard sprints. Linemen, two, then hit the weight room. Jenkins, Keary, and Johnson, see Coach Duggin in his office after showers. Backs and ends first on the line . . . on one! DOWN, SET, HUT!"

Ty stood in the crowded hallway unlocking his school locker for the first time by himself when he was bumped roughly by Melvin Summers. "Watch it, Nance, you can't take the whole hallway."

Ty ignored the fat senior who stood four inches taller than himself. Summers, a self-proclaimed Indian hater, had plagued Ty since childhood. To make matters worse, he was the principal's son.

"I'm talking to you, Nance!"

Ty took an English book from his locker and shut the door. "No, you're not, Summers, you're oinking at me. Do yourself a favor and quit feedin' your face."

Ty turned his back on the red-faced senior and started down the hall.

"Half-breed motherfucker," Summers mumbled under his breath.

Ty spun around and shot his partially bandaged hand out, sticking two pink fingers roughly into the boy's throat. "Pig, you say that again, you won't be able to eat for a month."

Summers backed up, gagging from the surprise blow, just as Becky approached. Ty turned, ignoring the pain in his hand, and looked directly at his brother's girlfriend, who quickly grabbed his arm and hurried him down the hall.

"Ty, don't start the year by getting in trouble. Melvin isn't worth it."

Ty relaxed and slowed his pace. "I just stole his spirit. It had to be done. It's better we got it over early."

Becky shook her head. "He's trouble, Ty. He and Billy Ray Stevens have been saying horrible things about you. Stay away from them . . . I promised Jay I'd watch out for you."

Ty stopped at the door of the English class and winked. "I'd say you'd better put on forty pounds to help me with those two fatasses, but thanks."

Becky laughed and hit his arm playfully. "I'm finding you a girlfriend. That's the only thing that will you keep you out of trouble."

Ty rolled his eyes and walked into the classroom. "Forget it."

Jason stood under the showerhead, feeling sick and drained. Beside him, Clarence Keary sat exhausted on the tiled floor, letting the gushing water beat on his back. Keary, a freshman, was Jason's roommate and had been recruited from Rush Springs, where he had been an all-district split end.

Keary raised his head in dejection. "Jay, he's going to can us just like he did the others."

Jason turned around so the water could massage his lower back. "Those guys quit. If we stick it out, we'll make it."

Keary motioned toward the locker room. "They treat us like shit. We started with thirty freshmen, and now there's only ten of us left. Don't you get it? They're sifting through us to find the cream and tossing the rest out."

Jason turned off his shower. "We're on scholarship, they can't throw us out."

Keary shook his head tiredly. "You're dreamin', Jay. Half of 'em that are gone were on scholarship. They have their ways to get us out. Didn't you read the small print in your contract? If we get hurt, it's all over."

Jason felt a wave of depression creeping over him. Keary was going to quit like the others, he could see it in his eyes. "Look, Clarence, if we hang tough we can get through this thing together. Maybe we can make the special team."

Keary walked toward the locker room. "Come on. Coach is waiting for us. I wanna get this over."

Twenty minutes later, Keary walked out of Coach Duggin's office with his head down. He looked up for only a second to acknowledge Jason and tell him he was next. Jason didn't need to ask what happened; it was apparent in his friend's posture. Jason stepped into the small office of the head coach feeling like he wanted to vomit.

Duggin sat behind his cluttered desk, still wearing his blue ball cap and short-sleeved yellow coach's shirt. He motioned to the only chair and waited until Jason sat down before speaking. "Johnson, you're not progressing as we'd hoped. For a player to make our team he has to give one hundred percent. You're only giving us seventy-five. The way things are going right now, we don't think we can use you."

Jason held back his anger. He'd only seen the head coach twice in three weeks. He'd stayed with the varsity players on the upper practice field and left graduate assistants to coach the freshmen. Duggin had no idea how he was "progressing."

Jason's jaw muscles rippled. "I'll give you a hundred percent."

Duggin's eyes immediately showed disappointment. This was not going to be as easy as the Keary kid. "Johnson, you don't understand. You're not cutting it. I want you to quit."

Jason held back the bile in his throat and stared at him. "I'm not quitting."

Duggin returned Jason's stare for several seconds as if looking for a weakness, then stood up. "Okay, tomorrow you report to the red team. See Coach Stewart. He'll be expecting you."

Jason got up from the chair in silence and opened the door to leave. Duggin sat down, staring at a pencil on his desk. "Johnson."

Jason turned around as Duggin leaned back in his chair and spoke almost apologetically. "It ain't nothin' personal, it's just the way things are. I can only keep the best, and I need that scholarship back so I can get the best."

Jason turned for the door, maintaining his stoic expression. He didn't want to give the bastard the satisfaction of knowing he understood his twisted philosophy.

* * *

Ty walked out of the school building heading for the buses when he felt a rough hand on his shoulder. He turned around and looked into the jowled face of Mr. Ernest Summers, the principal.

"Mr. Nance, I understand you assaulted one of the students in the hallway today."

Ty looked directly into the puffy slits of the principal's eyes. "No, sir, there was no assault, just insults from your son."

Summers's eyes narrowed, and small veins rose to the surface of his cheeks and nose. "Mr. Nance, I will not tolerate your hostility this year. Melvin tells me you started the whole unpleasant affair and embarrassed him in front of his fellow students. In light of your previous performance over the years in this school, I believe his story. Consider this a warning, Mr. Nance. I will be watching you very, very closely."

Ty took in a deep breath for control, knowing he was against a wall. "Yes, sir."

Summers released his grip. "I will also be conveying my concerns to your father."

Ty kept his eyes fixed. "Stepfather, not father, sir."

Summers turned without reply and waddled toward his office, leaving Ty with the feeling he was sinking in quicksand.

Jason returned to his room after eating dinner in the cafeteria and found Keary boxing up his clothes to move. Jason sat down on his bed. "Do you have to move?"

Keary tossed his books into a box. "Yeah, this floor is for jocks; I'm moving up two floors." He looked at Jason. "He moved you to the red team, didn't he?"

"Yeah," Jason said, "but it'll be all right."

"No, it won't, and you know it!" blurted Keary. "The red team is nothing but a bunch of blocking and tackling dummies for the varsity. Damn, Jay, you're nothing but red meat for them . . . the injury rate is criminal on the Reds."

"I don't have a choice. If I quit, I gotta drop out of school. I don't have the money for tuition and books, let alone the dorm room and meals."

Keary felt stupid. He hadn't realized his friend's plight and wished he hadn't been so negative. "I'm sorry, Jay, I didn't know it was all or nothing for you. Look, you have one chance on the Reds. Beat them at their own game. Show 'em you can take more than they can dish out. Kick ass and you'll get them off your back, and they'll give you a shot on a special team."

Jason thought about the greasy garage and the disgrace of going home a loser. He knew there was no going back, no matter what happened. Keary was right; he still had a shot to show Duggin he was wrong about him.

Ty watched the last of "Wagon Train" and got up from his chair. Mea reached out and touched his arm as he passed by her. "Bob Hope is on next."

Ty motioned toward the kitchen. "I'm gonna get something to drink, then I have to read a couple of chapters."

Mea turned her attention to the television, glad he was doing so well despite the call from Mr. Summers about the trouble in school. She was just glad Duane hadn't been in and she'd been able to reassure the principal that Ty would behave. She would have been more concerned if the reports from his teachers hadn't been so positive. In a way, the accident had been a blessing in disguise. He hadn't been able to write, so he had to read and give oral reports to his teachers. At first, the reading had been boring for Ty, but later he had become genuinely interested in his subjects and had read far more than was required. He had several library books in his room that a month ago would never have been there.

Ty walked back from the kitchen, and Duane put down the evening paper. "Ty, when you get the rest of the bandages off, ya ought to think about going to work and makin' some money. You can have Jason's job and make a buck-fifty an hour."

Ty faced his stepfather squarely. It was now or never. "No, thanks. I'm renting the hill out for grazing, and the place needs a lot of work. Thanks, anyway."

Duane tossed the paper to the floor. "I'm offering you a chance to make money for college. Quit thinking about that damn hill and think about your future. You can't live with your mother and me all your life. You have to make something of yourself."

Ty's eyes narrowed in anger, and he was about to answer when Mea stood up. "Leave it be, Duane. He has his own life to live."

" 'Life to live,' my ass!" said Duane, seething. "He's gonna end up being a moocher, just like George."

Ty spun around and walked into his room, slamming the door. It took every bit of resolve he had not to pounce on his stepfather and rip his throat out. The bastard could say all he wanted about him, but not about his granddad. Many Moons had been ten times the man Duane would ever be.

Mea opened the door and stepped in. "He didn't mean it, honey. He's just upset that you didn't take his offer. It was his way of making amends, and you wouldn't accept."

Ty lay down on his bed and stared at the ceiling. "I couldn't work for him, and you know it. He'd badger me like he did Jason, and I can't take it like Jason did. I'm gonna make it, Mom. I'll make something of myself. I just don't want him pushing me into something I don't want."

Mea sat down on the bed. "I'm not worried about your future, Ty. I'm worried about you and Duane. It's got to end. It's tearing you both from me, and I love you both. Try, honey, try for me to be tolerant of him. You don't have to work for him, but at least show him some respect. He needs that."

Ty rose up and looked at his mother. He was in misery over the worry in her eyes. "I'll try, Mom. I'll really try."

Mea turned to go, but Ty touched her arm. "Thanks for not telling him about what happened in school."

Mea nodded with a faint smile and walked out, quietly closing the door behind her.

5

Jason sidestepped a guard's block and lowered his head, hitting the fullback below the knees, upending him. The red defensive team yelled their approval, and Big Chuck Halloway helped Jason to his feet with a toothless smile. "That'a way ta bust his ass, Johnson."

Jason pounded the huge lineman's shoulder pads in elation, then grabbed his helmet and exchanged head butts. "We're BAD! WE'RE BAD!"

Chuck turned to his defensive teammates, holding his arms up as if in triumph, and growled, "Ya gotta LOVE IT, CRAZIES!"

His red team members responded fanatically. "YOU GOTTA LOVE IT!"

Coach Duggin stomped toward the offensive huddle and threw his cap at the quarterback. "What the hell was that? You're not thinking! They were in a five-four look, for Christ sake! You can't run a thirty-thirty dive against a five-four defense!''

Jason smirked. The varsity was finally getting a taste of their own medicine. Usually it was the other way around. The varsity didn't have a game that week and were preparing for Angelo State by using the meat squad to run Angelo State's defenses. They had walked through the different plays several times and had gone full speed on the last four. The meat squad had stopped them cold. The reason was Chuck Halloway.

Chuck had been a first-team tackle but had flunked his business math quarterlies and was declared ineligible. Coach Duggin was washing his hands of the sophomore and had put him on the red team two days before to get rid of him. Chuck would be able to play out the rest of the season with the meat squad and wouldn't lose his scholarship unless he quit.

Jason lined up behind the 240-pound tackle and slapped his backside. "They're not going through us! Hold 'em, Chuck. Hold 'em!''

Jason glanced around him at the rest of the team and could see the determination in their faces, determination that had not been there before. Chuck had sparked the meat squad with his total commitment to bringing misery and destruction to his former teammates and the head coach who spurned him.

Jason couldn't help but get motivated, seeing Chuck beat his chest and growl menacingly as he waited for the offense to line up again. Because Chuck was twenty-four and had been in the Army before coming to school, he was considered the "old man" of the team. He looked like a throwback to prehistoric times, with his heavy brow and long, muscular arms. His neck was as thick as a normal man's thigh, and he always looked as if he wanted to rip out your heart and eat it. He was mean, vulgar, and uncouth, and the meat squad loved him.

Before Chuck came to them, the red team had been a collection of losers. Everyone knew it was only a matter of time before they were going to be hurt. The only question was how badly. Most were like Jason, those who wouldn't quit and were holding on to their scholarships and playing scared. Chuck turned things around with his attitude and fierce playing. At first, he was the only one who helped his teammates up with a word of encouragement and a call for more effort. He led by example, giving one hundred percent effort on every play, and was a one-man terror that no one could stop. He would get up after a tackle and deeply growl to his teammates, "You gotta love it, Crazies!''

The day before, during a water break, Jason had asked the huge

tackle why he kept telling them they had to love it. Chuck looked
at Jason and the other team members who had gathered closer to
listen with the eyes of an old, experienced warrior. "'Cause it
ain't gonna get no better. None of us wanna quit, and they know
it. They just keep kickin' us and tryin' to break us, but they can't.
You know why? 'Cause we fuckin' love this shit! What can they do
to us if we love it? NOTHIN'! We're fuckin' crazy! They hit us
and we hit them harder. Play after play they know they gonna get
popped, and they start thinkin' about it. But we don't think shit,
WE KNOW! We know it ain't gonna get no better for us, and we
gotta love it to survive."

Jason smiled to himself, recalling how the team changed after
Chuck's pep talk. It started as a joke at first, but soon they began
calling each other "Crazy." Then they started acting the part, mim-
icking Chuck's actions, helping one another up, and bashing their
helmets against one another. For the first time practice had become
fun.

Jason broke from his reverie as the varsity offense lined up on
the ball. The quarterback barked out the signals and was snapped
the ball. Both lines clashed in an explosion of pads, forearms, and
grunts as the quarterback faked a handoff to the plunging fullback
and quickly pitched to the halfback Simmons.

Jason was hit by the right end but spun off the block and ran
laterally along the line for the halfback. Seeing a hole, Simmons
cut back inside, but the hole closed a split second later as Jason
filled the gap and lowered his shoulder for the impact. Simmons
didn't have time to react and was hit in full stride. The blow caught
him in the stomach and he fell backward, only to be hit again by
Chuck Halloway, whose blow caught him across the helmet.

Jason jumped to his feet and embraced Chuck. The two began
to beat each other's helmets when Coach Duggin grabbed Jason
and shoved him back, screaming, "You stupid fool! You hurt him!
What the hell do you think you're doing?"

Jason looked at Simmons, who was slowly getting up with the
assistance of the trainer, then back to the red-faced coach. His eyes
turned cold but he spoke evenly, trying not to show his disdain.
"I'm giving you one hundred percent."

Duggin's face contorted in rage, and he began to shake as if he
were about to explode. The trainer's squeaky voice broke the silence. "He's just stunned, Coach."

Duggin pointed his finger at Jason's face. "Smart-ass, you're
lucky you didn't hurt him."

Jason held his ground without blinking and spoke with the same level tone. "It wasn't nothin' personal."

Duggin glared at Jason with a loathing stare for several seconds, then spun around and blew his whistle. "That's it for the day. Varsity, hit the showers, then report to the team room for reviewing Angelo's films." He turned around and stabbed a finger toward Jason. "YOU, smart-ass, run ten laps."

Coach Stewart waited until Duggin turned his back and walked over to Jason. "Don't worry about it, Johnson. Duggin is stretched pretty thin right now. He wants to win the conference. It was a hell'va tackle. Good job."

Jason nodded in silence and jogged to the cinder track as the team walked toward the locker room. Chuck walked along with the others but suddenly stopped and turned around. He saw Jason in the distance and began to run toward him.

Jason ran slowly to conserve his energy and heard footsteps behind him. He turned and broke into a grin. Chuck was coming up behind him and, farther back, more of the meat squad were coming to join him. Jason lifted his arms skyward. "YOU GOTTA LOVE IT, CRAZIES!"

Mea handed Duane a glass of lemonade and sat down beside him to watch the evening news. Walter Cronkite's reassuring voice filled the room.

". . . and today the Selective Service announced a call-up of forty-five thousand men for the month of December. This is the largest draft since the Korean War. A White House spokesman said the call-up was necessary to meet the Communist buildup and escalation of insurgency in South Vietnam. To date, eight hundred and ten Americans have died in the conflict and . . ."

Mea's eyes watered and she lowered her head to hide the tears. The news was like that of fifteen years before, news that had ultimately taken her husband. She hadn't even known where Korea was, and yet Americans like John had gone because their country had called. He had died so young and she still didn't know why. And now, after all these years, the country was calling for more young men, men like her son.

Duane didn't notice his wife's distress and spoke as he kept his eyes glued to the television. "Ty will probably get drafted after school. It'd be good for him . . . maybe he'd learn a little responsibility."

Mea looked at her husband with tears streaming down her face. "How can you say that? There's a war going on!"

Duane looked at her with shock. Never once had she yelled at him. He knew immediately he'd made a mistake, forgetting that her former husband had been drafted. He rose from his chair and stepped toward her. "I'm sorry, honey, it was a stupid thing to say. Of course I don't want him drafted."

Mea stood and backed up, not wanting him to touch her, but his large arms encircled her. "I'm truly sorry; I didn't mean it, Mea."

She looked up into his eyes. "He can't go, Duane . . . he just can't."

Duane hugged her tightly and spoke softly to soothe her. "Don't worry, honey, he has his hill and we can get him a farmer's deferment. Don't worry about it. I'll take care of everything, sweetheart, everything."

Jason was about to go to bed when his door flew open and Chuck staggered in. The big tackle flopped down on the empty bed across from Jason and lifted a Budweiser to his mouth.

Jason quickly got up and checked the halls before shutting the door. Drinking was forbidden in the dorm, and if Chuck was caught he'd be suspended. "Damn, Chuck, if Duggin finds out he'll can you."

Chuck smiled cruelly. "Fuck him! Fuck him and the horse he rode in on. I needed a few beers and I'm drinkin' a few beers."

Jason sighed and sat down on his bed. "Sleep it off, buddy. You can sleep here tonight so nobody sees you."

Chuck sat up with a strange look. "What'd you call me?"

Jason had to think what he had said and shrugged his shoulders. "I said, 'buddy.' "

Chuck grinned and lifted his beer can. "To us buddies. WE'RE BAAAD!"

Jason couldn't help but return his smile and lift an imaginary can. Chuck guzzled the last of the beer and crushed the can in his hands before tossing it to the floor. He looked back at Jason and became somber. "Ya know we're on Duggin's hit list, don't ya? He'll never give you a chance to play, no matter what you do."

"Yeah, I figured as much," Jason said. "But I gotta hang in and hold on to the scholarship, no matter what he does."

Chuck leaned back against the wall. "Ya ain't got no money to finish up yourself, huh?"

Jason shook his head. "How about you? You gotta hold on, too?"

Chuck burped and scratched his crotch. "Naw, Uncle Sam is footing the bill. The GI Bill keeps me in school and beer."

"Why do you knock your brains out then? Hell, he's after you, too."

Chuck's eyes shifted to Jason and lit up. "'Cause it makes me feel good. I like it. I like kickin' ass and takin' names. There's nothin' else that gives me that feeling." The light went out and his eyes softened. "It's all I got."

Jason felt worry for the big man and changed the subject. "Why'd you join the Army?"

Chuck's eyes rekindled. "I was like you are right now, but it wasn't a fucked-up coach that screwed up my scholarship. I flunked out. I didn't have the bucks to try again, and I couldn't go home, so I joined up. I figured I'd spend my two years, then come back with Sam paying the bills."

"How come you couldn't go home?" Jason asked.

Chuck lay down and looked up at the ceiling. "Pride, I guess. Everybody expected me to make the big time. I couldn't face 'em. Ya probably wouldn't understand, but I just couldn't go back and see their faces, all pitying me and really thinking the big ox couldn't hack it. Well, FUCK 'EM, I made it. I'm gonna play until I can't play no more and get me a degree and wave it in their faces."

Jason did understand and felt the same way about going home if he didn't make it. He lay there several minutes in silence thinking about his future and raised up to ask Chuck more questions about the GI Bill. The effort was wasted. Chuck was asleep, snoring.

Ty sat at the counter of the Coffee Cup Cafe looking up into the tired face of Ptomaine Toni. Toni Watkins was a hard-looking, bony woman who appeared ten years older than her thirty-eight years. Her hair was dyed jet black and contrasted horribly with her ghost-white skin and bright red smeared lipstick. She usually looked as bad as her food, but Ty thought she was a genuine sweetheart of a lady.

"Toni, let me have the special, but hash browns instead of grits."

Toni leaned over the counter with a mischievous glint and took the grease-stained, one-page menu from his hands. "You up kinda early, ain't ya, or you just gettin' in from a hot date?"

Ty grinned at the owner, waitress, and part-time cook of Meyers's only cafe. Toni knew everybody and everything that happened in town, and what she didn't know she made up with her vivid imagination. "I'm up early 'cause I've got work to do on the hill."

Toni seemed disappointed at his answer and turned toward the grill, speaking loudly to her husband, who was frying eggs. "Need a special, hold the mush, and throw on spuds!" She looked back at Ty with a raised penciled eyebrow. "You gonna work on the new shack, huh?"

Ty's eyes widened, surprised that she knew of his secret project. He couldn't help but be impressed by her ability to pick up information. The bandages had been removed from his hands the week before and he had immediately begun work building a new cabin to replace his granddad's shack. Despite the initial pain of using his hands again, the cabin had to be rebuilt. It was his way of making the Hill like it had been.

He forced a smile, "Yeah, I am, but it's a secret for the time being. I'd appreciate it if you'd keep it just between us, okay?"

Toni drew her thin fingers across her lips as if zipping them closed. "My lips are sealed."

6

Jason felt bad that he hadn't told the truth, but it was just too complicated to explain. He sat in the front seat of the Olds as his father drove through Meyers. Duane had picked him up two hours before from school and was taking him home for the day. His dad didn't understand the complexities of college football and assumed that if he was still on the team he was going to one day play on varsity. Jason didn't explain that he was only a glorified tackling dummy going nowhere. It would serve no purpose and spoil the beautiful Sunday. He had given his dad nothing but positive reports about school and his "advancement" to the red team.

Duane pulled into the long driveway leading to the house and honked the horn. Mea and Ty came out the kitchen door all smiles, making Jason's heart sink. He knew it would be difficult to keep up the show for the rest of the family and even more difficult when he went to see Becky.

Mea hugged him as he got out of the car and patted his back with concern. "Aren't they feeding you, honey? You're skin and bones!"

Jason was about to answer but was saved by Ty, who held out his hand with a smile. "Aw, Mom, he's workin' his butt off in practice. . . . Good to see ya, Jay. You look lean and mean to me."

The family moved into the living room. Duane and Mea brought Jason up to date on the goings-on in Meyers and asked what seemed like a hundred questions about school and the football team. Jason noticed that Ty seemed interested but was silent during their conversation. He could tell Ty was reading between the lines of his evasive answers to when he'd be playing on varsity. Ty saved him again by getting up and saying he was going to Red Hill, asking if Jason wanted to go along.

Ty and Jason climbed into Duane's pickup and drove the mile up Highway 81 to the dirt side road that led to the hill. Ty pulled in beside the gate. "Whadya think?"

Jason was taken aback by the sight before him. He got out of the pickup and followed Ty up a short flight of steps. Flooring was nailed down, and the two-by-four frame of one wall was up.

Ty brushed a nail off the floor with his foot. "I started Monday, just after I got the last bandages off. My hands are stiff as hell, but it's good to be working again. I come up and work on it after school."

Jason looked at Ty's handiwork and sat down on the new front steps. "When you gonna tell 'em?"

Ty lifted a two-by-four and tossed it up to the flooring. "They'll find out soon enough . . . like they'll find out about you."

Jason looked at Ty as if he'd been caught stealing. He lowered his head, knowing Ty had seen through him. "Is it that obvious?"

Ty put a hand on Jason's shoulder. "Come on, let's go to the top. I wanna show you something."

Jason wanted an answer but stood up and followed Ty as he walked the worn path through the trees. Jason slowed in awe as he stepped into the cool, shaded darkness under the huge trees. He felt like he had entered another world. The old monarch's gnarled and twisted limbs reached skyward, displaying brilliant autumn leaves of yellow and amber, forming a canopy of gold. Overcome by the majesty of the place, Jason found himself stepping lightly so as not to disturb the silence and serenity. Ty turned around to see what was holding him up.

"It's like being in a cathedral," Jason whispered.

Ty looked up at the small funnels of light that broke through the canopy and spoke softly. "Granddaddy called this place his heaven on earth." He held his hand out to one of the shafts of sunlight and let the brilliance fall into his open hand. "And this was his riches."

Jason smiled in understanding.

Ty walked slowly to let his brother enjoy the hill and felt closer to him than he ever had before. He now understood why his grandfather told him beauty was best when shared.

The two strolled into the clearing. Ty stopped by the log bench and pointed ahead. "Looks pretty good, doesn't it?"

Jason continued walking and halted just short of the new white picket fence surrounding the small cemetery, but his attention was focused on the wooden flagpole centered behind the markers. He looked up at the American flag fluttering in the light wind and stepped closer. The replanted grass looked like a golf course putting green. Not a single blade was higher than the rest. He turned around to tell Ty it was beautiful, but his brother was seated on the bench looking at the view below him. Jason joined him on the bench and patted his leg affectionately. "It's something very special, Ty. You did a great job."

Ty seemed embarrassed. "I had to do something. I rented the land last week for grazing to make some money and needed to do something to keep the cattle from stomping over the headstones. I got carried away, I guess, but . . . well, I figured they deserved it."

Jason lowered his eyes in reflection. "I wished I'd spent more time with George. I feel like I missed something very special."

"No use in lookin' back," Ty said, sitting up. "Now tell me what's *really* happenin' at school."

Jason had prepared himself during the walk up the hill and told Ty about his trouble with the head coach. When he had finished, he leaned back and shut his eyes. "So that's it. I'm never going to play as long as Duggin is there. The man tried to make me quit and I wouldn't. It's become a test of wills with him."

Ty stood and looked at their house far below. "Have you told Becky?"

"No, she's like Dad and wouldn't understand. I'll let them both figure it out next year when I'm still not playing varsity."

Ty turned around with a look of shock. "You're not going to keep playing?"

"I'm sure as hell not quitting! As long as I make all the practices and don't get hurt I hold on to the scholarship. Duggin is just going to have to get used to me."

Ty could see the determination in his eyes and tried to erase his worried expression with a smile. "Come on, hard-head. It's time I shared something with you that's very special to me."

* * *

Ty pushed back the boughs of a nearby cedar and walked down some natural steps made by time in the red sandstone. This side of the hill was his favorite. He could have followed the twisting trail blindfolded. He knew every bend, switchback fold, and rock. South of the hilltop the land gradually sloped down to where the cabin and dirt road were located. But just across the road, past a stand of tall cedars, the gradual slope abruptly stopped, dropping off into a wide ravine. Countless years of rain and wind had created a natural wonder. It was a miniature Grand Canyon, but with trees, special evergreens that clung to the craggy red rock walls with thick twisting tentacle roots. The trees were stunted, and with their twisted branches and sparse foliage looked like Japanese bonsais, adding yet another dimension to the surreal beauty of the hidden canyon.

Ty and Jason made their way down into the bottom of the ravine, which was scattered with barren dogwoods and red oaks. They followed a trail running by the side of a creek that fed from a natural spring at the head of the draw. Ty couldn't help but remember how years ago he had imagined the ravine as the pass in Korea where his father had died. He had fought alongside his dad a hundred times, trying to save him from the attacking Chinese. He'd charged down the trail, stabbing and slashing, but had always been felled by a Chinese bullet. He had always died after reaching out and grabbing his father's hand.

Ty continued walking for a hundred yards before slowing and holding up his hand. Ahead was Crystal Pond. The water's surface was partially covered with wild ducks. Jason knew the pond. It was where he and Ty had caught their first fish, gigged their first frogs, shot their first ducks, and learned to swim. The pond backed up against a sandstone bluff covered in cedar and oak trees.

They followed a snaking trail around the pond up to the bluff that overlooked the water. Ty strode past a large oak before halting. Twenty yards ahead, the bluff ledge met the ravine rock wall that rose straight up for almost forty feet. He motioned Jason forward. "Clear your thoughts. We're about to enter."

"Enter what?"

Ty motioned toward a huge sandstone rock in front of the ravine wall. He closed his eyes and stood motionless.

Seconds passed before Jason noticed a sound—the wind in the rocks sounded like a soft moan. Ty led him forward and they walked around the huge reddish-brown rock. Jason's eyes opened wide in astonishment. Behind the rock was a gap in the cliff wall. The gap was ten feet wide at the mouth and went back another ten feet before quickly tapering to only a few inches. Carved in the far rock wall within the gap was a shallow cave. The entire floor of the gap was carpeted in rich green moss.

"The Hunter's Place," Ty said. "The Kiowa hunters of Grand-dad's father's tribe would go to special places away from their camps like this one and cleanse themselves before a hunt. It was a time for mental preparation, clearing the mind and concentrating on becoming the buffalo. They believed they had to think like buffalo, gain their spirit before the hunt."

Ty raised his head, looking at the rock above the cave blackened from past fires. "Granddad brought me here before we went to Fort Sill. He wanted me to have the chance to hunt the buffalo like his ancestors. It was important to him. He left me here and told me to come back to the shack when I thought I was ready for the hunt. I stayed here two days.

"I was somebody else that day. I don't even remember the car ride. I found the buffalo, I knew where they were. I'd never been there before, I just knew. It was the most . . . most wonderful feeling I've ever experienced. It was the proudest moment of my life. When we came home afterward, we dropped you off and Granddad brought me back here. He told me stories about the great-est Kiowa hunters because I had proven I had the gift. I had joined their ranks. I would be able to tell the same stories to another gifted hunter. I was to pass on the heritage of countless generations who lived and hunted this land. He explained that becoming the buffalo was a gift. It was a state of mind, and that I could use its power when facing danger or if I needed strength for something important. His son, Richard, came here and prepared himself before going to war."

He was silent for several moments before speaking again. "After the hunt, I had to stay here alone again before going to the house. Granddad called it 'truth time.' He said it was a time to realize what was gained and lost in the hunt. I felt good for a couple of hours, still on the high, but slowly, very slowly I began to think like the buffalo again. I didn't want to lose that strange, wonderful feeling. I couldn't do it. I only felt incredibly sad. Then I realized the reason: I was thinking of the buffalo whose spirit I'd taken. I was feeling his loss.

"I told Granddaddy what I felt when I went back to the shack, and he hugged me. He said during truth time a hunter experiences the loss of the spirit he's taken and gains understanding, but the real lesson was I couldn't live in the past when on a hunt. I couldn't think of the past buffalo, for I had beaten him. I had to think of the next one who had an even greater spirit. Only that way could I grow.

"The hunters were also the warriors and used their special place to prepare themselves, become the buffalo, before a battle. Once they had become prepared, they couldn't return to their loved ones, or it was said they'd lose the feeling. After the battle they would return to their place, where the spirits of friends and fellow warriors who'd died in combat were released to join the Chosen. The badly wounded couldn't go back to their families until they were healed or certain to live. You see, in their special place, they were almost in the spirit world. If they died, they died as great warriors and would ride with honor among the Chosen. . . . Granddad said when the wind blows just right you can hear the warrior's death song."

Ty shifted his gaze to Jason. "I've never told anyone those stories that Granddad passed on to me, or showed anybody this place. I didn't want to share that part of granddaddy with anyone . . . until now."

Ty lowered his head. "I've missed you and wanted you to know why the Hill is so special to me. Your dad and I never got along because of Granddad and this hill. Duane never understood but I think you do. This place and this hill are part of me, like you are."

Jason put his arm around Ty's shoulder with a warm smile. "I've understood that for as long as I've known ya. Hell, we're brothers and don't worry about pleasing dad. He grew up poor and had to work all his life to make ends meet. He doesn't understand how land is like blood, that it can flow through your veins and become a part of your being. Be *you*, Ty, never feel guilty about loving this hill."

Jason looked around him at the beauty and shook his head. "It's funny, but I get the feeling this hill needs you more than you need it." Jason broke from his reverie and slapped Ty's back. "C'mon, I've got to see Becky and get me some hugs before I go back. You've got a hill to love and I've got the best-lookin' gal in Meyers!"

7

Mea ran her hand over the hood's glossy black finish. "She's beautiful, Ty. I never dreamed you could fix her up like this."

"I didn't do much," Ty said, opening the car door for his mother. "The guys in shop class did most of the work."

Mea sat on the maroon Naugahyde seat and admired the interior. "Does the radio work?"

Ty motioned his mother over and slid in behind the steering wheel. "Yep, but it's not the original. We pulled one from another Ford in Brogan's junkyard. Willy Farris tucked and rolled the seats, and me and Jimmy rebuilt the engine." Ty turned over the ignition switch, starting the engine. "The ol' Black Widow is finally back."

Mea couldn't help but smile, hearing the name her father had given the car. She remembered when he'd first brought the black 1950 Ford home. He'd gotten out of the car in a cold sweat and said he'd almost killed himself three times driving home. He hadn't been used to such power and lost control on some turns. That day he named the Ford his "Black Widow," for she was deadly and had to be handled with care.

Mea put her arms around Ty's neck and gave him a gentle hug. "I love it. Dad would have been thrilled to see what you did with her."

Ty smiled with pride and shut his door. "Sit back and relax. I'm gonna take my favorite girl on a ride."

"Where we going?" Mea said, grinning.

Ty eased the car down the driveway and turned on the radio. "We're gonna drag Main, then tool around the Dairy Boy so I can show you off . . . and if ya give me a kiss, I'll buy ya a Dr Pepper."

She laughed and lightly slapped his arm. "I hope that's not how you get kisses from the girls."

"Naw, *they* buy the Dr Peppers."

41

* * *

Jason wiped his hands on his jersey and lined up behind Chuck. "Stick 'em, Chuck. We're baaaad!"

The defensive coach stood beside Coach Duggin and motioned toward the field. "Look, I know you don't like Johnson, but be reasonable. He isn't good enough to be a halfback, but he's one hell'va linebacker. I could use him right now, since Watley got hurt."

Duggin kept his eyes on the quarterback as the offense broke from the huddle and lined up on the ball. Monday was the infamous "Toilet Bowl." The varsity players who didn't get a chance to play in Saturday night's game scrimmaged against the red team. The past few Toilet Bowls had been as fierce as Saturday's game. The "Crazies," as they called themselves, had been giving the second- and third-teamers a real battle. Today's scrimmage was no exception.

The second-string quarterback received the snap from the center and immediately raised up and threw a short pass toward the end, who had buttonhooked. Jason read the play at the last second and threw his hand up, deflecting the ball into the air. The defensive cornerback caught the ball in midflight and streaked down the sideline. A halfback prevented him from scoring by a last-ditch flying tackle.

Duggin's veins along his neck popped out as if he were about to explode. He spun around and glared at the defensive coach. "Never! That kid is playing over his head. I've seen his kind before."

He blew his whistle and stomped out onto the muddy field. The assistant coaches conducting the game immediately jogged toward the irate head coach for his blasting. Duggin ignored them and yelled at the offensive team. "Terrible! You've lost the ball on three damn possessions! . . . Give me the ball!"

The defensive back tossed the football to Duggin, who marched toward the end of the field. He slammed the ball down on the five-yard line and pointed at the quarterback. "You have four plays to score on these idiots, or you and your offense run twenty laps! You think you can manage making FIVE DAMN YARDS?"

The quarterback yelled at his team, "Let's show him!"

Chuck shook his shoulders like a maddened bull and snarled, "He called us 'idiots'!"

Jason grabbed Chuck's face mask and yanked his head down so he could look into his eyes. "We're gonna hold 'em! They're not gonna score on us Crazies!"

Chuck beat Jason's shoulder pads and turned to his defensive team that had huddled up. "Let's make them bastards run!"

The Crazies yelled in determination and broke the huddle. The offense lined up and tried a draw play, but Chuck buried the quarterback before he could hand off, for a four-yard loss.

Duggin blew his whistle and put the ball back on the five-yard line over the protest of Jason, who shook with anger. "He was down back there!"

Duggin just looked past Jason. "Tough! They get the ball on the five!" He went back to the offense and called the play.

Chuck patted Jason's back. "It don't matter; we're gonna hold."

Jason lined up. The quarterback took the snap and quickly handed off to the halfback. Jason was hit by the tackle but shucked the block and met the halfback in the hole, stopping him cold in a shattering pop of shoulder pads and helmet plastic. Chuck jerked Jason to his feet and pounded his helmet screaming, "WE'RE BAD! We're bad CRAZIES!"

Duggin knelt down in the offensive huddle, trying to contain his anger. "You gonna let a bunch of losers whip your ass? BLOCK, goddamnit! Right, Y out, sixteen, on two."

The team lined up and the quarterback barked out the signals. He took the snap and faded back to pass.

Jason was blitzing behind Chuck and no one had picked him up. The quarterback saw him coming and began running to his right. The offensive halfback saw Jason pass by him and threw himself at the back of the charging linebacker's legs. Hit unexpectedly, Jason pitched forward to the ground with his left arm under him at an odd angle. His momentum and body weight popped the elbow out of joint in a jolt of excruciating pain.

The quarterback managed to make three yards on sheer determination before being smothered by an even more determined host of defensive tacklers. One of the assistants had thrown a flag on seeing the halfback clip Jason and blew his whistle while running to see if he was injured.

Jason got to his feet, holding his elbow. The stabbing pain had passed into throbbing agony. The assistant looked at the injury and could see the ball end of the bone jutting out grotesquely just under the skin. "It's dislocated, Johnson. You'll be back for spring ball."

"No, he won't," Duggin said, with a smirk as he walked up. He quickly glanced at Jason's arm and shook his head with exaggerated concern. "Too bad. Looks to me like a permanent injury."

The assistant, who didn't know about the bad feelings between the two, spoke innocently. "No, Coach, I've seen a couple of these, and it'll heal in a month or so."

Duggin glared at the assistant as if he were about to tear his head off. "Get him to the trainer!"

Jason looked at Duggin with defiance. "It's fourth down." He brushed past the assistant and walked toward the defensive huddle.

"Get off the field, Johnson," Duggin bellowed. "You're through!"

Jason turned around, forgetting the pain. "You got what you wanted, you bastard, but it's still fourth down."

Duggin's lips curled back cruelly. "It doesn't matter anymore. Like you said, I got what I wanted."

"It matters to me," Jason said. He turned around, taking his position, and challenged Duggin with a stare.

The assistant spoke pleadingly. "Coach, you can't let him play with . . ."

"Fourth down and two yards to score," Duggin yelled, cutting him off. "Huddle up, offense!"

Chuck looked worriedly at Jason. "Don't do this, buddy."

Jason's jaw muscles tensed, and he spoke in a rasp. "It's personal now."

Chuck nodded and faced his teammates. "Crazies, the bastards ain't scorin'!"

The team growled their defiance as Duggin squatted down in the offensive huddle and looked at the right guard. "Strong right, twenty-four on one."

Jenkins, the right guard, was to pull and lead through the hole and hit the linebacker, Jason. Jenkins shook his head, "But coach, he's hurt."

Duggin grabbed the 220-pounder's face mask and hissed, "You hit him or tomorrow you'll be playing on the red team! You understand?"

Jenkins glared at the coach. "Yeah, I understand."

Duggin repeated the play to the rest of the team and broke the huddle. The offense lined up slowly, each man eyeing Jason to see if he was really going to play. Jason ignored their stares and moved into position behind Chuck. The quarterback glanced nervously at Duggin, who motioned him to hurry up. He turned from the coach and looked at Jason before beginning his cadence. "Down . . . set . . . hut!"

The quarterback faked a pitchout to the right halfback and handed off to the left halfback, who was to follow Jenkins through the hole. But there wasn't a hole. Chuck had bulldozed himself into the gap and, despite Jenkins's efforts, held his ground, plugging the route. The halfback lowered his head and launched himself over the mass of bodies to travel the two yards to the goal line.

Jason saw the halfback leap, and he lunged upward to meet him. The two clashed in midair in a loud explosion of popping pads. The blow spun the dazed back around and the ball flew free. The two players fell onto the mass of bodies that were scrambling for the ball.

Duggin lowered his head, seeing Chuck jump up from the pile holding the ball and the Crazies go wild in exultation.

Jason got up feeling faint. The adrenaline high was gone, leaving him with tremors of pain shooting up his arm. Chuck gave him a toothless smile and helped him up. "You've loved it enough . . . ya damn Crazy."

Duggin turned around and bumped into the defensive coach, who was standing behind him. Duggin smiled and tapped his clipboard. "That's one more scholarship we'll get back for the spring."

The defensive coach stepped out of the way and shook his head. "You gained a scholarship but lost a kid who had heart."

"Heart isn't good enough," Duggin snorted.

The coach motioned toward the field. "Case you didn't notice, 'heart' just whipped your offensive team's ass."

Ty left the school gym and got into his car feeling good. He'd tried playing a little basketball and found he hadn't lost any of his skills. His hands had regained their flexibility, and he'd start practicing and try out when the season started in late November. He pulled into the driveway of the house and walked into the kitchen as the phone rang. Mea answered and saw him in the doorway. "Ty, it's for you, honey."

Surprised, Ty walked into the living room and picked up the phone. "Hello?"

"Ty, act like you're talking to one of your friends. This is Jason, and I wanna tell you something that I don't want Mom to know just yet."

Ty leaned forward and peeked into the kitchen and lowered his voice. "Mom's in the kitchen. What'sa matter?"

Jason spoke evenly. "I had a little accident playing ball today, nothing serious, just dislocated my elbow. The doctors have already popped it back in place and have me in a sling. It'll be fine in a couple of weeks. I don't want Dad or Mom to know about it, or they'll come over. You know how they are."

"Sure, I understand," said Ty, trying not to sound alarmed.

"Good. Ty, could you do me another favor? Could you pick me up Friday night and take me back home? I want a little time for the swelling to go down, and I can explain better in person if I'm there."

"Sure, I'll be there. You take care, huh?"

"Thanks, brother, I will. See ya Friday."

Jason handed the phone to Chuck and sat down. Chuck hung up the receiver and joined him. "Don't be hangin' your head. Ya got the rest of the semester paid for. Hell, ya can drop out for a semester and make enough money to come back next fall."

Jason sighed and looked at the sling. "Nah, I'm like you . . . I can't go home and face them. Dad would only go in hock and make me stay in school. I talked to some people and took some tests a few weeks ago . . . I have some options."

"What options?" Chuck raised an eyebrow suspiciously.

Jason stood up and walked for the door. "You oughta know; you gave me the idea."

Chuck quickly caught up with a pained expression. "You didn't."

"Not yet, but I passed all the tests with flying colors, and they said I could be an officer by next fall. What is OCS, anyway?"

Chuck's shoulders sagged. "Damn, Jay, there's a war on now. It ain't the same as when I was in. You're gonna finish the semester, aren't ya?"

Jason looked up at the fall night and took in a deep breath. "Yeah, Duggin can't pull my scholarship till after Christmas. The Army can get me on a bus the first week in January for basic training and then send me to this OCS place to be an officer."

Chuck couldn't help but smile. "It ain't a place, it's a school . . . shit, you an officer. God help us all. A Chuck-trained Crazy defendin' our great country from the Communist horde. Now, don't that beat all?"

Jason laughed so as not to cry. He'd never felt so low in all his life. The Army was a way to finish school. There were no other options for him. Working meant living at home to save money. Borrowing money was impossible, and taking borrowed money from his dad was unthinkable.

Jason patted his big friend's back. "I have two dollars to my name. Will you buy us some beer?"

Chuck gave an expression of shock. "You don't drink!"

Jason looked down the darkened road toward his future. "You're right, but tonight I think I need one . . . just one to kill the pain."

Chuck laughed and threw his arm over Jason's shoulder. "One, my ass, I got a couple of bucks my ownself. We gonna drink up

enough to drown your worries away. Hell, I might even join . . .
naw! Not again! Come on, we got some serious painkillin' to do.''

Ty picked up Jason's bag and tossed it in the backseat. Jason
whistled and kicked the Black Widow's front tire. "Nice, brother,
real nice.''

Ty lifted the hood and motioned toward the spotless engine.
"Flathead V8 that's made for draggin', rolled and tucked seats
for cruisin', and a stud behind the wheel ready for lovin'. Jay,
I'm R-E-D-D-Y, RED-Deeee for action!''

Jason laughed and threw his good arm around Ty. "Just get me
home, will ya?''

The two got in the car and in minutes were on the open road. Ty
couldn't help but cringe as Jason told him how he had dislocated
his elbow and of the doctor popping it back into place. Jason lifted
the slung arm. ". . . and since then it hasn't hurt that much. Throbs
a little, but the sling really helps.''

Ty glanced at Jason with concern. "Will you be ready for spring
practice?''

Jason was silent for a moment and looked out the window. "I
won't be playing this spring. I lost the scholarship.''

"What?''

Jason spoke evenly. "Duggin is pulling my scholarship at the
end of the semester. Don't say anything to anybody . . . and don't
be shocked when I flat out lie to Dad and Mom when they ask me
about spring ball. I don't want them going into debt to keep me in
school.''

Ty couldn't concentrate and pulled off the road, stopping the car.
"What the heck ya gonna do?''

Jason smiled and raised an eyebrow. "Would you believe, join
the Army?''

Ty's jaw dropped. "The Army? No way, brother. Duane and
Mom will never let it happen.'' Ty broke into a nervous laugh.
"The Army, are you crazy?''

Jason's smile dissolved. "It's too late; I joined. I'm leaving the
middle of January for Fort Bliss, Texas.''

"Damn, Jay, you can't mean it!'' Ty could see by Jason's expression that he wasn't kidding, and he spoke softly. "You shoulda
told me. I have four hundred dollars left in the bank, I would have
given it to you.''

Jason shook his head. "Thanks, but I couldn't have taken your
money or anybody else's. I gotta make it on my own . . . come on,

I need a hug from Becky. Kick this black bucket in the ass and get me home.''

Ty pulled onto the road, upset at the news, knowing his mother would take it very badly and Duane would become even more of an ass to live with. "When ya gonna tell 'em?''

Jason leaned back in the seat. "After Christmas. Until then it's just our secret, okay?''

Ty didn't like it but nodded. "Okay, but you know it's gonna break Mom's heart.''

Jason didn't respond as he looked at the passing plowed fields.

Becky tried to catch her breath and lightly pushed Jason back. "Let's get in the backseat.''

Jason sighed. The Mustang's bucket seats sure weren't made for making out, but getting in the small backseat wouldn't be any better. He held his sling out. "You know how you are. You'd probably break my arm. Let's go somewhere with some room.''

Becky brushed back her hair and quickly started the car. "Let's go to my house and watch the late movie. My folks will be in bed.''

Jason leaned over the stick shift, giving her a light kiss before sitting back. "I've missed you so much. Now that football is over I can come home every weekend and make up for lost time.''

"You've got me shaking all over. Do you know how good it's going to be next year when I get to Central with you?''

Jason nodded in silence, feeling his stomach twisting into a knot. He wanted to tell her, but it wasn't the right time. He closed his eyes, knowing deep inside that there would never be such a time.

Ty pounded the nail into the stud as Jason held the board flush with his one good arm. Ty had gotten up early to work on the cabin and was surprised to find Jason sitting at the kitchen table waiting for him. He'd said he couldn't do much with one arm, but he wanted to help. The two had worked all morning putting up the wall siding.

Ty finished pounding in the nail and slipped the hammer into his apron loop. "Jay, I gotta be honest with you, I didn't want ya to help me. I had it in my mind I'd build the whole thing by myself.'' Ty broke into a smile and patted Jason's back. "But I gotta say I'm sure glad I changed my mind. You're darn good help.''

"You're just saying that 'cause I'm cheap.''

Ty laughed and picked up another board. "You got it.''

Jason was about to pick up the other end of the board to help him when a car horn honked.

Ty let the board drop, seeing Becky's blue Mustang pull up to the gate. She got out of the car carrying a large basket and a jug of iced tea. She was wearing blue jeans and a football jersey.

She raised the basket as she approached. "Lunch time, guys. Take a break and eat some of my good fried chicken."

Ty tossed down his hammer and slapped Jason's back. "I'm the boss and I didn't hear any lunch whistle. We've still got work to do."

"Come on, boss," Jason said, "we need a break. We can't turn down a good-lookin' woman."

Ty looked around. "Where?"

Becky threw paper napkins at him in mock anger. Ty opened the basket. "Okay, okay, I'm easy. Let's eat."

Thirty minutes later, the three of them climbed up the hill to see the view. Becky stepped gingerly along the trail, avoiding the piles of cow manure.

Jason abruptly halted and said to Ty, "What kind of tracks are these?"

Ty glanced at the prints in the soft soil. "A badger. He was huntin' last night and probably got himself some young rabbits."

"Badgers don't eat rabbits, do they?" Becky said, making a face.

Ty squatted down, looking more closely at the animal's tracks. "Yep, they sure do. Badgers are bad news and meaner than snakes . . . y'all want to see where this one lives?"

Becky glanced nervously at the ground around her feet. "You know where his hole is?"

"No, but we can track him right to it."

Becky shook her head in disbelief. "There aren't any more tracks. You'd never find it."

Jason laughed and patted Ty's back. "You've got to be kidding. This here is Ty Nance, a gifted Kiowa hunter who has the spirit of the buffalo. I've seen him track coyotes, raccoons, even wild turkeys. Who do you think has put the turkey on the table for the past four years?"

Becky rolled her eyes. "Bull. You guys are full of it."

Jason shrugged his shoulders. "Woman, you are doubting the very best." He waved his hand at Ty. "Brother, if you would be so kind as to demonstrate to this nonbeliever."

Ty smiled and took a few steps and waved Becky over. "Look at this carpet of leaves. See how they're not broken or crumbly? Now look at this one and this one. See the difference? They've been stepped on. He's heading straight, so that means he's going back to his hole. If his trail meandered it'd mean he was searchin' and sniffin' around for his meal. These tracks tell us he found what he was looking for, got full, and headed straight home. They're nasty in their eating habits, 'cause they leave the rabbit heads to mark the boundaries of their hunting grounds. Even coyotes won't mess with 'em."

Becky nervously looked around her feet with renewed interest. "I've seen enough, I believe. Now let's go on up the hill. If that thing eats bunnies he might decide to munch on my feet."

Ty laughed. "Okay. Come on. This Kiowa hunter is boss and we've got work to do."

"What about me?" said Becky, pouting.

"You're going to help," Ty said.

"Great, and I thought with the good food I could convince your brother to ravish my body."

Jason winked at Ty. "How about it, boss, ravish or work?"

Ty pointed toward the trail. "Work first, ravish later."

Jason put his arm around Becky and started toward the path. "Somehow I knew he was gonna say that. I haven't taught my little brother worth a damn."

8

Deep within the rugged, jungle-covered mountains, just seven miles from the Cambodian border, an American battalion began its march up a narrow valley known as the Ia Drang. North Vietnamese scouts of the Sixty-sixth Regiment, Eighth Battalion, stood on a hill overlooking the valley and saw the unit's first company break out of the jungle and cross a small elephant-grass meadow. The scouts immediately ran down a narrow path to report what they had seen to their commander.

The tall, silver-haired regimental commander sat by a huge sayo tree pondering the information he had just received. His regiment had already had two battalions decimated in the past week's fighting, but this was an opportunity he could not ignore. The Eighth had time to set up an ambush and pay back in kind what American artillery and bombs had done to his men. The Americans were moving to a large open area at the mouth of the valley and would walk directly into a well-set trap.

Standing, he spoke to his operations officer, who was seated by a radio. "Tell him to wipe out the Yankee battalion."

The Eighth Battalion's colonel smiled, seeing the lead American company approaching. He would please his leader with the victory. Newly promoted General Bin Ty Duc would be leaving the regiment command position to become the newly formed First Division's commander. If the ambush was successful, his leader would surely ask him to join his command as a staff officer. General Duc was a true master of warfare and would be a prominent leader after the reunification. To be with such a man assured a prosperous future.

The colonel turned and nodded to his company commander, who immediately dropped his hand. The valley's silence was shattered by machine-gun fire.

The first Americans were caught in tall elephant grass with no place to take cover and were mowed down along with the green stalks. The noise of battle steadily increased into an ear-shattering roar as more and more of the colonel's men brought their weapons to bear on the exposed enemy.

Taking cover behind a tree, the colonel yelled over the noise to his radioman, "Tell General Duc we are engaging!"

9

Jimmy Higgins pushed open the gym door and looked out into the rainy night. "Ty, can I hitch a ride with ya?"

Ty walked out of the locker room toward the door. Basketball practice had lasted until seven again. "Sure, Jim, you can ride, but for a price."

Jimmy shrugged his thin shoulders, "All I got is a dime, man."

"Naw, I don't want money," Ty said, "but how's about letting me score a few points next practice? Ya makin' me look bad."

Jim smiled shyly. Ty hunched his shoulders before making the dash toward his car. "Come on, Skinny, ya ain't gonna melt."

Ty ran into the parking lot and swore as he approached his car. The side window was down. He opened the door and slid into the seat, hitting something. He began to feel for what it was when an overwhelming odor hit him. "What the . . ."

Jimmy got in the car but quickly got out, waving his hand in front of his face. "Damn, Ty, you openin' a liquor store?"

"Aw, shit!" Ty got out of the car and swept a soggy paper bag holding a broken bottle of liquor from the front seat. "Some son of a bitch is gonna pay for this. Damn, Skinny, somebody threw a busted bottle of booze into my car."

Jimmy got back in the Ford and rolled down the window. "Come on, I got supper awaitin'."

Ty mumbled as he slid in behind the steering wheel again and started the car. "Who the heck would do somethin' like that?"

He pulled onto Canal Street and sped up to thirty-five. He was about to push down the signal lever when a red light began flashing behind him. "Damn, ain't Cliff got nothing better to do than hassle us?" he said. Twenty-five was the limit on Canal, but nobody ever kept to that.

Ty pulled over and rolled his eyes at Jimmy. "This will be the normal five-minute lecture."

Sheriff Hamby leaned into the car window with a flashlight in his hand. He began to speak but smelled the whiskey and jerked back. "I'll be damned, it's true! Get outta the car, boys, and put your hands on the hood."

Ty slumped his shoulders. Cliff had an official tone to his voice tonight. He musta been watching "Highway Patrol" again. "Come on, Sheriff, it's rainin'," he complained.

Hamby opened the car door and waved his flashlight in Ty's face. "I got a call says y'all was drinkin' in the school parking lot, and it sure smells like it to me. Git out, boy, or I'll run your butt in right now."

Ty slid out of the seat as Jimmy tried to explain what happened. Hamby shined the light on the floor, then leaned over and looked under the seat. He froze for a moment and reached under it, pulling out a half-empty bottle of Jack Daniels. Ty's eyes widened, and he began to speak, but Hamby barked, "Shut up, both of ya. You're both in serious trouble."

In the darkness, parked two blocks away, sat two men in a red Chevy. Melvin Summers smiled.

Duane paced back and forth in front of the sheriff's desk as Hamby read the list of charges. "Speeding and possession of an alcoholic beverage with the seal broken. The charge of driving under the influence is dropped for insufficient evidence." Hamby raised his bloodshot eyes from the report. "Neither one of the boys had liquor on his breath, and both of 'em passed the sobriety test. I don't like it no more than you do, Duane, but I gotta charge Ty with the first two counts."

Duane stopped pacing. "Who called and said they were drinking?"

"Don't know who it was," Hamby said, leaning back in his chair. "It was a man's voice. He just said he was a concerned citizen."

Duane slumped in one of the side chairs. "Can we handle this between us?"

"Wish I could, but I can't when it's dealin' with liquor. Ty is gonna have to go before the justice of the peace and get his fine pronounced. It'll cost him seventy-five for the open bottle and fifteen for speedin'. I ain't a lawyer, and I'm not supposed to tell you this, but the best bet is just pay the fine and forget it. He's still a minor in the eyes of the law. It's a good lesson, and nothing will go on his permanent record."

"Shit! I knew something like this was going to happen."

Duane began his verbal lashing as soon as Ty was released. Ty remained silent and walked directly for the table to collect his keys and billfold.

"Look at me, goddamnit!" Duane snarled. "You have shamed your mother and me. The whole town will know about this tomorrow morning. How are your mother and me gonna face them?"

Ty put his billfold in his back pocket without looking up. He started for the door, but Duane grabbed his arm, spinning him around, and pushed him toward the table. "No, you don't! You're not going anywhere until you apologize to me and tell me where you got the bottle!"

Ty jerked his arm free from Duane's grip and glared coldly. "I'm not apologizing to you or anybody else 'cause I didn't do anything."

Duane stepped forward, menacingly raising his hand. Hamby

quickly blocked Duane's path. "Settle down, Duane. You can't be hittin' your boy!"

Duane backed up, shaking with rage. "Then lock him back up! I'm not signing for him. A night in jail will change his mind about drinking."

Hamby ran his hand through his thinning hair with annoyance. "Be reasonable, Duane. It don't look good for the kid to be locked up. Mea ain't gonna like it, and it costs the town five dollars. Take him home and settle down, will ya?"

Duane ignored Hamby and pointed a finger at Ty. "This is a lesson you won't forget!" He picked up the release form he'd signed earlier and tore it up as he went out the door.

Ty got up stiffly from the mildewed mattress and blinked his eyes to accustom himself to the light. Hamby tiredly opened the cell door. "Your mom signed for ya."

Ty shivered as he glanced at his watch. It was midnight. He walked into the office and saw his mother sitting by the desk with a look on her face that broke his heart. She held an expression of worry, love, and disappointment that only a mother could have.

Mea hugged him without saying a word and handed him his car keys and billfold. Ty began to speak, but she raised her hand and touched his lips. "Just go home, honey. I know you didn't do it. We'll talk tomorrow."

Ty began to leave but turned and hugged his mother again. "I love you, Mom."

Mea nodded in silence and motioned him to go. She wiped her eyes and sat down, looking at Hamby. "Cliff, tell me exactly what happened again, please."

Jimmy saw Ty leave Coach's office with his head down and knew something was wrong. "What's up, Ty?"

Ty walked to his locker and suddenly exploded in anger, slamming his fist into the metal door. He threw the door back and ripped off his jersey.

Jimmy sat down on the bench behind Ty and spoke softly. "What happened, man?"

Ty threw his shoes into the locker and spun around. "The damn school board voted to throw me off the team! That asshole Summers told them I'd already made trouble this year. Can you believe those bastards! They said because of my 'history' and because I paid the fine I had admitted guilt."

"What'd Coach say?"

Ty's eyes lost their fire. "He did everything he could. He even pleaded with them, but the do-goody assholes wouldn't listen. I'm through."

Jimmy looked up at his friend with sympathy. "I'm sorry, Ty, it just isn't right."

Ty lowered his head. Damn those self-righteous bastards!

Ty walked in the school cafeteria door and paid his quarter to see the first game of the season. The Meyers High cafeteria was a long, single-storied brick building attached to the gymnasium. Both buildings had been constructed several years before and were the only modern additions to the fifty-year-old school.

He had mixed emotions about going to this first game of the season, but he didn't want people to think the school board had gotten the best of him. Besides, he had to get away from the house. Duane had become impossible to be around. Every time his stepfather spoke to him the words were venomous. The tension had been so bad between them that even Thanksgiving had been ruined. The family had sat through the entire meal in nervous silence.

Ty sat alone and watched the first half, fighting a sickening feeling of frustration at not playing. During halftime he walked into the crowded cafeteria and bought a Coke. Taking a sip, he was about to go back to get away from the stares but noticed Clifton, Becky's younger brother, standing in a corner of the cafeteria in what looked like a heated argument with Billy Ray Stevens.

Ty walked up behind Billy Ray as he snickered, "Come outside, you little shit, let's see if you're as tough as your mouth."

Ty brushed past Billy Ray and leaned against the wall beside Clifton. "Howdy, Cliff. Ya enjoying the game?"

Clifton pointed with contempt at Billy Ray. "He's drunk and saying nasty things about Sis!"

"Billy Ray has a bad habit of talking like that. He didn't mean nothin' by it." Ty's eyes narrowed and shifted to Billy Ray. "Did ya?"

Billy Ray met Ty's stare. "This ain't your concern, asshole."

Ty took a sip of his Coke, ignoring the senior's foul alcohol-laden breath, and looked up at the ceiling. "Well, ya see, it is my business. Clifton here is a friend of mine, and so is his sister."

"Bullshit, Nance. That big-titted bitch will drop your brother's sorry ass!"

Clifton pushed off the wall toward Billy Ray, but Ty put his hand out, stopping him. "Relax, Cliff, he's half-drunk and pissed 'cause

Becky laughs at him when he asks her out. He's lookin' for trouble. Let's go and let him find some grade schoolers to pick on.'' Ty took Clifton's arm and began to lead him toward the gym door.

Seething, Billy Ray snarled at Ty's back, ''She ain't worth fuckin'. I'll bet it ain't just your brother. I'll bet your filthy Indian cock's been in her, too.''

Ty spun around, but Billy Ray was already swinging and landed a blow that glanced off the side of Ty's forehead. Ty went down to one knee with the punch but savagely jabbed a fist into Billy Ray's groin, doubling him over. With teeth bared, Ty rose and viciously jerked his knee up, smashing Billy Ray's nose and face. Billy Ray tumbled back onto a table, with Ty following. Then, grabbing his hair and jerking his head up, Ty ruthlessly slugged him in the jaw, knocking him to the floor, and fell on his chest, grabbing for his throat.

''STOP IT! STOP IT, TY! You're killing him!'' screamed Clifton, grabbing Ty's shoulders. Ty heard nothing. He applied more pressure, wanting to rip out Billy Ray's windpipe. Several more people tried to pull him off, when suddenly everything went hazy.

Sheriff Hamby shook his hand in pain and threw his other arm up. ''Back up, people, it's all over. Back up!''

The crowd backed up, avoiding stepping in the expanding pool of blood coming from Billy Ray's broken nose and busted mouth. Hamby lifted Ty up, but his legs were still wobbly and he sunk to his knees. The sheriff knelt beside Billy Ray, who was gasping for air in panicked desperation. Hamby spoke calmly. ''Easy, kid, take a deep breath . . . easy now . . . breathe in . . . now out. Good, do it again.'' Hamby looked up and spoke quickly to one of the onlookers. ''Virgil, go call Doc Riddle.''

Mr. Summers waded through the crowd and raised his hands. ''Folks, we need your cooperation. Please clear the cafeteria and go back to your seats. Please, folks, we need the cafeteria cleared!''

Ty shook his head, still feeling dizzy, and got up with the help of Clifton. Blood trickled down his face from the cut above his eye as he looked at the faces in the crowd. They stared at him and his blood-covered hands with fear and shock as if he were a crazed animal. He turned away from their stares and looked at Billy Ray lying on the bloody floor. He'd hurt Billy Ray worse than he'd intended. He couldn't help it. He didn't remember a single blow or punch he'd thrown. It was just a blur in his memory, except for the loathing hate he'd felt.

* * *

Miss Applegate, the home economics teacher, dabbed Ty's cut with a cotton ball as the sheriff questioned him. ". . . so Billy Ray says what to you?''

Ty looked at the teacher with embarrassment and turned his eyes to the sheriff. "I don't think Miss Applegate would appreciate what he said.''

She glared at Ty, then at Hamby. "I was a nurse before I was a teacher. I'm sure I've heard worse than you two can imagine. Tell him, Ty. Don't mind me. You've got a nasty cut that needs cleaning.''

Ty exchanged glances with Hamby, but the sheriff nodded. Ty told him what was said and all he could remember about the fight up until the moment he blacked out.

Hamby raised his bruised hand after Ty had concluded. "It was me that hit ya that last time. Sorry, I guess my ring caused the cut, but damn, you was killin' that kid. Sure glad I stopped by to see how the game was goin'. You messed him up pretty bad, but your story checks with Clifton, so there won't be any charges pressed against you.''

Hamby sighed and tossed his hat to the table. "But you sure went beyond shuttin' his mouth for insultin' you and the girl. Jesus, you was killin' that boy. You can go home tonight, but come by the office tomorrow and write me a statement for the record. I'm having Billy Ray write his statement at Doc Riddle's office tonight so his folks won't have no lawyers sniffin' around. Far as I'm concerned, it's history, but you'd better watch your p's and q's. You're gettin' a bad rep, Mr. kid.''

Mr. Summers followed Ty outside and tapped his shoulder roughly. Ty turned around.

"Mr. Nance, your conduct was uncalled for,'' Summers said, scowling. "Violence is never the answer to life's problems. You are on probation, and you are forbidden to attend any school extracurricular activities for a month. I cannot condone your or Billy Ray's actions, and I must make an example of both of you. Do you have anything you want to say for yourself?''

Ty looked at him with contempt, knowing he'd practiced his little speech and was waiting for a retort so he could slap him with another month of probation.

Ty wanted to grab Summers's tie and jerk him over his shoulder, but instead he shook his head in brooding silence.

Summers wasn't satisfied with the wordless answer and pushed his luck by extending his hand. "As gentlemen, I want you to promise me you'll shake hands with Billy Ray.''

Ty ignored him. He turned around and headed for his car.

Summers lowered his hand and puffed out his chest. "Two months' probation, Mr. Nance."

10

Ty gave Sa Tonkee a bucket of oats for his Christmas present and left the warmth of the small barn. The biting wind tore through his flannel shirt, chilling him to the bone before he reached the backdoor steps. The smell of the cedar Christmas tree welcomed him into the quiet house. The family had gone that afternoon to visit Duane's parents in Oklahoma City and would be back tomorrow.

Ty walked into the darkened living room and sat down in the rocking chair. The blinking Christmas tree lights reflected off his face as he stared at the tree he and Jason had cut down on the hill. He wasn't in the Christmas spirit, knowing his brother would soon be telling his mother about leaving for the Army. The TV news had been reporting heavy fighting, and the recent toll of American deaths had gone over a thousand men. A huge peace rally in Washington was still making the news, and many were claiming the war was a mistake. A young Quaker had gone so far as to pour gasoline on himself in front of the Pentagon and burn himself to death in protest against the war. Hardly a season of love and peace, he thought.

Jason adjusted the throw pillow and tried to get comfortable on the lumpy sofa. He hated staying the night at his grandparents' house. They were wonderful people, but there was nothing to do but sit around and talk about the old days. Becky had been a good trouper and had looked at all the family photo albums with the appropriate laughs and giggles, but he'd known she was bored. She had been the lucky one. She had gotten a bed in the den. His dad and mom were staying in the guest room upstairs and he'd gotten the couch. Great, he'd never get any sleep.

Jason shut his eyes but felt strange, as if someone were watching him. He raised up and saw Becky standing in the doorway. The light in the stairway was on, silhouetting her. She was wearing a light cotton sleeping gown that revealed every sensual cleft and mound. He gasped, thinking it was a dream, but she walked toward him whispering, "I'm cold."

He swung his legs off the sofa just as she sat down and pulled the blanket around her. "It's no wonder, Beck. That thing is too thin. Didn't you bring anything else to wear?" She snuggled next to him shivering. "I have you. Hug me, I'm freezing."

Jason nervously looked toward the hallway but knew they couldn't be heard. Becky raised up and kissed him passionately and pushed him back on the sofa. She whispered huskily, "Get me really warm, like you do."

She maneuvered her hips between his legs. His body responded immediately as she began rubbing against him.

Jason groaned in pain; his pajama bottoms and underwear were binding in the wrong place. Her rubbing was like sandpaper against his sensitive skin. He grabbed her in a death grip, stopping her gyrating.

Becky raised up, looking at him in astonishment. "That was quick. What about me?"

He laughed and lifted her off him, then stood up and smoothed down the bunched-up material around his groin. "I know I haven't got much control, but this time my underwear got me."

Becky giggled as he sat down and ran her hand down the waist of his pajamas while pulling up her gown. "I like this just as much. Touch me, I need to . . ."

Jason lifted her hand up to his face. "Beck, let's get married."

Her eyes widened, seeing that he was serious. She leaned over and kissed his chin. "We can't. We have to plan for the future. We . . ."

"T'hell with plans," Jason said, pulling back. "Let's get married."

Becky didn't like his tone of voice. He was talking crazy and meaning every word. She pushed down her gown, suddenly feeling self-conscious. "Jay, we can't get married now, we're too young. We have years to have fun and . . ."

Jason picked up the blanket from the floor and lay back on the sofa. Becky had returned to the den after kissing him good night.

She'd left, believing her wonderful plans were back on track. He
shut his eyes, knowing he would have to tell her, but not until after
the new year began. He needed the time, time to figure out how to
tell her that the Army had plans, too.

11

Ya think your elbow is gonna be okay?'' asked Ty, lifting the
suitcase to his lap.

Jason extended his arm and flexed like a bodybuilder. "Strong
as ever; I've been doing push-ups every night."

Ty nodded with a weak smile and looked around the small bus
station. There was only one other passenger sitting in the waiting
area, an older woman behind them who was staring blankly at the
wall clock. Ty was glad Jason had insisted the good-byes be given
at the house. It had been worse than a funeral. His mother and
Becky had cried the whole time. Even Duane had broken down
before they left. Jason had remained dry-eyed throughout the ordeal
and reassured them all that he'd be fine and be back on leave in
four months. Mea had loaded him down with boxes of food, and
Duane had slipped him twenty dollars. Becky smothered him in
kisses and gave him an expensive watch. Whatever Mea might think,
one thing about Becky was for sure in Ty's eyes—the girl had style.

Ty squirmed in his seat. Like Mea, he hated his brother going to
the Army. The news was getting worse: 1,643 Americans killed
and 8,000 wounded. The North Vietnamese Army was reported to
have two hundred thousand men in the south. President Johnson
had said in his State of the Union address that the U.S. would stay
in Vietnam until the aggression stopped, and he would continue to
build a great society here at home. Ty couldn't help but wonder
who was going to do the building if all the young men were fighting
in Vietnam.

Jason glanced at his new watch; there wasn't much time. "Ty,

I'm sorry about you and Dad. I wish there was something I could do.''

Ty shrugged his shoulders. "Don't worry about it. Things are gonna get better.''

"I'm worried about you," Jason said.

"Heck, don't worry about me. I'm gonna move into the cabin in the spring and start work helpin' ol' man Randall on his farm. He's gonna pay two-fifty an hour. Things are lookin' up.''

Jason wasn't convinced. He had seen the way his father looked at Ty. Coach Duggin had looked at him in the same way. It was a test of wills, and Ty was winning by feigning indifference. The frustration in his father was building and turning more bitter. His dad had become so short-tempered he couldn't stay in the same room with Ty. Perhaps Ty's moving out of the house and being on his own would be best, but it would be terrible for Mea. The sun rose and set on her son. She would be the real loser in the conflict.

The big Trailways bus pulled to the curb and its door swung open. Jason remained seated and hugged Ty to him. "Ty, I didn't tell you this too many times, but I love ya. Take care of yourself and promise me one thing, will ya?''

"Sure.''

Jason stood and looked into his eyes. "Promise me you'll finish school. No matter what happens between you and Dad, you hang tough in school and finish. Don't drop out to pay bills, 'cause I'm going to send some money to you. Just keep that temper of yours under control.''

Ty held out his hand. "No sweat . . . and keep your money, I'm not gonna need it. Now promise me somethin' . . . don't get your butt shot off, huh?''

Jason smiled and took Ty's hand, pulling him to his feet. "It's a deal.''

Ty watched the bus pull away, feeling like a piece of him was missing. He had only shaken Jason's hand and hadn't told him how he felt . . . he loved him, too.

"Down people! Get on down and knock out ten!'' barked the drill sergeant, his hands on his hips. Private Jason Johnson was the first to complete the push-ups and snapped back to attention. The sergeant noted Johnson was first again, but that wasn't anything new. Johnson was a model soldier, and the sergeant had selected him to be his platoon guide.

The stiff-backed noncom eyed his recruits from beneath his wide-brimmed campaign hat and began pacing again. "Dummies, either you listen or you gonna push up Texas higher than the grrreat state of Colorado. If I see anybody sleepin' in my class again, you gonna paaay.''

Jason looked around to make sure his men were paying attention. He'd found basic training nothing more than an extended college football practice. It was all the same except that the hours were much longer. The intent was to weed out those who were weak and build a team of winners. The hollering and screaming were at times unnerving, but he'd learned quickly enough that if you did well, you were rewarded for your efforts. The training was a mental game that he saw through the first couple of days. The sergeants wanted and demanded blind discipline. If he gave them what they wanted and listened to their every word, it wasn't too difficult. The soldiers having the hardest time were those who rebelled against being told what to do. The classes were mostly a matter of staying awake. Nothing was complicated, only repetitive to the point of boredom. Marching, drill and ceremonies, manual of arms, guard duty, and weapons training were all new to him, but easy to pick up, though physically demanding in the extreme. The physical training part was where he excelled. Surprisingly, most of the young men were in poor condition and were always behind the power curve. They were so sore and miserable from PT that they didn't listen to instructions and instead concentrated on their own aches and pains. They paid for being out of shape by having to do more PT, starting the vicious circle over again. The benefits of being platoon guide included not having to pull KP or guard duty. Both duties meant the victim would lose some of the most valuable commodity in basic training—sleep.

The last month had passed by in a blur. The only bright spot in training was mail call. Becky had been writing almost every day, keeping him up on events in Meyers. Her letters made him feel like he was back home for a while.

The sergeant finished his class and motioned Jason to him. "Johnson, the company commander inspected your platoon barracks this morning. You did good. Your people will get a forty-eight-hour pass this weekend. You made it happen, so you get to tell them." The sergeant began to turn around but stopped. "Johnson, I've seen a lot of dummies go through this zoo, but you're one of the better ones I've had. If you don't get a big head or get lazy on me, you'll be this company's honor graduate. 'Course, it won't buy you a cup of coffee, but it'll make me look good." The sergeant smiled and spoke with pride. "I've had the last two honor grads, so I know what I'm talkin' about. You're doin' good, Johnson, real good. I'm proud of you.''

Jason also felt pride and knew he'd made the right decision in joining. The Army liked him and he liked the Army. It was a marriage of understanding. He knew what they wanted, and he was willing to give it.

He formed the platoon and told them about the pass. Their smiles started goose bumps running up his back, and he stood a little taller. A month before, his men had been civilians from every part of the country and from every conceivable background. The past weeks, they'd become leaner and tougher as they struggled to become soldiers. They were slowly being shaped and molded to fit into the green machine, but Jason knew every one of them by name and where they were from. To him, these men were not numbers or cogs in the green machine's grinding wheel. They were his people, and he cared about them. They responded to him, confided to him their hopes, dreams, and fears. Some cried at night in loneliness and others still wet the bed, but they were becoming soldiers, young men he was chosen to lead.

Jason smiled with pride, knowing he was partly responsible for their success, but he also knew they still had a long way to go. He gathered the platoon around him, feeling confident. It was time for Crazy Chuck's spirit to get them over the top. ''Third Herd, we're half through and you know what we've put up with so far . . . well, it ain't gonna get any better. They're gonna keep pushin' us, screamin' at us, and tryin to get rid of some of us, but we ain't losin' another man! They *can't* get rid of anybody in the Third Herd. You know why? 'CAUSE WE LOVE THIS SHIT! What can they do to us if we love it? . . . NOTHIN'! The Third Herd is gonna be the craziest bastards in this company 'cause WE LOVE IT!''

The drill sergeant stood behind the barracks and smiled, hearing his dummies holler and scream that they were ''Crazy.'' The dummies *were* crazy. Johnson was good. He was a natural leader who knew how to motivate men to perform above their capabilities. The dummies were gonna need it. Johnson had done what none of the other trainee leaders and other drill sergeants had: he'd made his platoon a team. He had found the key that would unlock the door to success for the platoon, teamwork. As individuals, they'd fall on their ass, but as a team, they'd be unbeatable.

He chuckled to himself and headed for the orderly room. It was standard practice to bet a few bucks with the other Drills on who would have the honor platoon. Today was the day to put down his twenty greenbacks. Tomorrow the highly motivated Crazy Third Herd would be a sure thing.

Becky picked up her pen and stared at the light blue stationery. It was hard to know what to say. Over the past few days, it had become more and more difficult to write and be positive. Her friends felt sorry for her. Jason's stupid pride had ruined everything. She'd known he couldn't change his mind once he'd signed up, so she hadn't made a scene when he left, but the consequences of his joining the Army were all too clear. She'd be going to college without a boyfriend to take her to parties and to help her enjoy campus life as she had planned. Instead, she would have to be lonely for three years. Three years! She'd be a junior before he got home!

She tossed the pen down and lay on her pillow. All her plans for the future were gone. Jason had said he'd be an officer within the year and be making enough money for them to live comfortably, but she didn't want to get married next year. Nor did she want to follow him to some godforsaken Army post. She'd promised herself she wouldn't be like the other girls that married after school. She wouldn't do it!

She looked at Jason's picture on the nightstand and lowered her eyes. Tears trickled down her face as she rose and picked up the pen. She'd tell him now . . . no, next month when he came home. Yes, she could wait a month. One month more and her girlfriends wouldn't think badly of her. They would understand.

12

Becky leaned back in her chair, tired of the history teacher's rambling. She looked across the aisle at Ty, who seemed to be genuinely interested in Nazi Germany of 1939. She tried to get his attention and show him her acceptance letter from Central State College, but he was totally engrossed. Minutes later, the bell rang and she followed him into the crowded hallway. She was about to speak when she saw Mr. Summers standing at the end of the hall, pointing his finger toward Ty. "Mr. Nance, come here!"

The milling students hushed and made a path for Ty as he walked toward the principal. Becky moved closer. Ty stopped in front of him and spoke clearly. "Yes, sir?"

Summers jerked his other hand up, which was holding a wrench. "You recognize this, Mr. Nance? You should; it's the wrench you stole from the school auto shop!"

Ty glanced at the wrench, then shifted his eyes back to Summers. "I don't know what you're talking about, sir."

Summers leaned closer. "You're lying. I found this wrench in the front seat of your car just minutes ago. There was a theft at the shop last night, and I got a tip from someone who said they saw your car there."

Ty backed up to get away from the principal's foul breath and snarled a warning. "Don't call me a liar. I didn't do it."

Summers's face turned red and he was about to retort when he saw Sheriff Hamby walking toward them. Summers pointed at Ty. "Here he is, Cliff; get him out of here."

Hamby took one look at the other students in the hallway and spoke firmly. "Ain't you all supposed to be in class? Move along." His eyes narrowed on seeing Ty, and he shook his head.

Summers realized he'd lost control and waved his hand. "Go to class. The law will take care of this." He led Hamby and Ty to his office and shut the door. Hamby sighed, and reopened the door, and motioned Ty out. "Sit out here and don't be goin' anywhere, boy."

Hamby closed the door again and spun around. "What the hell ya doin'?" he whispered angrily. "I told ya when ya called me not ta do anything until I got here."

"But I found a wrench. . . ."

Hamby shook his head as if dealing with a naughty child. "Ya didn't ask permission to search the car, did ya? Ernie, ya messed this all up by taking the wrench out of the car. Ya moved the evidence and put your hands all over it. I can't prove a damn thing unless someone saw the kid doin' it. All I got is circumstantial evidence that won't get no conviction."

Summers's pudgy jaw went slack. "There must be something we can do."

Hamby frowned and grasped the doorknob. "Just keep your mouth shut and we'll see what happens." He opened the door and approached Ty. "Boy, I want permission to check your car."

Ty shrugged his shoulders. "Sure."

He led Hamby and Summers to the parking lot, while Hamby questioned him. "Where were you last night? Did anyone see you?"

Ty didn't show any discomfort as he spoke. "I was on Red Hill, working on the cabin I'm building. Nobody was there but me."

They stopped at the Black Widow. Hamby held out his hand. "Give me the key to your trunk."

Ty smiled. "It's open; the lock doesn't work."

Hamby opened the trunk. Ty's legs suddenly felt weak. Sitting on top of the spare tire was a toolbox he recognized immediately. It was from the auto shop.

Summers tapped Hamby's shoulder with a grin. "You got yourself a thief."

Billy Ray Stevens backed away from the window in the men's room. He stopped in front of a sink and leaned forward looking in the mirror above the sinks. The scar above his lip had healed, but his nose would be forever crooked. He smiled, exposing his new porcelain front teeth, and ran his tongue over the scar tissue on the roof of his mouth. He winked at himself and walked out.

Jason stood stiffly at attention as the brigade commander and sergeant major marched directly toward him. They halted two paces in front of him as the master of ceremonies spoke into the microphone. "Ladies and gentlemen, receiving the distinguished honor graduate award of the Third Basic Training Battalion is Private Jason Johnson. Private Johnson is a member of Bravo Company, Third Platoon, and his hometown is Meyers, Oklahoma. He received the highest composite training scores in the battalion. Colonel John Davis will now present the Distinguished Honor Graduate Trophy and special diploma to Private Johnson."

Colonel Davis took the bronze statue of a soldier standing at attention from the sergeant major and handed it to Jason. "Young man, you can be very proud of this accomplishment. There are over six hundred men behind you who would like to be standing where you are."

Jason took the trophy in one hand and shook hands with the other. "Thank you, sir. I wish my platoon was up here with me; they deserve it, too."

The colonel smiled and handed him his diploma. "Son, today *you* are the top dog. Enjoy it."

The two men exchanged salutes. "Private Johnson also received the company leadership award, and his platoon received the company honor platoon streamer. Private Johnson will next be attend-

ing Advanced Individual Training at Fort Benning, then attend
Officer Candidate School. . . . The recipient of the marksmanship
trophy is Private Lloyd Simms, a member of . . .''

The drill sergeant waited until the platoon returned from the
graduation ceremony before calling Jason over. He smirked. ''You
keep grinning at me like that and I'm gonna think you're queer,
dummy.''

Jason came to attention as the sergeant, rocking back on his
heels, continued. ''Johnson, you will not be going on leave, I can-
celed it. You will be boarding a bus in three hours for Fort Benning
to start an AIT course in two days. I found out this morning your
OCS class that was to start in July was delayed for a month. Knowing the Army the way I do, you might get sidetracked in that time
and not ever get in. I pulled some strings and fixed it so you could
attend the earlier AIT course and start the June OCS class.'' The
sergeant's scowl dissolved and his voice softened. ''The Army needs
leaders like you, Johnson. God knows we got a bunch of managers,
but we need leaders. You did a hell'va job, dummy. The best of
luck to you. I'd be proud to serve with you anywhere.''

Jason's eyes moistened, knowing he was receiving the highest
compliment he could ever receive from the sergeant, whom he respected more than any man he'd known.

Jason began to speak, but the sergeant squared his shoulders and
barked, ''Move out, dummy! You got a bus to catch!''

Jason spun around, conditioned to the sergeant's commands, and
began to run but stopped and turned. He knew he was supposed to
salute only officers, but there was one way to transmit his respect
toward the sergeant. He snapped to attention and raised a rigid hand
to his cap. ''Thank you . . . for everything.''

The sergeant brought his hand up in a perfect salute. ''Good-
bye . . . Crazy.''

Jason looked out the bus window into the darkness, unable to
sleep. On his lap was the box of inexpensive stationery he'd picked
up at the El Paso bus station. The box was still unopened. He turned
from the window, knowing he had to write the letter. He had to
release her. Becky had written only three letters that second month,
and they'd been considerably different from the others. He knew
after the first time he walked away empty-handed from a mail call
that he'd asked too much of her. Those last mail calls were the most
painful times he'd experienced in his life. The sergeant would hold
a handful of letters and call off the lucky soldiers' names. There
was no rhyme or reason to the process, and the entire platoon would

stay compressed together, each man hoping and sometimes praying he would be called. The last letter was the worst. The sergeant would hold the letter up and every man would hold his breath until the name was read. For those whose letter didn't come there was an moment of incredible loneliness, a quiet time that everybody respected until, finally, hope returned—there was always tomorrow.

Finally, after a week, the sergeant held up the light blue envelope that made Jason's heart skip a beat. The familiar writing on the envelope was like a miracle drug to a dying man. He savored opening the letter slowly. He read the lines, searching. Then he read them again. Something was missing. Where were the words of love and commitment? Gone, replaced by others that he didn't understand, that were vague, like a mist over their future. He knew. It was over.

From that day on he didn't want any more pain. Her letters only hurt. The unwritten words between the lines were like red-hot knives twisting in his stomach. His dreams were gone, as were hers. He couldn't hold on to the sky or stars and he couldn't hold on to her.

Jason called for strength from within and opened the box. He would tell her of his love and because of that love he would free her. He had to be the one to write the letter because he couldn't take such a letter from her. All he had left was pride. She'd taken everything else.

Ty and Mea stood in the aisle by the replacement light bulbs and anti-freeze. Sheriff Hamby stood beside the part-time justice of the peace for Meyers and the owner of the hardware and car parts store, Fred Tate, who pulled on his long nose as he read the charge sheet and statements. He squinted and looked up. "Well, Mea, I'm glad Duane has been off ta that sales conference this week. He sure wouldn't be none too happy reading this. Ty here is charged with larceny of school property. The tools are estimated to be worth a hundred dollars new, but used they wouldn't be worth forty, which ain't enough ta take ta court. The charge stands as petty theft and is a misdemeanor that I can handle."

He shifted his eyes to Ty and shook his head. "Ty, ya oughta be ashamed of yo'self. I been knowing your folks for twenty years . . . sure not fittin' you makin' all this trouble for 'em. Mr. Summers don't want you back in school, and he wants ya in jail."

Leaning on the desk, he held out the statements. "Only because I know your folks so well am I gonna be light on ya. I'm finin' ya fifty dollars and ya gotta work for the city as a trash collector for two months. You're on probation, and if anything else happens, you'll go ta court. Mr. Summers don't like it none, but ya can go back ta school but can't be takin' part in any activities up till ya graduate. You're lucky I didn't do more." He lowered his head and looked up at Mea. "Mea, I'm surely sorry 'bout all this. I know it upsets ya."

Mea kept her head held high during the entire proceedings and only nodded at her old friend while Ty had stared blankly at the rows of fan belts feeling like he was caught in a whirlpool. No matter how hard he fought and screamed, he was still hopelessly being sucked down.

Mea took Ty's arm and walked toward the door without showing any emotion. She would not show weakness to her son's false accusers. He was innocent, she knew it in her heart; no matter what they said she believed her son. His eyes would have told her if he'd been guilty.

Ty stopped outside and Ty put his arm around her thin shoulders. "What's gonna happen when Duane comes home?"

Mea looked at her son with adoration. "He'll be angry, but he will have to understand. Don't worry about it, honey, go on to school. I'll talk to him when he gets back this afternoon."

Ty kissed his mother and hugged her for her belief in him. He got into the Widow and backed up before the tears finally broke free. He loved her so much and hated himself for what he was putting her through.

Ty went to English class amidst the whispers and stares of the other students. He sat at his desk, feeling like a paroled criminal, when Mr. Summers appeared in the doorway and strode straight toward him. Mrs. Alberton stopped reading and rose to meet him. Summers waved her back and stopped in front of Ty. "Mr. Nance, take off that letter jacket. You might be able to attend this school, but you sure aren't going to shame Meyers High School by wearing our school jacket."

Ty glared but spoke quietly. "Mr. Summers, I paid for this jacket. The only thing the school gave me is the letter." He stood up, took off the jacket, and pulled out his pocketknife. He cut the corner free and ripped off the letter. He handed it to Summers and sat down.

Summers's face turned red. He spun around and waddled to the door, throwing the cloth letter in the trash can as he walked out.

Mrs. Alberton composed herself and tapped her desk for attention. "Now, if you all will turn to page twenty-three we'll discuss the . . ."

Ty stared at his jacket, wanting to scream. The son of a bitch almost pushed him too far. He should have cut the bastard's heart out and handed it to him instead.

He tried to relax, but it was impossible. Loathing was running through his veins, needing release. He crossed his arms and dug his fingernails into his arms, wanting the pain.

Classes ended at three and Ty walked out to parking lot but stopped in his tracks, seeing Duane leaning on the hood of his car. The big man stood erect and stared coldly. Ty took a deep breath and headed straight for him.

Duane clenched his fists. "You really did it this time, didn't you?"

Ty spoke evenly. "I didn't do it."

Duane rolled a stone over with his shoe. "You can cut the shit, I'm not your mother. Oh yeah, she did talk to me, but you and I are going to have it out right now. People are staring at me when I walk down the street, and I don't like it. And I don't like what you've done to your mother and this family."

Ty shrugged his shoulders. "I didn't do it. You can believe what you want, but it's the truth."

Duane smiled as if Ty had told a flat joke. "You're lying again, just like last time." He jerked his hand up, pointing his finger at Ty's face. "You've hated me since the day I first walked into that damn house. You and George resented me. I know it and you know it. Well, let me tell you something, I didn't like you either, yeah, there it is, the truth. I hated you an' George, AND that damn hill. I hated it always throwing its shadow over me and everything I ever tried to do. You and your wonderful hill! You hide behind it like your mother's skirt. It ain't nothin'! It ain't nothin' but dirt that should have been sold a long time ago!"

Ty lowered his eyes and closed his mind to his stepfather's angry words. He couldn't say or do anything to change Duane's mind about him. His mind was made up years ago.

Duane stepped closer, his eyes widening. "Look at me, damnit! I want you to know I'm glad you're moving your lying ass into that shack. Maybe now you'll pay your own bills for a change." He snickered. "But there's a catch. Ya see, you're going to be drafted within a year unless you start farming that hill of yours. I checked with the draft board, and unless you're farming a minimum of a hundred and sixty acres, you don't get a farmer's deferment. You're gonna have to cut down trees and plow up that buffalo grass and work your ass off. You won't be able to swing a hammer now and then and lay around like George did. You're gonna have to be like the rest of us and work for a living.''

He grabbed Ty's jacket and pulled him within a few inches from his face. ''Live in the cabin, but don't you ever come around asking for handouts from your mother . . . and don't screw up again and shame me, or I'll burn the damn thing to the ground and let 'em throw your lying ass in jail until you rot! You got it?''

Ty stared coldly into his eyes. ''Get your hands off me and don't *ever* touch me again.''

Duane released his grip as if he'd held something filthy and backed up. Ty's eyes had actually sent shivers up his spine. The boy looked like a wild animal about to strike for his throat.

Ty advanced with his piercing eyes locked on his stepfather. ''You're gonna tell Mom we had a nice little talk, and *we* decided I should move into the cabin, aren't you? Who's the liar, you hypocritical bastard! You ever say another bad word about Granddad again, I'll kill you.''

Duane's face turned pale. He knew he'd gone too far. Ty brushed past him and threw open the car door, hitting him in the legs. He started the engine. ''I'm glad we had this little talk. Mom will be real glad you're so understanding.'' He popped the clutch and fishtailed out of the parking lot, showering Duane with dust.

13

Ty was cold, the most miserably cold he'd ever been in his life. He was shivering so badly his jaw was sore from clenching his teeth. He rode in the back of the open trash truck at 5 A.M. with rain pelting him in the face. He'd been working for an hour and was soaked after the first five minutes. The temperature was fifty degrees, but the damnable biting Okie winds that blew from the northwest were merciless, and there was no protection from the blinding rain.

The old Ford truck stopped by the stacked trash cans, and Ty jumped off the flatbed. His hands looked like white sponges, and they hardly had any feeling, they were so cold. He picked up the first large can and hefted it to his shoulder. He'd seen the modern trash trucks in Oklahoma City but never appreciated their efficiency until he began the trash punishment job. He had to lift all the cans to the truck, get up on the bed, and dump them. Then he would toss the cans down, get off the truck, and set them in their original position. He worked four hours picking up trash in the morning before school and another three hours after school, sifting through the dumped garbage for bottles and recyclable metal cans. The first week he was so sore he could barely move. The second week was a bit better, but his shoulders and arms still seemed as if they were full of lead bricks. His body hardened by the third week, and the job was even beginning to seem tolerable until the bad weather set in. The past week of constant rain was the most miserable in his life. Each day seemed worse than the last. Getting up in the morning was painful, getting in the back of the truck was agony, and lifting the heavy cans was torture. He actually looked forward to going to school, where it was dry and he could relax his weary body.

The truck finally pulled up to the last cans on the block. Ty slid off the back, filled with the relieved feeling of surviving the agony of another day.

An hour later, he walked into school wearing a change of clothes and his symbol of defiance, the letter jacket without a letter. It was a reminder to himself and others that he was an outlaw. The stares and whispers had stopped, but there was still an invisible barrier around him. It was as if he were dying of something contagious. He was vulnerable and everyone knew it. If he got in any kind of trouble, Summers would throw him out of school.

As Ty opened his locker, Becky came up behind him and tapped his shoulder. "You heard from Jason lately?"

Ty turned around, feeling sorry for the attractive girl. He'd known, deep inside, that when Jason joined the Army, the relationship was doomed. Rebecca was a free spirit who needed a man's constant attention. She still loved Jason, in her own way, but not enough to give up her college life for him.

He nodded. "Yeah, he's training at Fort Benning and doin' really good. He called the house the other night and said he'd been selected to be the student company commander."

"That sounds good . . . I guess he likes it." She smiled faintly and took his arm as they began walking down the hall. "I think of him a lot . . . but . . ."

"I know, Beck. Get your head up. He understands."

Becky squeezed his arm. "Thanks, Ty, you've been a good friend."

Ty shrugged.

"I hear you're moving into the cabin this week," she said, stopping by a classroom door.

He spoke over his shoulder, not changing stride. "Tomorrow's freedom day."

Ty hoisted the box of clothes from the trunk and walked up the stairs into the cabin. He'd made several trips to the house to move his things out of his room but felt too tired to make any more. The long hours of trash collecting drained him. He put the clothes in an old dresser and began to sit down when he heard a car pull up. He looked out the window and shook his head.

Becky came in, carrying a small portable television set. She held it out to him and said, "This is my house . . . I mean, my cabin-warming present to you."

"Naw, Beck, I can't take something that expensive from you. I . . ."

She frowned and snapped, "Hush your face, Ty Nance." She put the TV down and looked admiringly around the room. "It's perfect . . . just perfect. You've done a fantastic job."

The pine-paneled walls and exposed rafters gave the cabin the atmosphere of a hunting lodge, especially with the pot-bellied stove in the middle of the floor. The large single room had four distinct areas. First there was the kitchen, with its small refrigerator and stove, and pine shelving covering half the wall. The eating and study portion had built-in bookshelves all the way to the ceiling and a small heavy wooden table for two. The other half of the cabin consisted of the sleeping area and a small living area with an old couch and George's rocking chair. It had a cozy, lived-in look.

She kissed his cheek lightly. "I love it. You've really made something to be proud of."

Ty stepped back shyly but felt a surge of pride. His mother had cried when she came the day before. She'd hugged him as he took her around the room, showing off his workmanship. She'd been awed and kept saying she wished his granddaddy could see it. So did he.

14

Ty raked the garbage he had just sifted through into a huge pit and stooped over to pick up the bottles he had found. The sound of tires crunching on the gravel caused him to turn around.

Sheriff Hamby stopped his cruiser behind Ty and opened his door. "How's it goin'?"

Ty hefted the box of bottles to his shoulder. "Doin' good; found four bucks' worth of bottles this load."

Hamby got out of the car and followed Ty as he walked to the trash truck and tossed the box beside the other boxes of bottles he'd collected. The sheriff looked around the dump absently. "Ain't it amazing what people throw away. The town makes a lot a money on haulin' trash and what they find to resell. Most people don't know this side of their town government."

Ty was used to the sheriff coming around and checking up on him. He wiped his hands on the back of his jeans and tiredly leaned against the truck. "I've seen more of this side than I ever wanted."

Hamby chuckled and took out a folded envelope from his shirt pocket. "Well, boy, not anymore you won't. Here's a little somethin' from your town for all the hard work ya put in." He held the envelope out to Ty.

Ty pushed off the truck, wondering what Hamby was up to. He took the envelope and opened it to find a check. He looked up with a questioning stare. "What's this for?"

Hamby smiled. "For your hard work. Ya worked your ass off without complainin' or missin' a day. The justice didn't say nothin' about you workin' for free. The town owes ya two months pay."

Ty looked at the check blankly. "This mean it's over?"

"You're through, boy," Hamby said, patting Ty's back. "Pull the truck up to the lot; we gotta find somebody else to do the dirty work."

Ty looked at him strangely, not quite sure how to take it all.

74

Hamby noticed the expression and said, "Boy, I've seen a lot a men work this job, but ya outdid 'em all. You was never late, sick, or come up with no limp-dick excuses. Ya impressed me, boy. Ya ain't no punk like I was thinkin'. Ya keep your nose clean, huh?"

Ty put out his hand. "Thanks, Sheriff."

Hamby winked and shook his hand warmly. "Get cleaned up, boy, ya stink."

The next day, Ty walked into the Coffee Cup to pick up some food for dinner and sat down in the end booth.

Toni broke off her conversation with Johnny Barber and sauntered over to Ty with a warm smile. "Hiya, handsome, ol' Toni been missing you."

"You lookin' better than ever, Toni."

She blushed and patted her packed, dyed hair. "Lordy, ya keep talkin' like that I'll faint. I hear ya got a job with ol' man Randall."

Ty was mystified by her spy network. He'd only talked to Willie Randall that afternoon during lunch break. "Yep, I start work after school tomorrow and start full-time after graduation next Tuesday."

Toni patted his shoulder. "I'm proud a ya, handsome. You been through a lot, and I'll be right prouder seeing you walk across that stage and get that piece of paper. After all the hamburgers ya ate in my place, it's truly a wonder."

Ty laughed and put his hand on top of hers. "I didn't come in here for the food . . . it was always you."

Toni fanned her face. "There ya go again . . . what ya want this time, a couple of burgers and fries to go?"

"You got it."

Toni turned around to yell the order but thought of something else she'd wanted to know. "Oh, Ty, I don't wanna pry, but I was wonderin' how much they was payin' ya for the trees. My cousin has got some on his place that'll make good lumber and . . ."

She stopped in midsentence, seeing his puzzled expression. Her face turned even paler. "Didn't . . . didn't you know they was cuttin' trees on your hill? The loggers ate supper in here this afternoon and . . ."

Ty bolted for the door in a dead run.

"Oh, God," said Toni in a whisper. She turned toward her husband, who was looking to her for an explanation, and motioned toward the phone behind him. "Hand me the phone. I gotta' call Sheriff Hamby . . . there's gonna be trouble."

* * *

Ty braked hard and skidded into the turn off the highway. He floored the accelerator. His hands were white from gripping the steering wheel so tightly. Ahead he saw the logging truck parked alongside the road four hundred yards past the cabin. He felt nauseated, seeing the back of the truck half full of stripped trees and a winch dragging in another one.

The Black Widow skidded to a halt in a cloud of red dust, and Ty jumped out at a dead run, screaming for the two men with chain saws to stop their cutting.

One of the men, dressed in greasy overalls, looked up and held his hand on his ear, signaling that he couldn't hear over the roaring chain saw.

Ty leaped over two of the old cedars they had felled and grabbed the startled man's shirt, screaming, "STOP! STOP CUTTING!"

The man turned off the chain saw and yelled over the roar of the other logger's saw biting into an ancient tree. "What the hell is wrong?"

Ty pointed frantically at the other man. "STOP HIM! GOD, STOP HIM!"

"Who the hell are . . ."

Ty gave up and ran to the other logger who had his back to him and knocked him over with a shovel. The hill was immediately bathed in silence. The horrible noise still ringing in his ears, Ty turned to look at the damage, but was suddenly grabbed roughly and spun around.

The huge, bearded winch operator Ty hadn't seen pushed him to the ground. "What the fuck ya think you doin', asshole!"

Ty jumped to his feet. "You're cutting my trees! This is my land and you . . ." Ty was in tears and looked at the bleeding stumps, ". . . you can't cut them down."

The bearded man took out a piece of paper from his shirt pocket and quickly glanced over it as the two loggers walked up behind him. "I got a job here says I *can* cut 'em down. It was contracted by a Duane Johnson, Route 2, Meyers, Oklahoma. You be Duane Johnson?"

Ty turned to stone. "No, I'm Ty Nance, and I own this land and you get off it right now."

The operator glanced at the men behind him and cocked his head. "We don't know that now, does we? You could be crazy for all we know, but we do know we got a job to do. Ya find this Duane feller and work it out with him. Now git outta here and don't be gettin' in the way." He turned to the other men. "Git back ta work. We got two hours a daylight left."

Ty grabbed his arm and spun him around. "I said, get off my land!"

The big man pushed him back with a powerful shove. "I'm warning ya, back up, or I'll bust ya here and now."

One of the men started his chain saw, breaking Ty's stare. Ty ran to the Widow and threw open the trunk. Taking out his 12-gauge shotgun and throwing down the leather case, he jacked a shell into the chamber. Walking back toward the operator, he raised the gun and fired just over his head.

Pumping another round, he fired at the ground beside the logger whose chain saw was roaring.

"JESUS, KID, DON'T SHOOT US!" yelled the bearded man, holding his hands out. "Settle down . . . we'll go, shit, don't point that thang at me!"

Ty fired again over his head. "MOVE!"

Ty followed the three men to their truck. He waited until he saw a dust cloud kick up before he turned to look at his beloved trees. He counted nineteen stumps as he walked over the crushed and dying limbs they had stripped from his old friends. He stopped, hearing a faint noise. Pulling back two boughs he found what was making the sound and sank to his knees. Resting in the fork of a broken branch was a squawking baby red-tailed hawk, lying in a partially destroyed nest. Beside the nest, lying on the ground, were two more of the small birds, dead and covered with black ants. Trembling, Ty lowered his head. "I'm sorry . . . so sorry."

Duane was talking to one of the mechanics, who was lying under a tractor, and tossed him a new hydraulic pump. Standing up and stretching his back, he turned around. He never saw the blow that knocked him against the tractor. Ty grabbed Duane's shirt and hit him again, knocking him to the floor. Duane shook his head, spitting out blood, and tried to get up when Ty viciously grabbed his hair and jerked his head up.

Ty waited until his stepfather's eyes had focused before speaking in a venomous voice. "Why? Why did you have to do it? Wasn't hating me enough? Why?"

His arms were suddenly grabbed and he was jerked back by the mechanic. "Settle down, boy. Damn, why you hittin' your daddy?"

Duane got up, slowly wiping blood from his chin with the back of his hand. "Hold him right there!" he commanded. Stepping closer, Duane smiled cruelly. "I made your mind up for you, that's why. Two hundred acres to save your worthless ass from the war. That's the price, remember? I promised your mother you wouldn't get drafted, and you won't. The money from the trees will be more than enough to clear the rest of it for plowing.''

Ty struggled to free himself. "Never! You filthy son of a . . .''

Duane had turned his back but suddenly whirled, swinging his fist. Ty's head snapped back with the blow and he went limp in the startled man's arms.

The mechanic let go of Ty and grabbed for Duane. "STOP IT, DUANE! Goddamn, what's got into you two! Jesus, you're family, for Christ's sake.''

Sheriff Hamby walked into the work bay and felt sick at seeing Ty. Harry Sweet, the parts man, was rolling him over. "What the hell is going on?'' he demanded. "Harry, is the boy all right?''

Harry shook his head. "He's out cold and looks like he bit through his tongue. It's split open and bleedin' bad.''

"Call the doc; tell him to come on over here and bring his bag.''

Harry ran toward the office as Hamby stepped closer to Duane. "I just got through runnin' out to the hill 'cause Toni called me about some trouble. I missed the boy, but I saw those loggers you contracted. They flagged me down, comin' into town all upset. Did you get permission from the boy to have them trees cut?''

Duane rolled his shoulders back indignantly. "No, and I don't have to either. I'm his stepfather and . . .''

Hamby held up his hand. "Just hold it right there, Duane. The boy is over eighteen, and he owns that land. You had no right doing what you did. If the boy wants to file a charge against ya, I'll damn well carry out my duty . . . and like doin' it.''

Doc Riddle put the cigar back in his mouth and helped Ty sit up. "Don't try talkin' for a while. You have four stitches in that tongue of yours . . . you still dizzy?''

Ty glanced around the familiar office and faintly remembered getting into Hamby's cruiser with the doctor. He shook his head and was about to hop down from the table when Riddle gently pushed him back. "Whoa, just sit there a minute; I had to knock you out awhile to put them stitches in. Your mouth feels funny now because I numbed it up, but in about an hour you're gonna hurt like hell.''

Riddle took the cigar out of his mouth, blowing out a cloud of smoke, and motioned toward the door. "Your mom is sittin' out there waitin' on you. I'm afraid she and Duane exchanged some pretty heated words. I think she's gonna need you to be strong for her.''

* * *

Ty sat on the bank of Crystal Pond and leaned back on his elbows after reading the letter he had received from Jason. As in the other letters, his brother had written about the difficult training he had been going through and of how much he missed home, but the last paragraph was different—here Jason had written about the pain of losing Becky. Ty reread only the last two sentences:

Ty, it hurt me badly, but I guess time and distance heal everything. I love you and wish you the best.

Your Big Brother

Putting the letter in his pocket, Ty stood up and gazed down the ravine. He took several steps and slowly began to jog down the path, holding an imaginary M-1 rifle and screaming silently. Block, parry, jab! The bayonet sunk deep before he withdrew the bloody knife and met the next attacker. Savagely slashing upward, he suddenly stopped his attack. He shut his eyes and slowly lowered his arms. Nothing was ever going to bring him back. Over the many years the ravine had seen too many men die in his desperate charge, trying to right the injustice of his father's being chosen.

He looked around at the majestic beauty and walked back up the path to tell him his decision.

Minutes later Ty knelt by his father's grave and set a single honeysuckle rose beside the headstone. The flag popped in the breeze above Ty's head as he shut his eyes and felt the arms of his father hugging him to his breast.

Ty left the small recruiting office in El Reno and drove back to Meyers, thinking about his mother. He knew he had to make things right before he told her. She had made Duane move out of the house and boxed all his clothes. The bastard had finally gone too far . . . but he still loved Mea. He had pathetically begged her, but she had been strong and didn't shed a tear, until he had left.

Ty's hands tightened on the steering wheel, remembering her crying. He had never wanted to believe his mother really loved Duane. They didn't show their love outwardly, but he had always known in his heart it was there. The magic between them was just different. The fighting and bickering between him and Duane had only served to crush the woman they both cherished and had finally forced her to choose between them. The past days he had tried to comfort his mother and make her feel better, but he couldn't stop the tears or put back the gleam in her eyes. The decision in choosing him was no victory in winning the battle for her love. They had all lost.

The Black Widow rolled to the curb in front of the John Deere store. Ty stared at the front door, knowing deep inside he was responsible for his mother's grief.

Duane looked up and tensed. Ty strode directly to him and stopped in front of his desk. "It's got to end, Duane. I'm sorry for everything. I want you to come home . . . Mom needs you."

Duane shook his head. "It's too late for that."

Ty fought back his anger. "Mom needs you . . . and I need you. I joined up today. The Army is only for two years. The hill is forever, and I can't destroy it. I could have waited and got drafted, but you and I don't have the time. Mother needs us now."

Duane slumped in his chair. "Jesus, she'll be heartbroken havin' you go . . . that damn hill couldn't be that important to you."

Ty kept his voice steady. "I can't stand to see her cry anymore. She loves you. Come home and let's be a family again. I can't leave knowing she's unhappy without you. We can both make her happy again by becoming a family. Jason and I need to come back to a real home."

Duane looked into Ty's eyes. "She's still gonna be heartbroken having you go."

"But she'll have you . . . she'll have both of us. Distance and time heal. Maybe with time, you and I can heal the scars." Ty held out his hand toward his stepfather. "It's got to end."

Duane lowered his head. The hate he had felt for the boy had eaten him up inside and caused him to lose the most precious thing in his life. He hadn't realized how much Mea meant to him until she had forced him to walk away. And now, finally, he had come to realize what had driven his anger toward his stepson. He had been jealous all those years of Mea's love for Ty.

Duane stood and firmly grasped Ty's hand. "Let's go home."

Toni set a cup of coffee in front of Sheriff Hamby. "It's good to hear Duane and Mea worked things out, but where's Ty? I heard he wasn't in school today."

Hamby tossed his hat on the counter. "I talked to Duane this morning. He's up on his hill somewhere. He's gotta catch the bus day after tomorrow."

"He'll miss graduation!" blurted Toni, throwing down a spoon.

"Damn, Toni, don't get riled at me. I didn't tell him to sign up for the goddamn Army."

Toni shifted her weight from foot to foot. "It's not fair. It's just *not* fair. He's worked his butt off to get that diploma with what he's been through.''

Hamby picked up the spoon and stirred his coffee. ''He brought a lot of that on his ownself, so settle down. I'll take a hot roast beef sandwich and a . . . are you listening to me?''

Ty sat on the log bench watching the sunrise, trying to absorb the beauty and serenity into his memory. He knew it would be the last he would see from his hill for a long time. Now he would go on the great hunt of his life. He had spent the night preparing, meditating in his cave.

He lowered his eyes, knowing that trying to absorb his hill was wasted; it was already a part of him. His heart had been taken years before by its power.

Standing, he looked at the cemetery one last time and lifted his hand in a farewell salute to the resting caretakers of the hill.

The leather stirrups creaked as Ty threw his leg over the saddle and reigned his old friend toward home for the most difficult good-bye. His mother would be waiting.

15

Beneath the towering teak trees Private Bui Ngoc Duong shook the water from his soaked flop hat and squatted, shaking, by a small fire. A senior sergeant glanced at him. ''Be thankful for the rain. The Yankee planes cannot drop their bombs in this weather.''

Bui Duong only nodded, he was too cold to speak. His uniform was soaking wet, and he felt as if the rain had permeated his bones. He had been on the trail for two weeks, and each day was more miserable than the last. He felt hungry, cold, and sick. The rest stop had not come any too soon.

Two more replacements squatted by the fire and held out their hands to the warmth. One of them, who had gone through training with Duong, looked at the sergeant and spoke through chattering teeth.

"Sa . . . Sergeant, how much farther to the sanctuary? I am ill, as well as many of the men."

The sergeant snickered. "You are weak. This march is nothing. Be thankful you are not there yet and have not joined a unit."

"How . . . how much farther?"

The sergeant looked up at the canopy one hundred feet above him and glanced back at the soldier. "A week's march, if we are not bombed or detailed to repair road damage. A week and then you will pray to Buddha to be back on the trail as a replacement. We are joining the First Division. General Binh Duc needs your frail bodies to fill his ranks. Soon you will know why."

Bui Duong spoke with anticipation. "But we are engineers. We were told we would be digging tunnels in the base camp and not be fighting."

The sergeant studied the young soldier's face a moment before speaking. "When you are with the First Division, everyone fights. I was in the Sixty-sixth Regiment in the battle of Ia Drang. Nine of us engineers are all that is left of a company. General Duc was the regimental commander then, and I saw him cry. His regiment was almost wiped out by the helicopter soldiers. He lost all of his battalion commanders and almost all of the infantry units. He is a great soldier, but where he goes, so does death. Our leaders know if they give him a mission he will carry out the orders, no matter the cost, and the cost will be you and me. Be thankful you are on the trail."

The replacements exchanged looks of worry. Even more depressed, Bui Duong took off his pack and sat on top of the canvas bag. He had been an irrigation dam builder with his father and brothers prior to being called into the engineers of the People's Army. Two months before he had been happy in his home in Tuyen Quang province, working with his family in the builders' co-op. Now he was miserable and would soon be building fighting positions. He knew the reunification was important, but he could not help but wonder if building dams for future rice was not more important.

The sergeant stood and hefted his pack to his shoulders. "Put out the fires. Our general is waiting."

16

The young captain stood under the shade of an oak tree, watching his new platoon of officer candidates stand in formation under the hot Georgia sun. The prospects had just been inprocessed to the company and been given platoon assignments. Their instructions had been to form up in a military formation in front of the barracks and await further orders. The captain glanced at his watch.

Jason stood in the second rank, hoping someone would appear and take charge of the platoon. The sticky heat was oppressive and had already soaked his starched khaki uniform. He thought about the letter in his shirt pocket, hoping the ink didn't run and ruin his shirt. The words themselves had upset him enough already. The letter from his mother had said that Ty had joined the Army. It was good hearing that Duane and Ty had made peace, but he couldn't help but worry at the cost. His brother's temper was not suited for the Army's dehumanizing discipline. Ty would strike back, as he'd done all his life.

One of the soldiers standing in front of him began swaying, snapping Jason back from his thoughts. He knew he was in the best shape of his life after sixteen weeks of little food and too much PT, but the hot sun would soon take its toll on all of them unless someone soon moved them into the shade. He looked around and saw no one but a captain behind the formation, who didn't seem interested in them.

Jason didn't see the sense of it any longer. He stepped through the first rank and positioned himself in front of the platoon. "My name is Jason Johnson. I don't see anybody around to take charge of us, so for the time being, I will. Pick up your duffle bags and I'll move you into the shade of the barracks."

The men picked up their bags with no complaint and took Jason's commands as he marched the platoon into the shade and had them stand at ease. Jason kept his position in the front of the formation to keep a lookout for someone with authority. He didn't have long to wait. The captain who stood behind them strolled down the sidewalk in their direction.

Jason barked, "Platoon, a-tench-hut!" and brought his hand up in a rigid salute.

The captain, a short, wiry man, returned the salute and kept walking. Jason had noted that the officer was a veteran, by the ribbons on his chest, and a ranger, by the black and gold tab sewn on his left shoulder. Jason executed an about-face and gave the men an at ease.

The captain stopped and spun around. "WHAT ARE YOU CANDIDATES DOING?"

Jason turned around in shock, realizing it was the captain who'd done the yelling. It didn't seem possible that such a loud voice could come from that small body.

The captain set his narrow shoulders and strode straight for the staring men. "I said, WHAT ARE YOU DOING?"

Jason snapped to attention. "Sir, we are waiting on instructions."

The captain stopped only inches in front of Jason. "WHO GAVE YOU INSTRUCTIONS TO MOVE THIS PLATOON, CANDIDATE?"

Jason didn't flinch or blink an eye at the blast of words so close to his face. He spoke, staring straight ahead. "No one, sir."

The officer eyed Jason from head to black, low quarter shoes with a look of disdain. "You . . . you decided on your own to take charge of this mob? You have the audacity to step forward and lead? . . . Just who do you think you are?"

Jason kept his distant stare. "Sir, I am Candidate Johnson, infantryman."

The captain's eyes narrowed into slits as if about to explode when suddenly he stepped back and pointed a finger directly toward Jason's face and bellowed, "OUTSTANDING!"

He immediately dropped his hand and began pacing in front of the platoon. "Candidates, my name is Captain John Willis. I am your platoon tactical officer. This is the *Officer* Candidate School. For a while I was beginning to wonder if all of you had caught the wrong bus, no one wanted to take charge. WRONG! WRONG! WRONG! You will from this day forward. Always look for the opportunity to LEAD! You have one candidate among you who was willing to take the responsibility for your welfare and move you into the shade. He did, however, make a mistake. He said he was Candidate Johnson, Infantryman. Wrong! He is Candidate Johnson, infantryman *and* newly appointed platoon leader.''

Willis stepped back in front of his new platoon leader and came to attention. ''Candidate Johnson, you will appoint a chain of command, move this mob to the second floor of this barracks, and assign bunks. You will make a roster of all your men and give it to me and be ready for inspection in ten minutes. If you do not perform your duties in accordance with my instructions, you will be fired. Do you have any questions? Good. Take charge.''

Jason saluted smartly and executed an about-face. ''Anybody from Oklahoma?''

One rawboned redhead in the third rank raised his hand. Jason smiled. ''You're my platoon sergeant. Get me four squad leaders and move 'em into the barracks.''

Willis walked toward the company headquarters and pulled out a notepad from his pocket. He wanted to remind himself to watch the big, blond-haired candidate. He looked like a leader, but looks didn't count for much. He was the first to pass his little test, but there were plenty more. Maybe he had it, maybe he didn't.

Willis stopped and wrote ''Johnson'' in his book and placed a question mark by his name. In ten minutes he would know if he could erase the question mark.

''YOU TRAIN-NEES HAVE TEN SECONDS TO GET OFF MY BUS!'' Ty looked out the window of the large green reception station bus at a big-armed, barrel-chested drill sergeant, wondering if the sergeant actually thought he owned the vehicle.

The sergeant raised his wrist and looked at his watch. He began counting. ''ONE . . . TWO . . . THREE . . .''

Ty joined the scramble, picking up his two heavy duffle bags and trying to meet the impossible time limit.

''NINE . . . NINE AND A HALF . . . TEN, FREEZE! You people have pissed off Sergeant McCoy. Sergeant McCoy tells you get off the fucking bus, he means get off the FUCKING BUS! You now have ten seconds to get back on the bus and try it again. ONE . . . TWO . . .''

Ty had opened the back safety door and made it off the bus in time and was about to get back on, but he saw that the sergeant wasn't watching him. He stepped to the other side of the bus and stood by the tire so the sergeant couldn't see his feet. It was ridiculous to order forty men to get off a bus in ten seconds—just about like everything else the Army had wanted him to do the past few weeks. The reception station was nothing but staying awake for twenty hours a day, taking tests, undergoing inspections, formations, shots, eating slop, and undergoing more stupid inspections that no one could pass. Making a bed so tightly you could bounce a quarter on it was hardly what he'd expected. Nothing was what he'd expected. Sergeants didn't talk, they screamed. He'd heard his share of profanity in Meyers, but the Army didn't seem to know anything else. The whole thing had been a mistake. He should have joined the Air Force.

"NOW, YOU GOT TEN SECONDS TO GET OFF THE BUS AND IMPRESS ME! . . . ONE . . . TWO . . . THREE . . ."

Ty waited until "four" before stepping around the bus, only to look directly into the face of McCoy, who halted his count with "FREEZE!"

Ty sighed as the sergeant strode directly toward him like a hungry shark. "Scarface, did my eyes see you cheatin' on me?"

Ty shrugged. "Guess so, Sergeant."

McCoy smiled for an instant but suddenly grabbed Ty's fatigue shirt and yanked him to within an inch of his face. "You fucked up. You pissed off Sergeant McCoy. He got something for you. You cheated Sergeant McCoy and Sergeant McCoy don't like cheaters, cee-vilians, troublemakers, and attitude problems!"

Ty leaned his head back to put some distance between his nose and McCoy's foul breath. He tried to get his feet back under him, but the sergeant's grip was like a steel vise and held him just off the ground. Ty realized this man's strength was as incredible as his temper and spoke apologetically.

"Sorry . . . Sarge."

McCoy yanked Ty further up, causing him to choke. "Sergeant McCoy is not 'SARGE.' He is DRILL Sergeant McCoy to you, Mister Scarface Attitude Problem." McCoy tossed Ty back into the side of the bus like a sack of potatoes. "FIVE . . . SIX . . . SEVEN . . ."

Jason stood at attention as Captain Willis inspected his platoon. They'd been up most of the night polishing, shining, cleaning, and praying, trying to get ready for the equipment lay-out inspection of all their uniforms, field equipment, and wall lockers.

Willis picked up an entrenching tool and opened the blade. It was spotless and had been freshly painted. Damn, he hadn't found a single gig and only had four men left to inspect. This was a first. The second week's big inspection was always an opportunity to point out shortcomings and show his candidates they had a long way to go. OCS was a twenty-four-week course designed to take his men through progressive steps until they became certified leaders. The inspection was supposed to be a teaching vehicle. He was supposed to find countless gigs and chew them out because they hadn't become a team and weren't working together.

Willis sighed and tossed the small shovel to the candidate's bunk. There was no use looking further. He was wasting his time. This platoon was not like the last one he'd had. This platoon was a team. He could jump ahead of schedule and begin making them technically and tactically proficient. Vietnam was where they would all be going, and spit and polish would save none of them. Learning to be combat leaders was what was really important.

He turned around and strode toward the reason the platoon had jelled. He stopped in front of Jason and shook his head. "Candidate Johnson, your mob is undoubtedly the most squared-away platoon I have seen. You should be congratulated . . . but you won't be. You will fall your mob out in twenty minutes with full combat load for a road march. Today we begin REAL training!"

Jason couldn't help but crack a small smile. Weird Willis was living up to his nickname. The platoon had named him "Weird" because he constantly did weird things to the published training schedule. The schedule was supposed to be the gospel, but it was obvious Willis had his own religion.

Jason saluted smartly, knowing his platoon would march the pip-squeak into the ground. "Yes, sir, we'll be ready."

Jason swore and quickened his stride to keep up with Willis ahead of him. The "pip-squeak" was killing them with a blistering pace. Four men had already fallen out, and two more had dropped back.

Jason came alongside Willis and tried to speak between heaving breaths. "Si . . . Sir, we gotta . . . take a break . . . or we're gonna . . . lose the whole . . . the whole platoon."

Willis looked at his platoon leader with a smile as he kept walking. "Limitations, Candidate Johnson, we're finding the limitations in ourselves. Leaders must know their limitations."

Jason struggled to keep up again. "Sir, what . . . what happened to . . . taking care of . . . of your men?"

Willis quickened his stride. "These aren't ordinary men. They're future leaders!"

Ty looked up at the blazing sun, hating its existence. The huge star was trying to kill him, along with Drill Sergeant McCoy. Ty stood in the back of the extended platoon formation holding an M-14 rifle that also was quickly becoming an enemy. The platoon was practicing the manual of arms, but no matter how he performed the drills, McCoy found fault with him. He'd completed his fourth set of ten push-ups and was waiting on the sergeant's next command.

McCoy stood on a platform overlooking the platoon and spoke loudly. "By the numbers. RIGHT, SHOULDER . . . ARMS! READY, ONE . . . READY, TWO. GET DOWN, PRIVATE NANCE! YOU MESSIN' UP MY CLASS. READY, THREE."

Ty got down in the front-leaning rest position and placed the heavy weapon on the back of his hands before beginning the ten push-ups. He felt as if his chest muscles had turned to soft rubber as he got to the fifth repetition cycle and tried to push himself back up. It was useless, and he fell to the hot gravel, giving up. The past two weeks were the most miserable in his life. He'd already lost ten pounds and felt so weak he could hardly lift his fork during chow. He had not slept more than three hours a night, and the runs and PT in the mornings had made him so sore he could hardly move. He'd thought he was in good shape, but it wasn't good enough to withstand the torture McCoy was putting them through. The platoon had already lost eight men, and two more went on sick call that morning.

McCoy smiled to himself at seeing his "attitude problem" give up. He barked, "AT EASE. Shake it out and take a ten-minute break in place." He hopped down from the platform and strode toward his attitude case for personal one-on-one training.

"Attitude Problem, get up and get at attention . . . now, what seems to be your problem?"

Ty got up and stared directly into McCoy's eyes. "You're the problem, Drill Sergeant."

McCoy smiled proudly. "Good answer, you're right. I'm going to get rid of you, Mister Attitude Problem. You haven't learned a thing in two weeks. You're still thinking you can beat me, aren't you? You think you can get over on Sergeant McCoy and not give him one hundred percent. Well, I got news, Mister Attitude Problem, NO FUCKIN' BODY gets over on Sergeant McCoy. He gets your mind, heart, and soul and makes soldiers."

Ty rolled his eyes, not impressed. "You put me on KP every night, and I don't get any sleep. How am I supposed to learn anything?"

McCoy smiled cruelly and stepped closer. "You don't, that's how I'm going to get rid of you. You haven't got what it takes, Mister Attitude Problem. Your kind never do. . . . WHAT THE

FUCK IS THAT?'' McCoy pointed at the dog tag chain that had slipped out of Ty's shirt during push-ups. He fingered the silver wings Ty had placed on the chain with the ID tags.

''Those are my dad's wings, Sergeant,'' Ty said plaintively.

McCoy grabbed the wings and yanked the chain from his neck. ''You can't wear unauthorized awards, shithead! Your daddy must not be much of a man, having the likes of you. The best part of you ran down your mama's leg!''

Ty's eyes narrowed in rage and he began to shake, wanting to tear McCoy's smile from his face.

McCoy backed up a step, watching him in fascination. ''Well, I'll be damned. You scratch hard enough, I guess you finally get to the real man. You mad at me? You want to hit Sergeant McCoy? COME ON, ATTITUDE PROBLEM, TAKE A SHOT! You ain't got nothing to lose.''

Ty began to jerk his rifle butt up when a loud voice behind him barked, ''McCOY, WHAT THE HELL ARE YOU DOING?''

The sergeant came to attention and faced his approaching irate company commander. ''Sir, the private and I were having a talk, and he acted as if he wanted to strike me.''

The captain marched past Ty and angrily motioned to McCoy to follow him. They walked five paces and the captain spun around, red-faced. ''McCoy, I will not tolerate any further abuse of my soldiers. I saw you pull that chain from the private's neck. You will return the chain immediately. You have the highest attrition rate in the company, and battalion is asking why. You had the worst graduation rate last cycle, and you've already lost more men than last time. Get your act together and start training my men properly, or you'll be up to your ass in rice paddies in two months. You read me, Sergeant?''

McCoy was fuming. Shit, he'd been a drill sergeant for two years. He could just look at a trainee and know if the kid was going to make it. The captain was new and didn't understand that fuck-ups ruined a platoon and that it was best to get rid of them early. Screw the attrition rate. He was training soldiers, not playing numbers games.

''Sir, you don't understand how the system works. We . . .''

The captain raised his hand, ''No, Sergeant McCoy, YOU don't understand. This conversation is over. You have been given your last warning. You're dismissed.''

Ty had secretly smiled and jumped up and down inside. He'd heard every wonderful word and hoped McCoy would say something else. The way the captain looked, he was ready to axe the sergeant right there and then. Instead, McCoy raised his right hand in a perfect salute and spoke in a matter-of-fact voice. "Yes, sir."

The captain returned the salute quickly and stomped back toward his office.

McCoy strolled toward Ty with a swagger and smiled. "Don't worry, Attitude Problem, this doesn't change anything." He threw the chain at Ty's feet. "Next week we begin bayonet training, and I'm gonna use you as a demonstrator. I'm gonna get rid of you nice and legal. You're gone, Attitude Problem. You're gone."

Ty sat in the darkness on the back steps of the barracks looking at the distant airport. A lone plane was just taking off and rose into the night. Logan Heights basic training area was situated on a high plateau overlooking the outskirts of El Paso. The view constantly reminded him that there was still a normal world just a mile away. The view was known as 'AWOL Lookout,' because many a trainee had been overcome with homesickness and took off in the night to try and catch one of the sleek jets home.

Ty broke his gaze from the plane and continued shining his boots. The stars overhead reminded him of the hill.

"You thinking about taking off, Nance?" Warren Glinski asked, walking down the back steps and sitting down beside Ty.

"Naw, Ski, this coon dog ain't beat yet."

Glinski stared at the airport as if in a trance. "I am . . . McCoy put me on KP again. I can't take it anymore. He says he's going to get me one way or another, and he means it."

Ty frowned and put down his polishing rag. "He told me the same thing. Matter a fact, he's told half the platoon the same thing. Just keep doin' the best ya can."

"My girl understands," Glinski said slowly. "She told me she did. She said the war was wrong. She understands."

"Don't do it, Ski. Your girl might understand, but in a few days, you won't. You won't be able to look in a mirror again. Just hang in a little longer . . . it's gonna get better."

Glinski slowly rose and put his hand on Ty's shoulder. "He's gonna get you, Nance. Everybody knows it. Come with me."

Ty looked up at his eyes and knew McCoy had taken Glinski's spirit. There was nothing he could say to change his mind. Picking up his rag, he said dejectedly, "Take care, Ski."

Glinski patted his shoulder one last time and walked up the stairs in silence.

* * *

Ty stood in a circle of twenty-nine men watching two others in the center beat themselves senseless with pugil sticks. The platoon had finished bayonet training the day before, and the pugil-stick training was supposed to be like the real thing, except that the fighters wore helmets and chest and groin pads. Instead of real bayonets they were given sticks that looked like huge cue sticks with padded ends.

McCoy stood back from the flailers and held a whistle to signal when a "fatal" blow was delivered. The larger of the two had gone in hollering and bragging and had attacked with furious blows, but he was tiring now. It was just a matter of time before he was "killed." The smaller man feinted left and threw the butt up, catching his opponent with his arms down and knocking him off his feet. The finishing blow to the chest caused the ring of men to scream out in pleasure, like Romans cheering for the winning gladiator.

McCoy blew his whistle and raised up the smaller man's hand, proclaiming him the winner to even louder hoots and hollers. He glanced at Ty with a quick smirk and paced around the circle. "Has everybody fought?"

Ty had known it was coming when he hadn't been paired up. McCoy had set it up perfectly. They had an even number of men, but McCoy had sent one back to "secure" the barracks. It was time for him to carry out his threat.

Ty silently stepped into the circle. McCoy shook his head theatrically. "Damn, Private Nance, we don't have a partner for you. . . . I wouldn't want you to miss this training, so I guess I'll have to go a round."

The men looked at Ty in sympathy. McCoy had been riding Nance twice as hard as everyone else. It was clear the sergeant was going to make a lesson of him for their benefit.

Two men helped Ty put on his equipment and stepped back among the silent platoon members as McCoy held up his stick and yelled, "ON GUARD!"

Ty crouched and raised his stick, moving to his opponent's left. He'd been watching McCoy's demonstrations closely. He thought he had a chance.

McCoy played the cat-and-mouse game for only twenty seconds and lost patience. He wanted to finish the Indian off and get it over with. He screamed and attacked by lunging at Ty's head. Ty ducked and swung the stick at McCoy's feet, catching him just above his boot tops. The sergeant went down before he knew what had happened, but quickly recovered and rolled as Ty viciously swung again, just missing his head.

McCoy jumped to his feet and dropped into a low crouch. The kid was quick but not strong enough. He attacked again with a deep-throated scream, throwing himself at the smaller soldier's body.

Ty sidestepped him at the last instant and came around behind, swinging with all his might at the back of his helmet. The blow knocked McCoy forward, and he sunk to his knees. He shook his head and rolled right, but Ty was waiting for him and slammed the front of his faceguard with a horizontal butt stroke. McCoy reeled with the blow, falling to his back, and he felt the end of the padded stick strike his chest in the final deathblow.

The platoon erupted into pandemonium as Ty lifted his arms in victory. Seething, McCoy got to his feet and swung the stick at Ty's back, hitting him in the head. The powerful blow knocked him to the ground, knocking him out.

McCoy moved toward Ty's still form, lifting his stick, when the winner of the last bout stepped in front of him, blocking his path. "Drill Sergeant, we're late for company formation."

Two more men quickly joined him, then two more.

McCoy backed up, seeing the entire platoon push closer to form a wall of bodies to protect their gladiator. He knew he'd gone too far the second he felt his pugil stick hit Nance's head. If the captain had seen him or one of these scumbags said something, he'd be on the street with his bags. He'd have to let them get away with their little game for now, but they'd pay. The scumbags were gonna pay for their insubordination.

He quickly composed himself and held up his pugil stick. "You have just witnessed a lesson. Never let your guard down. The enemy might be playing dead and get up and stick his bayonet up your ass. I hope you all learned something. Now, GET FORMED UP! . . . Two a you help Attitude Problem to the barracks."

17

Candidate Jason Johnson confidently walked out of the wood-line and motioned the members of his platoon to move into their positions. Today would end the four-day field exercise that would culminate in an airmobile extraction. Thirty minutes before, under the watchful eye of Captain Willis, Jason had briefed the men on his plan for loading the choppers when they came in to pick up the platoon.

Jason looked south, waiting for the six Hueys to appear, and spoke to the radio telephone operator beside him. "Has flight lead reported in yet?"

The RTO lowered the radio handset. "This damn thing hasn't worked all morning. I've changed handsets and batteries and still get nothing but static."

Jason kept his eyes on the horizon. "It doesn't matter now. The last transmission said they'd be here on time."

Captain Willis came up behind Jason. "Candidate Johnson, are you sure you covered everything in your briefing that you wanted to?"

Jason nodded. "Yes, sir, I covered everything and double-checked with the squad leaders. We're broken down in chalks of seven men each, and every man knows what bird he gets on."

Willis backed up a step. "And what is the formation the flight of birds is going to use?"

"Sir, they'll come in just like we rehearsed, in trail formation, one right behind the other, like six ducks in a column."

Willis nodded his head in exaggeration. "I see."

Jason suddenly raised his hand. "I hear 'em." He turned and yelled toward the small groups of men spread out on line next to the trees. "GET READY, BIRDS INBOUND. REMEMBER WE HAVE TO BE ON IN TWENTY SECONDS!"

Jason looked back to the south and saw five Hueys streaking toward him just above the treetops. "Five? Shit, they said . . ."

"You want to throw a smoke," said the RTO, seeing that the birds were too far to the west and hadn't seen the landing zone.

Jason had forgotten the smoke and barked, "Throw it, quick!" He turned. "SIXTH CHALK BREAK OFF AND SPREAD OUT ON THE OTHER CHALKS . . . HURRY!"

The helicopters turned on seeing the smoke and came in for a landing from the north. Jason threw up his hands in exasperation. "They're coming in the wrong way! What the . . . what kind of formation is that! That's not a trail formation, that's a diamond!"

The helicopters landed in a screaming whine, kicking up dead grass and dust. The chalks of men were totally confused. They'd practiced getting the first chalk on the first bird in from the south, but the chalks were now gathered on the wrong end of the open field. The second chalk was supposed to get on the second bird in line, but the choppers were in diamond formation, and no one knew which one was the second bird. The third and fourth chalks had the same problem.

Jason watched in horror as the chalks crisscrossed and backtracked in mass confusion. Men were yelling commands, obscenities, and accusations, all unheard over the noise of the screaming turbine engines and whopping blades. Running back and forth from bird to bird, trying to find an empty chopper, the chalk leaders lost control. Soon it was every man for himself, scrambling in pursuit of a ride out of the mess.

Jason's shoulders sagged. He thought the disaster was a nightmare come true and couldn't get more screwed up until the excited RTO grabbed his shoulder and pointed. "FIRE!"

Jason turned and almost cried. The smoke grenade had started a fire in the dry grass.

Willis calmly walked up to Jason and spoke loudly in his ear to be heard over the turbine noise. "Are you still sure, Candidate?" Not waiting for a response, Willis shook his head and strode toward the lead helicopter, motioning for the flight leader to shut down.

Fifteen minutes later the platoon had put out the fire and sat under a tree with blackened faces, uniforms, and dispositions. Willis took off his helmet and put it under his arm. He began pacing in front of the platoon and suddenly halted, speaking in a surprisingly even tone.

"Candidates, I was truly awed, no, mesmerized by your unbelievable performance. Never have I witnessed such a spectacle. That was undoubtedly the best, most classic example of a Chinese goat rope that I have ever seen. You did absolutely nothing right. Congratulations are in order. This platoon will go down in the OCS history books. You have managed to completely, totally, and une-quivocally write a new chapter on how *not* to conduct an airmobile operation.''

Willis let his words sink in for effect and shifted his eyes to Jason, who was sitting in the front row. ''Your leader did NOT have a bump plan in case there were fewer birds than expected. He did NOT check the wind and know birds ALWAYS land INTO the wind. He did NOT have communications with flight lead, although his platoon sergeant had a radio that was working fine. He did NOT have a contingency plan for a different formation. He did NOT use arm and hand signals, but instead tried yelling commands. He did NOT have a hole dug for a smoke grenade, although it hasn't rained in two weeks.''

Willis had taken a step closer to Jason on each ''not'' and ended his last sentence standing directly in front of the humbled platoon leader. Willis shook his head in disgust. He spoke with the same even inflection. ''The lesson in all this, is that the best plan in the world doesn't mean a thing come time for execution. Conditions change, candidates. The enemy, weather, wind, chopper pilots, terrain don't know your plan. They don't care about your plan. They try and screw up your plan. *You* have to plan for the unexpected. *You* have to plan for Murphy's Law and think about everything that could go wrong, because it probably will.''

He paused, feeling a familiar tingling in his insides. He had to stop a moment and savor the feeling. He had them. He had their undivided attention, and they were actually learning. The blank stares were gone, and they were absorbing his every word.

Throwing his shoulders back, he continued. ''Candidates, this is a school. We are supposed to make mistakes, but we make them *here*. In combat, there is no room for mistakes. There you pay with blood. Today was a fantastic learning experience. We screwed up, but hell, look at what we learned.''

He suddenly broke into a smile and motioned Jason to his feet. ''Candidate Johnson, we learned a lot today. How about you trying it again. You've got thirty minutes to get organized, remembering all your mistakes.''

Willis backed up and spoke to the rest of the platoon.

''Candidates, let's show these aviators what an airmobile extrac-tion is supposed to look like.''

Forty minutes later the helicopters landed in a diamond forma-tion, and in twenty seconds, every man was loaded. Jason sat in the floor of the reverberating bird and smiled, shooting his thumb up at Willis, who sat beside the crew chief. The birds whined and lifted off.

"READY ON THE RIGHT? . . . READY ON THE LEFT? . . . THE RANGE IS NOW CLEAR. COMMENCE FIRING!"

Ty pushed the safety forward on the M-14 and squinted to align the rear aperture sight with the blade foresight. He let out a half-breath and held the rest before gently squeezing the trigger. The weapon's report kicked up a small dust cloud in front of his foxhole, but he didn't notice as he concentrated on the firing lane to his front, where silhouette targets were popping up at various distances. He took the teeth-jarring recoil of the rifle without flinching and fired again at another target that had just swung up.

"Hit," said the sergeant standing behind Ty's position, grading his shooting on the practice record fire.

BLAAAM . . . "Hit." BLAAAM . . . "Hit." BLAAAM . . . "Hit."

The sergeant excitedly stepped forward, keeping his eye on the 300-meter berm where he knew the next target would be coming up. There.

BLAAAM . . . "Damn! Hit!" He quickly marked the grade sheet on his clipboard and looked up just as the double targets began rising.

BLAAAM . . . BLAAAM . . . "Hit, hit."

Staff Sergeant Cody let the clipboard fall to his side and watched in awe as Ty expertly dispatched the last thirteen targets with thirteen shots. It was a first for him in the six months and countless trainees he'd graded since being assigned to the range committee. Never before had a soldier made a perfect score on his lane.

Cody jumped when the loudspeaker behind him blared, "CEASE FIRING . . . CEASE FIRING . . . CLEAR ALL WEAPONS AND PLACE THEM ON SAFE . . . SCORERS, MOVE FORWARD AND CHECK WEAPONS."

He looked into Ty's scarred face with curiosity. "Where'd you learn to shoot like that?"

Ty raised his weapon up to show it was clear and on safe. "Back home, I used to hunt a lot."

Drill Sergeant McCoy stood behind the range tower taking his platoon's score cards as they filed off the range. He looked at the cards as each soldier passed and became more and more angry. His men were doing poorly, and their scores would be perceived as a reflection of his previous rifle marksmanship training. The company commander would have his ass as soon as he found out. The platoon would be firing tomorrow for the real record fire, and if today was any indicator, they would disgrace him and the company.

Ty was the last man to leave the range. He handed the drill sergeant his card and continued walking. McCoy glanced at the card and blurted, "Freeze, Attitude Problem. Your card hasn't been marked for the last ten shots. You miss the whole range?"

Ty began to explain, when Sergeant Cody strolled up with several range committee sergeants. "That's my fault. I just forgot to mark the last hits. He was too much fun to watch."

McCoy motioned Ty to continue on and faced Cody in disbelief. "You mean that shithead hit every target?"

Cody arched an eyebrow. "That 'shithead,' as you call him, just set your company record. Nobody on this range has shot a perfect score in four months. I just checked. You got yourself the winner of the marksmanship trophy in that 'shithead.' But you set another record—despite what Nance shot, this platoon had the worst overall scores. You're gonna win the bolo award, McCoy."

McCoy walked away from the laughter of the range sergeants angered and humiliated. This ruined his plans. He was going to ensure Nance failed the last three weeks of training and be recycled, which meant starting training all over again with another company. The Attitude Problem would never make it the second time and would go AWOL or be forced out with a general discharge for unsuitability. This changed things.

Sergeant McCoy paced in front of his platoon shaking with rage. "You shitheads have done it this time! You all would fuck up a wet dream! You're scum, worse than scum, you're idiots! Well, scumbags, I got something for you. Unless you shoot better tomorrow, I'm gonna run your lazy asses into the ground and take away all your privileges. Never in my military career have I seen such a group of losers the likes of you. NEVER!"

Ty stood in the formation, tuning out the sergeant, and concentrated on thinking about something else. McCoy had become nasty and mean after the pugil-stick incident and had been taking out his wrath on the entire platoon. He had lost his effectiveness as their trainer, riding them with threats and constant demeaning screaming. He had destroyed the men's morale with his daily tirades. Not once had he said anything constructive or positive. Ty knew the platoon had good men, but none could meet the sergeant's impossible standards. The men had given up weeks ago and were all just struggling to survive.

McCoy finished his bitching and looked at the blank faces of the platoon, realizing he wasn't getting through to them. He was about to drop them all for push-ups, when the company commander yelled for him from his tent a hundred yards distant. He felt his stomach tighten, knowing what the officer wanted, and barked for his platoon guide. "Take charge of this scum and move them to chow."

Captain Treet looked up from the report on his field desk and locked his eyes on McCoy, who was standing before him. "At ease, Sergeant," he said. "I just read your platoon's scores on the range today. You have managed to ruin this company's chance of winning the battalion marksmanship streamer. In fact, your platoon's performance was so low, you pulled the other platoons down, and we're in last place. Even Bravo Company is beating us, for Christ sake!"

McCoy shifted his eyes nervously. The other platoons must have shot well, leaving him no excuse.

The captain shook his head and stood up, putting his hands on his hips. "Because of your inability to train your platoon properly, I'm going to ask the range committee to come over this evening and give your men remedial training."

McCoy's mouth opened in shock. To have others train his men was the worst humiliation a drill sergeant could endure. He wouldn't be able to go to the NCO club without his peers joking and making snide remarks about his teaching ability. The captain had gone too far!

"Sir, I messed up by giving the men PT before going to the range. I wasn't thinking. But tomorrow, we'll do much better. If you noticed, several men did very well, and one man fired a perfect score. I gave that soldier more training than the others, and it paid off. I think my abilities are proven by his score."

Treet hadn't known of the perfect score. He'd only received the platoon averages. His eyes lit up and he quickly thumbed through the individual score cards, knowing that if his company had the battalion's best marksman, he would be spared embarrassment, even if his company shot average. He found the score card showing all hits and held it toward the lantern. "Private Nance, huh? Well, I'll be damned. This is the first perfect score I've ever seen." He looked back to the sergeant with a questioning stare. "And you trained him?"

McCoy smiled shyly. "Yes, sir. I probably took too much time with him, and not enough with the others, but I'll square away the rest of the platoon tonight. We'll be ready for tomorrow.''

The captain looked doubtful. McCoy's platoon was doing poorly in all training subjects, and first sergeant had told him the sergeant was burned out and needed to be relieved. He lowered his eyes and sat back down at his desk. "I won't embarrass you by having the range committee come over, but I am going to have first sergeant give your men a block of instruction after chow.''

He looked back at the sergeant's face and raised his voice. "McCoy, I'm going to watch your men fire tomorrow, and especially Private Nance. You'd just better hope you haven't been blowing smoke up my ass, or I'll burn you. I'm not impressed by your platoon's performance, and it tells me you are failing as a drill sergeant. Things better change, and quick, or you're gone, with your record annotated appropriately. Move out, Sergeant. You have lots of work to do.''

Ty sat on the ground, eating a C-ration can of spaghetti, when a looming figure blocked the setting sun's glare. Ty looked up into the smiling face of Drill Sergeant McCoy.

"Private Nance, you shot good today. You must have been the only one who stayed awake during my classes.''

Ty immediately stood, as was the protocol when a drill sergeant spoke to a trainee, but he was surprised when McCoy motioned him back down and sat in the sand beside him. Ty looked at his sergeant suspiciously.

McCoy glanced around, making certain that none of the other men could hear, and set his eyes on Ty. "Nance, I showed you how to take up a good spot weld and how to breathe when shooting, didn't I?''

Ty honestly didn't remember anything but the push-ups during the sergeant's marksmanship training and shook his head. "I don't remember, Drill Sergeant.''

McCoy's facial muscles tightened, but he forced a smile. "Sure you do. Remember when just three days ago I showed you how to place your cheek tightly against your thumb as you gripped the stock and always to keep the same sight picture?''

Ty could see that the sergeant was desperate for the right answer from him and nodded—anything to get the man off his back. "Yes, Drill Sergeant, I remember now. You did show us that.'' And a hundred push-ups for not doing it right, you bastard, he thought to himself, remembering all too clearly his ranting and raving.

McCoy was satisfied and stood up, brushing the sand off his

fatigues. "Good. Well, I was just checking, and I'm glad you learned something. Tomorrow you'll be watched by the company commander when you're shooting, so remember all I taught you."

Ty stood up and spoke blandly. "Yes, Drill Sergeant." He waited until McCoy left and sighed in relief. What in the hell was all that about?

Ty Nance lowered his smoking M-14 as the loudspeakers behind him blurted, "CEASE FIRING . . . CEASE FIRING . . . CLEAR ALL WEAPONS AND PLACE THEM ON SAFE. SCORERS, MOVE FORWARD AND CHECK WEAPONS."

The range sergeant, Drill Sergeant McCoy, and Captain Treet walked to Ty's foxhole with broad grins. Treet put his hand out. "Congratulations, young man. That was some shooting."

Ty climbed out of his hole and shook hands with the captain. "Thank you, sir."

Treet patted his back. "You only have one more phase left, and that ought to sew up the trophy for you. Sergeant McCoy has taught you well."

Ty looked strangely at his commander. McCoy stepped back and gave Ty a warning glare.

Treet also noticed Ty's expression and quit smiling. "Private Nance, will you show me what Sergeant McCoy taught you? He said he spent a lot of time with you."

Ty slowly got down and into the front leaning rest position, and began doing push-ups.

Treet thought the young soldier had misunderstood and quickly ordered him up. "No, Private, show me the techniques he used for teaching you."

Ty got down and into the front leaning rest position again. "Sir, this is all I remember from the drill sergeant's instruction."

"Get up," commanded Treet. He turned and glared at McCoy, who was sweating profusely. "Sergeant McCoy, you will report to my office at zero nine hundred tomorrow morning. We are going to discuss your future in this company."

Treet spun around and walked down the berm, ignoring McCoy's salute. The sergeant lowered his hand and stepped in front of Ty. "Attitude Problem, you fucked up messin' with me. You're going to pay."

"McCoy, get off the range," said the range sergeant and motioned toward Ty. "Get in your hole. Phase two begins in one minute. Lock and load one magazine."

* * *

Ty awoke to a gentle nudge. "Nance, it's your turn to pull fire watch. It's almost midnight." Ty sat up in the small tent. "Same route as last night?"

Private Dodge crawled into the tent and pulled his poncho over him. "Yeah, same route for one hour, then wake up Smitty in the next tent over. He's got the next shift."

Ty put on his boots, stood up under the cloudless night sky, and looked down the quiet row of tents. They'd been bivouacked in the two-man tents for the past four days while range firing. Fire watch included an hour's tour of the perimeter of the company campsite, ensuring nothing was stolen, and time in the range tower to look out for range fires.

He made one round of the perimeter and crossed the road to check the tower. He had to climb sixty-two metal steps to a suspended tin hut that held communications equipment.

Ty stopped at the base of the tower and looked up at the countless stars. It was a beautiful night, with a trace of cactus flower in the light wind. He couldn't help but think of the many nights he and his grandfather had sat on the hill looking at the stars.

Reaching the top of the catwalk, he was about to check the door when he saw a dark blur out of the corner of one eye. He only had time to throw his arm up for protection before being knocked backward. He lost his balance and tumbled headfirst down the steps in a shuddering series of blows before jolting to a gut-wrenching stop, his foot catching one of the railing poles. He was dazed and was trying to get up when he heard the distinct sound of leather boots creaking as someone walked down the metal steps. Then his foot was freed and he felt his legs being lifted. Ty began to yell, when his legs were violently tossed toward his head and he tumbled down the steps.

"Sir? Sir, wake up, there's been an accident."

Captain Treet awoke and looked up into the face of his first sergeant. He sat up on his cot and shook his head. "What happened, Top?"

"Sir, one of the fire guards fell down the steps of the range tower and messed himself up pretty good. I don't think it's anything too serious, but he'll have to go to the hospital and get examined and get his foot checked. He's bruised all over, and he twisted his ankle pretty bad."

Treet stood up and walked toward the field phone. "Shit, the battalion commander won't like this. What's the soldier's name?"

"Private Nance, sir."

"NANCE! Shit, he's our shooter! It's not bad enough for him to be recycled is it?"

The first sergeant lowered his head. "I'm afraid it is, sir. He won't be able to train for at least a week with that ankle."

Treet's shoulders sagged, and he flopped down into his chair. "Damn! Of all the men in this company, it had to be my best shooter . . . there goes the trophy."

18

Private Bui Ngoc Duong wearily cleaned his hands in the creek and stood up. He shook off the water, wiping his hands on his shirt, then turned around. He took one step and froze in awe. Never had he seen such a wondrous sight. The sun was striking the jungle canopy in just the right way to bathe the base camp in green and gold radiance. The sight was breathtaking, like a landscape in a dream.

Bui Ngoc was afraid that if he moved he would break the magical spell. Two months before, when he had first arrived, he had been near death. Only in the past week had he begun gaining weight and recovering his strength from the arduous journey. During the trek, twelve men had died from sickness and another four from Yankee bombs.

The base camp was a sanctuary. Hidden in a small valley, it lay beneath towering teak and sayo trees. The forty huts and barracks had been built by the Montagnards and constructed on stilts with bamboo, sayo, and thatch. Their workmanship was better than anything he had seen in his own village.

The camp's buildings were lined in four perfect rows, with a path leading down the center of each row. Not a leaf, twig, or blade of grass was visible on the ground, which the mountain people constantly swept. Even the water buffalo sheds at the edge of camp were kept clean. The animals' waste, as well as that of the camp's inhabitants, was collected and used for fertilizer on small fields at the end of the valley.

Duong took in a deep breath of fresh mountain air. It was a good life. He was happy again. The job he had started was like being home. He was building a dam on the creek to divert water for a washing area.

Duong felt another presence behind him. It was Sergeant Ninh, who was admiring the shafts of golden light. "I have often thought I could live in such a place forever," Ninh said. "But tomorrow it will be different. The Sixty-sixth Regiment returns, and they are bringing many wounded. The battle was very costly."

Bui Duong thanked his ancestors every night that he had not been assigned to the famous Sixty-sixth. Instead he had been assigned to the 174th and had remained in the base camp. He knew that tomorrow every available man would assist the doctors and medics in helping the wounded.

Ninh glanced at the dam and placed his hand on the thin private's shoulder. "You are doing good work. You are blessed with skills that will be useful after the war. Perhaps we should . . ." The sergeant stopped speaking as a tall, silver-haired officer emerged from the nearest hut. It was the division commander. He wore a faded khaki uniform without rank. Men in the camp immediately stopped all work as he passed by.

Duong shook his head. "Look at the others. They look upon him as if he were a god."

Sergeant Ninh tightened. "You know nothing! He is a god to us. No man has given more victories to the fatherland." His voice suddenly softened. "And no man has shed more tears. He has seen more war than all of us."

Duong felt sorry for displeasing the sergeant. "I apologize, Sergeant, but I heard that the general is ruthless in battle, and we are the ones who pay for his career."

Ninh's eyes turned cold. "You are a fool! Go back to work. One day, if you live long enough, you might be able to talk to the Tall One, and then you will understand how much he cares for us. Go to work!"

Candidate Jason Johnson looked at the lensatic compass that lay on his map, then glanced up at the terrain around him. Nothing matched. He was hopelessly lost. He'd been on the land navigation course for three hours and found four of the five stakes, but he had become lost trying to find the last point. He'd thought he knew where the last stake was and hadn't used his compass until it was too late.

He picked up the compass, feeling as empty and lost on the inside as he was on the military reservation. The instructor had warned them to always use DDT when navigating: distance, direction, and terrain. He had left out direction by not plotting an azimuth and using his compass. He would fail the land navigation test because of the stupid mistake. He lowered his head, knowing the critical test was a must for graduating from OCS.

A limb snapped behind him and he quickly got to his feet, hoping it was one of the other candidates thrashing through the Georgia pines, trying to find the small stakes. If it was a classmate, he could ask for help. Jason ran toward the sound, feeling hope, but he swore when he saw the sweat-soaked soldier coming out of a thicket. Damn, of all people, it had to be *him*.

Captain Willis looked up from his compass, surprised to find one of his men staring at him. Shit, if he had been a dink, it woulda' been over. He was losing his touch.

Jason lowered his head, knowing he couldn't ask for help from his tac officer. The little bastard had been participating in all the training and taking great pride in leading the way. It was as if he were competing with them, against their youth, and he was winning. Weird Willis wouldn't help his own mother on a test such as this. He preached honor above everything else.

Willis hid a smile at the lost look on his candidate's face. "Candidate Johnson," he snapped, "do you have any idea where you are?"

Jason thought about saying "Yes, sir," and walking away, but he knew Willis would ask him to point out his location on the map. "Ah . . . Sir . . . I . . . I'm temporarily disoriented."

Willis marched toward him. "That answer is only used by qualified Rangers. You, Candidate Johnson, are LBS, correct?"

"Beggin' your pardon, sir?

"LBS is 'Lost Bigger than Shit.' "

Jason lowered his eyes. "Yes, sir. The only thing I know right now is I'm in Georgia."

"Johnson, you have given up. WRONG! Pull out your map sheet and show me that last stake you were at. . . . Okay, which direction did you take from there?"

"I thought I knew where it was and didn't use my compass. I thought it was due north but . . ."

"Think, Candidate. Did you go down hill, up hill, what?"

"I went down a slope and hit a creek at about five hundred meters."

Willis studied the map and Jason's last known location for several moments and pointed. "Look at this. You must have gone west. It's the only low ground and matches with the creek. Think what you did and what terrain you walked over, and point it out on the map."

Jason reconstructed his meandering, realizing he wasn't quite as lost as he had thought. He narrowed his location down to a thousand-meter grid square. "Sir, I gotta be somewhere in this area."

Willis cocked an eyebrow up. "Look around you, Candidate. What kind of terrain feature are we on?"

"Sir, we're on a ridge."

"And what direction is this ridge running, Candidate?"

"To the southeast, sir."

"Orient your map to north and you'll see there are four ridges that fit this description, but they all have one thing in common: if you were to go down them, they would all take you to Hewel Creek. If you were to go down this ridge and hit the creek and turn right, you'd eventually come to this bridge. If you stood on the bridge, you would know exactly where you are and you could plot your last stake . . . correct?"

Jason looked up from the map in awe. Willis had made it seem so simple. Of course, he was correct. "Thank you, sir, I mean really, thank you!"

Willis snarled coldly, "You gave up, Candidate. Don't you ever give up again. Leaders can't afford to panic and feel desperation, or their men will." He glanced at his watch and began walking away. "Candidate, you have only forty-five minutes to finish this course. According to the test instructions, you must make it on time or you fail, regardless of how many points you've found. I don't think you can do it; you've wasted too much time feeling sorry for yourself."

"I'll make it!" Jason yelled to the officer's back and spun around to align his compass. He set the azimuth toward the creek and broke into a dead run.

Willis stood behind the small field desk where the students had to report upon completion of the land navigation test. He glanced at his watch, then at the meadow in front of him. The students had to cross the open field to finish, and there were only thirty seconds left before time was up. In the distance, he saw a soldier emerge from the woodline in a slow run. It was obvious, even in the fading light, that the soldier was exhausted and barely able to move. Willis recognized the soldier and shook his head. I'll be damned, he did it. Johnson had to have covered two kilometers through the worst terrain on the course. The vegetation along the creek bed was thick with vines and laurel.

Willis glanced at his watch again. Shit, he was so close but . . . "MOVE IT, JOHNSON! FIFTEEN SECONDS! COME ON, RUN!"

Jason leaned forward with the last of his energy and tried to make his legs move faster, but they felt like rubber. He couldn't seem to bring air into his lungs, and everything was a blur. The familiar voice gave him a direction, and he lowered his head, pushing himself through the pain.

Willis stepped back, feeling guilty, and watched as the big soldier passed by him and slapped his map on the desk with barely a second to spare. Johnson's uniform was ripped, and his hands and face were bloody. He could envision the young soldier running and fighting his way through brambles and vines, trying desperately to stay on course and make it back on time. He, as tactical officer, was responsible for his pain and wounds. And why? For a test the soldier could have taken over in a few days? An officer's commission that might get him killed or maimed?

Jason held onto the desk as if it were a life buoy, and he tried to catch his breath while he waited for his score. The sergeant sitting behind the desk quickly checked the stake numbers and stamped his card with "PASS."

Jason turned around with a weary smile and walked to where the captain stood staring into the approaching darkness.

"Sir, I made it."

Willis studied the smiling face, and suddenly he had his answer. The candidate's smile was like those of the young soldiers he had led in Vietnam last year. He wasn't pushing the candidates for themselves; he was pushing them for the soldiers they would lead. Those young men who gave so much deserved the best their country could provide . . . and, by God, he'd make sure they got what they deserved!

Willis put guilt and sympathy out of his mind as he said with detachment, "Never quit on me again, Candidate Johnson. Inform the platoon they will not be taking the buses back as was planned. We will be force marching. We move out in ten minutes."

Jason's smile dissolved into a look of despair. It was twelve miles back to the barracks. He straightened his sore back and brought his hand up in a salute. "Yes, sir."

* * *

Private Nance stood in the ranks of Alpha Company, Second Battalion, Third Brigade, as they practiced their graduation ceremony on York Field. He'd finally made it through basic training and would be shipping out for Fort Benning in two days to begin AIT. Tomorrow morning would be the real graduation, and he'd finally leave Fort Bliss. He'd recovered from his ankle injury and been sent to Alpha Company, where he found the environment totally different. His drill sergeant had ridden him hard at first, because he was a recycle, but had finally eased up, seeing he wasn't a shitbird. He had even made him acting squad leader. He'd found the training to be much easier the second time around, because he was physically and mentally prepared. It was against the rules for a recycle to be listed as an honor student, or he would have been standing in front of his company receiving the training award and marksmanship trophy.

Ty lowered his eyes, feeling pride in himself, but he knew one more task had to be accomplished before he left for Benning. Tonight they would be released for a four-hour pass, and he'd have his opportunity then.

Sergeant McCoy left the NCO club feeling no pain; he'd drunk two six-packs during happy hour. He dug in his pockets for his car keys but couldn't remember where he'd parked. He swayed, then staggered into the darkness. Trying to keep his balance, he braced himself against a car, when suddenly he fell to the pavement in excruciating pain. His jaw felt like he'd been hit by a baseball bat. He looked up at a dark figure looming over him, unable to see his face.

"You got three seconds to get up! One . . . two . . . three. Freeze!"

The attacker put his foot on McCoy's chest, pushing him back to the pavement. "You fucked up, McCoy. Don't ever mess with an attitude problem."

"You!" said McCoy, feeling scared for the first time. "I . . . I didn't mean to bump you. . . . It was an accident . . . I swear it was, I swear."

Ty leaned over and saw the fear in the pathetic man's face and backed up. He'd planned to kick his teeth in, but this was better. He took the keys from the ground and threw them across the parking lot. Leaning down, he spoke evenly. "You just learned a lesson. Always keep your guard up, or some attitude problem is gonna pay you back. I got your spirit, McCoy."

Ty turned around and walked into the darkness, ignoring the sergeant, who was trying to get up. "You . . . you got what? What did you steal from me? You can't steal from Drill Sergeant McCoy. Goddamn you, come and fight like a . . ."

Ty sat in a large classroom, fidgeting in his seat and longing to get outside and march to the graduation ceremony. The company commander was giving a safety briefing before graduation to save time. As soon as the company graduated, they would return and immediately begin outprocessing.

The captain finished his briefing and motioned for the first sergeant, who stood and spoke in a deep, gravelly voice. "Anybody here want to volunteer for Airborne school, stay in the classroom for a short briefing. The rest of you move outside."

Ty stayed in his seat and pulled out his dog tags from under his shirt. Attached to the chain was the jump wings from his grandfather's treasure box. Touching the silver badge, he could hear two men calling out to him.

A tall sergeant, wearing glistening jump boots and an overseas cap with glider patch sewn to its front, walked down the aisle as if he were a king. He faced the small group and put his hands on his hips. "I am Sergeant Rolando, the Airborne recruiter. I need twenty men. Your legs don't look like much, but we'll square you away once you graduate from AIT. If you think you're good enough to be a paratrooper, see me when you outprocess this afternoon. I'll have a table at the end of the line. Have all your records in hand and a willing attitude.

"I can promise you fifty-five dollars extra a month and the best ride in town under a T-10 canopy of silk. The rest of your life will be pure hell. You'll be pushed harder than you were here at basic, and your reward will be a free, all-expense-paid one-year tour of the Republic of South Vietnam. You all will be going anyway, no matter what you do, so think about going over and joining the Army's most elite units, the 101st Screaming Eagles and 173rd Sky Soldiers. Both units need men now. Don't even talk to me unless you're sure in your heart you want to be a paratrooper. Think about it, legs. Jumpin' out of a perfectly good aircraft while in flight is most definitely not for everybody. You have a chance to volunteer and become a somebody. Legs, join and fight with the best, or be a nasty leg for the rest of your nasty leg life . . . the decision is yours."

Ty left the classroom, having already made up his mind the day he joined the Army. His father had worn the wings, and so would he. He was going to join the ranks of the Red Hill Paratroopers.

Ty hefted his duffle bag to his shoulder and walked toward the mailbox. Graduation and outprocessing were now nothing but memories. He'd received his paperwork and was to report to the transit billets for the night and catch the bus for Fort Benning tomorrow. Rolando had signed him up without even looking at his records and told him he'd be receiving orders at Benning.

He stopped at the mailbox and tossed the bag to the ground. Like all the trainees, he had found that going through the outprocessing pay line was an exercise in paying back the Army. Finance had taken out twenty dollars for a previous advance pay to buy required items for inspections. The executive officer had all of the company "volunteer" to buy a savings bond, because they had to beat Charlie Company in the Freedom Award contest. First Sergeant then collected ten bucks for the Army Emergency Relief Organization, five for a membership in the Association of the United States Army, and two for the company cup and flower fund. At the end of the official line were the merchants. He had been required to have a picture taken the fifth week of training, and now it was pay-up time. The cheapest pack of pictures was ten dollars. The catch was that if you wanted to send the pictures home, there was a mailer available for an additional dollar-fifty. Out of the original $79.20 he had gotten from Uncle Sam, he now had only $11.95 left to live on for the month.

Feeling guilty, he dropped an envelope into the slot. He'd send the pictures to his mother. He hadn't written her during the past few weeks because of his hectic schedule, but he had thought of her every night. He hoped she would understand.

He picked up his heavy bag and continued the long walk toward the transit billets.

Jason sat in the large classroom with two books and a map laid open on the desk before him. The acronyms seemed endless, as did the different rules and considerations used in planning combat operations. There was planning for route selection, planning for organization of the unit, communications planning, fire support planning, and planning for planning. But the only acronym that had really stuck and applied to all situations was the six P's rule: prior planning prevents piss-poor performance.

He leaned back in his chair and thought back over the past months of training. He'd learned everything, from how to address the commander's wife to what the dimensions of a slit latrine should be. He'd learned what fork to use at a dinner party and how to blow men to smithereens with plastic explosives. The day began at 4:30 with PT and a run, and ended at 10:30 at night with study hall or preparation for an inspection. The demanding training schedule and Weird Willis had cut the platoon by a quarter. Most had quit or failed a critical subject. The company, which had started with 220 candidates, was now down to 164 men.

Weird Willis was a human buzz saw who seemed to have endless stamina and boundless energy. He led all runs and participated in all training, constantly hounding his platoon to give a hundred percent and find their limitations. He was the most dedicated soldier Jason had ever seen.

Jason broke from his reverie, hearing the instructor call his name.

"Candidate Johnson, stand up and tell us what is the first step in troop-leading procedures."

Jason stood and faced the class. "Sir, the first step is to receive the mission and begin planning."

"Excellent. Now, Candidate McKenzie, tell us the second step."

Jason bought a Coke and stood in the huge hallway as the class smoked and joked during a ten-minute break. He took a sip and immediately snapped to attention as Willis stepped in front of him, holding a folder. "Candidate Johnson, you didn't volunteer for Airborne or Ranger school. Why not?"

Jason stared straight ahead. "Sir, I'm not making the Army a career. I didn't see any use in going to any more schools after graduation."

Willis shook his head in exasperation. "Wrong, Candidate. YOU WILL VOLUNTEER! Airborne or Ranger school is not for you, it's insurance for the men you might lead one day. Soldiers need an experienced leader. Experience comes from screwing up, and you'll have plenty of opportunities to screw up in Ranger school. You will volunteer and give your men the experienced leader they deserve."

Jason stared at him and saw the familiar challenging glint in his eyes. Willis had not approached the other candidates and forced them to volunteer. Jason knew he was being honored that the captain thought him worthy of attending the courses. Both Airborne and Ranger schools were difficult to obtain quotas for, and few candidates would have the opportunity. The platoon tactical officers made up an order-of-merit list, and Willis would put him at the top of the list, ensuring he got to both schools.

Jason sighed. "Yes, sir, I'll volunteer."

Willis hid his pleasure with a scowl as he opened the folder. "I thought you probably would. I have the necessary paperwork right here. Sign each copy, and I'll submit them to battalion for consideration."

Jason took a pen from his pocket and quickly signed both papers. "Sir, are you going to help me get ready? I hear Ranger school is a bitch."

Closing the folder, Willis looked as if he knew an inside joke. "Candidate Johnson, Ranger school is not a bitch—it's your worst nightmare come true. You fall out thirty minutes early for PT from now on, and we'll begin your training."

"Thank you, sir."

"Don't thank me, Candidate. You'll hate me every day you're in Ranger school. Believe me."

19

Outside the OCS theater, a cold wind blew down the deserted sidewalks and across the yellowed parade field. The sun had tried to warm the frozen ground for two hours but was failing against the chilling wind. Inside the theater, 139 graduating candidates and their guests sat listening to the assistant commandant of the Infantry School explain the significance of commissioning officers into the infantry. Many a mother and father wiped a tear with pride.

Captain John Willis nodded off to sleep, as did most of the candidates. They had all learned, after twenty-four weeks of training and listening to countless instructors, that words spoken from a podium had to be filtered through the brain only for relevance to future tests or usage in Vietnam. If the words were not in either category, they were considered irrelevant, and the brain blocked absorption. The company of candidates had received their orders last month. All would be reporting to Vietnam upon completion of their additional schooling and leave. They would now be tested in combat on what they had learned in school. There would be no rehearsals like they had performed for the graduation. There would be no breaking-in time to learn the ropes in a stateside assignment. They were going to play in the Rose Bowl of war without the benefit of previous games. They didn't care. They would not have wanted it any other way. In their minds, they were ready.

Twenty minutes later, Jason stood at attention as Captain Willis pinned a gold second lieutenant's bar on his right epaulet. "I'm proud that you asked me to do the honors," Willis said. "I'm just sorry your mom and dad couldn't be here to pin on the other bar."

Jason held his head proudly. "Sir, you taught me more than you'll ever know. Thank you."

Willis pinned on the other bar and shook the young officer's hand. "Congratulations, Lieutenant Johnson. You take care of our soldiers. They deserve the very best this country can give . . . and they're going to get it in you. The best of luck."

Jason raised his hand in a rigid salute. "I will, sir. I promise."

Willis stepped back one pace and returned the salute. He wanted to say more but knew he'd said enough in the past weeks. Johnson was ready. He was an exceptional leader who wouldn't let his soldiers down. "So long, Jay. Take care of yourself over there."

He lowered his salute and strode toward the door. There was no time for sentiment or reflection. Outside, standing in the cold, was another class of 220 young men wanting to learn to be leaders. And in the group there would be another like Johnson. There always was.

The large green bus squeaked to a halt and the door swung open, letting in the biting cold and a tired staff sergeant. "All right, people, this is it—the United States Army Airborne School. You will first be inprocessed at the IRP. Move off the bus with all bags and baggage and assemble on the white lines to your right. I will call your names and you will enter the building with your records in your hands. You will fill in the classroom from front to rear without leaving a chair empty. You will keep your mouth shut and your ears open until you have completed inprocessing. At no time will you smoke, spit, talk, or go to the latrine without permission. You will have one minute to clear this bus . . . oh yeah, welcome."

Ty picked up his bags and filed off the bus. The ride had been a short one. His AIT company had been located on the sprawling post of Fort Benning in a place called Harmony Church. There was no church or harmony in the desolate outpost nestled among tall pines, but there were World War II barracks and cranky sergeants

whose business it was to make infantrymen of basic soldiers. Ty
had spent eight weeks learning infantry weapons, radios, tactics,
land navigation, first aid, tactical formations, map reading, and
misery. Harmony Church was twenty minutes from the main post
of Fort Benning and thirty from the strip joints of Victory Drive,
but they might as well have been on the moon for all he had seen
of the post or downtown. They'd been kept in complete isolation
and never had a pass or leave. The bus ride through the main post
to the Airborne training area was like a ride through Disneyland
for young men who had not seen civilization for eight weeks. The
bus had been strangely silent. There was none of the usual smoking
and joking. Each man was living out his own fantasies as he noticed
cars, children, and women along the busy streets and sidewalks.
The bus driver had pointed out the three huge orange-and-white
towers looming up in the middle of the post. "Them's the 250-foot
jump towers you boys be jumpin' from."

Ty walked into the dilapidated classroom building and was about
to take his seat when he abruptly halted. On the other side of the
room was a lieutenant staring at him. Jason! Thinner, crew-cut,
and looking three years older, but Ty still couldn't mistake him.

"You, Private Nance," Jason bellowed, "report to the back of
the room."

He strode down the aisle and waited with a scowl until Ty halted
in front of him. Both men broke into smiles and embraced each
other, bringing stares from the others. Jason put his arm around
Ty's shoulder and led him to a back room. "Damn, little brother,
you look great, except for that skinhead haircut."

Ty ran his hand over the black stubble and looked over his brother's fitted uniform. "You don't look so bad either, Loo-tenant
brother, sir."

Jason laughed and hugged him again. "I've missed you." Ty
clapped his brother's back, feeling emotions he had forgotten he
possessed. He hadn't hugged a man since he had embraced Jason
a century ago.

Jason backed up a step and shook his head. "I've been trying to
contact you for a month. Didn't you get my letters?"

"Yeah, but . . . well, I . . ."

"I know," said Jason quickly, seeing his discomfort and giving
him an out. "You were busy as hell, same as me. But did you get
a letter off to Mom? She was really upset that you hadn't written.
You know she wrote a congressman to find out where you were?"

Ty smiled faintly. "You think Mom was upset, you shoulda'

seen my first sergeant when the congressional inquiry came down. He brought me in and chewed my ass for ten minutes for not writing and made me write a letter in front of him. He put a stamp on it and mailed it personally. I had to write one once a week after that, and he escorted me to the mailbox. Ya might say me and Top got *real* close.''

Jason chuckled, knowing the Army establishment hated congressionals because they had to be answered. ''Mom wrote and told me where you were. I called a couple of times, but your unit was in the field. They said you'd be reporting in for Airborne School today, so I thought I'd better see ya before goin' home on leave. Mom would have killed me if I hadn't.''

''Tell her I'm doing good, Jay. And yeah, I'll write once a week.''

''You bet, but you'll be home in three weeks yourself. We'll all be home for Christmas, and Mom is really looking forward to it.''

Ty nodded noncommittally. ''Yeah. . . . Hey, what's this Mom said about you going to Airborne and Ranger schools? You gettin' pretty gung ho, ain'tcha?''

Jason noted Ty's eyes when he mentioned going back home for leave and felt a stab of pain in his heart. He knew Ty wouldn't be coming. He covered his pain with a faint smile. ''Look who's talkin' about gung ho. I never thought you'd want to be a paratrooper. What happened, they draft you into it?''

Ty pulled out his dog tag chain. ''Remember these? I'm gonna be a Red Hill Paratrooper, just like dad and Richard. They both wore these wings, and in three weeks I'll be wearin' 'em.''

The staff sergeant stepped in the doorway. ''Lieutenant, I'm starting inprocessing in two minutes. The private needs to be in his seat.''

Jason nodded. ''He's coming, Sergeant, thank you.''

Ty put his hand out. ''I guess I'd better get goin'. Take care of yourself, Jay, and give Mom a hug for me . . . and check the hill for me.''

Jason ignored his hand and hugged him. ''I'm so proud of you . . . come home Ty, please.''

Ty gave Jason the same distant look and smiled. ''Sure, I'll see you then. Hey, take the 'Widow' out of mothballs and give her a spin.'' Ty turned to leave but stopped and looked over his shoulder. ''I'm proud of you, too . . . and, brother, I love you.''

He turned away so that Jason wouldn't see his tears and quickly walked out of the room.

* * *

Jason leaned back in his seat and shut his eyes. In fifteen minutes he would be landing in Atlanta. After a two-hour layover he would catch a flight to Dallas, then Oklahoma City. He would be home by eight o'clock that evening. Home. The small house that always smelled of fresh-baked bread would embrace him with its warmth and memories. Home. The smiles and hugs of love from his mother and father would be the same as before. The familiar faces in Meyers and the looming majesty of the hill would welcome him. Yes, home. It was going to be good to be back, but he knew it really wouldn't be the same. Ty wouldn't be coming home. It was in his eyes.

"Coffee, Lieutenant?"

Jason looked up to see who the stewardess was talking to and was surprised to see she was looking directly at him. "Lieutenant"; God, it sounded good. He'd forgotten. "No thank you, ma'am."

The hostess smiled. "Just holler if you need anything. Keep your seat belt fastened. It's a short flight."

Ty reported to 44th Airborne Company and was given a barracks assignment. Training would start on Monday morning, just three days away. He tossed his duffle bag down by his bunk and began unpacking. He stowed away his uniforms and boots, then picked up the large bundles of letters he'd kept and lay down on his bunk. The letters from his mother he tossed in his footlocker.

Her words of love and devotion caused immediate warmth to spread through him. He desperately wanted to see her and go home but he couldn't. He had prepared himself and couldn't go home until it was over.

A cloud of vapor puffed into the darkness from Jason's nostrils as he dug his boots into the red soil and churned his arms. Conditioned after twenty-four weeks of getting up early, he'd been rolling out of bed every morning at five and running up the trail to Red Hill. Today was no exception, despite the cold, biting wind that nipped at his ears and nose. A part of him was home, but another part was still at Fort Benning. One part was enjoying the love and warmth of the family, while the other fought to retain the regime of a soldier going to combat. Seeing the top of the hill in the early morning grayness, he pushed himself harder to feel the familiar pain that would signal he'd hit the edge. His body smoked as he topped the crest with the last of his strength. He slowed to a walk and felt elation in the challenge. His lungs burned with the cold air, but he'd won the race with the sun for the first time.

Jason faced east, just as the orange ball peeked over the purple horizon. He smiled at his small victory and walked toward the cemetery to complete the work he'd started two days before. Opening the gate, he knelt by the third tombstone to pull out the tall, yellowed grass.

Jason tossed the grass over the fence and looked back at the other markers where the two paratroopers rested. He knew they were smiling somehow, somewhere.

Ty stood at parade rest with five hundred other men, waiting. From up a small hill they came, their jump boots glistening in the early morning sunlight. Running in a small formation, in perfect step, wearing starched fatigue trousers and gray sweatshirts with master parachute wings painted on the front, the infamous Black Hats, the Airborne instructors, were coming to deal out misery and woe. Each of them wore a black cap with shining parachute wings pinned exactly one and one-half inches up and centered on the cap. They turned off the road onto the gravel, their boots crunching ominously on the stones. Five hundred pairs of eyes strained to watch the instructors as they came closer.

"COMP-A-NEEee, AH-tench-HUT!" the student company commander yelled.

A large Airborne instructor captain strode forward and positioned himself in front of the student company commander, who immediately raised his hand in a salute. "SIR, AIRBORNE CLASS NUMBER 46 DASH 66 IS PREPARED FOR INSPECTION!"

The captain looked at him with disdain. "We'll see about that, leg!" He quickly returned the salute and lifted his head. "IN-STRUC-TORS, CONDUCT INSPECTION!"

Ty was third in line in the first platoon and saw the instructors return the salute with precision and lower their hands, slapping their legs in the traditional "pop" of all black hats. The instructor assigned to his squad stepped in front of the first victim. "Leg, what did you shine those boots with, a Hershey bar? Drop! . . . Legs, this is the first stick. It is not a squad or section, that's nasty leg talk. You are the FIRST STICK." He stepped to the next man. "Leg, did you shave today?"

"Ya . . . Yes, Sergeant."

"Wrong, leg, you *thought* you shaved! THAT is a leg shave. You have nasty leg hairs under your nose. You said 'yes' to me. In Airborne you will say 'CLEAR, Sergeant.' Is that clear, leg?"

"Yes, Sergeant! Uh . . . I mean, CLEAR, Sergeant!"

"Drop, leg!" The sergeant took a step back. "First Stick, YOU

WILL spit-shine your boots. YOU WILL shave closely. YOU WILL wear a clean, serviceable uniform. YOU WILL wear your parachutist helmet properly with chin strap right side up. YOU WILL say CLEAR instead of yes. YOU WILL shine your belt buckle, and YOU WILL address me as Sergeant AIRBORNE!''

He strode to Ty and scowled. "Leg, you have the prettiest scar I ever saw. Who are you?''

"Sergeant Airborne, I am Private Nance!''

"Wrong, LEG! The tape on your helmet says Roster Number Twenty-two. Now, WHO are you, leg?''

"Sergeant Airborne, I am Roster Number Twenty-two!''

"OUT-standing! But your boots are cruddy, your belt buckle looks like something is growing on it, your chin strap is on upside down, AND your scar is too pretty. DROP!''

Ty began to get down in the front leaning rest position like the others and do push-ups when the sergeant bent over and barked, "REE-COVER, leg! . . . Leg, when I say 'drop,' you drop like you been hit in the head with a two-by-four soaked in motor oil. You got down entirely too slow. DROP!''

Thirty minutes later, the inspection was over and no one had passed. Ty had heard about the initial inspection and knew it was the tone setter. It established the high standards of Airborne. To-morrow, if a man showed up with a gig, he'd pay by having his name taken and would be sent to the gig pit, where a collection of specially selected NCOs "convinced" the offender that he didn't really want to be a paratrooper. Only a small group of men who went to the gig pit returned. Most would be "convinced" by the extra, exhausting PT to conform to standards or quit.

Following inspection, the company took a PT test consisting of push-ups, sit-ups, knee bends, pull-ups, and a two-mile run. Forty-five men failed and were absent from the ranks when the company formed up again to start training. Ty was now the second man in the stick when the platoon sergeant approached with four other instructors. "Legs, we have made the first cut. We started with 110 men in this platoon, and we now have 98. Look at the man to your left . . . now the one to your right . . . now the one to your rear. Legs, one of them other legs is not going to make it. It might be you! This is the mighty First Platoon. You will double-time every-where you go. And when you move, you move like LIGHTNING and sound like THUNDER!''

"Legs, you are about to jump from the thirty-four-foot tower. You have for the past two days learned to properly put on your parachute harness and reserve parachute. You have learned to hit the ground utilizing a PLF, Parachute Landing Fall, insuring to make contact with the ground with all five points of contact. The five points of contact are, again, the balls of the feet, calf, thigh, buttocks, and latissimus dorsi muscle, better known as the push-up muscle. You have learned the jump commands inside the aircraft and learned, utilizing the mock door, how to jump from an aircraft while it is in flight. Now you will have the opportunity to experience what it is like to actually jump outside of an aircraft. You will be hooked up to a set of risers that are connected to a cable. Once you exit the door you will receive an opening shock similar to that of the real thing and slide down the cable to the mound to your far right.

"Legs, you must remember what we taught you and take up a good door position with your head up, arms extended with palms facing out and barely touching the outside skin of the aircraft. Have your legs slightly bent and buttocks down. On the command of 'GO,' leap vigorously out thirty-six inches and up six inches. You snap your chin to your chest and pop your hands to your reserve. Keeping a good, tight body position, your legs should be together and you should be slightly bent at the waist, insuring to keep your eyes open and count the required four seconds.

"Legs, we have discussed the five points of performance. They are: keep a tight body position and count, check canopy, keep a sharp lookout during descent and avoid fellow jumpers, prepare to land, and land. Legs, move to the tower and remember everything I just told you . . . MOVE!"

Ty tried to run, but the parachute harness fit so tightly that all he could manage was a bent-over waddle. The soldier to his front approached the steps of the tower and stopped. "I ain't going up there, man."

Ty slapped his back reassuringly. "Look up, man, it ain't that high. No sweat, it's a piece a cake."

"No way!"

A Black Hat stepped in front of the scared soldier. "Roster Number Twenty-one, you have exactly five seconds to make up your mind whether you want to be a paratrooper and get up those steps."

The wide-eyed soldier shook his head. "I . . . I can't do it."

The Black Hat pointed to the harness shed. "Move out, quitter. You're gone! Next man, move up the steps!"

Ty reached the top of the tower, where there was an enclosed tin mock-up of the back of an aircraft. On both sides of the mock-up were exact replicas of jump doors. A Black Hat barked, "Come here, leg!"

The sergeant hooked up two risers to Ty's parachute harness and gave the jump command, "Stand in the door!"

Ty remembered to shuffle his feet and stomp his right foot into the doorway. He immediately crouched, raised his head to look at the horizon and threw his arms out, with the palms facing the skin of the aircraft. He remembered everything, but his eyes failed him and he glanced downward. Ooooh shit! It didn't seem that high from the ground, but from where he stood, it looked like it was a mile up. There was nothing out there to catch him. No soft sawdust to soften the blow if the risers broke. Nothing but lots and lots of empty space.

"GO!"

He tried to respond, but his body and eyes knew it was suicidal. He tried to leap, but his feet were glued to the floor.

"GO!"

Ty was about to turn around and ask for additional advice when he felt a powerful shove and was propelled into space. All the training, all the lectures, all the dry runs were forgotten. He did what instinct told him to do—he clamped his eyes shut and waited to die. The opening shock of the risers slapped his face like a boxer's one-two jab, and his testicles seemed to have been smashed up into his stomach by the harness leg straps. In excruciating pain, he opened his eyes, feeling himself sliding down the cable toward a huge mound of dirt. At the last second he remembered to raise his feet to keep from smashing his legs into the mound of dirt at twenty miles an hour. Barely clearing the mound, he slid up the cable to its stop, where two men caught him. They immediately unhooked his risers and pointed to the small, gray building under the tower. This was the grader's shack. Seated inside was an instructor who graded each door exit.

Ty checked to see if he would ever be able to have children and loosened the harness to ease the pain. Taking a deep breath to control his shaking, he jogged with an exaggerated waddle toward what he knew was going to be an ass chewing.

"Sergeant Airborne, Roster Number Twenty-Two reports."

"Twenty-two, you did absolutely nothing right! The only thing tight on your exit was your eyes. It was a night jump for you. Twenty-two, you were hit in the face because you didn't put your chin on your chest. You spread your legs and will probably talk like a girl for a week. Go up and do it again!"

Ty's face registered shock. AGAIN! He'd almost killed himself and the fool wanted him to do it AGAIN? The sergeant had just said he'd done nothing right. Maybe he wasn't cut out for this after all.

The sergeant shook his head, seeing his shocked expression. "Turn around and look at this next jumper!"

Ty looked up just as the frightened man tumbled out of the door forgetting even to stand in the door properly. The young soldier's lips were curled back in anticipation of dying, and his eyes were so tightly closed that his face seemed disfigured. The risers snapped his head up just as they had done to Ty.

The instructor frowned as he marked his clipboard. "Twenty-two, nobody does it right the first time. The first jump is just to give you confidence in the equipment. Now you know you ain't gonna die, so get up there and concentrate on what we have been teaching you. MOVE, LEG!"

Five jumps later, Ty slid down the cable without a trace of fear. It was getting to be fun. He'd messed up his vigorous leap several times but had learned to keep his head down and eyes open. He'd felt his last jump had been perfect. "Sergeant Airborne, Roster Number Twenty-two reports." The sergeant glanced up. "Twenty-two, that was a satisfactory exit. You're finally gettin' the hang of it. Exchange your harness with the next man, then move to the bench and watch this flying circus . . . good job."

Jason dragged the tree up the hill and sat down on the log bench to rest. The chopping down of the small cedar tree for Christmas had been surprisingly tough. The wood was either harder than steel or the axe was in desperate need of sharpening.

The cold wind whipped around him as he leaned back and absorbed the beautiful view. He now understood why Ty had loved his hill so. It was like a different world, unspoiled and so wonderfully quiet. No hustle or bustle, no time schedules to meet, no demands, no grinding of gears or whining of engines. The hill sat alone, untouched by time or altered by man, and seemed to exude a feeling of blissful peace. Quiet peace, a time to think and reflect. Constant, tranquil peace permeated everything growing and living on the magical red soil.

Jason felt the first chill and slowly stood. He didn't want to leave. He glanced at the headstones wishing the protectors well and picked up the tree. It was time to go back to the other world.

"You sure you know somethin' about building sheds?"

Ty struggled to keep up with the sergeant as he strode toward the closest 250-foot tower. "Like I said, Sergeant Airborne, I built three or four back home."

Master Sergeant Cherry slowed as he approached a large group of men snapping in a parachute around a large steel rim with cables attached to its top. The soldiers were performing the chore of rig and run. A specially modified parachute was attached to the metal ring and raised to the top of the tower with a jumper dangling under the steel rim. The parachute and jumper were raised by cable to a catch that automatically released the parachute from the ring. The parachute, already inflated, floated downward and performed exactly like the standard-issue T-10 parachute, giving the jumper practical experience in maneuvering and landing.

Master Sergeant Cherry motioned to the closest instructor, who immediately jogged over. "Sam, I want you to put Twenty-two up next. I know he's not in your platoon, but I got to get some grader sheds built, and this trooper knows how to build 'em. When he gets finished, send him over to supply."

The instructor smiled. "Sarge, you been scroungin' again, huh? Sure, no sweat. I'll square him away and he'll be over in a few minutes."

Ty was glad the sergeants were sure he would survive the 250-foot fall, but he wasn't quite as convinced. He now knew that when the tower branch chief NCO had asked if anyone had experience building houses or sheds he should have remained silent. He violated the rule of all low-ranking soldiers: never volunteer for nothin'. The master sergeant had taken him out of training on the swing landing trainer and brought him immediately to the tower to complete the critical tower jump. The platoons revolved in training, and he wouldn't have had time to build a shed and jump. Damn! The men who were jumping from the tower had received an hour class that he hadn't been present for. Maybe there was something he was supposed to do or know before going up the incredible height.

"Twenty-two, get over here!" commanded the instructor. "Put this harness on and stand right there. You'll be going up next."

"Sergeant Airborne, what do I do when I get up there?"

The instructor broke from the traditional scowl and smiled. "You look around at the view and then fall. Keep your feet and knees together and relax. Do a dynamite PLF once you make contact with the ground. Nothin' to it."

Ty put on the harness and placed his hands on his helmet for inspection. Nothing to it? He was going to be raised 250 feet in the air, suspended below a silk umbrella, and released into space. My God, how could he say "nothing to it"?

The sergeant quickly cinched the leg straps up tighter and slapped his buttocks, the traditional Airborne signal for "you're checked and okay. Move to the ring."

Ty moved in slow motion over to several men who fitted the parachute risers into his canopy release assemblies and stood back. The ring began rising, taking out the slack of the suspension lines, until Ty was suddenly lifted from the ground. Oooooh shit!

The ride up was short and spectacular. The view was breathtaking, but he wasn't interested in the view. He was trying not to move a muscle as he prayed that the contraption would hold together. Suddenly, he was lifted another six feet and released. The drop forced his stomach into his throat, and he quit breathing. The parachute billowed and popped into a full blossom of green silk, jerking him upward in a slight jolt. There was no pain, no noise, no sudden rush to the ground. He was floating. He yelled, "AIRrrrr-BORNE!" unable to contain his joy at surviving and experiencing the indescribable feeling of floating. It's great, super, unbelievable, it's . . . oh hell, the ground!

Ty hit the plowed field and crumpled into a green ball. He lay still for a moment and yelled again. "AIRrrrBORNE!" It didn't hurt at all. It was like jumping off a four-foot wall. Piece a cake.

The C-119 roared down the runway and lifted off into the crisp, cold air. Ty swallowed hard, and tried to concentrate on what he'd been taught. It was useless. His mind was a blank. It was the first airplane he'd ever ridden in, and he was going to jump out of the damn thing. The jumpmaster stood up and clapped his hands over the outside engine noise. He stomped his foot and held up his hands, yelling, "SIX MINUTES!"

Ty and his stick of jumpers yelled back, "SIX MINUTES," and began rocking their bodies back and forth to awaken anyone who might have fallen asleep. Ty knew the six-minute warning was one of the jump commands, but he couldn't imagine anyone sleeping at a time like this. A minute later, the jumpmaster stomped his foot forward again and commanded, "GET READY!"

All the jumpers stomped their lead foot out and slapped their legs while yelling, "GET READY!"

The jumpmaster yelled, "UNFASTEN SEATBELTS . . . IN-BOARD PERSONNEL, STAND UP! . . . OUTBOARD PERSONNEL, STAND UP!"

Ty fought to overcome the weight of his chute and struggled to his feet.

"HOOK UP!"

Ty unfastened the snap hook from his reserve carrying handle and hooked up the metal device to the cable above his right shoulder. He then formed a bite in the static line just six inches down from the snap hook and held on for dear life with his right hand.

"CHECK STATIC LINES!"

Each jumper kept his grip of the static line and traced the yellow nylon cord with his other hand to make sure that it wasn't frayed and that it was attached properly to the parachute pack.

"CHECK EQUIPMENT!"

Ty ran his hand over his chin strap, then looked at his harness. Everything was still in place and secure.

"SOUND OFF FOR EQUIPMENT CHECK!"

The last jumper in the stick stomped his foot and slapped the jumper's buttocks to his front, yelling "O-KAY!" Each jumper did the identical drill, passing up the okay signal.

Ty was the lead jumper and could hear the word being passed forward. "O-kay . . . O-kay . . . O-kay! . . . O-KAY! . . . O-KAY!" He felt his butt being slapped, and he stomped his foot down and pointed at the jumpmaster's face, yelling, "ALL OKAY, JUMPMASTER!"

The sergeant shot his thumb up and nodded toward the Air Force crew chief, who opened the side door, letting in a burst of light and icy cold wind.

Ty could see nothing but blue sky and prayed that the pilot knew what he was doing.

The jumpmaster grasped the door, and to Ty's horror, leaned out into the 120-knot wind. His face contorted in folds of blowing skin. What the . . . he's gone CRAZY!

The sergeant pulled himself back into the aircraft and held up his finger. "ONE MINUTE!" He leaned out the door again and rotated his head all around, making sure there were no other aircrafts nearby, and stepped back. "THIRTY SECONDS!"

Taking one more look to make sure the drop zone smoke was still white, meaning winds were safe, the jumpmaster stepped out of the door and pointed direcly at Ty. "DROP ZONE COMING UP . . . STAND IN THE DOOR!"

Ty shuffled to the sunlight and handed the static line to the jumpmaster before stomping his foot on the edge of the jump platform and extending his hands. He held his head up, ignoring the 120-knot winds tearing at his fatigue pants, but he couldn't ignore the ground speeding by 1,250 feet below. My God, they're serious! We're gonna do it! OOOOOh shit, I don't remember what . . .

The red light in the door frame went off and the green light came on. The jumpmaster slapped Ty's buttocks. "GO!"

Ty had no time to think or react. His repetitive training did it for him. He leaped without thinking and snapped into a tight body position. "Onethousand, twothousand, threethousand, fourthou . . . oooOOH!"

The jerk knocked the rest of his words out of him. With a "pop," the green canopy of silk settled over Ty, shading his face in the most beautiful sight in the world, his canopy fully deployed. "AIRrrrrrBORNE!"

20

"ROSTER NUMBER TWENTY-TWO, FALL OUT AND RE-PORT TO THE BACK OF THE SWEAT SHED."

Ty had just thrown his parachute onto the table when he heard his number called over the loudspeaker. He jogged down the crowded aisle of fellow jumpers to the back of the shed, where he saw Master Sergeant Cherry standing with his hands on his hips.

The sergeant looked more like an old football player than an Airborne instructor. His body was heavily muscled, and his neck was as thick as a tree trunk. The black cap cast a sinister shadow over his face. "Nance, I got a deal for you."

Ty immediately became suspicious; the sergeant hadn't called him by his roster number. "What is it, Sergeant Airborne?"

"Nance, you're not gonna be goin' to Vietnam as soon as you think. I just pulled a few strings and had your orders delayed a month. I got a bunch of grader shacks that need to be rebuilt and can't be waitin' on engineer support that probably will never come. I talked to Sergeant Major, and he fixed it for me. You're mine until the end of January. When you graduate today, you will be moving to the headquarters barracks and reporting to me tomorrow morning. I'll put you on leave until the first week in January, and then we can get started. I know you're thinking this isn't much of a deal, but trooper, I'm keepin' you out of da Nam for a month. Believe me, that's a deal.''

Ty had stiffened. "Sergeant Airborne, I wanna go to Vietnam. The sooner I get it over, the sooner I can get home.''

The master sergeant frowned. "Trooper, it's too late. I already got your orders cut. I can't go back now and change 'em. You can go home on leave, so it ain't that bad.''

Ty cussed himself for volunteering the week before and sighed in resignation. "I won't need the leave, Sergeant Airborne. I'll get to work after I graduate.''

Cherry eyed him more closely. "Don't you wanna go home for Christmas?''

Ty's eyes lowered. "I'd rather be busy.''

Cherry felt a pang of sadness for the young paratrooper, knowing that either he didn't have the money to go home or there were troubles there. "Okay, Nance, you start tomorrow. By the way, good luck to you today.''

Ty nodded and turned around to go back and chute up. Cherry sighed and barked softly, "Nance.''

Ty looked over his shoulder. "Yo, Sergeant Airborne.''

"Nance, since you're mine, I guess I should at least pin your wings on today. Don't you crash and burn on me, and I'll see ya at graduation.''

Ty grinned. "Piece a cake.''

Ty shuffled to the door wanting out of the aircraft. The plane had made several dry passes over the drop zone without dropping troops because of high winds. After the fourth pass, the jumpmaster saw white smoke, signaling winds were now within limits. The longer flight and anticipation had gotten to four jumpers, who vomited in the aisle and immediately caused a chain reaction from half the stick. The aircraft floor was slick with liquefied breakfast. Ty was in the middle of the stick and was trying to breathe through his mouth so as not to smell the sickening bile. He approached the door feeling no fear. He stomped his foot on the edge of the doorway and leaped.

The gusting wind tore at his body as he hurdled toward the ground. The static line became taut and pulled open the pack tray, releasing the folds of silk that quickly caught air and unfurled into a green half-sphere.

When Ty looked up and saw his canopy, he froze. Another jumper was heading directly for his chute.

The jumper's risers were twisted above his head, and he couldn't see where he was going. Ty began to scream a warning, but it was too late. The jumper hit the billowing silk and panicked. He grabbed hold of the skirt of the canopy.

Ty knew it was just a matter of time. He'd listened to the malfunction class and knew the other jumper's parachute would float over his and collapse. The instructor had explained that the lower chute takes the air so that a chute passing over another gets no updraft and collapses. It wasn't dangerous at high altitude because the upper jumper would fall below the lower jumper and his chute would reinflate. But if one of the jumpers didn't slip away quickly, they would continue the process of one chute stealing air from the other, a phenomenon known as "leap frogging," until the last jumper stole the air and the other plummeted the last forty feet to the ground without an inflated canopy. The instructor had warned all of them to never, never, NEVER grab another's canopy during leap frogging. If a man held onto the inflated parachute and his chute collapsed, his weight would pull the good canopy with him and cause the chute to collapse.

Ty screamed, "LET GO! LET GO OF THE CHUTE!"

The jumper's chute floated over Ty's and fluttered for an instant, then collapsed. The jumper screamed, feeling himself fall, and held on to Ty's chute for dear life. The canopy tilted with his weight and suddenly became a fluttering jumble of silk.

Ty was prepared to pull his reserve but wasn't ready for the sudden plunge. Without a parachute he was nothing more than a rock propelling toward earth. He yanked the reserve handle with all his strength and was hit in the chin by the small, spring-loaded pilot chute. The miniature chute ripped upward and pulled the rest of the white reserve parachute from its container. He was jolted upward, and then as fast was jerked down. The other jumper was dangling twenty feet below him, hopelessly entangled in Ty's original parachute.

Ty looked at the ground only 300 feet below and prayed the jumper's parachute fluttering in a jumble beside him didn't suddenly inflate and become entangled with his reserve. The ground was coming up fast. The reserve was smaller and designed for only one man, not two.

He yelled at the man below him to relax, but the other jumper continued kicking and yanking at the silk in a frenzy to free himself.

The huge speakers on the drop zone, known as the voice of God, were blaring, "JUMPER WITH THE ACTIVATED RESERVE, RELAX AND KEEP YOUR FEET AND KNEES TOGETHER. RELAX, RELAX."

Ty could see two jeeps racing toward him along with four drop zone instructors, who held megaphones. They were all yelling for him to prepare to land. He tried to keep his legs together for the landing, but the other man's fighting below was causing his body to sway. The entangled jumper hit the ground with a thud and the sickening pop of breaking bones.

The reserve without the extra weight slowed his descent just as Ty struck the ground, and he rolled onto all points of contact like he'd been taught.

Two instructors were on top of him before he could raise his head. "You all right?" asked one of the wide-eyed sergeants.

Ty got up slowly and checked his movement. "Clear, Airborne Sergeant."

Two more sergeants were kneeling over the other man. One stood up and shook his head. "That's one lucky dumb ass. He busted his leg and wrist but don't have no internal injuries." The sergeant looked at Ty and put out his hand. "Good thing you pulled your reserve so quick, or I'd be up all night filling out paperwork on two dead paratroopers. Good job and thanks."

As Ty extended his hand, he realized he wasn't shaking. He had never really been scared because there hadn't been time. The previous weeks' instruction had been drilled into him so thoroughly that he had responded without thinking. He smiled and pumped the surprised sergeant's hand. "No, Airborne Sergeant, THANK YOU!"

Ty stood in the first row of assembled men on the edge of the drop zone. Thirty feet in front of the formation was a crowded set of bleachers holding family, friends, and guests of the graduating class of paratroopers. The sunny December day held a tinge of crisp, cold air, but no one minded. It was a perfect day and a perfect place to graduate. Frayar Drop Zone had felt the boots of over a half-million paratroopers as they struck the grassy field and defied death. World War II, Korea, and now Vietnam: the old grass field ringed by pines was the true birthplace of all American paratroopers.

Ty looked around him at the yellow grass, feeling as if he were on honored ground. It seemed fitting to graduate on the ground where his dad and uncle had also made their jumps so many years before.

The Airborne School commander concluded his speech and raised his head proudly. "It is my privilege to now pronounce you, men of Airborne Class 46 . . . UNITED STATES PARATROOP-ERS!"

Ty had never experienced such a rush of pride. He seemed a foot taller and totally indestructible. He swelled out his chest and pulled out the special wings from his pocket. He'd had the wings on all the jumps. They had been his good luck charm.

A formation of Black Hats, holding small boxes of parachute badges, lined up beside the formation. The commander spoke into the microphone: "INSTRUCTORS . . . AWARD THE PARA-CHUTIST BADGE! Ladies and gentlemen, if you have loved ones or friends in the formation, please feel free to move forward and pin on their wings."

Master Sergeant Cherry strode toward Ty with a smile. He stopped in front of him and took out one of the badges he'd brought, but Ty held out his special wings. "Sergeant, my dad and uncle were pinned with these wings. My uncle died in Italy, and my dad didn't make it back from Korea. They're real special to me."

Cherry took the wings from Ty with reverence. "Private Nance, you're making me a very proud man today. These wings are a true tradition. We in the Airborne are the best because of tradition. Son, welcome to the fraternity of the few."

Ty held his bruised chin up proudly as the sergeant pinned the wings over his heart. Tears rolled down his face unashamedly. He knew there were two Chosen standing beside him, beaming with pride.

21

The tall, gray-haired general topped the crest of the familiar knoll and sat down at the base of a huge sayo tree. It was thirteen years ago, in this exact spot, that he had ordered his mortars to fire their final barrage on the French garrison at Dak To. The general's three regimental commanders sat beside him in silence as the division operations officer spread out a map in front of the group.

Binh Ty Duc, commander of the First Division, North Vietnamese Army, pointed at the large American outpost two kilometers distant. "Thirteen years ago I was commander of the 108th Battalion that destroyed the French garrison just to the left of the airfield you see before you. Today we begin planning for the destruction of our enemy again. The Americans are strong in numbers and in combat power. We will defeat the enemy's numbers and power by luring him out of his bases and fighting him on ground of our choosing. We will be everywhere, and he will not be able to concentrate his forces or his power. The Americans are single-minded with their doctrine of the offense. Should they believe this important area is threatened, they will send their units in strength to seek us out. This is precisely what we want."

Colonel Nguyen Van Huu, commander of the 174th Regiment, dipped his head reflectively. "General, I was but a platoon commander in the first revolution, but I know the American firepower and air support is far superior to that of the French. All of our units have had major casualties from their massive artillery and air support. What you say is true, we can break up their strength in numbers, but we cannot break up their dedicated fire support."

General Duc smiled and patted the tree behind him. "The sayo, teak, and ironwood are our friends and protect us. We will defend only the thickest hilltops. We will dig our bunkers and tunnels deep. We will force the Americans to attack on the narrowest of ridges and have our defenses in depth. Our enemy will find us and pound us but will not hurt us. He will attack, and we will be waiting. When he finally brings all his power to bear and attacks again, we will fade away to another position. Plan your defense for the offense. The Americans will be broken up and strung out, vulnerable to our concentration of strength at their rear or flanks."

He pointed at the map. "I have assigned sectors for each of your regiments. You have one week for selecting and planning your defensive positions. Send your company and platoon commanders to your sectors within the month and begin constructing your positions."

Colonel Thong, commander of the Sixty-sixth Regiment, studied the map and looked up. "Comrade, when will the Americans come?"

"They could come anytime," Duc said, looking at the view below him. "But we will only fade away until we are ready. General

Giap has given me ten months to prepare. Use your time to the utmost and dig deeply. The positions must be able to withstand the heaviest of their bombing. Use the tunnels that we used thirteen years ago. They are on the map. Expand and reinforce them.''

The meeting ended ten minutes later, and General Duc dismissed his commanders to return to the Cambodian sanctuary, one day's march away. Colonel Kinh, the division operations officer, collected the map and sat down beside him. ''You didn't tell them the plan was a diversion.''

Duc picked up a handful of red soil. ''Men who know they are a diversion will not dig deep enough. I will tell the commanders once the positions are ready.''

Colonel Kinh sighed and leaned back against the tree. ''It is difficult to understand the grand plan of General Giap. I know you must be disappointed in not leading the major thrust.''

Duc nodded in reflection. Thirteen years ago he had also been assigned a diversionary tactic while the main elements moved to ring Dien Bien Phu. ''We must do our part, or the grand plan will fail. The Americans must commit their main forces and leave the cities unprotected so that our forces can infiltrate and cache the necessary equipment and men.''

''But the cost?'' Kinh said with a worried expression.

The general rose and glanced one last time at the base. ''The cost will be paid in blood by both sides. When the Americans come to these mountains, my First Division will make them pay heavily. American power will ultimately prevail and they will claim victory, but in reality, they will have lost. We will be the real victors, for we will have given our brothers in the south time to prepare the cities for the Tet offensive one year from now. The grand plan will succeed, just as it did thirteen years ago. The cost, my friend, must be paid.''

Jason tried to focus his eyes and looked at his watch, knowing there must have been a screwup. It was only 2:30. The company had gotten to bed only two hours before. Nobody would start training at 2:30 in the morning. He ignored the lights that had just been turned on and lay back down.

''WHAT THE HELL YA DOIN' IN BED, GOLDILOCKS?''

Jason began to raise his head to see who was yelling at him, when suddenly he felt his mattress being lifted. He hit the floor in a sprawl and looked at spit-shined jungle boots. He slowly looked up. Apparently it wasn't too early. The pressed jungle fatigues and black beret on the gnarled sergeant standing over him meant BIG trouble.

"GET UP, RAGBAG. TELL ME WHY YOU'RE IN BED! ARE YOU QUITTIN'?"

Jason sprang to his feet and faced the meanest man he'd ever seen in his life. Staff Sergeant Childs, his Ranger class tactical NCO, had made his introduction the day before by having all the incoming students low crawl with their bags on their backs through the gravel to the barracks. Jason had just flown in to Columbus and had taken a cab to the Ranger Department to report for inprocessing. He was one of several who had to low crawl in his civilian clothes. Childs was only five feet eight inches tall and couldn't have weighed over 155 pounds, but he was all bad. He had the look of a cranky range rider whose wrinkled face showed the years of too much riding drag. He never smiled and never said anything without sounding like he hated everybody and everything, especially Ranger students. Childs had a permanent pissed-off expression that seemed to change only to higher degrees of pissed off.

Jason braced himself into the position of attention and fell back to the only response he could honestly give. "No excuse, Sergeant."

Childs stepped closer, his eyes narrowed to slits. "Ragbag, 'no excuse' is not an answer in my class. You say 'I fucked up,' or you say 'I quit.' I hope the hell you say 'I quit' so I can get rid of your long-haired ass."

Jason stared at him. "I fucked up, Sergeant."

"Yeah, ya did," Childs said. He backed up and pointed at Jason's head. "You got too much hair and ya stayed in bed when the lights came on. You see me in fifteen minutes when we have our company formation. I got somethin' for ya."

Jason got dressed, wishing he'd gotten a shorter haircut. During his leave he had gotten himself in prime condition but allowed his hair to grow out. He ran down the barracks steps and fell into the formation of 210 Ranger students who were trying to get over the shock of getting up so early. He saw Sergeant Childs in front of the formation and jogged over to him.

Childs saw him coming and motioned to a nearby pine tree. "Goldilocks, report to that tree and tell it 'no excuse' twenty-five times to get it out of your system."

Jason headed toward the tree and began complying, as Childs bellowed, "FAT MAN, REPORT TO ME!"

An ex-football player from Texas A&M broke from the back of the formation and ran to him. The soldier was six feet five inches tall and towered over Childs. "Sergeant, Ranger Miller reports!"

Childs shook his head. "NO! YOU ARE FAT MAN. How much you weigh, Fat Man?"

"Two hundred and forty-two pounds, Sergeant."

"Fat Man, you will report to me every day and give me a status of your weight problem. You will see me before every meal, and I'll help you become a lean, mean fightin' machine . . . MOVE OUT!" Childs paced a few times in front of the company, looking at the new class with disdain. He finally stopped and rocked back on his heels. "Ragbags, today you begin the course. You have no rank and no status. Ten of you will quit within the next hour. City Team is bad news and don't like wimps. You're gonna do an hour of PT, then go on a little run that's gonna kick your ass. Fifteen or so of you won't make it and will be gone. Ragbags, City Week is designed to make you miserable, sore, tired, and pissed off. It is a week of misery to see if you really want to be here. You can beat the City Team with motivation."

Childs pointed to the student company commander. "Move 'em out, ragbag!"

Jason helped a fellow student up the barracks steps and started back down to help another one. Childs had not exaggerated. The Ranger instructors who made up the "City Team" were animals who didn't know fatigue. The hour of exercises went nonstop from push-ups, sit-ups, flutter kicks, mountain climbers, bend-and-reaches, and body twists, then started over again. The three-mile run was at a fast pace and took its toll. Childs had been wrong about the losses; the company had twelve men quit, and another twenty-one fell out of the run.

As he was leading a young artillery officer up the steps, he heard a voice behind him.

"GET YOUR HANDS OFF THAT WIMP!"

Jason turned to face Childs, who had strode around the barracks. "He's cramped up, Sergeant."

Childs snickered. "The only thing cramped up on him is his brain housing group. Let him go! He makes it on his own or he doesn't make it! Come here, Goldilocks!"

"Yes, Sergeant."

Childs moved closer and spoke in a surprisingly moderate tone. "Ragbag, I noticed you're in good shape. That's fine, but it ain't gonna do any good trying to help these wimps that are hurtin' already. They're gone—they just don't know it yet. Tomorrow is worse, and the next day is even more miserable. Let 'em quit now or they might hurt themselves."

Jason couldn't accept the sergeant's fatalism. "Sergeant, if we help each other, we can beat it."

Childs frowned and shook his head. "What's your name, rag-bag?"

"Ranger Johnson, Sergeant."

"Well, Ranger Johnson, you're gonna learn a good lesson in the next couple a days. If you're still here at the end of the week, come see me and tell me what ya learned."

"Yes, Sergeant."

Master Sergeant Cherry strode into the work shed and stopped abruptly just inside the door. Six new grader shacks stood in a row directly in front of him. "What the . . ."

Ty didn't see the sergeant and walked from the back room carrying a sheet of plywood. Cherry broke into a small smile. "Nance, is your first name Noah by any chance?"

Startled, Ty spun around, almost dropping the wood sheet. "Oh, sorry, Sergeant Airborne, I didn't see you. What'd ya say?"

Cherry looked over the shacks as he stepped closer. "I know before I went on Christmas leave I said build me six shacks, but I didn't mean do it overnight. One a week would have been fine. Damn, when did you do all this work?"

Ty set the board down and shrugged his shoulders. "Over the holidays. There wasn't much else to do. I'm making a few signs for the parking area . . . hope you don't mind."

Cherry shook his massive head. "Hell no, I don't mind. Damn, Troop, you build whatever you want."

Cherry turned to leave but stopped at the door. He was responsible for training five hundred paratroopers a week but never really knew the men he trained. They were just faceless bodies passing through on their way to war. Nance reminded him that each man was unique.

He turned around. "Nance, you did a good job. I could give you plenty of projects, but that wouldn't be fair to you. You're not shipping out till the first of February, so we need to use that time and get you some good training. I've got some buddies teaching here on post who will show you some combat skills that you'll need. Come see me this afternoon, and I'll set it up. You can stay in the headquarters barracks and go full-time to the classes."

Ty frowned. "Sergeant Airborne, I'd just as soon work here than sit in some classroom for thirty days and get out of shape."

Johnson leaned against the door frame. "You ain't no student, so quit calling me 'Sergeant Airborne.' The guys call me 'Coach.' You ain't gonna be in any classroom. My buddy runs the Scout Dog

Tracking School. You won't have to mess with the dogs, but they have some of the best classes on tracking there is in the Army. They'll take you out on patrols and show you the ropes. That'll increase your odds in coming back from da Nam.''

Ty sighed in resignation. He knew the sergeant was trying to help him. ''Okay, Sergeant Air . . . Coach, but do me one favor: don't tell your friend I'm a carpenter.''

Childs waited inside the mess hall until Fat Man appeared through the door. ''Fat Man, get your tray and follow me.''

The big soldier followed Childs as he walked him through the food line, stopping in front of the servings. ''Let's see, bacon and sausage . . . no, too fattening. Fried potatoes? No, too fattening. Eggs? Yeah. Put on half a portion of scrambled eggs for him. . . . Good. Now, let's see. Pancakes? No, too fattening. Toast? Yeah, one slice.'' Childs let the cook put a piece of toast on Fat Man's plate, but he reached over and cut off the crust. ''Crust is fattening. Fat Man, drink three glasses of water and stay away from the coffee and salt. And Fat Man, don't be askin' for food from any of your buddies. Move out!''

Jason hid a smile as the soldier stared in horror at his meager rations and walked to a table.

''FAT MAN, REPORT TO ME!'' Childs bellowed.

Bob Miller broke from first platoon in a dead run. He slid to a halt in front of Childs, stirring up a gravel dust cloud. ''Sergeant, Fat Man reports!''

''How much you weigh today, Fat Man?''

''Two hundred and thirty-five pounds, Sergeant!''

''How much you weigh yesterday, Fat Man?''

''Two hundred and thirty-six, Sergeant!''

Childs shook his head in exaggerated disappointment. ''We're falling behind in our Ranger diet plan, Fat Man. See me before you eat breakfast. Oh, by the way, I have a little something for you to carry today.'' He pointed to an old wooden footlocker behind him. ''That footlocker is your buddy. I want you to carry it all day. MOVE OUT!''

Jason stood in the first platoon and couldn't help but smile as Miller ran over and easily picked up the footlocker and tossed it to his shoulder. Miller was an infantry second lieutenant like himself and had been a first-team tackle for the Aggies. He ran back to his position beside Jason and executed an about-face. The end of the locker hit Jason in the back of the head, knocking him forward to the laughs of the other men.

Childs began his pacing. "Ragbags, we have lost fifty-two wimps. Today you completed the last day of City Week. This morning, after chow, we're loading buses and going to Camp Darby, where we begin patrolling training. You will get only two meals a day and little sleep. This phase is the single most important part of Ranger School. You will learn the basics of patrolling, which you will be using through the rest of the course. Stay awake out there and learn what they teach you. Company commander, move these ragbags to chow."

Like the rest of the men in his squad, Jason went through the food line and picked up a small box of cereal. He quickly put the cereal in his leg pocket. Later he would give it to "Fat Man" Miller to keep him from starving to death. Childs had already led Miller through the chow line and again had allowed him only meager rations.

Miller carried the footlocker on his shoulder and the food tray in his other hand. He sat by Jason and put the locker on his lap to use as a table.

"Don't worry," Jason said, looking at the little bit of egg on Miller's plate. "The guys and me took care of you."

Miller wolfed down the egg in one bite and shook his head in despair. "If I look at another box of Frosted Flakes I'll puke. Jay, I need fooooood."

Jason smiled and slipped Miller a slice of toast. "Hang tough. Ya made the runs, so it's all downhill. It couldn't get any worse."

"GOLDILOCKS, COME HERE, RAGBAG!"

Miller gave Jason a look of sympathy as he got up and walked over to the cadre table where Childs sat.

"Sergeant, Ranger Nance reports."

Childs sipped coffee from a stained mug and raised his eyes. "Sit down, Goldilocks, and tell me if you saved any wimps."

Jason quickly took a seat and stared straight ahead. "No, Sergeant, I didn't save any of them. They quit or dropped out of the runs."

Childs nodded his head with pleasure. "Didn't I tell ya? What did you learn, Goldilocks?"

"Sergeant, I learned good men let their minds beat them."

Childs sipped from his coffee mug again and lowered his voice. "Johnson, it might surprise you, but I talk to every man who quits and give him one more chance to go back to training. None do. You wanna know why? They really didn't want it. Most of 'em swear they want the tab, but they don't feel they're cut out to be a Ranger. They're right. They know in their hearts they can't put up with all the bullshit. I'm telling you this because sometimes team-work and helping people don't do any good. This isn't OCS, where you can 'cooperate and graduate.' Men who know they haven't got it need a way out. We give it to them in the City Week. I wanted you to know how the system works so you wouldn't think we didn't give a shit. We do care. I care and it bothers me to see them drop out, but this is a leadership school like no other. I don't think you'd want it any other way."

Childs set his cup down and motioned his head toward Miller. "I saw you give that piece of toast to your buddy. You owe me fifty push-ups. I know; you got a box of cereal for him, too. You owe me another fifty push-ups. But Ranger Johnson, had you not tried to help him I'd have smoked your ass. Miller has proven he has what it takes. He is worth saving. You'd better have that squad of yours start getting two boxes of cereal a day."

Jason looked into the expressionless eyes of the sergeant in dis-belief. "Uh . . . yes, Sergeant, thank you for the . . . the . . . talk."

"MOVE OUT, Goldilocks!"

Jason returned to his breakfast and noticed Childs leaving. Miller leaned over his footlocker. "What was all that about?"

Jason sighed and tossed another piece of toast to his friend. "You wouldn't believe it if I told you."

Ty took two cautious steps and froze. Despite the biting cold wind, he was sweating. One step in front of him was a piece of fishing line stretched over the trail. His eyes followed the line as he slowly crouched down to see if it was a trip wire. A branch snapped to his left, and he immediately fell back on his side and rolled into a firing position. Ten yards away a man rose up from a spider hold and looked toward the trail. Ty fired his M-14 twice and jumped to his feet at a dead run. "AMBUSH!"

Sergeant First Class Winters stepped onto the trail and blocked the path. Ty came to a halt in front of him and waited for his critique. Winters eyed the scar first, then the eyes. "You knew somebody was there, didn't you?"

Ty looked behind him at the trail. "No, not really, but I had this feeling like . . . well, it just felt strange."

Winters nodded in understanding and smiled. "You was in the groove. When you're in the groove, you know. Remember that feeling and always listen to it. A point man lives on his senses and instincts. You have to be in the groove, or Charlie gonna light your ass in a heartbeat. Go on to Station 2, and remember to walk light and get the feel for the trail before you start movin'. Never think speed is important. It ain't. Speed is the quickest way to die. Don't ever push your luck or yourself when you in the groove.''

Ty nodded and walked to the next station as the man he shot approached Sergeant Winters. Winters shook his head. ''Willie, he kilt yo' ass bigger than shit.''

Sergeant Alcord rolled his eyes. ''I didn't hear him. I thought for sure he was still up the trail messin' with the false trip wires. Damn, he scared the crap outta me when he opened up.''

Winters threw a thumb over his shoulder. ''Get him a dog.''

''But he ain't one of the students. He don't know nothin' about handlin'.''

Winters grinned. ''You killed all our students on this lane, remember? We got us a natural, Willie, a real live natural, and they don't come around too often.''

Jason followed Miller, who was still carrying the footlocker on his shoulder. The company had arrived at Camp Darby four hours ago and had received their first series of classes on how to develop a warning order. The two men walked toward a large open area where the company was forming up, when an all too familiar voice rang out, ''FAT MAN, REPORT TO ME!''

Miller growled and ran, carrying the footlocker toward Childs, who stood at the edge of the field. ''Sergeant, Fat Man reports!''

''Fat Man, what is the maximum effective range of that one-each, OD, wood, government-issue footlocker?''

Miller looked perplexed. Childs stepped closer with a glint in his eye. ''Fat Man, this is obviously a secret Ranger weapon. I want to know what the maximum effective range of it is.''

Miller shifted the footlocker to his powerful right arm and took two strides for momentum, then threw the box with all his might. It smashed on impact to the hoots and hollers of the assembled company. Miller paced off the distance to the footlocker and jogged back to Childs. ''Sergeant, the maximum effective range of one-each, OD, wood, government-issue footlocker is twelve feet and six inches!''

Childs kept a straight face, despite the laughter from the company. ''OUTSTANDING, FAT MAN. THAT WAS AN EXCELLENT DEMONSTRATION . . . NOW, MOVE OUT!''

* * *

Ty let Major lead him through the darkness toward the sound of men talking. The voices were muffled and there was no light. They had to be in a bunker or tent. A cold sleet beat at Ty's face as he knelt down and whispered into the German shepherd's ear, "Stay."

The dog remained still as Ty crawled forward and pushed the safety off his rifle. The voices became familiar as he crept closer, but he still couldn't see anything but blackness.

"I see your twenty-five cents and raise ya a dime."

"You bluffin, Willie, you ain't got nothin'. Here's the dime and another quarter. Put up or shut up."

Sergeant Alcord picked up a quarter and tossed it into the pot. "Ray, I figure I got two hours before the first of them finds us. You're gonna run out of money before then. What you got?"

Winters held onto his cards. "Willie, my man, they been out for six hours, and the only team that hasn't been spotted or killed is Nance and Major. I'd be willing to bet whatever's in the pot that he makes it in without being detected."

"They're lost," Alcord said. "Nobody has ever made it through my test without at least one screwup. The Nance kid is good, I admit, but he ain't that good. He's lost or that stupid-ass dog has ate his leg off. Major ain't none too reliable. There ain't no way my men could have missed them."

Winters laid out his cards. "Three kings beats whatever you got."

Alcord threw down his cards in disgust. "You cheatin' son of . . ."

The tent flap swept back and an M-16 barrel pointed directly at Alcord's startled face. Ty walked the rest of the way into the warmth of the tent and lowered his rifle. He raised his hand and pointed at the sergeant. "Bang."

Winters burst out laughing, and Alcord rolled his eyes. "Don't say it. I know; the groove kilt my ass bigger than shit." He looked at Ty and broke into a smile. "What happened to your mutt? Major decide to go home and get out of the snow?"

Ty gave out a short whistle, and in seconds the shepherd was at his side. "Nope. The Major is in the groove, too."

Winters hooted and began picking up his money.

Jason was tired. He was past tired, he was dead on his feet. The company had moved to the mountain phase in Dalongeha, Georgia, and had broken up into small patrols. Jason's patrol had been moving for days without rest. It was just turning light and he didn't think he could take another step. So far, thirty-four men had been dropped because of frostbite and various other injuries. Jason would see a tree twenty feet ahead and shut his eyes for what seemed like only a second, and when he opened them again he'd be at the tree. He was sleeping while walking. It was an unreal feeling, like watching an old movie that had been spliced.

The patrol stopped to his front. He offered thanks to his maker and fell to the side of the trail to rest. He closed his eyes but jerked his head up to see if the patrol was moving again. They weren't. The man to his front was kneeling only ten feet away. Jason dropped his head again.

Miller was behind Jason and saw him dozing off again. He crawled over and tapped his leg. "Hang tough, it can't get any worse."

Jason lifted his head, too tired to smile. "Screw you, Fat Man."

Miller looked over Jason's shoulder. "Where is the rest of the patrol?"

Jason looked up and glanced at the man in front of him. "There, right . . . aw shit!" The man wasn't a man. It was a stump that his mind had tricked him into believing was something else. Jason got to his feet and listened for a moment. He could hear the others in the distance. "Come on. We gotta catch up before they find out there's been a break in contact."

He forced his body to move under the weight of the seventy-pound rucksack and took off in the direction of the sound he'd heard. In only minutes he saw the patrol ahead and breathed easier. He and Miller had no sooner caught up when the patrol halted. Both men fell in the snow beside the trail to rest when a voice barked out, "Patrol leader, you're dead. Ranger Johnson, come here."

Jason felt his stomach crawl up his throat and do a tap dance. The instructor was going to say the six worst words a Ranger student could ever hear: "You are now the patrol leader."

Jason stood over the seated instructor. "Sergeant, I'm Ranger Johnson."

The sergeant pointed his finger at Jason and said the six dreaded words. Then he said, "Your objective is five klicks away. What is our location?"

Jason knelt in the snow, having no idea where he was located. They'd moved all night, and it had been so dark he couldn't even see his hands, let alone read a map and follow along. The sergeant saw his expression and pointed to his map. "You're right here. What are you gonna do now, Patrol Leader?"

Jason reached down inside himself for the last reserve he possessed. The twenty-two-hour training days had drained his mind as well as his body. He weighed twenty pounds less than he had on the day they started. He was reduced to satisfying the basic needs for sleep and food, and nothing else. He would have killed for a peanut butter sandwich and a chance to rest for thirty minutes.

"Well, Patrol Leader, what are you gonna do?"

Jason struggled and fought through the fog in his brain and concentrated on the past miserable weeks of training. He raised his head and looked the sergeant directly in the eyes. "I'm gonna take charge of this patrol and accomplish the mission." He stood and motioned the assistant patrol leader forward and the team leaders. "Crazies, I'm now in charge. You have three minutes to disseminate the information to your men and get a status of weapons, equipment, and personnel, and report back to me. Send me the compassman and the paceman to go over the route, and make sure your men are alert and on one knee, not lyin' down. I'll be checking in two minutes. Do it."

The sergeant smiled to himself. His job was going to be easy. He had himself a patrol leader who knew how to lead.

Ty set his bags by the curb and faced the master sergeant. "Coach, thanks for everything. I really appreciate you settin' up the training for me."

Cherry put his arm around Ty's shoulder. "Ty, the way Winters talked it sounded like you taught them a few things. I'm proud of you. I want you to write me and let me know what unit you get assigned to. I got friends everywhere that can pull a few strings. You keep your butt down and don't play hero. I kinda got used to you and wouldn't want to hear any bad news."

The cab pulled up to the curb, and Ty reached into his pocket and pulled out an envelope. "Coach, there's one favor I want to ask of you."

"Sure, what is it?"

"My brother is gonna be coming through Airborne School the first of March. In this envelope is his name and what class he'll be in. I'd appreciate it if . . ."

Winter's took the envelope. "Consider it done."

Ty extended his hand. "Good-bye, Sergeant Airborne."

Cherry shook his head. "Paratroopers never say 'good-bye.' They just say 'see ya.' "

22

Private Bui Duong strained with all his might and felt the log finally move. He, along with forty infantrymen from his assigned company, was dragging an ironwood tree up the ridge toward the hilltop. Thirty minutes later, he was standing on that hilltop, covered in sweat, and feeling elated. Never had he seen such a view. The trees were even bigger and more beautiful than those in the base camp. He had been working a week on the hill, and every day he had grown to love it more. The trees were ancient, and the construction work had not destroyed a single one of them. The trees they had cut were from the valley.

A corporal motioned down the ridge. "Look! Now they bring the water buffalo? Why could they not have arrived an hour ago?"

Duong smiled and squatted down by the soldier. "How is your bunker coming along?"

The corporal looked disdainfully at the closest tree. "The soil is soft, but the damn roots make digging impossible."

"Be thankful of the roots. They provide strength to the soil and make the bunkers and tunnels even more bombproof. Use an axe to cut them."

"I am a fighter, not a digger like you engineers," the corporal said disgustedly. "You like this work, I hate it!"

Duong sighed and stood up, knowing he had to go back to work. The hill had a command bunker under the hilltop that had been used in the first revolution and was still usable. The ironwood they had cut down would finish replacing the one rotten support beam. The hill would become a fortress in time. The plan called for three defense lines all tied in with underground tunnels leading to the command bunker. The buffalo would ease the burden of dragging the trees needed for the bunkers.

141

Duong picked up a saw but stopped and took one more look at the view. Somehow he seemed to gain strength from the beauty.

Jason leaned forward and dug his paddle into the black water. The small rubber boat held ten men, all of whom were on the verge of collapsing. The class had completed the mountain phase the week before, but they had found only more misery in the flatlands of Florida. The Florida swamps were just as bad as the Georgia mountains, if not worse. There were only ten days left in the course, but he wasn't sure if he could make it. He had nothing left. He was totally drained, physically and mentally. Just making it the next ten minutes would be a miracle.

The late night quiet was broken by an ominous splash from the dark bank, startling Jason and the others. The instructor sitting in the center of the boat whispered a quick warning. "Gator. Keep your feet and hands out of the water."

The tired men came instantly awake and paddled harder. Ten minutes later, the river made a wide bend to the right, and the Ranger students knew it was time for the unthinkable. Under the light of the half moon they paddled the boat toward the far shore. They were to cache the boat and march five miles through the swamp to raid an enemy base camp. The boat reached the trees of the bank, but to their horror there was no bank, no sand dune, no dry ground.

The instructor pointed at the smallest man in the boat. "Get out and check how deep it is. Watch out for water moccasins."

Jason knew the instructor had to be insane. Get out of the boat, at night, in alligator- and snake-infested waters, in fifty-degree temperatures, and wearing seventy pounds of equipment? No way.

The instructor whispered again, but with command in his voice, "Do it."

Jason felt sorry for the other Ranger but didn't dare volunteer himself. Suddenly, the man behind him slid off the raft into the water. Jason turned around just as his big friend disappeared under the surface. Fat Man Miller was the last one he would have expected to display such bravery. Miller was deathly afraid of the water and had been staying as close to Jason as possible since the operation began.

Miller reappeared like a whale breaking the surface, spouting a huge geyser of water. He choked and spit and choked again as he frantically grabbed for the boat.

The instructor leaned over the side and tossed a rope out. "Pull us in closer and let me know when you touch bottom."

In the moonlight Jason could see Miller's panicked expression and prepared to jump in to help, but Miller suddenly rose two feet out of the water as if by magic. He'd finally relaxed and reached for the bottom. The water was only four feet deep. The sergeant pointed to a nearby cypress tree. "Tie us off. Good job, Ranger."

Minutes later, the patrol was in waist-deep water making its way through the swamp. The man who had been told to get out of the boat was beside himself with gratitude toward Miller, who just waved him off. Jason came up behind Miller and whispered, "That was a super thing to do, buddy."

Miller turned and whispered back, "I don't know what the hell y'all are talkin' about. I fell asleep and fell out of the damn boat. I thought the sergeant was going to throw me out of the course."

Jason contained a laugh by biting his lower lip.

The ten-man patrol walked the first thirty minutes through the swamp in total fear. They were certain that at any time an alligator would attack one of them and have a late-night snack, or a snake would strike from a low cypress branch. Every step in the stinking water was torture. Their bodies tingled with the expectation of being bitten by huge unseen jaws or struck by fangs to die foaming at the mouth. The fear slowly dissolved, replaced by bone-weary fatigue. Some even wished a gator would take a bite out of one of the other men and cause the mission to be aborted.

The eerie swamp forest of cypress and Spanish moss gave way to grassy marshland covered by two feet of water. The moon reflected off the tall head-high grass and the glistening water but also revealed they were still not out of danger. Beaten-down paths in the grass cut across the trail they were making. The paths were made by alligators, and the instructor had taken out his loaded .45 as a precaution.

Again the patrol was filled with fear and stepped lightly, but only for a while, as their overwhelming fatigue set in. The men moved in a column for an hour and stopped for a short rest break. Jason and the others lay back on their rucksacks in the water, hoping the instructor would doze off and give them the opportunity for precious sleep. Five minutes later, the sergeant stood and motioned everyone up to continue. Nobody moved. Every man in the patrol was out like a light. He kicked the nearest man and whispered harshly, "Wake up and let's go."

The Ranger got up groggily and turned to wake up the others. Soon the patrol was on its feet and moving. Ranger Boyd, ahead of Jason, took two sleepy steps and stepped on what looked like

a submerged log. The log moved and jerked upward.
"AAAAAAAAH!"

Boyd was thrown backward but kept on his feet and ran screaming through the tall grass. Jason had never heard such a bloodcur-
dling scream before and had never felt so helplessly caught by his
own fear. His heart pounded wildly as the entire patrol became
hysterical and jumped up and down, trying to stay in the air for as
long as possible and away from the deadly water where a monster
lurked. The instructor ran back to the scene just as the "alligator"
stood up and screamed hysterically, "IT CRAWLED OVER ME!
IT . . ."

The sergeant quickly glanced around with pistol ready to shoot,
but Jason stepped forward realizing what had happened. "Sergeant, it wasn't a gator! Watkins must not have gotten the word to
move out and was lying in the water. Ranger Boyd must have
stepped on him and thought it was . . ."

"Shit! Where's Boyd?"

Jason pointed at the path in the grass. "He went that way."

Ten minutes later, Jason and the sergeant found Boyd in a small
tree clinging on for dear life and whimpering like a scared child.
The instructor shined his flashlight into the man's wide eyes. Boyd
was shaking so badly the whole tree was vibrating. "Get down
from there, Ranger."

Boyd didn't budge. "Did . . . did you see it? It . . . it was ten
feet long!"

"Welcome to the 173d Airborne Brigade. You replacements are
now members of the best fighting unit in Nam. The 173d's nickname is 'Sky Soldiers,' but it's better known as 'The Herd.' The
173d is the first separate brigade in the Army and was the first major
ground combat unit to deploy to Vietnam. We were the first unit to
enter the Iron Triangle and War Zone C, and the first to use battal-
ion-sized helicopter assaults. You can feel very proud to be in . . ."

Ty listened for the first few minutes but dozed off to sleep. He
and thirty other men had just arrived at Ben Hoa from the inprocessing center, where they had spent twelve days and had experienced the Army's usual hurry up-and-wait routine. Ty and two
hundred others had made the twenty-four-hour flight from Califor-
nia to Vietnam and been bused to a replacement depot, where
nobody seemed to know or care about jet lag. The schedule was
hurry to clothing issue and wait for hours in the sun. Hurry to
inprocessing and wait for hours in a hot tin building before finally
filling out a stack of paperwork. Hurry back to the barracks and

wait for hours to be inspected and briefed. The powers that be had hurried them through the system because they had said that units needed replacements, but then they had pulled out the lower ranking enlisted men and put them on a sandbag-filling detail for eight boring days. Finally, on the twelfth day, they had called off names for unit assignments. Ty and thirty other paratroopers had been hurried to the airfield, where they waited all afternoon in the blazing sun for a C-130 to take them to Ben Hoa, home of the 173d.

The bus ride from the airfield and through several small villages had given the men their first real look at the country. The beauty of the countless geometric rice paddies, with their hues of green, was breathtaking, and was matched only by the soft blues of the distant mountains. The rusted tin and rice-straw huts of the villages harmonized strangely with the land, but not so the gawdy signs, sandbagged bunkers, and stink of trying to Americanize overnight. Black diesel smoke hung in the air from the convoys and combined with the stench of open sewers. Children played in filth wearing discarded GI clothing, while old women sold Cokes and cigarettes. Nothing seemed permanent except the land.

The sergeant completed his briefing and began calling off names for specific battalion assignments. Ty was wakened by an elbow jab and heard his name called. He was going to the Fourth Battalion, 503d Infantry.

He fell into a small formation that was hurried to a bus, which sat for an hour without a driver. Finally, a sergeant climbed on and woke everybody up. "People, I'll be taking you to the jungle school. The orientation school is a little indoctrination course that will familiarize you with the country and the way the 'Herd' does business . . . which is to kill people and destroy things. On behalf of the Fourth Batt and the 173d Airborne Brigade, welcome to da Nam.''

Jason stood at attention as a colonel pinned a black and gold Ranger tab to the left shoulder of his fatigues. He and fifty-seven other emaciated men were receiving the coveted tab on a small deserted airfield known as Field 7. It was over.

He felt both pride and sadness. Too many good men had quit, and the ones who had survived looked as if they had walked out of a Nazi death camp. Their bodies were shrunken and shriveled to bone and gristle. Fat Man Miller weighed 190 pounds and looked twenty years older. He was so thin that his uniform swallowed him. Jason was no better off. He was down to 160 pounds, and his facial skin was drawn tight across his cheekbones.

None of the men would have been recognized by a close relative at first glance. Their eyes were sunken and lifeless. Their fingers were split from cold weather and oozed yellow liquid. Their feet were wrinkled and peeling from immersion in swamp water. No one could take a normal step or pick up a piece of paper without pain. They were the survivors of fifty-eight days of hell and had paid the price for the twelve-cent Ranger tab. Jason knew more about himself than he wanted to know. The lessons he'd learned would stay with him forever.

It was just luck that he still stood in the ranks, Jason thought, blind, uncaring luck. Ranger School was the worst experience of his life and yet one of the best. He felt confident in his ability to lead men through the worst of situations, but he would never, never do it again, for any reason.

Childs waited until the colonel and reviewing party left before positioning himself in front of the formation. "At ease, ragbags. Today you join the ranks of the United States Army Rangers. You have a tradition to uphold. The men you lead will expect you to be better than other leaders. You are! You know misery, hunger, and fatigue. You know that you are capable of moving another five miles when you don't think you can move another five feet. You know you can lead, think, and plan, even though you haven't slept or eaten in days. But, ragbags, the most important things you've learned are your weaknesses. Not many men really know their weaknesses. They've never been forced or pushed hard enough to find out. You have. Leaders must know their own limitations and those of their men. You have found that the only limitations are the ones the mind sets. You've proven to yourselves you can drive on through anything and accomplish the mission. Be proud, but be humble. I wish the very best to all of you in the future. You've made me proud today. . . . Company commander, take charge of these ragba . . . no, RANGERS, and move 'em out!"

The survivors yelled and screamed their joy at finally being called "Rangers" as Childs strode to the camp without looking back.

The cloud of yellow smoke swirled and dissipated under the rotating chopper blades as the resupply bird settled to the ground. PFCs Ty Nance and Jim Deets scooted out the door and stood beside the shaking machine as four bare-chested men ran out of the woodline directly toward them. The tanned soldiers ignored the two new replacements and began throwing off boxes of C-rations and ammunition. One of the men held up his thumb, and the helicopter lifted off.

Ty exchanged glances with Deets and wondered if they were in the wrong place. The four men had disappeared into the jungle, leaving them all alone.

A voice rang out like a shot. "Get over here, cherries!"

Sergeant Jim Hammonds stepped out of the ferns and motioned them toward him. He eyed them. They had fat faces, and the fatter one was as white as C-ration toilet paper. Their clean uniforms were dark green and still smelled of mothballs. Their jungle boots were black and unscuffed, and their helmet covers were new and unmarked. Their new M-16s had no magazines and not a single scratch or mark on the plastic stocks. Their expressions revealed how they felt at the moment: lost and bewildered. They were most definitely cherries.

Ty halted in front of the lanky sergeant and was about to speak when Hammonds turned around and began walking back into the treeline. Ty shrugged his shoulders at Deets and hurried to catch up.

Hammonds strode down a muddy path through a bamboo thicket and broke into a small open area where the platoon was resting. He threw his thumb over his shoulder as he approached a tired, baby-faced lieutenant. "Look what I found, L-tee."

Lieutenant Brent Jenkins stood up with a smile. "Hot damn, I don't believe it. They finally sent us some meat."

Hammonds pointed at Ty. "I found 'em and want this one with the scar. He looks meaner than the pale one."

The lieutenant cocked an eyebrow as he scanned the faces of his new men. "We'll see. Get on back to your squad and we'll divvy them up later." He motioned for the two to sit down and took a seat on top of his rucksack. "Welcome to War Zone C and the first platoon of Bravo Company. I'm Lieutenant Jenkins, your platoon leader. Under the poncho over there is SFC Pop Berdenski, your platoon sergeant. We were on patrol last night, and he's catchin' a few z's. He'll meet you later.

"As you probably already know, the whole battalion air-assaulted in five days ago. We're the force blocking the VC from slipping into Cambodia. The operation is called Junction City, but we call it 'Junction Empty.' We ain't seen nothin'. The Second Battalion parachuted in and got all the glory and headlines in *Stars and Stripes*, but we'll show 'em something if the dinks ever stand and fight. Right now we're taking it easy because it's resupply day. I know you're wonderin' if this is really the war. Well, it ain't much, but it's all we got. Tomorrow we'll be movin', so maybe things will pick up."

He yawned and pointed at Ty. "You'll be going to Sergeant Hammond's first squad, the NCO that brought you here, and . . ." Deets puffed out his chest so the lieutenant could read his name tape. "Yeah, Deets, you'll be going to the third squad. Now, how about you cherries telling me where you're from and a little about yourselves."

Hammonds lifted his spoon and sucked the peach juice with a loud slurp. He looked at Ty from the corner of one eye and lowered the spoon into the can. "Don't worry, Nance. I know you can't remember all the men's names, but you will. Cowboy Williams is the first dude ya met. He's the skinny one from Texas. He's kinda slow in the head, but he can deal big time with the M-79 grenade launcher. Caddy was the light-skinned colored buck sergeant, and Silk was the big-mouthed nigger. Silk is aw'right if you don't let him get to ya. Goldie is the Jew with all the black hair, and Teddy Bear is the fat Yankee wearin' glasses. Paddy is the apple-cheeked kid, and Bugs is the bucktoothed guy you met last. I know we don't look like much, but we're the first squad."

Ty leaned back on his rucksack and studied the young sergeant's tanned face. Despite the man's professional air, Ty knew Hammonds couldn't be more than a few years older than himself. He was a raw-boned six-footer and looked as hard as a ten-penny nail. He had short brown hair and pale blue eyes that seemed too sensitive for a soldier. "And how 'bout you, Sarge, where you from?"

Hammonds scooped out a peach half. "Colorado." He swallowed the piece of C-ration fruit and raised the small can as if in a toast. "The first ain't pretty, but we sure is e-fective. Welcome to the family."

PFC Jim Deets was dead. He accidentally killed himself. He'd hooked two grenades to his harness, and a vine had caught one of the pins when he walked through a streambed. He'd heard the detonater pop and knew he had only five seconds, but he couldn't free the grenade in time. He died screaming.

Lieutenant Jenkins handed the handset back to his radio operator and angrily pointed at the third squad leader. "Goddamn it! I give you a cherry and you don't brief him on the basics, and he blows himself away. Shit. The ol' man is pissed off."

The squad leader nodded toward the body. "Sir, I told him. He didn't listen to a word I said. I just checked his weapon, and he had it on automatic. We were lucky he didn't shoot one of us in the back."

Jenkins waved the excuse away. "Don't give me that bullshit. You should have inspected him before we left this morning and checked him out a couple of times while we were moving. So now you can suffer. You're not getting the next cherry. You'll just go short until I fill the other squads to full strength. And maybe not then."

"Aw, hell, sir, I'm already two men short."

"No! Forget it! You blew yours away. Get back to your squad." Jenkins's angry eyes shifted to Sergeant Hammonds. "You better have YOUR cherry squared away."

"He knows the basics," Hammonds said softly.

Jenkins sighed and lowered his head. "Get him up here and bag Deets. Might as well break him in now."

Hammonds knew the procedure: new men place the KIAs in body bags. He motioned over his shoulder. "He's doing it now."

Jenkins only glanced in the general direction and slapped his weapon in frustration. "Deets had only one damn day in the field and . . . shit!"

Ty spread the body bag out and rolled the blood-splattered corpse onto it. He'd seen death before. It was nothing new, nothing to get upset about. Deets had been Chosen.

Hammonds watched for a reaction from his new man. After all, Deets's body didn't even look human anymore. But Nance didn't show the slightest hint of revulsion. Ty felt the sergeant's eyes on him and turned around. Hammonds studied the cherry's eyes. "You're supposed to be learning a lesson from this. Doesn't it bother you?"

Ty zipped up the bag and wiped his bloody hands on his fatigue pants. "Yeah."

Hammonds felt a chill go up his spine. He could tell the cherry was lying.

Cowboy Williams wiped sweat from his forehead with an olive-drab towel and sat down beside Ty. "Stay close ta me for a while and do what I do. It ain't gonna take long ta figure out the ropes. The main thang is don't be thinkin' 'bout nothin' but Charlie. Keep yo' eyes and ears open, and don't be half-sleepin' and thinkin' 'bout home. This is yo' home now."

Ty leaned back on his rucksack and looked at Williams. The thin soldier looked more like a clean-cut basketball player than a para-trooper. "Thanks for the advice. Why is it they call ya 'Cowboy'?"

Williams looked up at the blazing sun and shut his eyes. "'Cause I used ta do a little rodeoin' and made the mistake of tellin' Goldie.

He kinda hangs a handle on everybody. I reckon he don't want us callin' him Harold and done come up with nicknames for everybody. Goldie is the first Jew I ever knew. He ain't as tight as I heard about them people.''

Ty looked down the trail toward Goldman. He looked like an average GI—thick black hair, tan, average height. Ty shifted his gaze to Bugs Saben. Bugs was the point man. He looked a bit mongoloid, with his huge head and heavy brow, and his front teeth protruded badly. Bugs was from Iowa and was a constant talker when he wasn't on point. He liked most to talk about himself. He bored everybody to tears.

Sitting across from Bugs was Paddy McGuire, who was quiet and strikingly handsome. His rosy cheeks made him a target for Silk Davis, a foulmouthed troublemaker who always made sexual innuendos about Paddy's boyish face and self-proclaimed virginity.

Sergeant Hammonds strode down the trail, interrupting Ty's thoughts. ''Saddle up, first squad, we're movin' out. Second squad is leading, and we'll be in the saddle with the L-tee. Nance, you stick to Cowboy like stink on shit. Keep your finger off the trigger and keep your weapon on safe. Bugs, take point and keep the second in sight. Nice and easy now. Let's do it, First.''

Ty stood up under the watchful eye of Hammonds and ignored his searching stare. He could tell that the sergeant wasn't comfortable with him, but it didn't matter. Despite the first-day friendly introductions of the ''family,'' Hammonds seemed distant toward everybody.

23

Sergeant, alpha zero eight reports!''

''Alpha zero eight, that was a satisfactory exit from the tower, but you owe me ten for being a Ranger. Report to the bench and change your harness with the next man.''

"Clear, Sergeant Airborne!"

Lieutenant Jason Johnson dropped to the ground and knocked out ten push-ups. For good measure, he did one more, yelling, "One for the big Airborne Ranger in the sky!" He jumped up and jogged to the cement bench and gave his parachute harness to the next man waiting to jump from the thirty-four-foot tower.

Bob Miller scooted down the bench to make room and hit Jason's shoulder as he sat down. "Damn it, Jay, they warned us the first day not for us Rangers to show our ass, and here you go yelling that 'Airborne Ranger' shit. You're gonna get us in big trouble."

Jason smiled. "What they gonna do? Send us to Vietnam?"

Miller frowned and shook his head. "I know this ain't nothin' after what we went through, but ease up with the gung-ho Ranger stuff. These Black Hats will smoke our ass if they think we're screwin' with them. Keep a low profile so we can breeze through this without having to do extra push . . ."

"YOU, TALKIN' ON THE BENCH! GET DOWN!"

Miller immediately fell to the gravel and did his ten push-ups for the Black Hat instructor who had caught him talking. He was about to get up, when he looked at Jason with a grin and yelled out, "And one for the big Airborne Ranger in the sky!"

Jason sat back on the couch with a beer and looked at the television screen. The TV wasn't on, but it didn't matter. It represented civilization. After Ranger School, small things like sitting down for several hours without anything to do was ecstasy. Airborne School ran from 6 A.M. to 5 P.M., with weekends off. After fifty-eight days of averaging only a couple of hours of sleep a night and having something to do for every minute of the day, Jason was lost in time. Time to sit in a bathtub and soak away endless days of grime and soreness. Time to sleep eight hours in a bed, with sheets, not on the ground or against a tree. Time, precious time, to eat when he wanted and how much he wanted. Time to . . . damn, he was going crazy trying to figure out what to do with all the time.

He and Miller had reported to Airborne School after a week of recovery from Ranger training and found the course much easier than what they'd previously been through. The Black Hats were professionals and tried to make it tough, but with only a ten-hour day it wasn't the same. Airborne School was mostly a mind game, and to win you had to overcome fear. Jumping out of airplanes just wasn't natural.

* * *

Ty finished writing a letter to his mother and put the dirt-stained paper in his shirt pocket. He sat in a shallow foxhole and shifted his thoughts to deciding what he should eat. The C-ration chicken and noodles or the C-ration beef and spice sauces? The decision was a big one, and he wanted to weigh the options for at least another couple of minutes to kill time. He only carried enough food to eat two small meals a day, and it was important to make the meals count. Eating was an integral part of the routine. It was the only thing to look forward to besides sleep and mail.

So far, Ty had found the war boring. The platoon moved all day on what were called "search and destroy" operations, but they had actually been search, and search, and search some more operations. The platoon had found nothing and no one to "destroy" in the week and a half he had been with the squad. On a typical day, they would get up at first light and move until four in the afternoon, then set up a platoon or company perimeter. They would dig in and send out a few patrols, while the rest of the men would rotate all night on security or radio watch. The platoon would move for four days and be resupplied on the fifth by chopper. That was the big day, the highlight. The chopper brought mail, ammo, change of clothes, an SP—sundry pack—and one box of C-rations per man. The box of C's weighed twenty-five pounds and consisted of twelve meals. Nobody could carry that kind of weight or had the room in his rucksack, so only the meat and fruit were kept; the rest was thrown away. The mail lifted their spirits, and for those who didn't receive letters, there was always the *Stars and Stripes* newspaper. The sundry pack was a box of goodies for a platoon-size unit. It contained razors, blades, shaving cream, writing paper, envelopes, pens, cigarettes, candy, and chewing tobacco. The goodies were divvied up among the squads and given out to each man according to his time in country. Ty, being the newest, received only the stuff nobody else wanted, such as small boxes of terrible-tasting candy, Black Cows.

Still, he looked forward to resupply day, if only for the chance to change his uniform. After five days, his jungle fatigues were sweat soaked and stank to high heavens. Like the rest of the squad, Ty carried only necessities. His rucksack was his home. Inside the green pack were food, poncho, poncho liner, jungle sweater, shaving kit, block of C-4 plastic explosives, weapons-cleaning kit, extra socks, extra water, extra ammo, claymore mine, trip flare, and waterproofed bag, which held his letters, wallet, and writing paper. Attached to the outside of his rucksack was an entrenching tool. Around his neck was an olive-drab towel used as sweat rag and padding for his rucksack straps. On his fighting harness and across his body were three bandoliers of full M-16 magazines, two canteens, and a canteen cover with four fragmentation grenades, a smoke grenade, a first-aid pouch, and a compass. The idea was to travel light and be able to fight for an extended period of time.

The first day, Sergeant Hammonds had gone through Ty's pack and thrown away his extra uniforms, underwear, T-shirts, food, and paperbacks. He had explained that weight was a killer. To hump for long distances required light packs and good conditioning. After a few weeks of breaking-in he would be required to carry even more: extra M-60 machine-gun ammo and mortar rounds for the 81-millimeter mortar.

Ty had wanted to keep at least his underwear, but the sergeant explained that cotton underwear held in moisture and took a long time to dry. Wet underwear caused chafing, which was horribly painful while humping.

"Cherry, you gonna look at dem C's, or is you gonna eat 'em?"

Ty looked up into the black face of Silk Davis, who constantly hounded him. Silk was the blackest man Ty had ever met and the filthiest mouthed. The other squad members seemed to have accepted Ty into the "family," but not Silk. He was from Chicago and had worked on the loading docks until he was drafted. At five feet ten, he was a heavily muscled, 175-pound pain in the ass.

Ty selected the can of chicken and noodles and ignored him. Silk swept dirt, with his boot, onto Ty's back. "Cherry, when I talks to yo' ass, yo' looks at me."

Ty stood up slowly and faced him. "Back off, Davis. I haven't done a thing to piss ya off. Just leave me alone and mind your own business."

Silk's lips curled back in a snarl, and he pointed at Ty's face. "You IS my business, Cherry. You gots a attitude that pisses me off. I don't trust your red ass humpin' behind me. I think you is a Indian muthafuckin' nigger-hater."

Ty shook his head and sat back in his hole. He didn't care what Silk thought, and he didn't want to cause any trouble. Half the squad was on a watering party, leaving only him, Silk, Caddy, and Teddy Bear to sit on the barren hill and watch time pass.

Silk began to kick dirt again when Caddy barked from his foxhole, "Cool it, Silk. He ain't buggin' nobody. Leave him be."

"Shit, man, he's a nigger-hatin' muthafucker. Ya see the way he looks at me, man? I don't like it worth a fuck, man."

"Get back to your position and cool it," Caddy said coldly.

Silk knew better than to argue with the buck sergeant and walked away mumbling. Caddy climbed out of his hole and walked over to the edge of Ty's position. He sat down and watched Silk walk away. "Don't mind him. He's got a chip on his shoulder and rides all cherries hard."

Ty was opening his C-ration can with a p-38 opener and looked up casually. "He doesn't bother me; he pisses me off."

Caddy smiled. "He pisses everybody off, but he's a brother and I gotta watch out for him. Us colored boys gotta take care of each other. . . . You haven't been around many Negroes, have you?"

Ty set the opened can on top of a small stove fashioned from a C-ration can with holes punched in its sides. "Naw, we didn't have dark folks in my hometown. The first I ever talked to were the ones I met in basic."

Caddy kept his smile. "Where I'm from in L.A., I didn't talk to whites until I was sixteen . . . melt a tin of cheese into those noodles and it'll taste better."

Ty looked up into the eyes of Jerome Washington and felt as if he were reaching out for a friend. Caddy had smooth features and smiled a lot. He'd been in country for only two months, but he seemed to know his business. He told the squad he used to sell Cadillacs to pimps and had a prospering future until Uncle Sam sent him a letter of employment.

Ty motioned to his food. "Come on, Sarge, join me and eat some of this. And thanks for bustin' that up. I'm not prejudiced. It's just I don't like Silk messin' with me. If you could talk to him and smooth it over, I'd appreciate it. I don't want any trouble."

Caddy slid into the hole and squatted by the small stove. "It's past that. You and Silk are gonna have to work it out yourselves. Sorry, man. Where's your hot sauce and garlic powder?"

"Don't have any."

Caddy immediately stood and hopped out of the hole. He came back a minute later with a claymore bag filled with small bottles wrapped in tape. "Nance, the only way to enjoy this war is to become a connoisseur of C-ration cooking. Hot sauce kills the bland taste, and two shakes of garlic powder makes it like home cookin'. These dehydrated onions add flavor, but your farts will smell funny."

Caddy balled up some bits of C-4, which served as cooking fuel, and placed them inside the stove, then lit the white doughy explosive with a match. In fifteen seconds the noodles were boiling. Caddy opened a small can of C-ration cheese and spooned it on top of the noodles, then added the other ingredients. He stirred the concoction and lifted a spoonful to Ty. "It's time for heaven."

Ty took a bite and moaned. "This is great! Thanks, Sarge."

Caddy took a bite and nodded his approval. "Write your folks and have them send you a care package of these goodies, and you'll be set for the war. Till then, when you're ready to eat, come and see me and we'll make dishes made in heaven."

"I smell food!"

Ty glanced up at Theodore Cummings and quickly covered the can of noodles with his hands. "Get away, Teddy. You can't handle it."

Teddy Bear was a small twenty-two-year-old with an old man's build. He was thin-legged and narrow-hipped and had a large, protruding stomach. He wore thick glasses and was already partially bald. He was a complainer and whined when he talked. "Awww, come on, Nance. Give me a small bite, pleeeease."

Caddy waved him away. "Go on and mooch off somebody else. You ate all your food. You'll just have to wait until tomorrow for resupply."

Ty had been warned about Teddy by Cowboy and the others. Teddy couldn't restrain himself and ate most of his food by the second day. Ty had felt sorry for Teddy the first time and had shared some C-rations with him, but he ended up not having enough food for himself.

Teddy looked at Ty with basset-hound eyes. "Pleeease."

Ty threw Teddy a can of crackers and took another bite of noodles, avoiding Caddy's disapproving eyes.

The rest of the squad returned with the filled canteens and received orders to move to the north and search an area where a spotter plane had seen three VC crossing a canal. The first squad was to lead the rest of the platoon. Bugs Saben ran his tongue over his protruding teeth and led the way as point man, with Cowboy taking up the slackman position to cover him. Twenty-five yards behind were Hammonds and the rest of the squad.

The small unit broke out of a thicket of bamboo into rice paddies and were crossing a narrow dike when a single shot rang out. Teddy Bear stood for a full second before he sank to the dike and slid off into the muddy water. The rest of the men didn't know on which side of the dike to take cover. It was impossible to determine where the shot had come from. Ty threw himself into the water and mud and tried to become invisible. He raised up to take a breath, when three inches to his right the water kicked up in a miniature geyser followed a moment later by the report of the firing weapon.

Ty jumped up and tried to run to the other side of the dike, but it was like running through a foot-deep field of partially melted marshmallows. He churned his legs and arms but seemed to be going nowhere as the men on the other side of the dike returned fire. Ty fell, got up, and fell again. He reached the dike and crawled over Teddy Bear's body. Teddy's eyes and mouth were open as if he were screaming in silence. A perfect hole had been made in his earlobe, and a small trickle of deep purple-red blood seeped from the wound into the stinking water.

Ty threw himself to the other side of the dike and into the water. He took one look at his rifle and knew he couldn't use it. The barrel was choked with mud. If he tried to shoot it, it would explode.

The fire slackened, then stopped. There were no incoming rounds. Hammonds yelled from down the dike, "Anybody hit?"

Ty was going to yell back, but Goldman hollered, "Teddy got it!"

Hammonds put his helmet on the end of his M-16 barrel and slowly raised it above the dike. Nothing happened. He yelled out, "Nobody move till the gunships get here!"

Ty felt the heat for the first time. He hadn't noticed it when they were moving, but lying there in the mud made him feel as if he were in an oven. Half his body was in the cool mud, but his shoulders and head were exposed to the sun's baking heat. He had lost his helmet and rucksack on the other side and had no protection. He crawled over to Silk and asked for his cleaning rod to clear the mud from the barrel, but Silk snarled, "Get da fuck away from me, fool."

Ty vowed to himself to deal with him later and crawled down the dike to Goldie, who gave him his cleaning rod without complaint. Ten minutes passed before Ty heard in the distance the sound of the approaching gunships. Twenty seconds later they streaked over his head and unleashed a flurry of rockets into the woodline one hundred meters distant.

Ty lowered his head just as the rockets hit and exploded in a succession of thunderous cracks. The mud beneath him shook and the water rippled with the concussion.

Lieutenant Jenkins waited until the guns made their third rocket and machine-gun pass before maneuvering his other squads into covering position and ordering Hammonds's squad to advance. The first squad formed up and cautiously moved toward the woodline.

Ty recovered his helmet and rucksack as he waded through the mud toward the trees. He felt like a walking target for anyone hiding in the thick vegetation and tensed his body for the impact of bullets. There was nothing else to do but hope and pray the sniper was gone.

The squad labored through the paddies and finally made it to the island of thick vegetation where the sniper had fired. They swept through the bamboo, ferns, and banana trees only to find an empty firing position.

Goldie found the sniper's position and picked up two expended copper casings. Hammonds took one look at the casings and spoke with authority. "AK-47. The dude is long gone by now. Goldie, go get the L-tee and tell him what we found."

Ty finished his sweep and walked over to the position. He bent down and studied the flattened grass, then lay down on the ground. Hammonds looked at his new man as if he had lost his mind. "Get up, Nance. This is no time to be layin' down."

Ty lifted his head only a few inches and motioned Hammonds out of his line of sight. The sergeant stepped out of the way but shook his head in disgust. "You're wastin' your time trying to spot his escape route. He fired a couple of times and took off."

Lieutenant Jenkins approached with his radioman and saw Ty lying on his stomach with his head lifted up as if he were trying to align a putting shot on a golf green. "What the hell is he doing?"

Ty got up in total concentration and began walking toward a clump of bamboo. Hammonds shrugged his shoulders. "Sir, he's trying to find the escape route of the dink."

Ty took a few steps and crouched down again. He had that strange feeling Winter's had called "in the groove," and what he knew as "becoming the buffalo." He could sense that the killer was close. The rest of the squad stayed behind him as he rose up and followed the path. When he had lain down he had noticed that the grass was bent toward the east. The sniper had run directly back and turned north at the clump of bamboo. Ty stopped and lay down again at the base of the bamboo thicket. The sniper had stopped running when he had made his turn. The distance between his strides was much shorter. The path was clearly evident for twenty yards and suddenly ended as if the man had picked up his feet and flown.

Ty rose to a crouch and stepped forward lightly. The son of a bitch was there. He knew it.

Jenkins watched in fascination as Ty crept forward toward nothing but banana trees. There wasn't a thing suspicious that he could see. Ty stopped again, extended his rifle barrel toward the ground, and circled to his right, keeping the barrel pointed at a bare spot.

Ty had seen the faint outline and wanted to get behind the trapdoor. He had his man. Sucking in a deep breath, he took out a grenade and lowered himself to the ground. There was no latch or handle. The cover was simply fitted to the spider hole. The sniper had gotten into his hiding hole and set the perfectly camouflaged cover into place to wait out the searchers. He'd made one mistake.

Ty motioned the others to take cover and pulled the pin. He set the grenade on top of the cover and ran back to a nearby palm tree.

The grenade exploded in a vehement blast, and Ty rushed the hole. The cover was only partially blown away, revealing a five-foot-deep, perfectly square hole with a figure covered in dust kneeling in the bottom trying to raise up. Ty fired a quick burst into the man's back. The sniper jerked with the impact and slumped forward to his knees.

Ty rolled to his right and waited for the other man to pop his head up as Jenkins walked toward the hole in disbelief. Ty heard the officer coming up behind him and threw his hand up to halt him. It was too late. A burst of fire cut the air just above Jenkins's head. Ty saw the muzzle flash and crawled toward the position. The second hole was twenty yards away, beside a banana tree. The squad was down firing wildly in the general direction, but the fire was ineffective. Ty stopped and took aim. The spot in the earth lifted only a few inches and the barrel of a weapon protruded. Ty fired a single shot, and the rifle barrel beneath the matted trapdoor fell to the ground.

Hammonds picked himself off the ground as Ty pulled back the camouflaged cover and waved him forward. Jenkins joined them and motioned toward Ty. "How did he know? I thought he was a cherry."

Hammonds shook his head, still in shocked disbelief. "I don't know."

Jenkins passed by the first spider hole and strode toward the second hole, where Ty was pulling out the body. "Nance, how did you know where they were?"

Ty slid into the hole and tossed out a rifle and several pouches. "Sir, the first one left the cover to his hole beside his position too long and flattened the grass, leaving an imprint. When I lay down, I could see where the moisture had built up on the grass. It was a dumb mistake. The second one I wasn't sure of until he opened up."

The lieutenant inspected the spider hole and lifted the earthen cover. The hole was like a bedding box but with angled insides. The cover fit perfectly on top of the hole and would not have been seen. "But how did you know there were two of them?"

Ty climbed out of the hole and pressed his magazine release.

"The rule is, where there's one, there's two. The dinks don't leave men by themselves . . . they're like us."

"Where'd you learn all this? You sure didn't get it from books."

Ty knelt over the body and checked his shot. He had hit the VC just below the nose. "Sir, I went to the scout dog tracking school, and they showed us a lot of pictures and told us what to look for. These holes are even better than the pictures. If there's time, it would help the school if somebody took some snapshots of these and sent them back to Benning."

Hammonds couldn't get over Nance's reaction. He wasn't even shaking. He knew Nance was cold when he'd seen him bag up the dead cherry, but it was obvious he was past being cold. He was ice.

Jenkins turned around and yelled at his radioman, "Get me the old man on the horn." He looked back at Ty and spoke quickly, "You stay right here and I'll send up one squad at a time. I want you to show them what you did. Give them a class on what to look for." He pointed at Hammonds. "Your squad gets the first class, then move back and cover the second when you're done."

Ty sat down by the body and looked into the dead man's face. He was smaller than he'd imagined the enemy would be—probably no more than five feet tall and about a hundred pounds. He was young, too young. Eighteen at the most. Ty scanned his clothes and equipment, feeling respect for the young soldier. He was barefooted, wearing only a pair of dirty khaki shorts and a black nylon shirt. He had only two magazines for his older Chinese-made AK-47 rifle, but he had put up a fight trying to protect his friend.

Silk yanked the first body out of the hole by grasping his black hair and pulling him up. "Looky here at dis gook, man. He pissed his pants." He tossed the body to the ground and pulled the man's pants down. "Man, no wonder the dink broads dig us. These gooks ain't got but two inches of dick. I think I'll take his and send it to my hole back in the big windy." Silk pulled his knife and squatted down but was suddenly knocked over by a butt stroke to his helmet.

Ty lowered his rifle barrel into Silk's face. "You kill your own dink to cut up."

Hammonds didn't see the incident and spun around. "Nance, put down that weapon!"

Ty ignored him and leaned closer to Silk, touching the still-warm barrel to his nose. "And don't you ever refuse me or any other man in this squad when we need help."

Hammonds grabbed Ty's shoulders and pulled him back. "What the hell you think you're doing? Jesus, we're on the same side!"

Ty stared at Hammonds with expressionless eyes. "Tell that to Silk."

Caddy walked with Cowboy and Goldie toward the second squad to take their place so they could receive Ty's class. Caddy looked over his shoulder as he walked. "I've never seen anything like it. He was like a cat stalking its prey, the way he moved and crouched down."

"Just be glad ya gave him your cleaning rod," Cowboy said, patting Goldie's back. "I wouldn't wanna be Silk. He wasn't kiddin' none when he put that there sixteen in his face. No sirree, I wouldn't want the Cat Man mad at me. He's bad news."

Goldie smiled and pushed back his helmet. "Cowboy, I think you just named our cherry. 'Cat Man' is kinda catchy."

Caddy nodded. "Yeah, 'Cat Man.'"

Ty sat back on his rucksack after giving the classes and felt Silk's eyes burrowing into his back. He tried to ignore the stares but couldn't take it anymore. He turned around to face the black man. "Look, we're all in this together, so let's make a truce. I'm sorry for knocking ya over and pointin' the rifle at ya."

Silk kept his scowl. "Fuck you, Indian!"

Ty kept his stare for several seconds before getting to his feet and stepping to within striking distance of Silk. He extended his hand. "Truce?"

Silk turned his back to Ty and looked into the faces of Caddy and Goldman, who eyed him coldly.

Ty dropped his hand and began to walk away, when Silk turned around slowly and softened his glare. "Nance, you nothin' but a lucky muthafucker, but you're right. We is in it together."

"Family?" Ty said. He extended his hand.

Silk hesitated, then grasped Ty's hand in a firm grip. "Family."

Jason walked toward the back doors of the roaring C-119 feeling good. Today was the last jump. No matter what happened, once he jumped he would be a paratrooper. The entire company was riding a high, knowing they would be receiving their wings. He climbed the ramp and sat down in the last seat. He would be first out the right door, and Fat Man Miller would be first out the left side. The plane rumbled and began rolling down the runway.

Miller looked across the aisle and held up his right thumb. "Feet and knees to the breeze time!"

Jason yelled back over the engine's roar, "It don't get any better than this!"

The plane lifted off and crossed over the Chattahoochee at five hundred feet. Gaining altitude, the silver bird banked left and began to make its approach to the drop zone. The jumpmaster had already completed his commands and pointed at Jason. "STAND, IN THE DOOR!"

Jason yelled over his shoulder to his stick, "Ya gotta love it, Crazies!"

The men screamed back, "YA GOTTA LOVE IT!"

He stood in the door with a smile on his face.

"GO!"

He leaped out and snapped into a tight body position. The parachute yanked him from his fall and fully inflated in a billowing pop of silk. He looked up to check his canopy and grabbed the risers, pulling them down to his chin to avoid Miller, who was floating thirty feet away.

The parachute immediately responded and drifted to the right. Jason looked down and could see the grassy field far below and the small creek that ran down its center. The water glistened in the sunlight like an aluminum foil ribbon. The wind was blowing directly toward the creek. Damn!

Jason pulled down on the risers again, but the winds had died down. The chute glided to the right and lifted up, caught in an updraft. Jason was suspended for ten seconds, going neither up nor down. Suddenly, he began descending again. Keeping his legs together and relaxing his body, he prepared to land when the wind caught him again and glided the parachute over the creek. Jason hit the shallow water in a splash, then made a bigger splash as he rolled forward in a wet parachute landing fall. He jumped up soaking wet but thrilled. It was the softest landing of the five jumps he'd made. "AIRBORNE!"

An hour later, he stood in the company formation and listened to a colonel praise their accomplishment in becoming paratroopers. Jason only half-heard the speech. He was thinking of catching his flight out. He was going home for fifteen days on leave before shipping out for Nam.

The colonel concluded his speech and asked the visitors in the audience to move forward and pin the wings on their loved ones. Jason ignored the throng of people and waited for an instructor to pin on his wings. A large sergeant wearing his Class A Army greens stepped in front of Jason and pulled out a crumpled envelope. "Lieutenant, I'm Master Sergeant Cherry. A young paratrooper

asked me to present your wings to you today.'' Cherry eyed Jason
from head to foot. ''You didn't know it, but I've been watching you
the past three weeks. I wanted to make sure you were worth what
I'm going to give you. I'm proud to say you are. You're like your
brother . . . a real paratrooper.''

He handed Jason a small piece of paper. ''This will explain things
a little better.''

Jason looked at the note and smiled. It was from Ty.

> Dear Jay
> Congratulations, paratrooper! Today is a very special day. You
> are going to join the ranks of the Red Hill Paratroopers. I have
> asked MSgt. Cherry to do the honors and pin you with the wings
> that my dad, uncle, and I were pinned with on graduation day
> making us America's best. I'm proud of you, brother. Take care
> and keep your butt down.
>
> Love ya
> Ty

Cherry took the parachute wings from the envelope and held
them up for Jason to see. ''Lieutenant, Nance has asked me to
give you his wings. They are very special to him. He must care
for you very much.'' He pinned the wings over Jason's heart and
stepped back with a rigid salute. ''Congratulations, Red Hill
Paratrooper.''

Jason returned the salute with tears in his eyes.

24

25 April, Central Highlands

General Binh Ty Duc set down his pack and rotated his tired
shoulders. The tour of the defensive positions was taking its toll on
him. He felt ancient as he sat down on the hilltop and looked at the
valley to the east. He felt as if he was home. Years ago he had sat

for many days in the same spot, thinking about home. The hill had been his headquarters during the preparation for the attack on the French outpost at Dak To. The hill had been special to him. It sat alone, standing taller and more beautiful than its brothers, and had for him an inexplicable allure. Every time he saw the hill, his heart would soar. Even now, after so many years, the hill had the same effect on him. Nothing had changed. The place still strangely moved him. He could feel its strength and needed its powers of rejuvenation. He shut his eyes. Thirteen years ago he could have marched the same distance without fatigue. Since then, the years and wars had taken away his youth and vitality. The young men who were digging the bunkers and connecting tunnels were constant reminders of his age.

Colonel Kinh walked up the hill, holding a cup of cool tea. "General, you need rest. I have told the company commander we will be staying the night."

General Duc nodded, knowing his plans officer was looking out for his best interests. Kinh had taken it upon himself to be his keeper. The sad thing was that he knew he needed Kinh to make sure he didn't push himself too hard.

Kinh smiled as he gave the general his tea. "The positions are excellent. The digging is a week ahead of schedule, and we expect to finish the tunnels next month."

General Duc pulled two maps from his pack and spread them out on the ground. He prized his captured American map for its detail and preferred it to his own. He traced his march from the lower ridges to the hilltop and pointed at a spot on the map. "This is Hill 875. Years ago this was my headquarters, and my men built the command bunker that is below us. The hill was known then by my men as the 'Refuge.' It was here that we knew we would be safe." His eyes saddened. "And now, my friend, I must use the old one as a fortress. This is key high ground, for it commands the valley to the east. This is our last defensive position."

Kinh felt his commander's sadness and spoke softly. "We can inspect the positions tomorrow. You should rest."

General Duc slowly stood and gave a last lingering look at the valley before facing Kinh. "No, we do not have time. Show me the positions."

Kinh stepped out of the way, allowing the general to look out of the bunker's firing portal. They had already inspected the command bunker and had walked through the newly constructed communications tunnels to check the first line of fighting bunkers.

A young soldier wearing a dirt-stained uniform stood in awe as they went by. He and his squad had been working on the position for months.

General Duc nodded in approval and patted the sayo logs above his head. "How many meters of soil do you have on top of your support logs?"

The senior sergeant standing in the bunker entrance began to speak, but the general looked at the young private for the answer.

Private Bui Ngoc Duong nervously shifted his stance, having never before spoken to a senior officer. "Comrade General, we placed five meters of soil on top and packed it tightly."

General Duc smiled and patted his shoulder. "Your work is very good. Do you understand why the bunker is located here?"

Duong wasn't sure if he should answer the question, for he thought the bunker was in a poor position. The general seemed to sense his concern and motioned toward the firing portal. "You question the position because of the trees blocking your sight? Come, let me explain the plan to you."

He stooped and walked through the communications tunnel leading toward the trench line. Then he climbed nearby steps up to the slope that overlooked the bunker twenty meters down the ridge. Waiting for the private to join him, he motioned down the hill. "Sadly, the trees that are around us will not be here when the enemy attacks. He will use his artillery and planes to destroy the beauty of the old hill. There will be nothing left but debris."

Duong tried to imagine the destruction of the towering teaks and ironwoods. The trees were over thirty meters in height and three to five meters thick. The rain forest blocked out all light, leaving the jungle floor in semi-darkness.

General Duc squatted down and drew a circle in the red soil, then extended lines from the circle to the north and south. "The hilltop has only two approaches and both are narrow ridges. The enemy must use the ridges to the north or south because the east and west approaches are too steep. He can only attack using one of the ridges and has very restricted room to maneuver. The first time he comes up the hill, he will not know where your bunker is located, and you will cut the lead element to ribbons. You can easily stop him, for you will be protected inside your bunker along with the others to your sides and behind you. The enemy will fall back and destroy the forest with his bombs and attack again. The fallen trees will add more cover to your bunker, and he will have to expose himself by climbing over the debris. It will be impossible to attack in any strength, and again you will be able to stop him. If your bunker becomes damaged or the portals blocked, you can use the tunnel and fall back to the trench or the next bunker and fight again.''

Duong shut his eyes. He could see the battle unfold as the general had described. The bombing would be horrible, but the senior sergeant had already explained that they would be hiding in the tunnel for protection. Once the bombing was over, they would return to their bunkers and wait for the attack. He felt more confident but sad at the loss of the magnificent trees. He looked at the general. "Is there a chance they will not come and destroy the old ones?"

The general put his hand on the boy's shoulder and looked down the ridge. "This hill is the highest of those that run along the valley to our east. It is called key terrain by us old warriors who study war. The enemy must take this hill to command the valley. He will come, my friend. He will come, but you will be ready.''

"They will not take the hill, my general,'' Duong said. "My comrades and I will stop them.''

General Duc faced him. He knew the horror the boy would experience and felt remorse. Such dedicated men. The awful truth was the hill would be taken. No position could be held if the attacker was willing to expend the necessary men and firepower.

He forced a smile. "The reunification of our country will be your reward. Take care, my young friend. Keep digging and take care.''

The general felt his age again as he walked down the steps into the trench to visit the next bunker. The determination in the boy's eyes had touched his heart and weakened him. He would have to sacrifice the hill's beauty and perhaps the young soldier's life for the greater good. The truth of it hurt and aged him more than his years.

Duong could still feel the silver-haired officer's hand on his shoulder. The sergeant who had chastised him so long ago had been right. The general cared.

He walked back to his bunker and leaned against the logs he had cut and emplaced. There was much work remaining on the other tunnels, but this bunker was his. He had supervised and helped build it. He was an engineer, but he would fight alongside the infantry of his assigned company and protect the hill. This hill and others like it were Vietnamese, not the Americans' or the puppets'. It was his hill. He would fight those who dared think they could take it from him. This was his home.

* * *

In single file, the twenty-three men of the First Platoon snaked their way up a winding trail leading to a series of small, tree-covered hills.

Every man was drenched in sweat, but not from the heat. They were sweating from apprehension. They had been moving for two hours, watching where they stepped and making sure they kept at least ten yards from each other. Earlier that morning there had been twenty-five men in the platoon. A booby trap had killed one and badly wounded another.

Lieutenant Jenkins reached for the map in his leg pocket. A muffled explosion from the front of the column froze him in his tracks. "Shit."

No one got down or moved to the side of the trail. Every man remained motionless, carefully eyeing the ground around his feet. Then slowly, cautiously, they all stepped lightly to the side of the trail and studied every inch of soil, grass, rock, and trees to their front. They had learned their lesson that morning. The lieutenant had made everyone look at the body. The second squad had been leading, and their point man tripped a fishline attached to a grenade. He had heard the pop of the detonater and yelled as he ran for cover. The slack man also ran and flung his body to the side of the trail, empaling himself on hidden pungi sticks. The sharpened stakes stuck only ten inches out of the ground and, covered in grass, were almost impossible to see. His momentum had driven three of the stakes completely through his neck, shoulder, and right arm. The rest of the stakes had only partially stabbed him, suspending his entire body off the ground. He'd lived for several minutes, choking on his own blood. The point man had run into the stakes just off the trail in a desperate effort to get away from the grenade. The angled pungi stakes had caught him just above the boot tops and had ripped open his legs. He had fallen backwards just as the grenade went off. The shrapnel tore through his buttocks and back. His wounds had been nasty but not fatal.

Jenkins pushed the sidebar of the radio handset to find out the situation but heard the anguished cry from up ahead. "Medic up! Medic up, booby trap!"

He turned around to Doc Weaver, but the twenty-year-old platoon medic was already running past him. Jenkins followed as he spoke into the radio handset requesting a medevac.

Doc knelt over the blue-faced soldier and quickly opened his aid bag. He knew the explosive device must have been in a tree, for the airburst had caught the point man in the face and shoulders. His helmet had protected him from most of the shrapnel, but a big piece had hit him in the mouth and chin. He wasn't breathing. Shattered teeth, shrapnel, and destroyed tissue were blocking the air passage.

He pulled out a scalpel and felt along the soldier's throat for his Adam's apple. Finding it, he punctured the skin and cartilage just above the protruding bump. Air immediately began filling the soldier's lungs. Doc held the incision open with his fingers and nodded toward his chest. "Get the ink pen out of my shirt pocket and unscrew it. Use the scalpel and cut the small end of the casing off to make me an air tube."

The squad leader compiled and quickly held up the makeshift breathing tube. Doc inserted the plastic device into the incision and taped it to the soldier's neck before attending to the other wounds.

Lieutenant Jenkins watched the entire procedure while talking on the radio. He had a medevac coming in, but the closest area suitable for landing was on top of the hill, still another five hundred meters away. He turned around and yelled down the column, "Cat Man, up!"

Several minutes later, Sergeant Hammonds strode up the trail followed by his squad. Jenkins motioned the sergeant to the side of the trail and lowered his voice. "Before you start bitching, I know it isn't your squad's turn on point, but I need the Cat to get us to the hilltop."

Hammonds eyed the officer coldly. "Damn it, sir, he was on point yesterday. What happened to the rotation system?"

"Fuck the system. I need the best, and he's it. Get him up here and move out."

Hammonds turned around in disgust. "Cat, up."

Caddy heard the word being passed back and cussed under his breath. Ty walked up beside him and changed his magazine to all tracers. "They're calling for us."

Caddy shook his head despondently. "Being your slack man is bad news. My nerves can't handle it much longer."

Ty smiled and patted his friend's back. "No sweat. We're in the groove."

Captain James Elliott was tired. He took off his helmet, sat down, and looked up at his new lieutenant. "Jesus H. Christ, L-tee, don't stand at attention like that. We're not at Benning. Sit down and relax."

Feeling ridiculous, the second lieutenant quickly sat down.

Elliott lit a Camel and inhaled deeply. "L-tee, I know you just got off the chopper, but I gotta put you to work. You'll be taking the second platoon . . . my problem child. The last platoon leader was a dip shit and got himself blown away three weeks ago doing something stupid. He stood up to adjust close-in artillery. The platoon is now being run by Sergeant First Class Ramirez, who is about as bad. He's a by-the-book noncom who doesn't know how to read, a real dumb-ass. I want you to take charge of that bunch of prima donnas and get them back in the Army. They're good men, but right now they're livin' in the past and totally undisciplined. Most of them made the parachute combat jump in February and think their shit don't stink, but they're worthless to me. They do what they want when they want and don't respond to Ramirez, who has lost control. Before I'm through, Alpha Company of the 503d is going to be the best damn company in the Second Battalion and in the whole damn 173d Airborne Brigade. You look like you're big enough to handle the job, and I want you to do it quickly . . . like yesterday was too late. I want you to take three days and work on whatever you want. I suggest the basics. The area is pretty quiet, so take the time to get to know your men and train them the way you want. On the fourth day, you will start search and destroy operations east of your platoon perimeter. Take charge, Lieutenant Johnson. Take charge of that second platoon, or I'll fire your ass in a week.''

Lieutenant Jason Johnson nodded and stood up. After two and a half weeks in Vietnam of going through inprocessing, jungle school, and briefings, he was anxious to finally see the war. He had been thrilled while at Cam Ranh Bay when he received orders for the same unit as Ty, the 173d, and later at Ben Hoa when he learned he was going to be a platoon leader. He had reported that morning to the company headquarters on the firebase and been issued an M-16, fifteen magazines, four bandoliers of ammunition, a web belt, load-carrying suspenders, one bottle of insect repellent, a rucksack, a compass, a map, and a one-page history of the 503d Infantry. He was told he was ready for the war and escorted to the landing pad, where he had been flown out on the resupply chopper. Fifteen minutes before, he had been dropped off, and now he was already being challenged by his company commander.

Jason turned to leave but stopped. He had one slight problem. ''Sir, where is the second platoon?''

Ty broke out of the trees onto the open, grass-covered hilltop. He held up his hand to halt Caddy and searched around the woodline for wind mines. He had circled halfway around the hilltop before he spotted what he was looking for. Thirty feet up, tied to a tree trunk, was an American claymore mine that pointed toward the hilltop. The VC had a mortar flare parachute dangling in the branches with a string tied to it. When the chopper winds caught the miniature chute, it would inflate and pull the string, releasing the pin and detonating the deadly mine. Ty continued his search, but finding no more, returned to Caddy and Sergeant Hammonds on the trail.

Lieutenant Jenkins strode up to find out what the delay was. "Let's go. We gotta get the medevac in."

Ty held out his rifle, blocking him from moving any closer, and nodded toward Caddy. The sergeant lifted his M-79 grenade launcher and fired. The shell exploded in the branches by the flare chute, ripping the silk in half and yanking the string. The top third of the tree toppled over with the thunderous explosion and was consumed by black smoke. The steel ball bearings of the mine tore into the side of the hill and kicked up a debris cloud of dirt and pieces of grass just fifty feet in front of the stunned officer.

Ty lowered his rifle. "Now you can bring in the bird."

Thirty minutes later, Hammonds took off his fatigue shirt and tossed it over a small tree. "Get your shirts and boots off and let the sun dry up the jungle rot."

Ty and the other squad members began unbuttoning their shirts as they moved closer to hear the sergeant's briefing. The resupply bird had not brought out a change of clothes in several weeks, and their bodies and uniforms reeked with dried sweat and rice paddy muck. The Fourth Battalion had been choppered out of War Zone C and had moved to Xuan Loc three weeks before to conduct search and destroy operations. They were to clear VC tax collectors from the area. There was no significant threat, so the company had been broken up and had worked in independent platoon sectors to cover more area. The platoon had only two minor contacts with the VC but had been mauled by their booby traps. Six men had been lost in the past three weeks.

Hammonds motioned Bugs to his feet and had him turn around. "You see these white spots on his back? It's nothin' to get worried about. It's just a fungus that eats up the pigment of your skin. Sun is the only cure for it." He took out his notepad.

"Looks like the second squad's point man is gonna make it. They called from the rear and said he made it back to the evac hospital in time. Doc Weaver and Cat Man pulled the platoon out again. Okay, for your information, we are now in an operation called 'Fort Wayne.' I know it doesn't make a shit to you what the hell the brass calls our humpin', but that's the official title. We're assigned to check out the small hills to the north. Intelligence says local VC units are operating there that harass the government villages along the road and are responsible for the booby traps we've been hitting. The lieutenant wants us to send out a recon patrol this afternoon and an ambush patrol tonight. Cowboy, you take Cat, Goldie, and Paddy on the recon, and the rest of us will pull the bush tonight. Plan on going out in an hour, and be back before sixteen hundred hours. Remember, the hills are in a free fire zone, so grease anything that moves.''

Silk stood up with a scowl. "Fuck this shit, man. We doin' everythang for the platoon. We pullin' point out a turn, and having ta recon and bush is fuckin' bullshit. The lieutenant is gonna get us all waxed.''

Hammonds sighed. He was used to Silk's complaining. "All the squads are sending out recons and bushes, so cool it.''

Silk eyed Ty coldly. "What about point? The lieutenant thinks Cat is Superman and keeps puttin' us up there to cover him. Man, the odds are runnin' against us if we keep playin' Indian scout. Even Cat ain't that good. Sooner or later he's gonna trip the big one that'll blow us all ta hell.''

"Shut up, fool," Caddy snapped angrily. "The Cat is savin' your black ass. He's in the groove, man.''

"Fuck the groove! The dude is crazy. He loves this shit, man. He digs it, and he's gonna get us wasted.''

Hammonds looked at Ty for a reaction, but as usual, he didn't seem to be listening. He pointed at Silk. "Second squad needs a new point man. I'll be glad to give them you if you want to volunteer.''

Silk glared at the sergeant, knowing he was bluffing, but didn't dare call him. "Fuck it, man. Fuck the whole fuckin' thing.''

Hammonds snickered. "I didn't think you would . . . shut the fuck up and sit down.'' He looked at his watch and nodded toward Cowboy. "One hour.''

Lieutenant Jenkins had walked up behind the squad and had heard most of the argument. He waited until the men had gone back to their positions before approaching Hammonds, who was heating a cup of coffee. "You handled that pretty well.'' He sat down and took off his helmet. "You think Nance is crazy?''

Hammonds raised an eyebrow. "Naw, but three weeks ago I would have probably said yes. Nance is just different. Like Silk said, he loves it. I've just seen one other guy like him. He feels good being the point man because out there he relies on this senses. He believes in his instincts and honestly thinks he can see, hear, smell, and feel the dinks first. The Cat is about as good as they come.''

Jenkins looked over his shoulder at Ty, who was sitting by himself and soaking up the sun. "I always see him alone. Doesn't he have any friends, someone to talk to?''

Hammonds smiled. "Everybody is Cat's friend. He's family, but he doesn't let anybody get real close. He likes being a loner, and we all respect that. None of us want to mess with success. I honestly don't believe Cat needs or wants close friends . . . I think he knows.''

"Knows what?'' asked Jenkins.

Hammonds sipped the hot coffee and stared at the officer. "He knows the odds. Point men don't last long.''

Jason's new uniform was drenched in sweat by the time he arrived at the edge of his platoon's perimeter. He had made the two-klick movement across the open rice paddies with only a scared eighteen-year-old replacement for company. Jason had refused a guide and had decided to make the trek on foot instead of waiting all day for a copter ride.

He strode past three men sleeping under a palm tree to the middle of a small open area, where four others were playing cards. A transistor radio was blaring. One of the men looked up from his cards and tapped the player next to him. "The new L-tee is here, man.''

Sergeant Ramirez kept his hand and slowly stood up with a fake smile. "Good to see you, sir. We didn't expect you till later.''

Jason took off his rucksack and looked around. "Yeah, I can tell. How about you tellin' your cardplayers to turn off the radio and gettin' me the squad leaders so we can make the introductions?''

Ramirez motioned to the three seated men who were looking at him indifferently. "These are the squad leaders.''

Jason contained his anger, remembering what the Fort Benning leadership department had taught. The instructor had stressed that, when arriving at a new unit, never make changes based on the assumption that things are messed up. Rather, go in nice and easy and ask questions and see first how the unit performs as a whole.

He spoke softly. "You all wait right here and don't move.'' He walked to the first position he had passed and looked at the sleeping men. None had shaved in days. He picked up an M-16 laying on the ground beside one of the soldiers and quickly made an inspection. The rifle was filthy and the barrel was red with rust. He kept the weapon and walked around the small perimeter checking each position. In every case he found the same things: dirty, sleeping men and neglected weapons and equipment. He walked back to the center, where the sergeants had resumed playing cards.

Jason took a deep breath and set his shoulders. He had seen enough. He wasn't assuming the platoon was screwed up; he *knew* it was. He kicked the blaring radio across the perimeter. The stunned squad leaders looked up as he threw the rusted rifle on top of the stack of cards. "Since none of you squad leaders stood up and introduced yourselves, I'll just do it this way. You, you, and you will get your asses up and assemble your squads. Since nobody was pulling security and I heard that radio three hundred meters away, security must not be a problem. You will have two minutes to tell your men that I, Lieutenant Jason Johnson, am now the platoon leader. You will then instruct half your men to shave while the other half clean weapons. They will switch at the appropriate time. You will then inspect all weapons and equipment and provide Sergeant Ramirez with a list of discrepancies. I will make my inspection in one hour. I don't think any of you have questions, do you? Good, move out!"

"We don't have formations in the field," Ramirez protested. "It's dangerous and . . ."

Jason cut him off by picking up the rusted rifle and shoving it into his arms. "No, *this* is dangerous. Sleeping men are dangerous and goddamn radios are dangerous. And as far as I'm concerned, *you* are dangerous. Get me the platoon RTO and medic, then give me a status of your men and how this platoon is organized. Don't say another word until you are ready to brief me. Move."

He sat down on his rucksack and looked up at the replacement, who was staring at him. "Well, Sawyer, did I get their attention?"

Sawyer smiled weakly. "Yes, sir, I'd say you most definitely did that."

Paddy McGuire sat down beside Ty. "Cat, Mickey hit his five hundredth."

Preoccupied with cleaning his rifle, Ty set the oily rag on his lap. "Huh?"

"Mickey Mantle hit his five-hundredth home run against the Orioles. He's from Oklahoma, isn't he?"

Ty began to put the weapon's receiver group back together. "Yeah, he's from Spavinaw, up in the northwest part of the state. It's just a podunk town, but they sure play some mean baseball. Better check your magazine and see if your ammo is cruddy."

Ty was worried about the apple-cheeked soldier. He knew Paddy had gotten his information from *Stars and Stripes*. Paddy always read the paper cover to cover eight to ten times out of desperation for contact with the outside world. He was in Nam in body only. His mind was always back home.

Paddy took off his helmet and took out the folded paper from inside his helmet liner. "Things aren't going so good at home. In New York City they had a peace rally protesting the war. One-hundred-thousand people walked from Central Park to the United Nations building."

"Is that a long hump?" Ty said. He inserted a magazine and stood up.

"It isn't very far, but that's not the point, Cat. Those people think this war is wrong."

Ty let the rifle bolt slam forward. "Wonder what Deets and Teddy Bear would think about that. Come on, we have our own little protest march to make."

A minute later, Ty and Paddy joined Cowboy in the center of the platoon perimeter. Sergeant Hammonds approached with Goldie, who was carrying the radio. "The dinks haven't had any GI's around lately, so you might catch them half-steppin'. If you see something, give me a call and we'll come like the cavalry. Don't take any chances, and take it slow and easy."

Cowboy smiled confidently. "If they're there, we'll be findin' 'em."

They moved to the north for thirty minutes, with Ty leading and the Texan covering. Goldie was third, followed by Paddy, who was rear security.

Ty stopped at a small creek at the base of a hill covered with scrub trees and motioned Cowboy up to him. "This trail we're on hasn't been used in a while. If there are any dinks around here they'll be close to the water. I think we should follow the creek."

Cowboy looked at his map. "Yep, you're right. This is the only creek for several klicks. Take it to the west 'cause it flows through a small valley between the hills."

They had walked only four hundred yards along the creek when Ty froze. He heard voices coming from around a bend in the stream. Cowboy heard them, too, and cautiously moved up. Both men exchanged glances and smiled at each other. Cowboy signaled for Goldie and Paddy to be quiet and follow closely behind.

Ten long minutes later, the four men had made it to the far bank and began crawling. The jungle was thick next to the streambed, but farther inland it thinned out, except in spots where the sun penetrated the canopy of branching hardwoods. Ty led them around a thicket of twenty-foot yellow bamboo and stopped. Twenty yards ahead he could see four Vietnamese men and one woman sitting on a log in front of a small thatch hooch. The men were making pungi stakes by whittling sections of bamboo down to razor-sharp ends. The woman was fire-hardening the ends by placing the sharpened stakes onto the coals of a small fire. It was an assembly line, and they had amassed seven large bundles of the nasty weapons. Ty noted that each of the workers kept a rifle within arm's reach.

Cowboy crawled up beside Ty and broke into a grin. "We gonna capture all of 'em," he whispered. "Cover me."

Ty began to protest when Cowboy rose to his feet and stepped from behind the bamboo. He took three steps and yelled, "DUNG LAI!"

Two of the startled men began to run, but Cowboy fired a burst over their heads, yelling, "DUNG LAI! DUNG LAI, ya dumb sonofabitches!"

The men froze in place and stared with horror at the smoking rifle. Ty and Goldie quickly got up and stood beside Cowboy, who was grinning from ear to ear. "The L-tee is gonna give us R and R for this 'un."

Suddenly a soldier appeared in the doorway of the hut and fired a long burst from his AK-47. Ty had seen the movement and was already flinging himself to the ground when the bullets cracked by his head. Goldie screamed in pain and spun around, falling into the shallow stream. Cowboy cussed as a bullet creased his hip and another shattered the plastic stock of his rifle. Ty rolled and fired at the shooter. The bullets flung the VC back like a rag doll jerked on a string. Paddy ran around the thicket to fire but pushed the magazine release instead of the safety. The magazine fell out and hit his knee. He grabbed for another but the woman lifted her weapon, shot him, and swung her rifle toward Ty. Ty ran directly toward her, spraying her and the men who were grabbing for their rifles.

The woman toppled over the log, and three of the men were lifted or knocked off their feet by the impact of bullets. The fourth ran for a stand of trees nearby but was cut down by Cowboy, who managed to fire his broken M-16. Ty was out of ammo. He was about to reach for another magazine when the woman raised up screaming hysterically and grabbed his rifle. Ty let the weapon go and hit her in the face with his fist. Her head snapped back, showering him like he'd hit a balloon filled with blood. He hit her again and felt her front teeth and bone give way with a sickening crunching, popping sound.

One of the VC Ty had shot in the legs picked up his rifle and fired wildly. The bullets stitched the log beside Ty as he threw himself over the fallen tree and grabbed the woman's AK-47. He crawled down the log a few yards before leaping up and shooting the soldier in the head with a short burst. Lowering the rifle to his hip, Ty strode forward, jerking the barrel left and right and firing a round into each body.

Cowboy grabbed Ty's shoulder as he bent over a bloody corpse to get another magazine. Ty spun around and jammed the rifle barrel under his neck. Cowboy jerked back and screamed as he shot his arms skyward, "NOOoo, IT'S ME! God, Cat, it's me."

Ty's eyes focused and he felt pain for the first time. He stared at his friend for an instant, then lowered his eyes to his bleeding hand. The woman's front teeth had laid his knuckles open to the bone.

Cowboy lowered his arms and limped toward Paddy, who was choking and writhing on the ground. He had been hit in the chest. One bullet had ricocheted off his ribs and struck his arm, but the other had passed through his chest, collapsing the right lung and lodging in his back.

The Texan lifted Paddy's shirt with shaking hands. "Jesus, Cat, come here and help me! He's got a fucking chest wound!"

Ty picked up his rifle and inserted a new magazine. He stepped over the log and walked over. He glanced at the wound and kept walking. "Get an airtight bandage on it."

He waded into the creek, where Goldie sat in the water holding a tourniquet, fashioned from his towel, around his thigh. Goldie looked up at him with a pained expression. "I never saw him . . . not till he opened up . . . it hurts, Cat, really hurts bad. Is . . . is Paddy gonna make it?"

Ty squatted and inspected the wound. "Yeah, he'll get to read the papers at home, like you will. Keep the pressure on the tourniquet, and I'll drag you out and fix another one." He took hold of Goldie's radio straps and pulled him to the bank. The bullet had passed through the thigh muscle and gone out the back of his leg, leaving a one-inch hole. Ty used his belt to replace the towel and cinched the buckle down tight before beginning to dress the wound. "You were lucky the bullet didn't hit any arteries."

Goldie leaned back on his elbows, his face contorting in pain. "It hurts real bad . . . God, why'd I stand up!"

"Cat, I'm losing him!"

Ty quickly joined Cowboy, who was trying to tie a bandage around Paddy's chest. Paddy's eyes were fluttering, and he was wheezing in tortured breaths.

Ty slapped Paddy's face and lifted his head. "Relax. You hear me? Quit trying to breathe so fast. Relax and take short breaths. You're gonna be fine, but ya can't go in shock on us. You're going home. Ya hear me? Home. Open your mouth and relax, relax . . . think about home . . . relax."

Paddy's eyes stopped fluttering and became focused. Ty patted his arm and checked the plastic wrapper that Cowboy had used to seal the wound. It was airtight and holding. The color was coming back to Paddy's cheeks.

Cowboy was shaking so badly that he couldn't kneel anymore and fell back on his buttocks. "It was stupid! I shoulda never stood without makin' sure. Jesus, Cat, I hurt Paddy and Goldie."

Ty took out his knife and unwrapped the towel from around Paddy's neck. He split the towel in two and handed half to Cowboy. "Take off your pants and wrap this around that hip wound. You're losing too much blood."

The lanky soldier looked at his blood-soaked pants and stared at Ty. "I'm responsible for all this. I fucked it up, didn't I?"

Ty wrapped the other piece of towel around his hand and looked into Cowboy's guilt-ridden face. "It's over, forget it."

Tears welled up in the Cowboy's eyes. "But it's all my . . ."

Ty tossed the radio handset to Cowboy and spoke roughly, "Forget it! Call the platoon and get 'em here. Quit worrying about the past and get these two a medevac."

Jason sat under his poncho hooch and glanced over his notes, but he wasn't really concentrating. He was looking busy while thinking. The inspection had been a disaster. The weapons looked a little better, but he could tell that the men hadn't put much effort into it. So far, nothing was like he had expected. Of the thirty-four men assigned, only twenty-six were in the field. Ramirez had reported two men on R and R, three in the hospital for malaria, two in for clap, and one in with a light shoulder wound.

He leaned back on his rucksack and wished that the Infantry School instructors had mentioned the possibility of having fewer than the forty-one men he was supposed to have. Instead, they had based all their instruction in tactics, planning, and organization on a full-strength platoon. Three-fourths of what they taught wouldn't help him. He was on his own, hoping he was doing the right thing, and right now he wasn't sure he was.

"Sir?"

Jason looked up at his first squad leader, Staff Sergeant Taloga, a barrel-chested Samoan who looked as if he had pumped weights all his life. "Sit down, Sergeant. What's up?"

Taloga knelt and lowered his head. "Sir, I just want to apologize for this afternoon and the way my men looked during the inspection. We're better than that. It's just that we've been pretty slack lately. Sir, give me another chance and we'll show you the best squad in the platoon."

Jason felt hope bubbling up in his chest. He had needed a spark, and Taloga was going to give it to him. He was about to respond when Sergeant Ramirez strolled up and smugly held out a piece of paper. "Sir, I wrote a memorandum for the record that states you held an inspection in a hostile environment, jeopardizing the safety of the men. I also wrote that you attacked me verbally in front of subordinates, displaying unprofessionalism and a lack of respect to a noncommissioned officer."

Jason sighed. He pointed to the west. "Sergeant Ramirez, I want you to personally take your memorandum of record to the company commander. You have five minutes to pack your shit and get out of my perimeter. You're relieved for negligence."

Ramirez's jaw dropped. "You can't do that! I've got ten years in service, and I know the regulations. You can't . . ."

"Four minutes and forty-five seconds," Jason said, looking at his watch. "You better get moving before the sun sets. Sergeant Taloga, you are now the platoon sergeant. Appoint a new squad leader for the first squad and come see me to plan out tomorrow's training."

"Training, sir?" asked Taloga.

"Yep, training. We're going back to basics for the next few days."

Taloga surprised him with a grin. "No sweat, sir. We need it. I'll get the squad leaders together and see what we need to work on."

Jason nodded and picked up the radio handset. He wanted to tell Captain Elliott to expect Ramirez. His self-doubt was gone. The second platoon wasn't going to be a problem child anymore.

Ty got out of the chopper and motioned for the three new replacements to follow him. He'd been sent in with the other wounded the day before and had had his hand stitched.

Sergeant Hammonds ignored the rotor's wind and strode directly toward his point man with a smile. "Good to see you, Cat. I thought you'd be gone for several weeks."

Ty was surprised to see the sergeant smiling as if he had really missed him. "They gave me a Purple Heart and I left," he said. "The REMFs were hassling me. They wanted to put me on detail."

Ignoring the much needed replacements, Hammonds threw his arm around Ty's shoulder. "Come on, I've got some hot coffee. Tell me how Cowboy is doing."

Ty looked around for Bugs, Caddy, and Silk. He sat down on the edge of the sergeant's foxhole, preparing himself for bad news. "Where are they, Sarge?"

Hammonds laughed and tossed his head toward the north. "They're on a watering party."

Ty lowered his head in relief. He didn't want to admit it, but the squad had really become family to him. Waiting in the evac hospital had been a nightmare. All he could think of was returning to his squad and getting back the feeling, getting back in the groove.

Hammonds glanced at the three bewildered replacements standing a few feet away. "You cherries report to the center of the perimeter and see the lieutenant." He looked back at Ty. "You know something? Losing you and the others upset the hell out of me. I felt like a real asshole for not getting to know you and the other guys better. I couldn't sleep worth a shit worrying about . . . well, you know what I mean. I guess I'm saying things are going to be different."

Ty smiled for the first time. "Same here."

"Cat, what the hell you doin' back?"

Ty turned as Caddy, Bugs, and Silk approached carrying filled canteens. Caddy tossed the canteens aside and hugged Ty. Bugs pumped his hand, and even Silk broke into a smile and offered to shake.

Caddy cocked an eyebrow. "How were the nurses? Pretty, big-titted, round-assed, willing, what?"

Ty frowned. "The only ones I saw were officers, and they were bitches to the max."

"Damn, too bad. How's Cowboy?"

"He'll be back in a couple of weeks. Paddy and Goldie were sent to Japan. They'll be goin' home."

Bugs looked at Ty's hand. "You get your purple?"

"Yep, a fat colonel gave it to me this morning."

"Cool man, you can be a postman now."

"What da fuck you talkin' about, postman? You crazy as Cat," Silk said.

"Back off, Silk. I know what I'm talkin' about, man. You get ten points on a civil service test for being in the Army. You get another ten for being a veteran, and another ten if you get the purple. Cat's got thirty points going in. He's got a postman job sewed up.''

Silk eyed Bugs. "Really, no bullshit, man? That's cool. They give points for being a bad-assed dock worker, man? How about ten inches of pile-drivin' dick? Man, if they do, I be the fuckin' general of da post office.''

Ty smiled and felt at home as he backed up unnoticed and walked to the hill's crest.

Jason shook his head and yelled, "Cease fire! I don't want anybody firing automatic. I want to see if you can hit the target with well-placed single shots.''

Private Fontaine rose up from his prone firing position. "Goddamn, sir, put a dink out there instead of a lousy C-ration can, and I'll blow his head fuckin' off for you.''

The other members of the platoon laughed. Jason also smiled—he was about to make his point. "Okay, Fontaine, show us your stuff. Hit the can.''

The soldier knelt and took aim. The small can was twenty-five yards away on a rice paddy dike. He fired. The bullet kicked up a spout of water a few inches to the right of the can. The men's laughter made him angry. His second shot hit even lower.

Jason held up his hands, quieting the laughs and snide remarks. "What you've seen is what most of you do when you shoot. You'll be close, but you won't hit the can. Fontaine, what is the zero of your weapon?''

"Zero? Aw hell, sir, that's basic training shit. I don't know.''

Jason motioned Fontaine to join the others. "I'm going to tell you men the truth. I don't know a damn thing about these new M-16s. I fired an M-14 in basic and never qualified on the 16. This is for my benefit and probably just a refresher for you all. Bear with me. We're going to put some C-ration boxes out twenty-five meters and zero all our weapons. Remember to zero. Shoot three times trying to keep a close grouping. If you're off target, move the windage and elevation knobs the required number of clicks to bring the shot group into the center of the target. I want every man to know the number of clicks it takes to find your zero and write it on his helmet cover so he won't forget it. If we miss a can at twenty-five meters by three inches, we'll miss a man at fifty yards by a foot. First squad, you put up the targets.''

Sergeant Taloga stepped up to him as the men were loading their magazines. "I saw you messin' with Fontaine's rifle this morning

when he was still sleeping. You didn't happen to add a few clicks
of elevation to his sights, did you, sir?''

Jason smiled. "Prior planning can prevent or help poor performance. I needed him to miss.''

Taloga grinned. "You don't play fair, do you?''

Jason arched an eyebrow. "Nope.''

25

Ty smelled it first, the dusty smell of grain. The light, warm
wind carried the distinctive odor like a warning. Crouching down,
he looked left, then right, and froze. He knew he was dead if there
was a soldier at the other end of the green tunnel. He lifted his eyes
only a fraction and gasped. An orange tongue from the end of a
rifle leaped directly toward him. The AK bullet passed a fraction
beneath his ear and hit the rim of his helmet, knocking the steel
pot from his head. He reeled backward and frantically clawed the
ground for cover as a second bullet thudded into the ground beside
his boot. Caddy didn't see the muzzle flashes of the sniper but fired
a round in the direction of the shots.

Ty crawled toward Caddy and leaped behind a large above-ground
root just as the trail behind him lifted and disappeared in a brown-
black cloud. The shattering explosion knocked him over, and he
cried out from the intense pain in his eyes and ears.

Caddy was thrown to the ground by the blast. He picked himself
up and ran into the debris cloud as Hammonds and Bugs sprayed
the sides of the trail with automatic fire. He grabbed Ty's collar and
dragged him up the trail away from the choking dust and black
smoke.

Ty lay stunned, his head feeling as if it were going to explode.
He could see, but his eyes stung as if they were sunburned and
covered with gritty sand. Hammonds was apparently talking to

him. He could see the man's mouth moving, but he could hear nothing but a steady ringing.

Hammonds screamed again. "MEDIIIIC! Goddamn it, Doc, come on! MEDIIIC!"

Doc Weaver ran down the narrow trail and slid in beside Ty like he was sliding in to home. He took one look at his face and pulled out a canteen.

Out of breath from running up the trail, Lieutenant Jenkins knelt beside Hammonds. "What's the situation?"

Hammonds motioned Caddy to him. "What the fuck happened?"

"I saw Cat get down and then heard an AK open up," Caddy said excitedly. "Cat jumped back and crawled to me, and the trail behind him went up like . . ."

Ty sat up and squinted. The ringing in his ears was almost gone but was being replaced by a strange crackling noise. He looked around and realized he must have passed out.

Doc Weaver knelt in front of him and smiled. "How's the head?"

Ty nodded and tried to stand up, but he suddenly felt woozy. Weaver helped him to sit back down. "Take it easy, you passed out on me. You were a little too close to the 105 round they had rigged to blow us all away. You'd been any closer, your eyeballs would have popped out like marbles." Weaver motioned at the thatch huts beside them. "Just twenty yards behind the hooches is the trail we were on. Looks like you led us into a VC rice-storage area. The L-tee called the CO, and he flew in a little while ago. He's tickled pink and is promising us all an in-country R and R."

Ty tried to talk, but he felt as if a dentist had gone wild with novocaine inside his mouth. Weaver turned him around and propped him up so he could see the fire. The squads had stripped to the waist and were throwing bags of rice on top of a raging bonfire that sent up a black cloud through the single canopy. Standing beside sacks of rice was Jenkins and the company commander, who was smiling like a Cheshire cat.

Weaver clicked his tongue and picked up his aid bag. "We didn't find a single dink or spider hole. They must have left one man to fire you up and trigger the booby trap. He's halfway to Hanoi by now thinking he blew you to kingdom come."

Ty felt a hot wave run up his back. His stomach knotted into a ball, and he broke into a sweat. "Na . . . na, naaaaOO!" He tried to get up.

"What's wrong?" Weaver said, helping Ty to his feet.

Ty struggled and looked for his rifle. "Tha . . . they're . . . they're here!"

Weaver's eyes widened in disbelief. "Oh, shit. L-TEE!"

The company commander threw up his hands in exasperation. "The battalion commander is flying in here in five minutes, and you want me to tell him not to land? You didn't tell *me* not to land. What the hell is going on?"

Lieutenant Jenkins ignored him and yelled toward the second squad, "MOVE IT! GET ON LINE!" He spun around. "Sir, one of my men says there are dinks here. We're going to conduct another search and see if we can find their holes. Until we do, this area isn't safe."

The captain smirked. "One of your men tells you he *thinks* there are dinks under us, and you stop the whole operation? Shit, Jenkins, we've been here for an hour and haven't seen a damn thing."

Jenkins was tired of trying to explain and spoke over his shoulder as he strode toward Doc Weaver. "Sir, when Cat Man says they're here, they're here."

Weaver stood up as the lieutenant and captain approached. "Sir, Cat is back on his feet. He and the first squad are heading for the trail. Cat said to tell you he's gonna check out a spider hole"

Jenkins immediately broke into a run toward the trail.

Hammonds took one peek and jerked back. "I'll go, you cover me."

Ty checked his magazine and lay down. "No, he's mine."

"You sure? Are you feeling all right?"

Ty nodded and began crawling down the trail.

Hammonds quickly motioned the squad up and followed his point man. Ty stopped just short of where his helmet had been shot off and cautiously peered into the green tunnel. The camouflaged cover was down. Without hesitation he continued crawling. Hammonds positioned himself behind Ty to cover him and kept his finger on the trigger. The firing lane was invisible when walking by, but when on the ground it was like a miniature highway. The VC had cut and cleared only the lower branches and ferns, making a small firing tunnel. Their tactic was to let several men pass then shoot the third or fourth man in the legs. The sniper would usually wait until another soldier tried to assist his wounded friend and shoot him, too, then finish both off with head shots.

Crawling closer, Ty felt strangely light and powerful. He knew the VC soldier; he had seen his eyes in that split second before the soldier panicked and jerked the trigger. Ty had caught him day-dreaming, maybe thinking about home or his girl. The soldier was his age, with a new haircut cropped on the sides—not a typical VC peasant or farmer. He was hardcore cadre. His eyes had been looking directly at Ty, but without comprehension until they suddenly focused, showing fear just before jerking the trigger. The war had been reduced to a battle between just two men, the way Ty wanted it. The better man would survive. The young enemy soldier had his chance but had shown weakness. He'd lost his spirit to Ty. Confidently, Ty inched closer.

Hammonds ignored the beads of sweat running down his face as he kept his rifle pointed just over Ty's bare head. Lieutenant Jenkins and the captain had crawled up behind him, but he didn't dare to look at them.

Ty saw the faint outline of the larger than usual cover and slowly withdrew his knife. He cautiously rose to his knees and readied the rifle in his right hand. With his left hand, he began to gently work the knife into the hairline crack of the cover. He carefully pushed through the soil and felt the knife pierce wood. He pushed a bit farther to get a better bite and stopped. Sweat stung his eyes, but he ignored it as he took a breath and tightened his grip on the knife handle. With a lunge, he embedded the blade deeper and pulled the cover up.

The startled soldier sitting on the firing step looked up and instinctively raised his AK but was blinded by the sudden light. Ty had his weapon pointing at the man's head but lowered the barrel at the last instant, firing a single shot into the Vietnamese's shoulder. The small soldier was slammed against the far wall from the impact and screamed in pain from powder burns. Jumping into the large hole, Ty immediately saw the tunnel entrance and extended pistol. He ducked and fired a long burst at the second soldier, who was squatting in the darkness of the tunnel.

Hammonds heard the rattle of the M-16 and the pop of a smaller caliber weapon. He jumped up and crashed through the thornbushes to the edge of the large spider hole. He lowered his rifle but instantly jerked the barrel up. Below him, Ty was dragging a torn body into the sunlight. Another VC with a shoulder wound was sitting against the earthen wall, clutching his stomach with bloody hands.

Ty looked up and his eyes widened. "Get down!"

Hammonds flung himself to the side of the hole and yelled at the men behind him, "Spider hole with a tunnel! They could pop up anywhere!"

Ty gagged. The smell of the blood, defecation, and the sweet musty odor of the men's uniforms was overwhelming. He'd smelled that odor before and it sickened him. The countless fires the Vietcong had squatted beside permeated their bodies and uniforms with the smoky, fishy smell. The second soldier had been stitched from groin to head with ten rounds. His watery bowel excretion stained through his pants with his blood. Ty looked at the torn corpse at his knees and threw up. The top half of the man's head was gone, and his brains were oozing out over what was left of his face. Ty struggled in the tight confines to stand up and vomited again.

Hammonds looked into the hole and jerked his head back, overcome with the stench of death and bile. "Jesus, Cat, get out of there!"

Ty leaned against the earth wall and stared into the eyes of the man he'd purposely not killed. The soldier was dying anyway. His comrade in the tunnel had gotten one shot off, missing Ty but hitting the young man in the stomach. The mortally wounded soldier returned Ty's stare as if he recognized him and tried to speak. Ty knelt in the filth and took his hand. He knew him. He knew the fear he had felt and the pain. He knew he was a soldier like himself and didn't want to die in a stinking hole.

Ty started to pick him up when he heard the staccato of gunfire in the distance. The soldier seemed to smile and closed his eyes. Ty heard men screaming for the medic as the man's body went limp and fell over into the coagulated blood and vomit.

"Get out of there, Cat. Third squad found another position and has a man wounded," Jenkins yelled.

Ty recognized his voice and stood up. "Sir, it looks like this tunnel goes back a helluva long ways. I'd bet this place is honeycombed with them, and they go down to several levels. We're going to need more men and the engineers to get them out."

He began to climb out but remembered the pistol. He held his breath and squatted down. Grasping the blood-covered weapon, he began to leave but noticed the soldier's uniform for the first time. "Sir, one of these dinks isn't VC. I think he's NVA."

Jenkins quickly crawled to the edge of the hole and peered in. "God almighty . . . are you all ri . . ." He jerked back, gagging.

The captain had heard Ty say "NVA" and yelled from the trail, "Jenkins, get the body and pull your men back! I'm going to call for more support!"

Jenkins shook his head to clear his senses and steeled himself. "Cat, I'm coming down to help you."

* * *

Jason pushed back the ferns and looked over his objective. Two hundred yards away across dried paddy fields was a small hill covered with grass mounds. It was the cemetery for the village only fifty yards behind him. The burial mounds looked like they had been placed on the hill with a giant ice cream scoop.

He backed up and exchanged worried glances with his RTO, Specialist Fourth Class Bagley. The freckle-faced radioman knew they couldn't use artillery because of the closeness of the village. Bagley shook his head. "Why is it the ol' man always wants us to do the company's dirty work?"

"'Cause we're the best," Jason said, motioning the squad leaders to him.

Sergeant Taloga and the others knelt in front of Jason, who had taken out his map. "The CO has ordered us to check out the cemetery. One of the villagers reported seeing three VC on the hilltop yesterday, and they were digging into one of the mounds. I'll take the first squad; we'll go up the hill while the rest of you cover from the tree line. Make damn sure the machine guns keep the hill covered as we start up. Any questions?"

Taloga leaned back with a frown. "Sir, you ain't got no business going with the first squad. We're gettin' kinda of used to you."

Jason smiled and stood up. "This is what I get paid for."

Jason looked at his watch and nodded for Sergeant Redford to move out. The squad of eight men rose up and stepped out of the tree line. Jason positioned himself in the center of the formation and set his eyes on the hill.

The small group of men crossed the dried, cracked paddy fields without incident. Jason took his first normal breath on reaching the base of the hill and reached for his canteen. He felt incredibly thirsty. Suddenly, the silence was broken: CRACKCRACK-CRACK, CRACKCRACK.

Simon, the PFC beside Jason, doubled over and fell backward. Shot in the lower abdomen, he sat looking at his wound, not saying a word, as the rest of the men fell to the ground and sought cover.

Taloga and the others saw the muzzle flash and opened up. The two M-60 machine guns rattled and threw out a continuous stream of red tracers toward a mound at the crest of the hill.

Jason forced himself to his feet and tried to yell for the squad to follow him up the slope, but his words were lost in the din of chattering weapons. He began running up the steep incline, hoping the squad would follow and knowing the protective covering fire wouldn't last forever. His legs felt like rubber and his lungs screamed for oxygen as he scrambled up the barren slope on all fours. The sound of the platoon's bullets passing overhead became louder and louder, as if he were approaching a beehive. Twenty feet directly ahead stood a large burial mound, which the machinegun tracers were striking. He fell to the ground and pulled out a grenade. He yanked out the pin and tossed it over the mound just as the supporting fire ceased. The ensuing silence racked his nerves. He could hear his heart pounding and the sound of the grenade hitting the dirt. Sergeant Redford began to run past and Jason tackled him. Both men tumbled down the slope, as the grenade detonated in a vehement blast.

Jason jumped to his feet and ran up the sandy slope again, with Redford following, screaming obscenities at him.

Taloga stood up on seeing his platoon leader disappear behind the mound. He unconsciously cringed and waited for the sound of AK fire.

Jason sat down on the side of the mound feeling dizzy. He tried to spit out the white, sticky substance from his mouth but his mouth was too dry.

Redford peered into the hole in the mound and fell to his knees. "How fuckin' dumb can you get?" he said.

Jason pulled out his canteen and swished out his mouth as the rest of the squad assembled around the mound and peered into the death trap. Two VC had dug a cave into the mound and made a small bunker supported by American ammo crates. They had dug out too much of the protective dirt, and the M-60 bullets had penetrated the position, riddling their bodies.

He stood and spoke tiredly. "Carter, you and Smitty pull out the bodies and check out the bunker. Report what you find to me. I'm going down and check on Simon."

Redford sheepishly looked up as he passed. "Sorry, for yellin'. I didn't see you throw the grenade."

Jason nodded and quickened his stride.

Sergeant Taloga and the medic tried to pull Simon's hands away from the wound, but it was impossible. Simon was in shock and looked and felt like a concrete statue. He was still seated and clutching his abdomen. His expression was frozen in horror.

Jason knelt in front of him as the medic tried to put an IV into the young soldier's arm. "Simon, you have to let us see the wound so we can bandage it." Simon didn't respond, and Jason tried to move one of his hands. The hand didn't feel human. Simon was like a man who was thawing out after being buried in ice for a decade. He was shaking but rock hard. "What can we do, Doc?" Jason asked in desperation.

Doc Porter gave up trying to put the needle in Simon's arm and moved to his leg. "Pray the damn chopper gets here quick."

The CO sat down by Lieutenant Jenkins and took off his helmet. "Jenkins, I have to apologize. The engineer tunnel-rat team has just reported finding a huge underground storage area, a small hospital, and a classroom of some kind. We're sitting on top of a VC base camp. Looks like you found them before they could get their rice underground. The old man sent out an interpreter with the dog team, and he's looked over the papers you found on the NVA soldier. The dead NVA was a logistics captain assigned to the VC as an adviser. The dog team found two more entrances four hundred meters to the east and reported a bunch of tracks. Looks like whoever was here in the tunnel complex escaped several hours ago while we were waiting on the engineers. I called your platoon up because the company is being lifted out by chopper in a hour and returning to base camp. I want your men to go out first—they deserve it for the good job. Start organizing for the lift and . . ."

A muffled explosion to the east stopped him in midsentence. He put his helmet on and stood up. "What now, for Christ sake?"

The radio buzzed with static and an excited voice spoke in a rush. "Talon six, this is three six. Engineers and dog handler hit a booby trap. Need additional medic ASAP, over."

The captain spoke calmly into the handset. "Roger, three six, medic en route and will call dust off for you. Keep me informed, out." He lowered the handset and spoke quickly to Jenkins. "Send a squad with your medic to the Third Platoon and help them out. I'm going back to my RTO and call the old man."

Jenkins turned around and yelled, "Doc, first squad, saddle up!"

The third platoon lieutenant moved his people back and approached the growling German shepherd. "Nobody is going to hurt you." The dog backed up and bared its teeth. The officer squatted, keeping his eye on the animal, and checked the neck pulse of the prone soldier. He knew the man was dead by the gapping hole in his back, but he wanted to make sure before having to destroy the tan and black shepherd. There was no pulse.

He stood and backed up to his platoon sergeant. "He's dead. Do we have to do this?"

The young sergeant kept his eye on the dog. "Yes, sir, it's policy. The dog ain't gonna let none of us move the handler without taking one of our arms off. He's already bit two of the men. We gotta kill the mean sonofabitch before he puts one of us in the hospital."

The lieutenant turned his back to the dog and nodded toward the sergeant, who raised his M-16.

"Hold it!"

The sergeant lowered his rifle and turned around. Ten steps in front of him stood a black-haired soldier with a purple scar running down his tanned cheek. He was holding an M-16, and strapped around his waist like a gunfighter was a brown leather NVA belt and holster. The shiny belt buckle, with its raised red star, reflected the sun's rays like a mirror.

"Who the hell are you?" the sergeant blurted.

Ty ignored him and turned to the lieutenant. "I'm a handler. I'll take care of the dog. It'll take a few minutes, and I need your people to back off a ways."

Glad to be relieved of the gruesome duty, the officer motioned to the wounded engineers lying a few feet behind them. "Move those men to the LZ."

Ty sat down by the handler's body and pulled the leash and muzzle from his belt. Burned into the leash was the name "Rex." The dog snarled and lunged forward, nipping at Ty's hand. Ty sat perfectly still, not showing fear, and stared into the shepherd's eyes. "Easy, Rexy, easy. It's just you and me, buddy." He slowly moved his hand out and spoke softly. "Take your time and smell me. You're confused, and you don't have a friend in the world anymore, but it's all right. This ol' coon dog understands."

Hammonds and Caddy approached and stopped in their tracks as Ty signalled them to freeze. He spoke as if talking to the dog. "Y'all back off and let me see if I can get Rex here to let us take the body. I'll be along in a while."

"We can't leave you alone out here. Shoot the mutt and let's go," Hammonds said impatiently.

Ty kept his even tone. "Nobody is killin' the dog. Leave me alone. I'll holler when I need you." He took out his canteen and poured water into his hand. "Come on. I know you're thirsty. Just relax and come here."

Rex backed up snarling and paced back and forth in a small circle, keeping his eyes on the strange-smelling man.

Hammonds tapped Caddy's shoulder and began walking away. "Come on, we've got to tell the L-tee what's holdin' us up."

Caddy sat down. "Not me. Somebody has got to stay with him. You go on."

"Not you, too? Shit, it's just a goddamn dog, for Christ sake. Come on!"

Caddy shook his head. "I'm covering Cat. Go on."

Hammonds sighed and sat down. "I guess we'll all get blown away together. Shit!"

Sergeant Taloga positioned the men into seven-man teams for the helicopter extraction and walked back to Jason, who was sitting under a banana tree. "Sir, we're all set. Any word on when the birds are due in?"

Jason stared into the distance. He was lost in thought about the man he had watched die of shock. Taloga motioned for Bagley to take a walk, then took off his helmet and sat down on top of it.

"Sir? . . . Sir!"

Jason broke from his stare and looked at Taloga. "Are the men ready?"

Taloga's eyes narrowed. "Yes, sir, they are, but you're not. Lieutenant Johnson, you're gonna have to snap out of it. You're the best damn officer I've ever worked with. You've turned this platoon around in just three and a half weeks, but you're fuckin' up with this guilt thing about Simon. L-tee, you are going to lose men. This is a fuckin' war. Men die and get hurt. Face it and start leading this platoon again . . . we need you. You can't be worrying about the past. Fuck the past. It's history. You got thirty men who need you *now.*"

Jason's shoulders sagged. "He shouldn't have died like that."

"Nobody should die, but they do. And they'll keep on dying because that's the way it is. You're good, L-tee, but you're not that good; you'll never save all of them. All you can do is what you've been doing, making them better soldiers and hoping they don't die because of stupid mistakes or poor judgment. That action on Cemetery Hill was by the book. It was executed perfectly. You did everything right. Shit, the company commander wants to put you in for a Bronze Star. But we lost a man, one man, and you turn to shit on me. Snap out of it, L-tee, or these men you've worked so hard with are going to lose their confidence in you. They might piss and moan about the training and constant questions you ask, but they respect you because they know you care enough to make them better. You've got yourself a platoon of men who believe they have a leader. Don't fuck it up now."

Jason lowered his head and stood up slowly. The image of Simon's face faded away and was replaced by the faces of the men waiting for the choppers. He looked at Taloga and said softly,

"Thanks." He turned and yelled, "Bagley! Call up and see when the birds are coming in! Redford! I still need the list of shit you found in the bunker for the ol' man. You've got three minutes to give it me!"

Taloga smiled and turned around, hearing the distant whopping sound of the incoming Slicks.

Hammonds and Caddy strained with the weight of the poncho-covered body as they approached the LZ. Lieutenant Jenkins sighed with relief on seeing them. "About damn time. Where's Cat?"

The two men set the body down, and Hammonds gestured behind him. "He's coming, sir."

The captain walked up behind Jenkins. "I want to meet this 'Cat' fellow and personally thank him for . . . what the hell is that?"

Jenkins glanced over his shoulder at the approaching soldier and dog. "You can meet him right now; that's him."

The captain stiffened at the sight of the young soldier straining to hold the muzzled German shepherd. "Ah . . . that's okay, I'll meet him later. Make sure he turns in that pistol he's wearing. It's unauthorized. And find him a helmet."

Jenkins smiled to himself. "Yes, sir. I'll take care of it."

Sergeant Hammonds gathered his squad next to the LZ and lay back on his rucksack. "I just got briefed from the L-tee. The entire company is being lifted out in a few minutes, and we're going back to base camp for a five-day stand-down. We'll all be drinking cold beer tonight."

Silk, Bugs, and Caddy all broke into big smiles. Hammonds smiled, saving the best for last. "The L-tee also said he got word that Cowboy is in the rear waiting for us. He'll be linking up as soon as we get off the birds."

The smiles became bigger, and Silk turned around and yelled at Ty, who was keeping the dog away from the commotion. "Ya hear that, Cat? Cowboy is back, man. He gonna have us some stories about da nurse holes, man."

A captain whom Hammonds didn't recognize walked up. "Which one of you men has the K-54 pistol captured this afternoon?"

Hammonds stood up and eyed the pressed jungle fatigues and spit-shined jungle boots the officer wore. "Beggin' your pardon, sir, but who are you?"

The captain stiffened. "I'm the assistant battalion S-2, intelligence officer. The pistol was reported by the interpreter we sent out, but it wasn't with the effects of the deceased. I want the pistol. Who has it?''

Hammonds cocked an eyebrow. '''Deceased'?'' Hammonds said. ''Oh, you must mean the fucker who tried to kill us. Sir, the reason we don't send in war trophies to the S-2 is you people never give them back. Somehow, they're always conveniently lost. I gave all the necessary information to our lieutenant. It was a Chinese 7.62 standard-issue K-54 with holster.''

The captain's face turned red. ''Sergeant, you are obstructing the intelligence effort of this battalion. I want the pistol turned over to me right now, or I will speak to your company commander.''

Hammonds heard the approaching helicopters. ''Saddle up, First.'' He looked at the officer as he hefted his heavy rucksack to his back. ''Sir, you'll find the company commander over there by the hooches. I'm sure he'll appreciate your 'intelligence effort,' since you people said there were only VC tax collectors in the area and didn't mention booby traps, spider holes, or hardcore VC. Yes, sir, I'm sure the ol' man will appreciate your 'effort' just about as much as me and my squad do.''

The captain angrily responded, but the first helicopter settling to the ground drowned out his words. Hammonds ignored him and ran to the first chopper with the squad. Ty bumped into the intelligence officer as he labored under the weight of carrying the dog in his arms. The captain caught his balance and saw the pistol strapped to Ty's waist. He yelled for him to stop, but Ty hopped on the Huey. The captain was still yelling as the bird lifted off with the smiling men of first squad waving good-bye with their middle fingers.

Jason left the officer's tent and walked down the dusty road toward the enlisted area. It seemed strange to be away from his men. In the field he was with them twenty-four hours a day, but back in civilization, the traditional separation of officers and enlisted ranks prevailed. It was a strange war. The rear area was nothing more than an island surrounded by barbed wire and bunkers. The only ground that was secured and safe was the ground you stood on. Base camp was a place to drink a beer or Coke, buy a few things from the PX, and sleep without having to rotate on guard or radio watch. It was also a place where the field soldiers had to get haircuts, shine their boots, and salute. The secret was to stay away from sergeant majors and everyone else who wore starched fatigues and spit-shined boots. For some reason, they didn't seem to know a war was going on and insisted on appearance standards that would make more sense at Fort Benning.

He stopped on a slight rise overlooking the platoon tents. His men were outside filling sandbags from a huge pile of dirt. He saw Taloga supervising the loading of the green bags onto a truck and yelled to him.

The big Samoan jogged up the rise and saluted smartly. "Yes, sir."

"What the hell y'all doin'? You're supposed to be taking it easy."

Taloga relaxed and shrugged his shoulders. "Sir, the Sergeant Major said we had to fill six hundred sandbags and haul them to the officers' area before we could kick back."

Jason's jaw muscles tensed. "Stop right now and get our men to the shower point and club. We came here for stand down, not for filling sandbags."

"Sir, this is NCO business and . . ."

"The hell it is! It's my platoon and this is *my* business. Sergeant Major doesn't run this platoon. Get the platoon moving, *now*!"

Taloga turned away but immediately spun around again and saluted. "Yes, sir."

Jason noticed his smile and returned a quick salute.

Taloga jogged down the rise yelling, "The L-tee wants us at the shower point and then to the club in less than thirty minutes. MOVE IT!"

The men hooted and hollered as they threw down their shovels and sandbags, and ran to the tents for their towels. Jason smiled and began to walk back up the road but saw the starched fatigues of the thin sergeant major, who was striding directly toward him. He squared his shoulders.

The sergeant saluted offhandedly, as if he had more important things to do. "Lieutenant, what the hell you think you're doing?"

Jason returned a perfect salute. "I don't *think*, I *know* what I'm doing, and that is, I ordered my men to the shower point."

The senior sergeant rolled his eyes as if he were dealing with a stubborn child. "Lieutenant, I'm Sergeant Major Littlejol, the camp sergeant major. You just fucked up. I'm going to have to get those men back and fill the sandbags. Why don't you go back to officer country and let me . . ."

Jason raised his hand. "No, Sergeant Major Littlejol, *you* fucked up. Those men belong to me. Unless you have a written statement from my company commander or he tells me, you aren't saying shit to my people. This conversation has ended. Good evening."

Littlejol's face contorted and turned beet red. Jason started up the road, his mind already on other matters. He had heard from other officers that the entire brigade had come in for the stand-down, and he was eager to find Ty.

Littlejol turned and spoke with disdain. "You'll hear about this, Lieutenant!"

Jason didn't look back.

Silk glanced up from the letter he'd received and gave the rest of the squad a quick warning. "Trouble, dudes."

Hammonds stood up from his cot and blocked the lieutenant's path. "Sir, can I help you?"

The big blond officer smiled. "Sure can. I'm looking for PFC Nance. A sergeant two tents up said I'd find him here."

Hammonds eyed the officer with suspicion. "Are you from Battalion S-2?"

Jason frowned. "Hell no. I'm from Second Batt. Ty . . . PFC Nance is my brother."

Hammonds grinned and put out his hand. "Sorry about that, sir. Good to meet you. We've been looking out for S-2 REMFs hassling the Cat. Cat said he had a brother over here, but I didn't know you were in the Herd."

Silk stood up. "Dig it, dudes. The L-tee is the Cat's bro."

Jason cocked his head. "Cat?"

Silk strode up with Caddy, Bugs, and Cowboy. "Yes, sir. The Cat is a baaad muthafucker. He deals big time with da Charles. He's the baddest point in the Fourth Batt. He done . . ."

Jason followed Bugs to the perimeter after hearing all about Ty's exploits. They stopped behind a bunker.

Bugs pointed. "Cat is in there. He's kinda keepin' a low profile. S-2 has been looking for him. Hey, Cat, I got a visitor for ya!"

Jason put out his hand to Bugs. "Thanks for bringing me here, I . . ." He stopped in midsentence as Ty emerged from the bunker. My God, Jason thought, he wasn't nineteen anymore. He looked ten years older, and every inch of him was hardened combat vet-eran. His face showed the effects of the field by its leanness and dark tan. The sweat-stained, dirty uniform was faded and his boots were scuffed white. The NVA pistol belt strapped around his waist rode low on his right hip, as if he were looking for trouble. The men in the squad were right. The man before him wasn't Ty—he was the Cat.

Ty felt weak-kneed as a flood of memories and emotions swept through him. He had put away all the thoughts of home and family for another time and wasn't prepared. A thousand pictures of himself and his brother passed through his brain and stopped at the one when they were on Red Hill so long ago in another lifetime. He brought up his hand in a salute. "I never saluted a Red Hill Paratrooper before."

Jason started to raise his hand in a salute but got only halfway before reaching out and embracing his brother. Then he stepped back. "Damn, if you don't look good. C-rations do right by you."

"Ya lookin' good yourself," Ty said, thumping Jason's chest. "A little skinny maybe, but ya look like a real field soldier. When did ya get here?"

Jason looked at his watch and patted Ty's leg. "I guess I'd better get back. We've been jaw-jackin' for over an hour. I'll come by and see you tomorrow."

Ty rose up and took his brother's hand, pulling him to his feet. "Jay, it's really good seeing you. We're going to be here five days, so let's make use of the time. I wanna know more about home and how the hill is lookin'."

Jason was about to speak when Caddy jogged up. "Excuse me, sir, but all hell is breaking loose. We just got word to pack up a basic load and get ready to move. It looks like tomorrow the whole brigade is flying in to Pleiku. Word is we're going to join the Fourth Division for an operation in the Ia Drang valley."

"I gotta get to my platoon," Jason said. He put his arm around Ty and gave him a quick hug. "You take it easy out there and be careful. Mom wants us Red Hill Paratroopers to make it back in one piece. She told me to tell ya she loves ya . . . and so do I. Good-bye, brother."

Ty smiled and patted his brother's back as he began to walk away. "Us paratroopers only say, 'I'll see ya.' "

Jason grinned as he looked over his shoulder. "I'll see ya, Cat."

"Love ya, big brother," Ty said. "Keep your ass down."

26

The C-130's ramp lowered, exposing the rugged mountains of the Central Highlands and a huge lake with a muddy island in its center. Sergeant Hammonds stood and hefted his rucksack. "This is it. Let's go, First."

Bugs took one look at the flooded landscape and shook his head dejectedly. "I already hate this place. What's the name of it again?"

"Dak To," said Hammonds, as he walked down the ramp into an inch of water covering the tarmac.

A sergeant stood on the runway, pointing across the lake toward a small colllection of buildings on high ground. "You people head straight across to the base camp. Watch your step. There are some deep holes."

Hammonds saw a long line of men already crossing the flooded ground and stepped off the tarmac into six inches of muddy water. "Come on. It only looks deep."

Silk balked at the edge of the runway. "I ain't in the damn Navy! Shit, Sarge, I thought we was gonna be in the mountains. This fuckin' place looks like da delta."

"Move your ass. You're holdin' up the rest of the platoon," Hammonds barked. He lifted his rifle and pointed. "Seventeen klicks to the west is Cambodia and Laos. The mountains all around us are supposed to be crawling with NVA."

Silk waded into the water and snickered. "Yeah, sure man, just like the Ia Drang valley was supposed to have 'em. Man, we humped for almost a month and only seen blisters and leeches. All I see here is water and straight-up humpin'. This mutha sucks, man."

Cowboy looked around at the mountains covered with rain forest. "Cat, this place is bad news. I hope to hell them NVAs ain't holed up in them hills, or we gonna be in big-time trouble."

Ty nodded in agreement. The airfield and Dak To Special Forces

Camp sat in a river valley surrounded by mountains. The monsoon rains had flooded the river and all the low-lying areas. Any entrenched NVA in the mountains would enjoy all the advantages. They would know the terrain and could pick the ground of their choosing to defend.

He looked up at the circling C-130s. Jason was in one of those planes. The Second and Fourth battalions of the brigade were taking part in Operation Greeley, checking out reports of increased enemy activity in the area. His stomach tightened with worry. He had thought about Jason constantly since last seeing him.

Caddy followed Ty and glanced behind to check on the three new men. "Come on, cherries, I told you all to stay close to Cat and me. Catch up." He increased his pace and joined Ty. "One good thing—at least getting these cherries almost brings us up to strength."

Ty turned and looked at the bewildered faces of the replacements. It was strange but he wasn't worried about them, as he was his brother. In fact, he wasn't worried about anybody in the squad. He knew they wouldn't walk into anything they couldn't handle. He, the Cat, would make sure of it. He was good and felt completely confident. No NVA could beat him, regardless of the terrain. He didn't worry about himself or his squad, but Jason was different. Jason was part of home, and he was alone. He was probably a good leader and soldier, but he didn't understand. He didn't know how to become the buffalo.

Jason looked up at the threatening sky. More misery was on the way. He stood beside a bunker overlooking the swollen Poko River. The company had flown in an hour before, just behind the Fourth Battalion. His platoon had been ordered to the southern sector of the Dak To airfield perimeter to guard against attack. Bagley had summed up their situation accurately when he said, "The only thing that can attack us across that river is the U.S. Navy."

He walked into the bunker where his squad leaders sat around a small fire, trying to dry out their boots. "Looks like it's going to rain some more," he said. "I don't know how long we're going to be here, but let's get as comfortable as we can while we have the chance. I want squad positions instead of fire teams so we can get maximum rest. We don't have a threat, so there's no use pretending there is. Get back to the squads and move them into the bunkers and report to Taloga when you're done. I'm going to the company CP and see if I can find out what we're going to be doing the next couple of days."

Sergeant Redford smiled as he stood up, "L-tee, don't be volunteering us for anything. We'd just as soon stay right here for the rest of the war, protecting the fishes."

Jason chuckled. He felt the same way. For the past twenty days, his men had humped everyday in the Ia Drang valley, searching for an enemy that never materialized, although the intelligence reports kept saying they were there.

Jason tossed his rucksack in the corner. "Don't worry, I'll keep my mouth shut. You all just keep your eyes out for the North Vietnam Navy while I'm gone."

He was halfway to the command post when the monsoon storm unleashed its torrent. In half a second, he was soaked to the skin. Never had he seen such rain. He stopped, unable to see where he was going. It was as if a huge bucket of water were being poured over him. The rain beat against his helmet. He couldn't see, hear, smell, or feel anything but the pounding water.

A dark object approached, and he heard a muffled voice. A man's face broke through the curtain of rain only inches from his nose. "Follow me."

Jason stayed on the soldier's heels, barely able to make out his form as he tried to keep up. Finally, he saw the tent and ran the last five meters.

Captain Elliott rose from a folding chair sunk in six inches of mud and half-yelled over the sound of the beating rain. "I saw you coming just before it hit. I took an azimuth with my compass and sent out the RTO to fetch you. Monsoon rains are something, aren't they?"

Jason took off his helmet and shouted back, "How long does it last?"

"Sometimes days," Elliott said. He looked out the tent flap as if in a trance.

They had to wait fifteen minutes before the rain let up enough for the other platoon leaders to find the CP. When they were assembled, Elliott spread a map over his lap and began his briefing. "The Second Battalion got lucky. We're not going to be moving very far. Tomorrow we'll be choppered into the hills due south of us to look for mortar and rocket positions the gooks have been using to shoot at the airfield. We're only going out six to eight klicks and landing on a small hilltop. From there we hump up into the higher mountains. We'll be leaving at zero nine hundred tomorrow morning, if this damn weather clears up. Any questions?"

Jason raised a wrinkled finger. "Sir, if NVA are in the mountains, isn't it kinda dangerous moving in company size?"

"It's not a problem. The intelligence people haven't confirmed anything that looks big. Mostly small stuff. The Mohawk snooper missions have picked up a little bit of activity on the hilltops and ridges, and they just want us to see what's up there. If we hit something, we'll pull back and call in arty and air support. I think this is going to be pretty much like the Ia Drang operation. The NVA know better than to tangle with us. They'll pull back to their sanctuaries in Cambodia and Laos."

He folded the map. "That's it. You guys get back to your platoons, and I'll see you here tomorrow at zero seven hundred to discuss details."

General Binh Ty Duc studied the wall map for several minutes and turned to Colonel Huu. "Can the Americans be so confident as to send only two battalions to find us?"

Colonel Huu set the rice paper on the bamboo table. "The radio reports come from three different scout elements of the Sixty-sixth Regiment. They all reported the same thing. Only two infantry battalions plus artillery have arrived at Dak To."

The general lowered his head, thinking aloud. "Their intelligence planes have spotted our preparation as we knew they would, yet they only sent two battalions. The Americans must believe us to have only small units and not be a threat."

Colonel Huu did not understand the general's concern. "What is wrong with that, my general? If they sent more units they would find our defensive positions. Should we not be rejoicing?"

Duc stared out the thatch hut door at the drizzling rain. "General Giap's master plan is based on the Americans' believing we are capable of overrunning Dak To. He also believes, as I do, that the Americans would react by sending many of their units to search for us."

He broke his gaze from the rain and turned it to his operations officer. "Don't you see? Today is a rehearsal for what is to come. I have ordered my commanders not to fight, but to pull back. The Americans will find no units to destroy, and they will leave. In October, when we occupy the defensive positions to execute the master plan, the Americans will send only a small unit, as they did this time, believing we will pull back. General Giap and I have overestimated the intelligence capabilities of the Americans. They will not react as we had planned, and the diversion will fail."

Colonel Huu nodded. "I understand. We must make them believe we are a major threat, but what can we do?"

Duc turned around and looked at the map. "We must teach the

arrogant Americans a lesson they will not forget . . . a lesson in respect.''

Caddy tore open the envelope and smiled. ''Sweet Cynthia came through. Guys, we now have a new collection of drive-on pictures.''

Silk leaned over Caddy's shoulder and whistled in admiration. ''Man, that hole is baaad. Give me da one where she's got 'em spread.''

Bugs and Cowboy quickly hurried over. Cowboy took one of the Polaroids and shook his head. ''Caddy, ya sure this lady don't mind ya given' us a picture of her doin' this? She know somebody was takin' her picture?''

''Damn, Cracker, you're dumber than dirt,'' Bugs said. He held up a photo. ''Look at this one. She's lookin' at the camera and smilin' while she's humpin' this guy.''

Lassiter, a short Californian with blond wavy hair, took a picture and stared in awe. ''Why do you call them drive-ons?'' He was one of the cherries.

Caddy smiled. ''Surf, when it gets hot and nasty in the toolies and you don't think you can take another step, you pull out that picture. Man, with one look you forget the heat and drive oooon.''

''Yeah, man, it's what we's fightin' for,'' added Silk.

Holding up his picture, Bugs slapped Silk's back. ''Yeah, home, baseball, apple pie, and round-eye poontang!''

Ty exchanged glances with Sergeant Hammonds and smiled. The squad was feeling its oats. They had been given the skate job of guarding a bridge that crossed the Poko River into the Dak To base camp. For four days they'd had the duty, and now the mail had finally caught up.

Caddy held out a picture to Hammonds. ''Sarge, there's one here for you.''

Hammonds lifted an unopened letter. ''Naw, my Betty would get upset with me lookin' at another woman.''

''A picture is worth a thousand words,'' Caddy said, shrugging his shoulders. ''Cat, you want one?''

Ty shook his head. ''Naw, it's hot enough without those.''

''Give 'em to me, man,'' Silk said as he grabbed the extras. ''I'll send one to my hole for an example of what I want in my next pony.''

''Pony? What is 'pony'? asked the bespectacled new PFC who looked like a Harvard lawyer and always seemed lost.

Silk rolled his eyes. ''Book Man, you been wid us a week and still ain't got the lingo. Pony, man, the mail, like in Dear Johns and care packages. Da pony express, man.''

Ty started to get up but noticed Hammonds reading the familiar yellow stationery from his girl. He wasn't smiling as he usually did when reading her letters. He was staring blankly and trying to hold back tears.

Ty stood and silently signalled Bugs and Caddy. They both understood and motioned the others to take a walk with them. He sat down beside the sergeant and waited.

Hammonds lowered the letter and snarled, "Leave me alone!"

When Ty didn't move, Hammonds angrily tossed the letter at him. "Here, read it! It's a fucking classic! She even said, 'I'll remember you always.' Read it! Read it and get a good laugh in this goddamn hell hole!''

Ty collected the three scattered sheets of yellow paper and folded them up neatly. Without saying a word, he handed the letter back. Hammonds stared at Ty, knowing it was no use. The Cat would wait him out all day if need be. If he got up to leave, the Cat would only follow and wait.

He lowered his head, knowing why the Cat was doing this. Nobody in the squad had the luxury of being down or having moody days. Problems had to dealt with immediately or they would become squad problems. Problems meant minds not on business, which would lead to somebody's getting hurt. And besides all that, Cat was letting him know he cared.

Hammonds looked up at Ty and spoke softly. "Why? Why couldn't she wait just a little longer?"

Drenched in sweat, Jason looked behind as his men walked up the twisting trail. He couldn't help but feel proud. His platoon was leading the way for the rest of the company. They were selected to lead because the CO had said he wanted the "first team" up front. For a day and a half the company had searched the smaller hills at the foot of the mountains looking for NVA, but they had found only freshly dug positions. That afternoon they had been ordered to march up a mountain ridge and had entered the rain forest, the thickest one Jason had even seen. It was like a different world under the darkness of the triple canopy. The huge trees dwarfed those on Red Hill, and there was no feeling of serenity. Instead, there was a lingering, ominous smell of rot and decay, and the feeling that the forest was slowly, methodically devouring them. Life was two hundred feet above, in the green majesty of the countless leaves, but below was a brownish, intangible hell.

Bagley held out the radio handset. "L-tee, it's Six. He wants you to find a night laager."

Jason cringed. The thought of sleeping on the steamy, decomposing forest floor was repulsive. He felt like a small child afraid of a monster and shook his head to clear away the absurdity. "Tell the ol' man 'Roger.' We'll hold up as soon as we get to the top of this ridge."

Colonel Van Thong ran his finger along a line on the map and tapped a spot. "Here is where they will be tomorrow. They carry heavy packs and move slowly. The Americans love high ground and will rest on this hill tonight."

Major Hai Xuan took the cigarette from his lips and smiled, exposing yellow teeth. "I know that area well. It will be perfect."

Colonel Thong backed up from the small table, eyeing the major closely. He didn't like him. Xuan was without emotion, and he was headstrong. The major was one of Thong's best fighting leaders, but he lacked formal military schooling. He had no refinement or education, and relied solely on brutal discipline and unmerciful killing to impress his leaders. Xuan was a product of the war. War was all he knew and lived for.

He tapped the map again. "The general's orders are clear. You must ensure that the lesson is inflicted without great loss to our own forces. Pick your ground carefully, and if the Americans seem to be cautious, wait until another time. If the time is right, hit them quickly and fade away."

"It is about time the general unleashed us," Xuan said as he inhaled on his cigarette. "My men do not like this running. They want to fight. We will show the general the Yankees are not worth running from. I am honored that you chose me to teach this lesson."

Thong shook his head. "No, I didn't choose you. The American unit that has come the farthest into my area happens to be in your sector. Fate has chosen you."

Xuan felt the colonel's disdain but didn't care. He was used to it. The other battalion commanders were treated as brothers, while he alone was looked upon as an uneducated, simple-minded nephew. He tossed the cigarette to the bamboo slat floor and picked up his floppy hat. "Then I thank fate. You can radio our cautious general and tell him the Third Battalion will not just teach a lesson to the Yankees. We will show him—and you—that wars are not won by hiding."

* * *

Jason awoke and quickly packed his poncho and liner into his rucksack as the dark, gray morning sky began to lighten. He was hungry, but there wasn't time to eat. The company had received word late last night to begin walking back to Dak To that morning. He stood and looked at the magnificent view below him. Six klicks away, nestled in a narrow valley, was the Dak To airstrip and base camp. He was standing on the edge of a grassy knoll just below a hilltop. The only open spot for miles around, the hilltop was like an island in a sea of rain forest.

Captain Elliott spotted Jason and called him to his location. "Jay, I want your platoon to lead us again. Third Platoon will follow you, followed by headquarters, weapons, then First. This hilltop is a good spot to observe the airfield. I'm having First scatter CS gas crystals all over it so the gooks won't be able to use it. Go ahead and move out in five minutes."

Jason looked to his left and saw men from the Third Platoon still sleeping. "Sir, I don't think the rest of the company is going to be ready in that time. We're gonna get awfully strung out."

"Don't be telling me my business," Elliott snapped. "Just move your ass straight north and get us out of these goddamn mountains."

Jason could tell that the lack of sleep and the strain of the humping had taken its toll on his commander. He nodded, with a weak "Yes, sir," and strode toward his platoon.

Fifteen minutes later, the Second Platoon was making its way down the ridge and was completely swallowed by the rain forest. Jason followed the lead squad, knowing he wouldn't be able to see the base camp or daylight again until they broke out of the trees five and a half klicks down the slope. The ridge dropped off steeply from the hilltop for two hundred yards, then became more gradual. The narrow finger was void of all underbrush or vegetation but had a series of dips and small knolls. The triple canopy far overhead killed all sunlight, leaving the men in semidarkness.

Sergeant Taloga came up alongside him and spoke in a whisper. "Why we moving so slow?"

Jason pulled out his map. "The company isn't ready to follow, and I don't want to get too far ahead. Plus the ol' man didn't send out clearing patrols this morning. You can see here on the map this ridge is like a downhill roller coaster with these two little knolls and saddles. We're going to take it slow and easy and not take any chances. I told Redford to hold up his point team once they reached the second small knoll that's just ahead. We'll wait there for the Third to catch up."

"I knew you'd have an answer," Taloga said, smiling. "The men wanna hurry and get back. They don't like it up here."

Jason walked down the first small barren knoll into a saddle and halted. His point man, Perkins, was thirty yards ahead and kneeling on top of the second knoll. "I don't like it here any better than they do. Go back to the rear and let me know when Third links up."

Taloga began to take a step, but Jason suddenly grabbed him. Perkins had thrown up his hand, signalling for everybody to freeze. Jason slowly lowered himself to one knee, keeping his eyes on Perkins, who was crawling backward, obviously frightened. Redford stopped the point man by blocking his path and whispered, "What's wrong?"

Wide-eyed, Perkins whispered back in a rush, "Dinks, lots of 'em just ahead. I heard 'em first, then I saw them. They're coming up the knoll!"

Redford spun around and motioned the six men in his squad to follow him. He immediately crawled up the mound and peered over the crest. He had raised his head only an inch when he jerked his rifle up and began firing.

Jason had watched the whole event unfold but still jumped at the sound of the shooting. Whatever Redford was shooting must have been close. The sergeant was on his knees, firing his automatic, when he was suddenly knocked backward. The back of his head seemed to explode. Perkins raised up to shoot but immediately turned and ran. Then Jason saw them: a line of khaki-clad NVA topping the mound. They were running and firing from the hip.

Perkins screamed as bullets tore through his legs. The rest of the squad fired at the point-blank targets, but there were too many to stop.

Jason jerked his rifle up and shot three NVA in less than two seconds and was still too late. Taloga lowered his smoking rifle and screamed for the second squad to come on line behind him. There were no more enemy. They were gone, leaving behind their dead mingled with those of the first squad. They had run up the hill on line and fired, then turned and ran.

Jason could see two of his men moving and began to get up to help them. Taloga grabbed his shoulder and pulled him back. "Get on the fucking radio!"

Jason's stomach was balled into a painful knot, and his mouth seemed like it was full of sand. Up until that second he hadn't thought or spoken a single command. His mind was still trying to comprehend what had happened. It was all so quick, the shooting, the charging enemy, the dying. A minute ago Redford was alive, and then in an instant he was dead. The noise, the confusion, the instant reaction of killing men without thinking, watching his men die without thinking, getting up without thinking. He wasn't leading or in charge of anything.

Bagley held the radio handset out to him. "Sir, the old man wants a situation report!"

Jason looked at the bodies lying on the slope and took the handset. He yelled toward his men, "Second and third squads, get down here and form a perimeter at the crest of the knoll! Bring the machine guns up! Move!" He put the handset to his mouth. "Six, this is two six. We made contact with an NVA reinforced squad. I am forming a perimeter five hundred meters from your location. I need artillery support and medevac ASAP, over."

The captain spoke calmly. "Roger, the Third will link up with you in a few minutes. Artillery is coming up on our radio push any minute now. Keep me informed."

Captain Ky Trung lowered his head as he reported to his battalion commander. "The Yankees surprised the First Platoon as they were moving into their ambush position. The Americans must have left much earlier then we expected. Our lead two squads attacked immediately but withdrew under heavy fire. Our losses are eight dead and three wounded."

Major Xuan lit a cigarette and blew out a cloud of blue-gray smoke. "Where are the Yankees now?"

"The unit my squads attacked is one hundred meters up the trail," Trung said, pointing up the ridge. "The scouts radioed that another element is five hundred meters farther up, just below the hilltop."

Xuan nodded and squatted down. "Attack the Yankees again. Get close and keep them pinned down. I am going to send the Second Company's platoons to their flanks and have the Third Company move around to their rear. They will attack as soon as they are in position."

"You are committing the entire battalion?" Captain Trung said, He looked concerned.

Major Xuan smiled cruelly. "Yes, it is time for us to fight."

Jason moved his platoon to the right side of the mound that was no bigger than forty yards in diameter to make room for the Third Platoon. He had checked the left and right flanks of the ridge to see if he could possibly maneuver around the enemy, but the ground was too steep. Counting his men, he found he had twenty-four who could still fight. Four men in the first squad had been killed, and two were wounded.

After situating his headquarters in the bottom of the saddle between the two knolls, he went to check on the wounded. Both men had been shot in the legs and were lying on their stomachs. The medic had already given them morphine. He knelt down beside them. "We're gonna be moving you both back to the hilltop once Third gets into position. Hang tough, guys."

He looked up and saw Lieutenant Dike approaching and waved the Third Platoon leader to him just as an artillery round exploded far to the north. Jason lifted the radio handset and spoke quickly. "Redleg, one three, this is two six, drop one hundred and try it again. You're still hitting long." He glanced at Dike, who seemed mesmerized by the NVA bodies. "Jim, have your boys take the left side of the knoll and tie in with my guys on the right."

Dike bent over an NVA and stared in fascination. "I've never seen regulars up close."

Jason impatiently grabbed his shoulder. "Move your men in now. I've gotta get these wounded back."

Dike nodded absently and strode up the knoll. Stopping at the top, he pointed out positions for his men to occupy. Jason began to yell for him to stay low when rifle fire broke the silence. Dike spun around, clutched his neck, and tumbled down the slope, stopping by the NVA bodies. Jason ran to him, but he was already past help. The bullet had passed through his neck, severing the carotid artery. Blood was spewing from the wound like water from a miniature fire hose. Jason clamped his hand over the wound but Dike's neck began to expand grotesquely.

The medic knelt by Jason and shook his head as another artillery round exploded with a CRACK BaaLOOOM! Jason looked at the smoking, hot blood covering his hand and wrist. He spun around and yelled, "Bagley, tell the artillery to fire for effect and keep it coming!"

Taloga screamed from the hilltop, "They're attacking!"

Captain Elliott sat on his rucksack and listened to the radio reports. He had been writing the information in his notepad. Johnson's platoon had made the first contact at 0700, and Dike's had linked up at 0730. He had sent five men from First to their perimeter with extra ammo and a machine-gun team, and they had linked up at 0745. The enemy had attacked the perimeter twice but had been repulsed. The casualties numbered twelve dead, including Dike, and fifteen wounded, with an estimated forty enemy killed.

The First Platoon leader looked over Elliott's shoulder. "Sir, don't you think we should join the Second and Third platoons? Jay said they were just barely holding on."

"It's almost over," Elliott said. He looked up from his notepad as if upset with the distraction. "The A-1Es are going to be here in just a minute, and the gooks will pull back. The worst is over . . . we won."

"Sir, you heard what Jay reported. The artillery fire is almost useless. It's hitting in the canopy and exploding too far up. The tree limbs are taking most of the shrapnel. The helicopter gunships can't spot the perimeter because of the trees, and their fire is worthless. Shit, sir, Jay is begging for help. The bombers can't do any good if they can't get a fix on Johnson's position. We're all he's got that can really help."

Elliott stood up and looked at his watch. "It's zero eight hundred. By eight-thirty, it'll be over."

The RTO held out the handset. "Sir, the pilot is calling you."

Jason covered his head as the plane streaked over. Please, oh God, please! Please! The air suddenly disappeared and he couldn't breathe. A whooshing noise, like the sound of a freight train going two hundred miles per hour, filled his ears, then the napalm heat wave struck. The wet forest floor began steaming, and a resinous smell, like that of model airplane glue, caused him to feel faint. He closed his eyes, then opened them again to reality. The line of wounded in front of him told its own story.

He grabbed up the handset. "Six, have them drop again, but this time twenty-five meters closer."

The radio buzzed with static as Captain Elliott answered in a whisper. "That was their last run. We've only got gunships on station until another pair of fast movers get here."

Jason felt like smashing the handset. The gunships had already killed two of his men and wounded seven others. He lifted it and began to speak, but gunfire broke out. "God, not again," he mumbled.

Taloga yelled over the shooting, "They're hitting the Third Platoon!"

Jason ran down the line of wounded toward the platoon's sector and could hear the chattering of AK-47s. The din was like a rifle range, with a hundred rifles firing at once. He tripped over a tree root and stumbled forward, stopping himself just short of a small, deep crevice. He hadn't noticed it before and backed up cautiously. The split, which carried runoff from the saddle, had eroded a narrow trench that ran down the side of the ridge. It was a good twenty feet deep and had ugly, twisted roots sticking out from the inside walls. He bypassed it and began climbing up the hill, when he saw at least ten NVA were climbing up the steep slope of the ridge. They were only twenty yards away. He ran up to the crest and fell beside the left flank. The entire platoon was facing northwest, shooting at NVA who were behind trees no more than fifty yards away.

Grabbing the soldier next to him, he screamed and frantically pointed. "They're coming up over there! Get the next five men and tell 'em to swing around!"

Jason shoved the soldier toward the other shooting men and pulled out two grenades. He crawled a few yards until he could see the NVA clearly. They were climbing barefooted up the steep slope on all fours, their AKs slung over their shoulders. They had almost made it to the top when Jason pulled the pin on the first grenade and tossed it underhand. Then he tossed the second and ducked. The first blast knocked three men over, and they slid down the slope. The second exploded directly in front of an NVA, whose body seemed to disintegrate. Jason rose up firing at the stunned men and was joined by three more soldiers of the Third Platoon. The NVA could do nothing but hug the slope and slide down, praying a bullet didn't find them before they reached a tree or some cover.

Jason emptied his magazine and was reaching for another when a horrifying thought occurred to him. The other side! They would be trying the same thing on his side of the perimeter. He jumped up and slammed in a new magazine. Motioning for the three men to follow him, he had taken only a few strides when he heard the first shots. The NVA popped up in perfect line and swarmed over the wounded and his headquarters element, shooting the screaming men. Jason fired from the hip as he ran toward them.

Elliott nervously looked at his watch and motioned the First Platoon leader to him. "Ruffin, take your platoon down and reinforce the others. And take a squad from weapons platoon with you to carry back wounded. Report as soon as you link up."

The lieutenant glanced at his watch. It was nine-fifteen. He stared at Elliott with disdain. "Aren't you coming, sir?"

Elliott turned his back, afraid to face the accusing stare. "Uh . . . no, I've got to monitor the radios and keep the battalion commander informed. Go on, hurry up!"

* * *

Taloga knew something was different but couldn't figure out what. The silence! All the shooting had stopped. He raised up and looked down the ragged line. He couldn't tell who was dead and who was alive. They all looked the same, lying in the shallow holes they'd dug with their hands and the butts of their rifles. He began crawling to get a head count of effectives.

Jason stared into the freckled face of Bagley and pried the handset from his hand. The young soldier's eyes were open and staring into eternity. He had been killed instantly, shot in the heart and head. The radio was dead as well. Jason stood and looked at the bodies lying in a row. The NVA had killed half the wounded, including Bagley, the medic, and two men from the First Platoon. He sighed, knowing grief was wasted. There was nothing that could be done now.

Taloga walked wearily over to him and sat down beside an NVA body. "Sir, I just checked our platoon and the Third. We've got only twenty-one men left between us who ain't been shot up. Nine or so of the wounded can still shoot and I'm leavin' them on the line. The Third's radio got hit, so that just leaves ours."

"We don't have any," Jason said. He shut his eyes and let himself sink to his knees. "Bagley and Doc both bought it. The radio is gone."

Taloga looked at the remaining wounded and shook his head. "Out of sixty men, we have just over twenty left. Where the hell is the rest of the company? Jesus, we've been beggin' for help."

"We can't worry about that now," Jason said. "We've got to tighten the perimeter and get the badly wounded off the line." He took a deep breath and got back to his feet. "Send the walking wounded down with the badly hurt, and I'll have 'em move the dead and consolidate the other wounded. Get ammo redistributed and strip our dead of anything we can use. Might as well get the dinks' ammo, too; we can use AKs if we have to. Come on, let's get our people movin' before they start thinkin' it's a lost cause."

Taloga raised his head. "Is it? Is it over for us?"

Jason clenched his teeth, trying to find a source of strength, and looked into the bloodshot eyes of the sergeant. "Not yet."

Ruffin followed his point team as they cautiously walked down the ridge. Twice he thought he heard movement to his right flank but motioned his men forward, determined to link up with his sister platoons. The point man began to make his way up a slight rise when he saw three NVA standing by a tree with their backs turned. They were talking loudly as if arguing. Ruffin joined the point man, and both men fired, ending the argument. He lowered his smoking rifle and motioned his men forward.

Jason sighed with relief as Ruffin walked over and shook his hand. "Sorry we took so long. The old man kept thinking the dinks would pull back."

"Jesus, we're glad to see you," Jason said. "Now we can get the hell out of here. I've got over twenty wounded. I figure you can protect our rear as the weapons platoon and us carry the wounded back up the ridge."

Ruffin lowered his eyes. "Jay, I've only got five men from the weapons platoon with me. The rest of weapons and headquarters didn't come. The old man is still back at the hill with them."

Jason's mouth dropped open in disbelief. He looked at the wounded men and lifted his head. "Bill, they're going to overrun us here. We gotta get back to the rest of the company."

Ruffin motioned for his radioman and took the handset. "Six, this is one six. I have linked up with the Second and Third. We are taking the WIAs and falling back to your location."

Lieutenant Ruffin adjusted artillery and had his men take up positions on the knoll with the dead as Jason and his men organized litter teams. In ten minutes the Second and Third Platoons, carrying their wounded, were moving back up the ridge, with the squad from the weapons platoon leading. Jason topped the second small knoll and breathed easier. Every step was closer to making it back home.

Taloga caught up to him and motioned over his shoulder. "The First just left the knoll and are following behind. We . . ."

CRACKCRACKCRACK, CRACK CRACKCRACKCRACK CRACK!

Jason fell to the decaying soil as bullets passed inches over his head. The screams of his men echoed through his brain with the sound of the AK-47s. He shut his eyes, pressing himself into the ground and wanting to disappear. He thought of sunlight and the quiet of Red Hill. God, he just wanted silence—no more sounds of gunfire, dying, and pleas for help. No more screams, no thinking or moving, no worrying.

He opened his eyes and forced himself to his knees. The gunfire was coming from up the ridge. The NVA had cut them off. He yelled for his men to pull back. The only thing that he could do was form a defense behind the second knoll with his remaining men and have Ruffin's platoon stay on the first one. They would have to wait for reinforcements. The saddle would have to again serve as the location for the wounded and CP. He stood despite the fire and looked at Taloga, who was staring at him as if Jason had lost his mind. Jason shook his head with anger. "I know what you're thinking', but not yet. NOT FUCKIN' YET!"

Captain Elliott stood on the edge of the knoll and listened to the gunfire down the ridge. He had just radioed the battalion commander and reported that his three platoons were surrounded. The colonel had promised two companies for reinforcement, but they wouldn't be there for at least two hours. There were no landing zones nearby, and the companies would have to walk to reach them.

He cursed himself for spreading the gas crystals on the hilltop, rendering it unusable for a landing zone. He knew by the sound of the exchange of weapons fire that his men would run out of ammunition long before the rescue force arrived. He turned around and spoke dejectedly to his weapons platoon sergeant. "Form a perimeter and prepare for an attack. Have three of your men dig a foxhole large enough for me and the two RTOs."

The sergeant nodded and began to turn around but stopped. "Sir, we could try and break through. We've got enough men to do it."

Elliott lowered his eyes. "It's too late. They'll be coming for us next. Start digging."

Jason heard the swooshing noise over the gunfire and ducked. The Chinese B-40 rocket hit a nearby tree, exploding and throwing out its deadly shapnel and wood splinters. The men at the base of the tree didn't move or cry out. They were beyond feeling; they had been killed several minutes before during a frontal assault. He inserted his last magazine and let the bolt slam forward. He knew the remaining men couldn't hold off the next attack. Most were out of ammunition. Lieutenant Ruffin had sent a runner from the other knoll and reported that he was wounded and that his men were running low on ammo. The captain had radioed that reinforcements were coming but wouldn't arrive for several hours and that they were to hold on.

He crawled back from the crest and walked down the slope to Sergeant Taloga, who was tending the wounded. He put his hand on the sergeant's back and whispered, "I want you to take two of the lightly wounded and try and make it back to the company commander."

Taloga shook his head. "I can't leave you and the men. Get somebody else."

Jason forced a smile. "Nope. You're just mean enough to make it. The old man respects you, and he'll believe what you tell him. You're the only chance we've got left. Tell him we can hold if he will break through with ammo." Jason knew Taloga was going to refuse again and patted his shoulder. "Don't argue with me, you know I'm right. Just do it and don't look back. I'm counting on you."

Taloga put out his hand. "Good luck, sir."

Jason shook his hand warmly. "Thanks for everything you've done. Go on . . . I'll see ya."

He walked back to the crest and minutes later watched his platoon sergeant slip down the west slope with two other men. He wished he'd said more to Taloga and asked him to look up his brother and tell him . . . No, he didn't want Ty to know how he'd died. It didn't matter.

An out-of-breath runner ran up the slope and fell beside him. "Sa . . . Sir . . . L-tee Ruffin said the dinks are massing in front of his position. He says it looks like the big one, and he wants your help."

Jason nodded tiredly. "Tell him we're on the way."

Ruffin pushed the NVA body over so he couldn't see the man's face and propped his M-16 on the dead soldier's bare leg. He had ordered the use of the bodies as frontal protection. The sound of the Vietnamese voices down the ridge had told him he and his men were going to need all the help they could get. The NVA leaders were shouting commands, and by their numbers he knew the next attack would be big. There were no M-79 ammo or any grenades left. There were only two hundred rounds of machine-gun ammo, and his men were down to two magazines apiece.

Jason crawled up beside Ruffin just as the NVA machine guns opened up and stitched the top of the hill. Ruffin tried to crawl backward, but his wounded leg was numb and wouldn't respond. Jason grabbed his trousers and pulled him back.

Ruffin rested his head in the dirt. "Jay, this is it; they're going to keep us pinned down with machine guns until the assault force is almost on top of us. We could stop the bastards if we had grenades."

Jason could envision the swarm of NVA rushing over the top of the knoll and began crawling backward. "Bill, I'm going to set up a second defense line in front of the wounded so they don't think we've abandoned them. Good luck."

Ruffin raised his head. "We did our best, didn't we?"

Jason stopped and looked into the watering eyes of the young officer. "Yeah, we did our best."

The suppressive RPD machine-gun fire lasted several minutes, then suddenly increased with the addition of two heavy machine guns that raked the top of the knoll, making it impossible for the defenders to raise their heads. Three platoons of NVA jogged up the ridge without receiving a single shot of return fire and deployed on line at the base of the knoll. The lead platoon commander raised his rifle above his head and screamed for his men to attack. The machine guns immediately ceased firing as the men ran up the knoll.

Ruffin forced himself to his knees and readied his rifle to meet the onslaught. He saw the first of the attackers and screamed as he fired. "COME ON, YOU MOTHERFUCKERRRRRS!"

Jason had six of his men positioned in front of the wounded in a last stand. He stood with a fixed stare as the first of the NVA swarmed over the platoon and ran down the slope. His men knocked eight of the enemy down, but it was like trying to stop a dam from bursting. The small trickle turned into an unstoppable flood. Jason raised his rifle and fired until it was empty. He picked up the AK he'd positioned by his feet but was knocked violently backward. He fell hard on his back, feeling as if his shoulder had been hit with a red-hot sledgehammer. Fighting to regain his feet, he stumbled to his right and suddenly dropped into darkness. His head banged into the side of the crevice wall as he slid down the narrow dirt chute, the roots tearing at his face and body. He fell ten feet before his shirt became snagged on a root and jerked him to a jolting halt. Screaming in pain, he fought to free himself, but he couldn't move his arms within the tight confines. He looked up at the hole of light and heard the battle overhead. Suddenly, the light was partially blocked, and he could make out a face. It was one of his men, Sawyer, whom he had positioned in front of the wounded. The soldier lowered himself into the crevice, pulling a body over the top of the hole. Dirt fell into Jason's face and he coughed. Startled, Sawyer almost lost his grip on the roots he was holding and looked down, whispering in disbelief. "You're alive! Jesus, I thought you were dead, L-tee."

Jason clenched his teeth to fight the pain in his shoulder. "Did they fall back? What's happening?"

Sawyer dug his boots into the earth wall, knocking more dirt on Jason. "They ran past us and up to the other knoll, but the second wave is coming. I was out of ammo and played dead. I saw you go down and figured this hole was worth a try. Jesus, sir, they were everywhere. I saw a lot of our guys holding up their hands to surrender.''

Jason began to speak when renewed gunfire broke out, and in a minute he could hear his men screaming. The sound sent shivers up his back. The screams were not in anger or desperation but in crazed fear. An explosion shook the earth around him and the gunfire stopped. The hole was a sauna without a source of air, and his eyes filled with stinging sweat. The silence was broken by men screaming in the distance and the sound of two quick shots. Again he heard wailing and crying, then two more shots. His body tightened and he fought to free himself. They were executing his men!

Sawyer began crying uncontrollably and beat his head against the dirt wall to try and clear the sounds from his mind. Jason gave up, overcome by pain and helplessness. His body went limp, and he let his head fall to his chest. He was trapped in hell, and there was nothing he could do but listen to his men being murdered one at a time.

Captain Elliott pressed the handset close to his ear to hear and spoke above the sound of the exploding artillery. "We are under attack from the northwest. I need air support and a resupply of ammo. I also need demo to blow a landing zone for my wounded. We have repulsed two attacks and are critically short of ammo."

He listened for a few seconds and yelled into the plastic mouthpiece, "Twenty minutes is too late! In twenty minutes you won't have anybody here but gooks! I need the resupply now, or what's left of this company is going to die! . . . Fuck, no I'm not going to settle down and stay calm! I've lost three platoons already and got four KIAs and nineteen wounded here! Get the shit to me NOW!"

Sergeant Taloga sat against the foxhole wall beside Elliott and concentrated on the sounds down the ridge. He'd arrived thirty minutes earlier only to find that the captain had been wounded during an attack along with many others of the weapons platoon. The hope of saving his men was gone. The captain's small perimeter had less than fifteen men who were not wounded or dead. The artillery was saving them. The trees were much smaller near the hilltop, and the exploding rounds were effective at putting up a curtain of protective steel. The sergeant stared at his hands, knowing the men he had been sent to save had perished.

Elliott tossed the handset to his RTO and looked at Taloga. "A resupply bird is on its way in. It'll have to kick out the ammo and demo into the perimeter. You and your two men will redistribute the ammo, then start blowing us an LZ.''

Taloga nodded tiredly. That morning the company had been 115 men strong and filled with confidence. Now, five hours later, the company was down to only fifteen men who were not wounded or dead, and the survivors were holding onto life by a thread. A resupply copter was their last hope. If they could blow an LZ, then additional men could be brought in and turn the tide. Again he was given the job of saving men. He inserted a fresh magazine and raised his head to look at the heavens. He hadn't prayed in years, but he hadn't forgotten how.

Sawyer mumbled as the gunshots just above him became louder. He could hear the Vietnamese voices as clearly as if they were talking to him. The body above him was suddenly turned over, exposing a shaft of light, and he screamed frantically, ''GOD NOOOOOoooo!''

Excited Vietnamese voices became louder and an AK-47 barrel was lowered to his head. Sawyer screamed louder and thrashed his head back and forth, trying to get the cool steel off his temple. The weapon fired and his head slammed forward into the dirt wall. His body slipped down on top of Jason's head and shoulders.

Jason bit his lip to stifle a scream. A second shot was fired, and Jason felt Sawyer's hot blood and brains roll down the back of his neck. The smell of gunsmoke and blood was overpowering, and the soldier's weight on top of him was suffocating. He couldn't breathe or see. Laughter and talking above seemed to melt into a fog as the pain and lack of air took over and released him from his tormenting agony.

Walking down the hill, Major Xuan stepped over American and Vietnamese bodies, until he reached a pile of stacked corpses. He glanced at his captain. ''How many Yankees died?''

Captain Trung responded blandly, ''Three platoons of infantry—approximately eighty men. We have collected their weapons and radios. My company lost thirty-eight men, and we have another forty wounded who will require medical attention.''

''What are the total losses to the battalion?''

Trung looked at a piece of rice paper. ''Comrade, our losses are heavy: 150 men have been killed and over 250 wounded. Enemy artillery wreaked havoc upon the thirteenth and fifteenth companies when they attempted to wipe out the remaining Yankees up the ridge. Reports from our scouts confirm two Yankee relief companies are en route. The scouts have been slowing them down with sniping, and they won't reach us here until later this afternoon. The victory is yours.''

Major Xuan lit a cigarette and inhaled deeply. As he exhaled he looked down at the blood-matted blond hair of a young paratrooper. ''Leave two squads to snipe at the reinforcements when they arrive and have the rest of the battalion retire. Take all our dead, and we will bury them where they will not be found. The lesson is over.''

Ty and Caddy were sitting behind sandbags and watching the far side of the river when Sergeant Hammonds walked up behind them. Ty knew something was wrong by the look on the sergeant's face. A shiver ran up his back. ''What's wrong?''

Hammonds tried to look Ty in the eyes but couldn't. ''The lieutenant has been monitoring the radio all day. It's your brother's company, Alpha, Second Batt. The last report said the company had seventy-eight men missing, presumed dead, four confirmed KIAs, and nineteen wounded. The survivors are coming in on helicopters in a few minutes. I told the L-tee about your brother, and he gave me permission to release you for a while. I thought you'd probably want to be there when the choppers came in.''

Ty picked up his rifle and began running toward the airfield. Caddy exchanged worried looks with Hammonds. ''Is there a chance he made it?''

Hammonds shook his head. ''Doesn't look good. The only guys to make it were the headquarters and weapons platoon. The line platoon grunts are the ones that are missing.''

''What the hell does 'missing' mean? Damn, don't they know what happened to them?''

Hammonds looked over his shoulder at Ty jogging toward the airfield. ''It means they haven't found the bodies yet.''

Jason awoke to the sound of moaning. At first he had thought he was dreaming and the sound was a part of a horrible nightmare, but the sound was real. So was the pain that racked his body and the crushing weight that still pressed on him. He tried to open his eyes, but they were covered in coagulated blood, dirt, and dried sweat. He tried again but couldn't tell if they were open. It was pitch black. Forcing his head up with all his strength, he moved Sawyer's body only a few inches, enough to free his right arm. The release of pressure sent a jolt of pain through his body as if he had been struck by lightning. For several minutes he shuddered and passed in and out of consciousness, until he finally regained enough strength to stand the excruciating throbbing. Moving his arm was agonizing, but he pushed the body up and moved his head to the side as far as possible. Sawyer's corpse shifted just enough and slid farther down, freeing Jason's head. Jason took in his first breath of fresh night air. His feeling of bliss was cut short when a man's low moan pierced through the blackness like a knife. The sound was docile and strangely homey as if he were moaning for a mother in the next room. It was a small child's moan. The voice was his own.

The point man for Bravo Company held up his hand, signaling for the lead platoon to halt. In front of him was what he had hoped he wouldn't find. The day before they had finally linked up with the Alpha Company commander at two in the afternoon but were stopped from trying to move toward the surrounded platoons. Every time they tried to move, snipers would pin them down. They had to wait all night and through the next day until one-thirty that afternoon before artillery finally cleared the ridge of the enemy. He hadn't slept the night before for thinking of the men only five hundred meters away.

The platoon leader came forward and looked at the grisly scene before him. He dropped to one knee. "God have mercy on their souls."

He posted security and ordered his men to begin the gruesome job of checking all the bodies. A sergeant found a man alive who had been shot in the head. Another soldier was found beneath two of his friends but had lost a lot of blood. The search continued for several minutes when the lieutenant noticed the crevice. He stepped closer and looked inside. Ten feet below he saw a creature looking up at him. It had two heads. "My God!"

Colonel Thong angrily slammed the table with his fist. "You did not obey my orders! You were to attack and withdraw."

Major Xuan tossed to the table an American dog tag chain with numerous tags. "The lesson you and the general wanted is there. Eighty Yankees are with their ancestors."

Thong ignored the evidence. "And over 150 of my men are with theirs!"

Xuan stood up, seething. "They are not *your* men. They are *mine*, and they are heroes. I did what you and the others are afraid to do: attack! Attack and wipe out the Yankee dogs. They are nothing! I saw them. They are overfed boys!"

The colonel shook his head, realizing he was talking to a madman. "Those 'boys' killed and wounded one-third of *my* bat-

talion," Thong said, shaking his head. "You are relieved. You are
no longer a part of this command. Get out now before I have you
executed."

The major's lip formed a cruel grin. "You will be calling me
back. I know the Yankees better than all of you. You need me."

Thong couldn't stand the sight of the man any longer and turned
his back, motioning for the operations officer. "Take him away
and . . ."

"Kill me?" Xuan said sarcastically.

The colonel finished his sentence. ". . . and make sure the general knows why he is returning to the base camp." Minutes later,
the operations officer stepped into the hut. "What will happen to
him, Comrade?"

The colonel lowered his head. "He will receive another command in another unit. Sadly, he was right. Some in the Fatherland
believe we need his kind."

Ty knelt on the tarmac beside a litter and held Jason's hand. Jason
wasn't looking at him; he was staring at Sergeant Taloga with blank
eyes. "They . . . they killed them all. Redford, Bagley, Fontaine,
Perkins, Billings . . ."

Taloga nodded and ran his hand over Jason's forehead. "I know.
You're gonna be okay, L-tee. You'll be going home. Don't think
about it anymore."

Jason mumbled, "And Sawyer, Carter, Smitty . . ."

Ty turned his brother's head toward him. "Jay? Jay, it's me. Look
at me."

Jason's eyes focused and tears began welling up. "Ty, my . . .
my men are gone."

Ty leaned over and hugged him, wanting to take away his anguish. Ty was still shaking with relief. He had been waiting all day
at the airfield for the final word. When he had seen Jason being
taken off the medevac, he had cried uncontrollably. The battalion
surgeon had cleaned Jason's wound and ordered another medevac
to take him to the hospital in Pleiku.

Ty patted Jason's arm. "Hang tough, big brother. You're going
home. Mom and Duane will be waiting for you."

Jason nodded and smiled strangely. "I'm a Red Hill Paratrooper,
aren't I?" He lifted his hand and pulled out his dog tag chain.
Attached to the chain were the silver jump wings Ty had given
him. "Take them, Ty. I don't want to be a soldier anymore. I wanna
go home to Mom."

"He's doped up pretty good," Taloga said softly. "Don't mind what he says. He'll snap out of it."

Ty nodded and pushed the chain back beneath Jason's shirt. "You keep 'em, Jay; they've been lucky for you. They're coming to pick you up now and get you to the hospital. You take care and hug Mom for me when ya get home."

"Home?" Jason said hoarsely. "I can't go home, I'm dead. I died with my men."

Two men picked up the stretcher and began walking to the Huey. Ty walked alongside, still holding Jason's hand. "I love you, Jay. I'll see ya, brother."

Jason looked at Ty. "I . . . I'll see ya."

Ty backed away from the helicopter and stood beside Taloga until the bird lifted off and became a distant speck.

Taloga looked south at the mountains. "He's right, you know. We all died up there on that ridge. We may be walking around and breathing, but something inside us died with our platoon."

Ty forced a smile. "Jay will be all right once he gets home. There's a place we know that will take away the bad memories."

"Only heaven can do that," Taloga said.

Ty closed his eyes and was back on his hill. "Yeah, I guess you could call it that."

27

Hammonds marched down the trail and tossed his rucksack beside Ty. "We're stopping again. The second platoon is trying to find a path through the bamboo up ahead; it's thicker than hair on a dog. It'll be at least ten minutes before we move out. Take a break."

He sat down beside Ty and took out his map. "This valley is the worst I've ever been in. I've never seen so much bamboo."

Ty looked over the sergeant's shoulder at the map. The valley they were in was shaped like a cigar pointing directly toward Cambodia. Unlike the mountains south of Dak To, the area to the west of the base camp was covered in bamboo that soared to fifty feet. The rain forest was locked in battle with the bamboo, and it looked as if the rain forest was losing.

Hammonds pointed to the west. "We need to get to the high ground on that chain of hilltops. Up there we could move a helluva lot better than in this shit."

Ty glanced at the mountains. "If the NVA are up there, it's gonna take more than a company to dig 'em out. I don't like it. I got the bad feeling they're playing cat and mouse, and we're the mouse."

"The brigade has had only a few small contacts since your brother's company got waxed," Hammonds said, putting the map away. "The dinks shot their whole wad or got real lucky with Alpha Company. They can't fight toe to toe with us and expect to win."

Ty lay back on his pack and shut his eyes. "I hope the dinks know that."

"How about a smile today?"

Jason forced a small smile at the prim, rotund nurse in the hope that she would leave him alone. Her constant cheerfulness had driven him crazy these past weeks.

"That's much better. I was beginning to worry about you, being so down and all. A little smile works wonders—just like this breakfast."

He sat up as she set the food tray on a rolling table and pushed it in front of him. "You know, Lieutenant Johnson, you should count yourself blessed that you're able to feed yourself. Some of the men on the other ward would give anything to pick up a fork, the way you do."

Jason glared at the woman. "Yes, Ma'am, you remind me every damn day."

The nurse's brow furrowed. "I will ignore that, because you're obviously tired. I can tell you didn't sleep again last night. But I suggest you ease up on me and the staff and put the war out of your mind."

Jason ignored her words and picked at his scrambled eggs. She stared at him for a moment, then lowered her eyes and pushed the cart down the aisle. He had to admit she had been right about one thing: he hadn't slept again. It was impossible to shut his eyes without seeing the enemy pouring over the knoll. He could see the wounded and hear their soul-wrenching pleas. He could feel Sawyer's warm blood dribbling down his back like syrup. The nurse wanted him to forget the war, but the war wouldn't let him go.

He began to pick up the glass of orange juice when a long-haired doctor strode up to his bed and began inspecting his shoulder wound.

Jason was tired of doctors making daily visits without ever telling him anything. He spoke coldly. "When am I going home? I'm gettin' real tired of this place."

The doctor raised his eyebrow. "Didn't anyone tell you?"

"Tell me what?" Jason said, figuring there was a typical snafu.

"You're being sent back for duty. The wound is healing nicely, and you should be able to return to your unit within a few weeks. Of course, you'll have light duty for an additional month, but you'll be as good as new and ready for whatever you do."

"No way!" Jason blurted. "I'm going home. They told me."

"Who told you?" asked the doctor, raising his voice to match Jason's.

"The medics, the doc that operated, the other guys on the ward. There's got to be a mistake."

The doctor raised his chin smugly. "Lieutenant, I have been specifically sent here to ensure that men who are fit for duty return to their units. You're a perfect example of a soldier who can still serve his country. I checked your records. You've served only four months in Vietnam. You can serve out the rest of your tour with no problem. Your wounds will heal."

Jason angrily pushed the table away. "You don't understand. I can't go back. My men are dead."

"Yes, well, many men have died, and more surely will. You will serve out your tour, and that is the final word. Accept it."

Jason could see the self-righteousness in the doctor's eyes. Any further argument would be wasted. The man had found his "perfect example," and he wouldn't back down. He lay back on his pillow. This doctor was like all the others who hadn't been there and could never comprehend real war. To them war was like the movies and *Life* magazine photos. But movies, books, and pictures couldn't capture the smell, sound, confusion, or feelings. Nothing could capture war. It was like filming only one play of a football game to represent the entire four quarters. Nobody truly understood except those who were there, living it every second, minute, hour, and day. The doctor didn't know where he was sending this "perfect example." But Jason knew. He was going back to hell.

* * *

General Binh Ty Duc paced back and forth in front of the large wall map as Colonel Kinh briefed him. ". . . and the Seventy-fourth Regiment reports five of their defensive positions have been found by the Americans, but none of the tunnels were discovered. The Sixty-sixth reports seven positions found, but again no tunnels discovered. The Americans find the bunkers and trench lines but make no effort to destroy them. We must assume they believe we will not use them.''

General Duc stopped in midstride. "I want our units to resume construction of their positions. The Americans may stay for days or perhaps months, and we cannot get behind schedule. The rains have slowed us enough already. Have the units post scouts for early warning and pull back if the enemy approaches. I also want selected scouts to follow the Americans, shadow them wherever they go when they are in our sector. Keep a map posted of all their movements so that we can track their presence. This will be good practice for the master plan."

Colonel Kinh rose from his chair. "General, there is one final matter: the Sixty-sixth Regiment's attack. You said you wanted to discuss the battle with me after some time had passed."

General Duc ran a hand through his gray hair. "The major who ordered the attack was a fool, losing so many men, but . . ." He looked at the map and tapped the ridge where the battle had been fought. "Xuan disobeyed orders, but the battle was a lesson for us all. The Americans were slow to react and sealed their soldiers' fate. They had their units too far apart to properly support each other. They have learned nothing from the mauling. They still make the same mistakes, and we could maul another of their separated units should we decide to. I want the lessons we learned from the battle given to every company and battalion commander. When the time comes, they will be confident in attacking the Americans.''

Kinh nodded and picked up his writing pad. "You asked weeks ago, 'Could the enemy be so arrogant?' I believe we found our answer by their recent movements. They seemed to have forgotten they lost an entire company."

"They haven't forgotten," Duc said. He walked to the hut door and looked out at the camp activity. "They just don't believe we can do it again. Their army is blind because of their poor intelligence. I have overestimated them, but I have learned. Their intelligence will now become my ally."

Ty smelled the freshly tilled soil and brought his hand up. Caddy tightened his grip on the M-79 and kept his attention on the frozen point man. Ty's eyes shifted to the right as he swung his rifle. He couldn't see the bunker, but he knew it was there. He slowly backed up to Caddy and lay down, keeping a low profile. Hammonds crept up to him and whispered, "What ya got?"

Ty motioned up the ridge. "Can you smell it?"

Hammonds lifted his head, taking in a deep breath, and immediately lowered himself. "Fresh-turned dirt. Yeah, I smell it. Shit, what ya think? A bunker or trench line?"

Ty shook his head. For the past week they had been walking the top of the chain of mountains along the western side of Cigar Valley and had come across numerous defensive positions. All had been occupied recently, but no one had seen a single NVA soldier.

Hammonds passed the word back for the lieutenant to come forward. When Jenkins arrived, he ordered Hammonds's squad to cover as third squad moved forward to check out the situation. The third squad moved only thirty yards before finding the first bunker.

The platoon reached the crest of the hill at noon after finding four bunkers and a partially dug trench line. Ty watched from inside the first bunker as the rest of the company came up the hill. He had crawled inside and stood on the firing step looking through the firing portal. Caddy joined him and peered over Ty's shoulder. "The dinks sure are dumb. They dug the firing hole at an angle instead of in front where they could see us coming from farther away."

Ty backed up, allowing his friend a better view. "They ain't so dumb. Look to your far left and you'll see the other bunker. It's covering this one. They'd blow anybody away who tried to attack from the front. They put their firing ports at angles so we can't spot them until it's too late. If there'd been somebody in here, he coulda waxed the third squad. If we would have come up to help, the other bunker woulda had us dead in their sights."

Caddy shivered. "Damn, Cat, this is a meat-grinder. You'd better give one of your stay-alive classes on this thing. I'll get Hammonds and the L-tee."

Ty was sitting on his rucksack eating a C-ration fruitcake, when he saw the company commander walking straight for him. He knew he was in trouble—he was still wearing the NVA officer's pistol.

The captain stopped in front of him. "Are you the one who showed your platoon the bunkers' fields of fire?"

Ty knew he should stand up to answer, but then the pistol would be visible. He remained seated and looked up. "Yes, sir."

"Outstanding initiative, young man. I have your lieutenant giving the other platoon leaders the same class right now. This is exactly what we need—an appreciation of enemy positions. One of these days, they might decide to stand and fight.''

He cocked his head to the side. ''Aren't you the one who found the rice cache that . . . damn, you're still wearing the pistol!''

Ty rolled his eyes. He was going to miss the pistol. It had become a part of him, like his rucksack and M-16.

The captain broke into a smile. ''Hell, I don't blame you. I'd have kept the damn thing, too. Just don't wear it back at base camp, or the S-2 will hang you on a cross in front of the mess hall as an example.''

Ty relaxed and stood when he realized that the company commander was one of the good officers who didn't play by the dumb rules. ''Thanks, sir.''

The captain held his smile. ''No sweat. What do you think about all these empty positions we've been finding? It doesn't make sense, does it?''

''Most of 'em aren't finished,'' Ty said, shrugging his shoulders. ''Maybe they're waitin' until they have all their positions done to start stopping us. Sir, I do know one thing: we have dinks following us. The other day, our platoon sent out a clearing patrol around the company's perimeter, and I saw sandal prints over the ones we had made going into the perimeter. There are four of them on our tail.''

The captain's eyes widened. ''I wasn't told that!''

Sergeant Hammonds watched the last of the company depart and nodded for Book Man to get a commo check. The soldier raised the radio handset to his mouth. ''One six, this is wild cat one, commo check, over.''

Immediately he heard a response: ''Roger, wild cat, I got ya lickin' chicken, out.''

Book Man looked at Hammonds strangely and whispered, ''He said something about licking chicken.''

Silk leaned over and grabbed Book Man's shirt and pulled him to within inches of his own face. ''Cherry, we done went over the lingo wid yo' dumb ass. Lickin' chicken means 'loud and clear.' ''

Hammonds sat beside Silk and motioned Book Man down. Silk leaned back against the bunker wall. ''Man, you gotta talk to Cat about his mouth. Dis stayin' behind shit is for da fuckin' birds. Da company is headin' for resupply and we is headin' for trouble.''

''We need to see if the dinks are following us,'' Hammonds whispered. ''We've got commo with the rest of platoon, and they're not going far. Just cool it and keep quiet. Keep your eye on Book Man, too.''

Ty peered through the firing port knowing his hunch would be proven or disproven within ten minutes. He brought his rifle up and pushed off the safety.

Caddy looked through the firing port on the other side and shook his head. "Cat, why in here? I hate it in dark, small places."

Bugs, sitting against the far wall, nodded. "Yeah, Cat, this bunker stinks like fish sauce. How come we couldn't wait on the outside?"

Ty kept his eyes on the first bunker, where Hammonds and the rest of the squad were located. "No place to hide. You two shut up and . . . we got company."

The NVA scout stopped on the trail and stood for thirty seconds, listening. He shifted his AK-47 and motioned to the others. Three men walked up the trail single file, all wearing packs and light green uniforms. The scout took several cautious steps and looked at the bootprints. He spoke to the soldier behind him, pointing in the direction the company had departed. The second soldier nodded and motioned the scout ahead. The scout took one step and Ty shot him between the eyes. The rest of the NVA never fired a shot or raised their weapons. Their bodies were riddled by small bullets that entered and rolled or flipped end over end, causing massive damage.

Ty kept the still forms covered as Caddy and Bugs crawled out of the bunker and approached the killing ground.

The company commander put down the handset and faced the small group of men. "The stay-behind ambush was executed perfectly. The battalion commander is very impressed and is notifying all the other companies to do the same. I wanted to thank you men personally and tell you that the documents and letters you got off the dead are very important. We already know the NVA you ambushed were members of the Sixty-sixth Regiment. Keep up the good work. By the way, PFC Nance, you are now a specialist fourth class. I just promoted you. The resupply bird brought in some cold Cokes, and I told your Lieutenant to save you all two apiece. Go on back to your platoon and celebrate."

Silk walked beside Ty as they made their way down the hill toward their positions. "Cat, next time youse get an idea, youse tell me and I'll tell the ol' man. Maybe I can get me some rank, too, man."

Jason sat on his cot and looked at the distant mountains through the open flap. When he arrived three days before, he had found out about the big shake-up. The battalion commander and company commanders had all been relieved after his company had been decimated, and Alpha was already back to full strength, filled with men from other battalions. Taloga had been sent to the jungle school as an instructor, and only a few men remained of the original company. He got the impression that the incident was an embarrassment and everybody wanted to forget it. Not a soul had mentioned a word or asked him a question about the battle.

He headed for the mess tent, where a movie was scheduled, but he stopped when he saw a long line of men waiting to get into the canvas theater. He almost turned around and went back, but he felt a wave of anger. The waiting men were field soldiers who hadn't seen a movie in months. He strode past the line and pulled back the tent flap. Sitting in folding chairs were the clerks and supply personnel of the unit. "Who's in charge?"

A sergeant first class rose up from his chair with a beer in his hand. "I am, sir. What's the problem?"

Jason gestured toward the line of men. "There doesn't seem to be enough room in this tent for all the men who want to see the movie. Why don't you move the screen outside so everybody can see it?"

The sergeant frowned. "Sir, if you want a chair, I'll get you one, but the rain could start anytime, and we don't show outside flicks."

"Who is 'we'?" pressed Jason.

The NCO rolled his eyes. "Sir, if you've got a complaint, see the S-1. He makes the rules. I run the projector."

"Where is he?" Jason asked, not liking the man's surly attitude.

"You can find him up at the Officer's Club." The sergeant turned his back and nodded toward the clerk to start the projector.

Jason stepped to the table and shut off the machine. "YOU, Sergeant, find the S-1! In the meantime, I'm taking charge." Jason pointed to the first four soldiers in line. "You men move the screen outside, then turn the table around and move it closer to the end of the tent. If it rains, the projector won't get wet." Jason walked down the line stopping halfway. "Men, you will all see the movie tonight, but you might get wet. I know you've all been wet before, being line dogs, so it's no big thing, right?"

The paratroopers yelled out their approval and gathered around the screen. Jason signalled the clerk to start the movie and sat down near two PFCs. They were wearing filthy uniforms and stank of sweat and jungle rot. Jason breathed in deeply, feeling for the first time like a soldier again. Their stink reminded him how he and his men used to smell. There was nothing like it. No one could understand but those who lie in the mud, sleep outside, swelter in the jungle heat, and shiver at night. Nobody but line dogs felt pride in their filth. They knew the real war. They knew there was no glory, no reward, no end.

28

Move it, Cat, we're the last ones.''

Ty broke his gaze from the mountains and followed Hammonds up the ramp of the C-130. He sat down on the red nylon seat and shut his eyes, knowing he was losing it. For the first time he didn't have the feeling. His company had been humping the mountains southwest of Dak To for two straight months without a break. They had not lost a man, but the mountains had taken a toll on their bodies and minds. The NVA were there, and everyone knew it. They had felt them and seen their tracks and freshly dug positions, but the enemy hadn't stood and fought.

Ty had constantly walked point, and next to the commander, had become the best-known soldier in the company. Every paratrooper breathed easier knowing the "Cat" was on point. His senses had become so finely tuned to the rain forest that he felt as if he were part of it. Day after day, walking alone twenty-five meters in front of the formation, the plants, trees, scents, winds, and light of the forest had become his closest friends. In the evenings he kept his distance from his squad and the others. Cigarette smoke ruined his ability to smell for a day. Loud talking or coughing caused him to cringe. Idle talk and laughter caused his mind to wander, and he had to force himself not to think about his other home. The men thought he had strange powers, but there was no secret to his success. The NVA were not as good as everyone thought. They made mistakes. Some had cut trees or bamboo too close to their positions. Others had collected the dead wood from around their positions for fires. Footprints, latrines placed upwind, freshly dug dirt, marks on trees from climbing—just one sign was all he needed. They had made their biggest mistake in leaving their defensive positions for him to study. They were victims of SOPs, just like the Army. Most of the bunkers and trenches were identical in size and spacing, depending on the hill or saddle on which they were built. He found position after position and saw that the enemy was constantly improving and upgrading. Connecting tunnels were being dug, as well as deep bomb shelters. It was clear that the enemy was preparing to fight. He told the company commander, who told the battalion commander, who told whoever would listen. It didn't matter. Their mission was to find the enemy, not positions, but the NVA had not cooperated.

Ty had truly become the buffalo. He knew the enemy and placed himself in their minds and bodies. He knew what they did and what they ate. He had grown to love the feeling when walking point. He saw a man's footprints and became that man. He could tell if the soldier was carrying a pack or limped, and he could tell if he carried a rifle or not. If he carried a rifle, his footprint on one side would be slightly deeper. When the soldier relieved himself, the spot he chose and the way he stood told him if the soldier was tired or fresh. A tired man wouldn't walk very far away from the trail.

Ty hadn't eaten a full meal. He preferred to remain hungry. Hunger had sharpened his senses. He never used soap to clean himself because of the lingering smell, and he hadn't bought along fresh uniforms for the same reason. The feeling had become an obsession that no one understood. Becoming the buffalo had become a way of life.

His slackmen had to be rotated every day because they couldn't take the mental strain of trying to keep up. They always thought of the rain forest as an enemy. Their nerves would be shot at the end of a six-hour movement, and it would take them days to recuperate.

Lieutenant Jenkins sat beside Sergeant Hammonds and leaned forward in his seat to look over his men. "The troops look beat. This new operation couldn't have come at a better time. I sure wish I could stay with you all the whole tour. I'm goin' to miss you guys."

Hammonds extended his long legs trying to get comfortable. "Sir, you're not going very far. Hell, as company executive officer, you still can take care of us. I'll tell ya, sir, I'll protect rice fields for the rest of my tour as long as they aren't in the mountains. I don't care if there are ten divisions of NVA around as long as it's flat."

Jenkins chuckled and leaned back. "Don't worry. Where you all are going is heaven compared to Dak To. The battalion is going in close to the coast, just west of Tuy Hoa. All you have to do is make sure this year's rice crop is harvested without the VC screwing with the farmers. It'll be skate duty after looking for the damn NVA. The VC in the area aren't too organized, and the briefing I got from the old man yesterday was good news: the big brass think we've pretty much kicked their asses. The VC attacks have dwindled down to almost nothing the past months.''

"We're winning?" Hammonds asked.

"Yeah, were kickin' ass. The big brass are only worried about the NVA. Reports say there are boocoo of them coming down the Ho Chi Minh Trail. The problem is they won't come out and fight, as well we know.''

Hammonds looked across the aisle at Caddy and Silk. "Sir, my squad is dead on their feet. The ol' man using us as point all the time has frazzled us. You think we could get a few days off at the R and R center to mellow out? I've really had it, and I know the men need it.''

Jenkins smiled. "I've already got it arranged for the whole platoon. It's a surprise once we get to Tuy Hoa. Oh yeah, before I forget, make sure Cat takes that damn pistol off when he lands. I saw him wearing it when he got on the plane.''

Hammonds leaned forward and looked down the aisle at Ty, who was sleeping. "He's the one I'm worried about most. He's nothing but skin and bones, and he's gettin' weird over the point job. I swear at times it seems as if he's enjoying himself out there. He needs this break more than any of us.''

"It's over now," Jenkins said. "He can take it easy." He relaxed and shut his eyes. "Dak To is just a bad memory.''

The major sat down behind the field table and looked up at Jason, who was standing in front of him. "Why do you insist on making trouble for me? The supply officer wants your head, and the adjutant wants you shot in front of the flagpole at dawn. Nobody in the rear likes you. I thought things might be different since we left Dak To, but we've been here two days and you've managed to piss off the entire camp staff. I've got four complaints in the past two hours. What the hell did you do?''

Jason was so angry that his hands were trembling. "Sir, those lousy sonofabitches wouldn't change their precious mess hall hours for our arriving troops. They were going to issue C-rations instead of getting off their lazy asses and cooking a hot meal. I made them stay open and cook. Then the bastard that runs the shower point decided our men would use up all his water, and he puts it off limits. We had a very heated argument, and he decided to change his mind. And the club NCO shut down the club and wouldn't serve our men and . . ."

The major held up his hand. "I know you changed his mind, too. I got news, Johnson—hitting an engineer second louie is not what I call a heated argument. It's called beatin' the shit out of people. And telling that club NCO you would gas his club every night we're here is called blackmail. The old man is spending all his time putting out fires you start, and he has better things to do."

Jason slammed his fist on the table. "These REMFs are supposed to support us, not hassle us! Sir, they oughta be given an M-16 and shipped to field for a week and see how it is for a change. They're workin' eight to five and have hooch maids. They think the war is rough when their goddamn ice machine breaks down."

The major laughed and stood up. "Damn you, Jay, you won't even accept an ass chewin' without arguing."

The battalion commander strode in the front door and immediately broke into a smile. "Johnson, you've done it again. You've made me the biggest asshole in Tuy Hoa. I had to see the colonel who runs this base and tell him you were my personal representative in charge of ensuring that my men were properly cared for. He blew his top and called Corps."

"I'm sorry, sir," Jason said despondently.

"Don't be sorry." The lieutenant colonel patted Jay's back. "It was great. They told that fat-ass leg to do his damn job and quit complaining. You won another one for the Second Batt. What the hell would I do without you? Keep up the good work."

Jason shot a look at the major, who quickly shook his head. He kept silent until the commander had walked into his office and shut the door. "You didn't talk to him, did you?"

"I can't afford losing you," Walker said. "You're the best damn assistant operations officer I've had, and I can't let you go to another platoon."

"Sir, you promised once we left Dak To you'd talk to him and . . ."

"Look, Jay, the old man won't let you go. We've got plenty of lieutenants for the field but don't have enough good staff officers. You are his best L-tee and he needs you here to keep the rear straight. Somebody has got to take care of the men, and you've proven your heart is where it's supposed to be—with them, the soldiers of the Second Batt. Do like he says and just keep up the good work."

Jason's shoulders sagged. He hated every minute of being a staff officer. He took out his frustrations on those who gave line soldiers a hard time or thought their job was more important than those who humped. He was hated by all the rear-area soldiers because he was unrelenting and unmerciful in demanding one hundred percent effort in support. He wanted another platoon, to be with real soldiers again. He looked at this operations officer who had become a friend. "Sir, you know I'm a duck out of water. I'm not a career officer. I'm just doing my time like most of them out there. I need to be with them."

The major put his hand on Jason's shoulder. "Jay, I know what you're feeling, but you've got to understand this part of the war is just as important. With a platoon, you'd be helping twenty-five or thirty men. Here you're helping seven hundred. You're doing more for the colonel and the battalion than you could do out there. We need you here."

Jason looked at the major and felt trapped. He knew the man was right, but he knew he couldn't take much more. His heart was breaking, seeing the cold stares of line soldiers when they came in. They thought he was a REMF—a rear-echelon motherfucker.

Colonel Kinh smiled broadly. "The last of the infantry has gone. Only a mechanized unit remains, and they can patrol only the lowlands."

General Binh Ty Duc rose from his chair. "Begin the next phase of the construction immediately. Every unit must work day and night. The South is holding its elections soon, and the new so-called 'president' will be placed in office. Our plan must be ready to execute."

Kinh pointed at the wall map. "We are almost complete except for clearing the flank approaches to our major defensive positions, as you ordered. Several of the commanders have questioned the need."

"The Americans will attack our defensive positions exactly as they have always done," General Duc said as he picked up a pen from the table. "They will find our first positions, then pull back and call in air and artillery support. This is when they are most vulnerable. We will keep ground units available and have them attack their rear and flanks while they are waiting. The Americans will think the ground to their flanks is too steep for us to maneuver, but if we clear and prepare hidden trails, they will be surprised and ill prepared. We can split their force as they are strung out along the ridges and defeat them in detail. They will have no choice but to call for more soldiers and help our diversion.''

Kinh shook his head, knowing what the cost would be. "I have grown to care for the men very much. How long must our soldiers defend for the diversion to be successful?''

The general sat down and stared at the pen in his hands. "General Giap has asked for twenty days. We have cached enough supplies and ammunition for that time.''

Kinh shut his eyes. "Twenty days will be twenty years to our men.''

Duc nodded silently, knowing twenty days of fighting would finish his division. American intelligence would not underestimate his strength again. He had a plan to make sure of it. The Yankees would come in large numbers, and his men would do their duty and die for the grand plan. The thought of the pain and suffering his soldiers would endure caused him to clench his teeth. He would die also. Perhaps not in battle, but his heart would surely die as it had done thirteen years before on seeing his men lying on the battlefield at Dak To.

Lieutenant Salias heard the loud buzzing and knew he was close. Sergeant Hammonds walked out onto the trail in front of the new platoon leader and pointed to a nearby sugar plum. "They're over here, sir.''

Salias swallowed the lump in his throat seeing the black cloud of flies and stepped closer. The two VC had been killed thirty minutes before and were already covered with insects. The flies were like pilot fish with a shark—they followed the platoon and waited for a kill so that they could reap the benefits. The flies had gotten grossly fat the past week. His men had killed seven VC in ten days and had captured five more. The platoon was working independently in its own sector and had been searching some small hills adjacent to a huge valley covered with rice paddies. The platoon was having good luck in finding VC who were poorly trained and equipped. The local villagers were solid backers of the government and were reporting anything they saw that looked suspicious.

He waded through the swarm of flies and made a quick inspection of the bodies, wanting to get it over with. The head shots told him who did the killing and caused a shiver to run up his spine. Nance had killed six VC in the past week. The young soldier was a merciless killer of the worst kind. He seemed to live for it.

Hammonds handed him a small plastic bag. "This is all we found on them, just some notebooks and pictures, not much. Cat heard them talking and snuck up to within ten feet before opening up. One got away, and he's tracking him now with Caddy and Book Man.''

Salias brushed flies from his face and felt sick, knowing what they had been feasting on. "I specifically told you to pull Nance off point. He's killing them when he could be taking prisoners. And quit calling your men nicknames; it shows too much familiarity.''

Hammond's jaw muscles tightened. He found the new lieutenant a jerk who didn't know the first thing about leading a platoon. He'd come to the platoon and immediately screwed up by saying Lieutenant Jenkins obviously wasn't any good as their past leader and he'd "correct the situation." He came on like a little general with by-the-book lectures on warfare, which would have made sense if he'd been talking about brigades and divisions, but none of his lectures applied to squad and platoon level. He had neither common sense nor tact in talking to the men, and he was already known as "Shitty Salias."

Hammonds tried not to show his disdain as he spoke. "Sir, Cat, I mean Specialist Nance, is the best there is. He doesn't take any chances when it comes to dinks. We lost some men trying to take prisoners. It's too damn dangerous for a point man. The third squad got lucky the other day capturing those men in the river. The dinks didn't have security posted, or it would have been body-bag-fillin' time.''

Salias strode back to the trail to get away from the horrible, incessant buzzing. "Sergeant, don't tell me what is dangerous and what isn't. War is a dangerous business and risks must be taken. Specialist Nance is nothing more than a murderer. He doesn't obey my orders, and he still insists on wearing that grungy uniform and unauthorized flop hat, not to mention the NVA pistol.''

"Shit, sir, he's the best point man in the brigade,'' Hammonds said. "He knows what he's doing. He doesn't wear a steel pot because he can hear better without it. He doesn't miss a thing. If there are dinks in the area, he knows and finds them. I thought that was what we were here for . . . to kill them before they killed us?''

Salias raised his chin indignantly. Nance was undisciplined, as was the entire first squad. The scar-faced soldier was obviously thought of as irreplaceable and beyond the rules of authority.

Silk stood up from his position and pointed. "They got the fucker.''

Salias looked down the trail and his stomach quivered. The men they called Caddy and Book Man were dragging a body by the feet. Nance followed carrying a small pack and Russian rifle over his shoulder. All three men had a sickening, nonchalant look on their faces, although they'd just erased a human life.

He glanced at the body and his face screwed into a grimace. "Did you have to kill him? He was wounded, for Christ sake."

Caddy tossed down the man's leg and sat down tiredly as the flies attacked the still form. "We didn't shoot him again. We found him this way. He bled to death."

Salias spun around before getting sick and walked down the trail. He had to do something. The troops of the first squad were nothing more than animals.

Hammonds approached the center of the perimeter, already knowing something was wrong by the sympathetic looks that the medic and RTO gave him. Salias stood up but averted his gaze.

"Sergeant, have Specialist Nance report to me with all of his equipment. He's being picked up in a few minutes and taken to the rear. The recon detachment needs men, and he's been selected. I'll have a replacement for him in a couple of days."

Hammonds looked at the ground and stepped on an ant before looking up with a defiant glare. "You selected him, so let's cut the bullshit. Why? Does he bother your conscience?"

"He makes me sick!" Salias yelled. "You and your whole squad make me want to throw up! You're not soldiers anymore, you're animals. It's going to stop. I won't tolerate it any longer. He's first, and you're next."

Hammonds spun around to keep from knocking the pompous officer on his ass. He took two steps and spoke over his shoulder. "We're not animals! We're the best goddamn soldiers you've got!"

Salias heard the sound of the approaching helicopter and smiled. "Not anymore you're not."

Ty got off the chopper and was met by a sergeant in pressed fatigues. "You Nance?"

He nodded. He already missed his friends. The sergeant smiled and put out his hand. "I'm Chigger from the Thirty-ninth Scout dog detachment. My buddy called me from the Long Range Recon platoon and said you were coming in. He said your records show you went to the Scout dog school."

"I didn't graduate. I just attended for . . ."

"Doesn't matter," the sergeant interrupted. "The letter in your file said you would have been an honor graduate if you'd had the time. We're short of people and you've got the credentials; a letter from Sergeant First Class Winters is a diploma in any Scout's book.

He's the guru of us handlers. We have priority over the recon unit, so you're going to us instead of them.''

Ty hefted his rucksack to his shoulder. ''I need to talk to my company XO, Lieutenant Jenkins, and get it cleared.''

The sergeant shook his head. ''Nance, you don't understand. A major is in charge of all us special units, and he already talked to Jenkins. I gotta tell ya, your XO was one pissed-off L-tee when he found out your platoon leader went around him and canned your ass. The major worked out a deal with Jenkins. You're going to be trained by us a few weeks to get refreshed and let your dog get used to you, then you'll be attached to Fourth Batt. You're going to be attached back to your old outfit.''

Ty grinned. ''I guess I'm lucky to get to work with you guys . . . my first name is Ty.''

The sergeant chuckled and began walking down the dusty road. ''No, we've already heard all about the 'Cat.' We're the ones that are lucky.''

Jason felt something wet on his cheek, then he felt the hot breath. He'd been asleep for only a few minutes and knew it couldn't be a nightmare. He very slowly opened his eyes and looked into the face of a wolf . . . no, a wolf didn't have one ear up and the other down. He heard a chuckle and looked up to see Ty's strange, sad smile. ''Damn you!''

Ty pulled him up and hugged him tightly. ''God, you look so much better than the last time I saw ya. Damn, I worried about you.'' He fought the tears back and gently pushed Jason away. ''And you came back to this hellhole? Why, Jay? You shoulda went home.''

''I told ya in the letter why. I didn't have a choice. But forget about me, I'm just a REMF now. Damn, if you don't look shitty. You're skin and bones. Have you been sick?''

''Naw, the humpin' took the weight off,'' Ty said. He patted the dog and sat on the cot. ''I feel the best I've ever felt.''

Jason smiled and sat beside Ty, putting his arm over his shoulder. He motioned to the dog. ''What the hell is that?''

'''That, Jay, is a half-shepherd, half-labrador, totally crazy Scout dog named Saber. He ain't your typical combat tracker dog, and that's why I picked him. He doesn't know how to attack, heel, stay, or freeze, but he sure likes to play. He's strictly a tracker, like me.''

Jason's eyes narrowed. ''You volunteered for the Scouts?''

''Well, not exactly. I had a little run-in with a new L-tee who thought I needed a change of scenery. Enough about me. How about you? How's your shoulder?''

Jason raised his arm. "Good as new. I'm the best pencil-pusher in the battalion.''

His brother was unhappy, but Ty was thankful that Jay was out of harm's way. "Somebody's got to do it," Ty said, shrugging. "Relax and enjoy it. Mom won't have to worry as much.''

"You're one to be talking about relax," Jason said and grinned. "You coming out of a line unit to the Scout's is like going from the frying pan into the fire." His smile faded. "Take it easy out there, brother. The dinks are better than most people think. When they want to fight, they know exactly what they're doin'.''

Ty could see the pain in his eyes. "What happened out there, Jay? I wanna know.''

Jason lowered his head, not wanting to remember, but the images were already in his head. He could smell the napalm and hear the screams again. He leaned back, shut his eyes, and was there.

As he listened to Jason tell what happened, Ty felt his brother's fear and helplessness. The enemy he was describing was still out there and capable of doing the same thing again. They were not like the VC. The enemy who had almost killed his brother on that narrow ridge was only warming up, testing his strength for another day. As Jason described the attacks of that horror-filled night, Ty could see the bodies and hear the pleas as the NVA killed the survivors one by one.

When Jason had finished, he looked at his brother with a distant stare that made Ty's skin crawl. "My men are still calling for me.''

"You've done enough," Ty said softly. He put his arm around Jason's shoulders. "You've seen enough of this war for a lifetime.''

29

General Duc stood at the head of a large table and motioned the assembled officers to take their seats. He waited until all eyes were on him before speaking. "Comrades, on the thirty-first of this month, the South Vietnamese government will inaugurate the first so-called president of their second republic. Today, General Giap has answered this hypocrisy with the orders we have been waiting for. We are to begin phase one of the master plan immediately."

The officers shifted in their seats exchanging smiles and confident nods. The general tapped the table for their attention. "Today, we begin moving our units toward Dak To to occupy the defensive positions. Our double agents have already been notified and are helping American intelligence by feeding them the information we want them to have. The Americans will believe our intention is to wipe out the Dak To base camp, and they will react by sending many units to stop us.

"Comrades, the battles before us will be watched by the entire world. We must maul the proud tiger. He will growl loudly and claw at us, but we must not be caught in his powerful jaws. We will strike his flanks, his belly, his tail, and when he is weak, we will strike his throat. The fight will last many days, and he will lose much blood. The tiger will limp away with scars for the whole world to see.

"My brothers, the tiger is coming. Go now and prepare to bring the beast to his knees."

Lieutenant Salias clenched his teeth as the familiar scar-faced soldier approached. He knew the bastard was taunting him by wearing the dirty uniform, floppy hat, and NVA pistol. Even the dog looked unmilitary. It was a big, floppy-eared, ugly crossbreed, not the pure-bred shepherd like most Scout dogs. The company commander had called twenty minutes before to say a dog team was being attached to him, but he was not prepared to see Nance again.

Ty held his new CAR-15 submachine gun in one hand and the leash in the other. He nodded instead of saluting. "Sir, I reckon I'm back for a while."

Salias wanted to tell him to go back to the captain, but he knew that wouldn't be a very wise move. The captain had been riding him hard lately because he was having so many discipline problems and he wasn't finding any of the enemy. He had no choice but to use the filthy soldier and mangy mutt. "Specialist, you and your mongrel report to first squad and be ready to move out in one hour."

Ty smiled. "Yes, sir. Glad to see you again, too."

Hammonds looked up and grinned as Ty walked down the trail with a dog at his side. "Well, I'll be damned!"

Silk sat up from his rucksack. "Dig it, dudes. The Cat is back with Rin Tin Tin."

The squad quickly surrounded him with backslaps and warm handshakes. Cowboy looked even skinnier, and Bugs was just as ugly as always. Book Man and Surf looked more like veterans, now that they had lost their fat cheeks and their faces had tanned.

But Ty didn't see his old friend. "Where's Caddy?"

Hammonds laughed. "He's bangin' his balls off on R and R in Bangkok."

Silk retorted quickly, "He better not, man. The dude promised!"

Ty looked to Hammonds for an explanation, but the sergeant only checked his watch and smiled more broadly.

Forty-five minutes later, Ty stepped onto the trail and unleashed Saber. Normal procedure was to keep the dog leashed, but Ty had learned over the past weeks that Saber worked better without restraints. Saber would walk only a few feet in front and zigzag back and forth, sniffing for a trace of Vietnamese.

Bugs watched as the dog moved lazily into his routine. He stepped up to Ty and whispered, "Saber ain't in a big hurry, is he?"

Ty looked at the buck-toothed soldier with a smile and held his finger to his lips. "He's gettin' in the groove."

Ty and Saber led the platoon for three hours without finding any sign of recent VC activity. Hammonds kept checking his map and his compass azimuth, but the terrain didn't match. He walked back to Salias three times to confirm the compass azimuth he had been given, and each time the lieutenant had told him he knew what he was doing and to continue. Hammonds finally stopped after another hour and passed the word back for the L-tee to come forward.

Salias stomped up the trail with his RTO. "Why are you stopping?" he asked angrily.

"You may know where we are, but I sure as hell don't," Hammonds said. He held up his map. "Nothing has made sense since we left the perimeter. Are you sure the compass heading you gave me is right?"

"We are right here," Salias said, pointing at a spot on the map. "Now let's move it!"

Hammonds looked at where the lieutenant was pointing and then at the surrounding terrain. "No, sir, we're not. If we were there, we would have small hills to our right. The hills are four klicks to our rear."

Salias quickly checked the map and pulled out his compass. He checked twice more before looking up. "Ah . . . well, I had us deviate a little to . . . we're doing fine. Just keep on this heading until we hit the highway to confirm our location."

Hammonds sighed, knowing the officer had screwed up again. He looked at the map, and shook his head. "We can't do that. I think we're here, which means we're two klicks outside our boundary. You gotta call the old man and tell him, so we don't get fired up by First Batt. This is their area."

Salias's eyes widened in fear. He couldn't call the company commander to tell him he had been lost and had wandered into another battalion's area of operation. To do so would be to commit career suicide. He nervously shifted his stance as he looked at the map again. "That's not necessary. We'll just turn around and go back the way we came."

Ty, who had reconned ahead while the discussion was going on, now walked back to the group. "Sarge, I think we're outside our boundary. Up ahead is a knoll, and five hundred meters down I saw a small village with GIs all around it. They . . ."

"We know exactly where we are!" Salias retorted hotly. "We don't need you telling us anything."

Ty shrugged. "Then I guess you know about the platoon coming this way."

Salias's face turned beet red. "What?"

Ty looked over his shoulder. "Saber picked up their scent, then I saw them. I waved at their point team so's they wouldn't shoot. They're right behind me."

Salias looked down the ridge and saw paratroopers walking up the slope with huge smiles on their faces. His body seemed to melt.

He had no choice but to call his commander and tell him he had been lost.

Ty sat up and patted Saber, wondering what was happening, as the squad began to gather around him. Salias had been told by the company commander to stay the night with the First Battalion soldiers, who turned out to be from Charlie Company. They had a small base camp outside the village. Hammonds and the men sat down around Ty and looked at their watches.

He couldn't take it any longer. "Come on, Sarge, what's up?"

Hammonds grinned. "We're having a little party we arranged with Caddy before he left for R and R. He promised he was gonna begin bangin' a broad at exactly twenty hundred hours, our time, and think of us."

Silk looked up from his watch. "Yeah, man, can you dig it? He's taking his clothes off right now."

Ty's mouth dropped open. "You gotta be kiddin."

Bugs patted his back. "Ain't it cool?" Bugs said. "Caddy told me he was gonna take pictures and give 'em to us to prove he done it on time."

Surf was grinning like a mad hatter. "This is most definitely cool. I'm gonna remember this one for when I get back to the world. The dudes ain't gonna believe it, man!"

Book Man raised his wrist. "Fellow mental voyeurs, the time is less than one minute away before our hero begins ravishing the young maiden."

Silk looked at Bugs with a confused expression. "What da' Book call us, man?"

Bugs shrugged. "Voyagers or somethin'."

Cowboy leaned forward. "You reckon that lady will mind him wantin' to do it right at eight?"

Ty leaned back as the men began counting down. He couldn't believe they were so engrossed in the mental fantasy. Book Man held up his wrist again. "Fifteen seconds until lift-off."

"Naw, fifteen seconds till 'put in,' " Bugs chuckled.

Their faces were all glued to their watches.

"Three . . . two . . . one," they all said together. "YEAH! Git it, Caddy!"

"Go, man!"

"I can hear her moaning! She's diggin' it!"

"OHHHHH, Caddy! Stroke! Stroke! Stroke one for ol' Silk!"

Ty couldn't help but smile. The "party" was, to say the least, unusual, but somehow they had figured out a way to share Caddy's freedom from the war. The squad would forget about it tomorrow when they were humping, but when Caddy came back, they would laugh again and recount the party many times.

He shut his eyes and felt a cold nose touch his neck. "What the . . . aw damn, dog." Saber had settled down and rested his head on Ty's shoulder. Since the first day they had been together, the dog had slept with his head on Ty's shoulder as if protecting him.

Ty pushed the animal away, but in a few minutes he felt Saber again. He gave up and patted the dog's head. "I thought once we got to the field you'd stop this. Okay, but only for tonight. You're a damn scaredy-cat, ya know it?"

Jason read the report and turned to Major Hanlon, who was updating his wall map. "Sir, this doesn't look good. The Fourth Division LRRPs confirmed boocoo dinks moving into the Dak To area. This confirms agent reports that the NVA are planning to attack the base. The Fourth Division is going to move its First Brigade headquarters into Dak To tomorrow, and our brigade has been put on alert to stand by to follow."

The major took the report and quickly read it himself. "Shit! The one thing we don't want is to be attached to the damn funny Fourth legs. I hope this is just another intelligence foul-up and we don't have to go."

Jason pulled out a folder. "Sir, here are the intelligence reports from the Dak To area for the past ten days. I've been reading them, and all the pieces are beginning to fit. The airborne personnel detector has been picking up strong concentrations since the twenty-fifth."

"Snoopy can't tell monkeys from people. Hell, it's probably a migration of apes."

Jason knew the major was trying to wish the evidence away. Nobody wanted to go back to Dak To. He began to put the folder away when the major put out his hand. "I'd better read those. You go ahead and notify all the companies to bring their platoons in. I'll brief the old man as soon as he gets back from the field and start planning a load out. It might not happen but . . . Shit! Why now, for God's sake? We just got settled in."

Ty held on to Saber as the chopper lifted off. The dog was panting heavily and couldn't keep his head up. Ty stroked Saber's head, wishing the bird would fly faster. He had awakened that morning to find Saber's stomach covered with leeches. The bloated parasites were gorged with blood and had sucked almost all of the life from the unsuspecting animal. Ty had burned most of them off, but the damage was done. Saber's only chance was a blood transfusion. The medevac arrived only a few minutes after the company commander called. A Scout dog rated the same treatment as a wounded paratrooper.

He hugged the dog to him. "Hang in there, buddy. We've only got a little ways to go." Saber had gotten to him. Ty had tried to keep the dog from taking a piece of his heart, but the animal, like a child, was desperate for affection. Saber never left his side. He depended on him for almost everything: food, water, and love.

The crew chief yelled over the engine noise, "The vet is standing by!"

Ty felt relieved as soon as the blood began dripping down the tube and into the vein. The captain took off his rubber gloves. "Saber doesn't look much like a Scout dog, does he?"

Ty gave the vet a plastic smile. "You'd have to know Saber to know why he ain't like most Scout dogs. He probably shouldn't even be here. I think he was given to the Army by a prison. He was used to tracking escapees."

"Well, whatever he is, he's going to be fine in a couple of days. You can report back to your unit and pick him up tomorrow."

Ty took off his rucksack and tossed it to the floor. "Ol' Saber and me have gotten pretty used to each other. I'd feel better stayin' with him."

The captain nodded. "Sure, I should have known better. I'll call your unit and tell them where you are and the status of Saber. By the way, did you hear the brigade is on alert to get back to Dak To? The NVA have moved into the highlands, and they're about to strike."

Ty patted the dog's side and spoke in a whisper. "They'll be waiting for us . . . it won't be like last time."

"How do you know?"

Ty turned slowly and looked at the officer. "I know."

30

Jason read the intelligence update and handed it back to the major. "That's bullshit. No NVA sergeant would know that much."

Hanlon handed the message to the battalion commander. "Sir, you can see my lieutenant doesn't put much stock in our intelligence. I think he's right. According to the message, an NVA sergeant from Sixty-sixth Regiment's reconnaissance unit turned himself in at Dak Ri, just a few miles west of Dak To. He said he was tired of the war and spilled his guts on the entire First NVA Division's plans to attack the Dak To base camp. He said his unit and the Thirty-second Regiment were going to attack from the southwest, and the 174th Regiment would attack from the northeast. The Fortieth Artillery Regiment was split and supporting all three infantry units. The attack was planned for the twenty-ninth of October but was delayed due to the arrival of the Fourth Division at Dak To."

The lieutenant colonel furrowed his brow. "How many sergeants in our battalion could tell us what the other battalions are doing in this brigade?"

The major shook his head. "Not very damn many, and they sure as hell wouldn't know a division's battle plans. This sergeant is a plant if I ever saw one, but the intell spooks are pissin' all over themselves with delight. They think they've broken the secret code of the whole fuckin' NVA army . . . and the top brass believe them!"

"What orders have been given to other battalions?"

"Sir, us and First Batt are still on standby alert, but Fourth Batt is moving right now to Dak To. The Fourth Division already has one brigade there and is about to send in a second. The dinks obviously want our forces to go to Dak To, but we have to ask, 'why?' Are they trying to con us into believing they're going to attack so we'll move troops, or are they really planning an attack?''

The colonel put on his helmet. ''Beats the hell out of me.''

Ty stared at the mountains to the south, where Alpha, Charlie, and Delta companies were taking different routes up the ridges to converge on Hill 823. The three companies had left the day before and had reached the foot of the first hills. They had found several old NVA camps and new trails. Their mission was to search for and destroy suspected concentrations of enemy from the Sixty-sixth regiment that were reported in the area. The three companies were to link up with Ty's company, Bravo, which was to air assault onto 823 that afternoon. Bravo's mission was to secure the hilltop so that engineers could clear back the rain forest and build a firebase for a howitzer battery.

The Bravo company commander had given the plan the night before to all the platoon leaders and attachments. The 173d Airborne Brigade was going to search the mountains one step at a time. One battery from the 319th Artillery was located at Ben Het, supporting the move to Hill 823, and another battery would move to the new firebase and support the next step.

Ty scratched Saber's neck. He was glad the brigade commander was being cautious, especially after what had happened to the two battalions from the funny Fourth three days before. Although the commander was being cautious, most of the men thought the operation was going to be a bust. They remembered the last time they were there and had humped for months, finding nothing but empty positions. They didn't believe the NVA would fight because of the large number of American units coming in.

The company commander saw his scout-dog handler sitting on a bunker and walked over. ''Cat, sorry I haven't had a chance to talk to you since you got here. Saber looks a lot better since the last time I saw him.''

Ty smiled and patted the dog's head. ''If it wasn't for you calling that medevac so quick, sir, he wouldn't have made it. I sure appreciate what you did.''

''No sweat,'' the captain said. He sat down beside Ty. ''Listen, I want you on the first bird that goes in this afternoon. It might be a hot LZ, so don't be in any hurry jumping off if the bird receives fire. The artillery is going to blow the shit out of the hilltop before we get there, but you never know. If it's a cold LZ, make a quick recon over the hilltop and try to figure out if the dinks have been there.''

Ty patted Saber again. "Sir, if they've been there, my buddy will know. He looks like a bird dog when he smells them. His hair stands up and he slobbers like he was crazy."

The captain looked at the dog. "You know, Cat, he's so damn ugly he's almost cute."

The helicopter approached the small hole in the rain forest and began losing altitude. Ty held his breath, waiting for the bullets to hit. The chopper was an easy, hanging target. The bird dropped suddenly and came to an abrupt hover four feet from the ground. Ty jumped, dragging Saber with him. They hit the ground and ran between blown-down trees and limbs to a large jagged stump. The Huey lifted off, blowing the pulverized ground into a choking dust cloud. Ty felt elated. Not a single shot had been fired at them. He looked around for the others that were on the chopper and saw two men lying on the edge of the LZ to his left. To his right was a huge crater made by a delayed-action thousand-pound bomb. The artillery had little effect, but the bomb had been devastating. The twenty-meter-wide crater was devoid of life, and surrounding the depression were only the battered wooden skeletons and jagged stumps of trees. Beyond the shattered trees, however, the green wall of rain forest and bamboo stood unaffected.

He heard the second Slick coming in and ran for the rain forest to secure the far side of the LZ. He and Saber crossed the crater's fine dust and fell into the tree line. Blinded by the dirt, Ty lowered his head to wipe his eyes. Suddenly, his arm was tugged and he looked up to find the dark hole of a bunker firing port. Saber was at the end of his leash digging into the side of the bunker, his hair standing on end and his muzzle frothing with foam. Ty shut his eyes, knowing he was going to die.

The sweat-soaked company commander tried to talk on the radio and inform the colonel that his company had secured the hilltop, but he couldn't get through. Alpha and Delta companies had walked into a nest of entrenched NVA and were in a firefight only two klicks down the ridge to the north. They were on the same frequency trying to get more artillery support and medevacs. They already had one killed and seven wounded and were fighting for their lives.

He gave up and looked at Ty. "What is it you were trying to tell me, Cat?"

Ty pointed to the right side of the perimeter and had to half-yell to be heard over the landing helicopters, which were bringing in the rest of the company. "Sir, the dinks were here just before we came in and had a defensive position in the trees! Saber picked up their scent, and he's going crazy! They're not far away!"

The captain stood and yelled to his platoon leaders, "Get outposts out and tighten the perimeter!" He glanced at Ty as he picked up the radio handset again. "Get over to where the dog picked up the scent and keep me posted."

Ty jogged to the Third Platoon sector and knelt down by the platoon sergeant. "Where's your L-tee?"

The sergeant pointed down the hill toward a small trail. "He's coming. He just put out the outpost."

The lieutenant strode up the trail and was about to speak when AK-47 fire erupted from where he had just put his two-man listening post.

"OH NO!" he blurted and spun around. Without hesitating, he began running back down the trail and yelled at three men lying beside the trail to follow him.

Ty stood up to follow when, to his horror, the lieutenant and two of the troopers who had gotten up were cut down by a burst of machine-gun fire. A split second later, from out of the trees only twenty meters down the hill, a squad of NVA burst out of the woodline shooting and screaming. Bullets popped by Ty's ears and filled the air like mad hornets. He fell to the ground and pulled Saber behind a fallen tree as the camouflaged NVA pressed their surprise attack.

An M-60 gunner lying in the crater began firing, catching the charging soldiers in the open. The red tracers were only visible for a millisecond before disappearing into bodies and bamboo.

Ty and the platoon sergeant began shooting along with the rest of the platoon. The charging enemy were riddled, but not before the last man had almost reached the crest. The only survivor of the three men who had gone with the lieutenant raised to his knees and called out for help. A PFC on the perimeter jumped up to make a dash for him, but an NVA stepped from behind a tree and shot the wounded paratrooper in the back. The PFC screamed in rage and ran down the hill, shooting from the hip. The NVA soldier was flung backward by a ricocheting bullet that struck his weapon, then his chin. The charging PFC jammed the rifle barrel into the NVA's face and pulled the trigger.

Shaking horribly, Ty lowered his rifle. The earsplitting noise, the smell of gunpowder, and the sight of charging men were terrifying. Tossing off his rucksack, he quickly took out his entrenching tool and began digging behind the fallen tree. He had to get Saber into a hole. Shrapnel or a bullet was twice as devastating to an animal.

The platoon sergeant was stunned by the death of five of his men and his platoon leader. He mumbled as he stared at his rifle, trying to figure out how to change magazines. His mind was blank. Ty stopped digging and took the weapon from him. He quickly inserted the new magazine and tossed the rifle back.

The sergeant's blank gaze evaporated and he stood up yelling, "Tighten up, Third Platoon, and fill the gaps! Buddy up and dig in! Jones, you and Kalanoski dig in by the trail! Baker, get that sixty dug in and break out the spare barrel! Everybody break out your extra sixty ammo!"

The company commander and first sergeant ran around the perimeter, checking positions and yelling out to the leaders. "Stay in your platoon sectors and be prepared to help another platoon! Get your grenades out and bring your mortar rounds to the crater, one man at a time!"

Ty dug frantically, feeling helpless. This was a different war. His skills as a tracker were useless. There were no tracks, signs, or smells to warn him of the enemy. This war was unfair. Skill meant nothing. This was nothing but raw force—gun against gun—and pure luck. These five dead men could not have done a thing to keep from being wasted. Their only mistake was being on Hill 823 in Bravo Company on the sixth of November 1967.

Ty's hands wouldn't stop shaking. He was thirsty, tired, and scared. His only consolation was that the dirt was soft and the hole was quickly becoming deeper. He didn't want to stop digging. The deeper he got, the farther away from the madness he got.

Suddenly, the air was filled with hornets again, and the log in front of him groaned with the impact of bullets. Two platoons of NVA broke from the trees and charged the perimeter as machine guns raked the hastily dug American positions.

The M-60 gunner couldn't raise up behind his gun without exposing himself, so he lay back in his shallow hole and waited for the first wave to appear. The captain screamed for the second and first platoons, who weren't receiving fire on their side of the perimeter, to turn around and shoot across their pinned-down buddies.

Ty lay on top of Saber, cringing. Bullets were crisscrossing only a foot over his head. He could hear the screams of the NVA as well as his own men. The sounds weren't human. A grenade went off only a few feet in front of the log and threw up a cloud of dust. He raised up only enough to ready his submachine gun when a North Vietnamese soldier jumped the log and ran past him. Another appeared and began to leap the obstacle. Ty shot him in the chest in midstride, knocking him backwards. He raised his head again and could see NVA running in all directions. Red and green tracers were whizzing past in a stream, and grenade explosions were shaking the ground like small earthquakes. Two NVA ran shoulder to shoulder, shooting and screaming in front of him. He fired a burst and hit one, but the other kept running. The soldier he had shot suddenly got up and ran straight toward him without his rifle. Ty fired again, hitting the wounded man in the chest, but his momentum carried him over the log. Ty deflected the falling body with his rifle barrel just as three more NVA broke out of the smoke only fifteen yards away. He swung his CAR-15 back and fired. The weapon recoiled twice, then nothing. He kept his finger on the trigger but realized the magazine was empty. The NVAs' fatigues looked brand new. They weren't wearing camouflage like the others, and they carried a full combat load of equipment. Their brown eyes were wide and fear-filled as they ran toward him, shooting wildly. Ty saw every detail as if they were stepping in slow motion. One jerked sideways, shot in the shoulder by a machine gun, and another abruptly fell face first, hit in the legs. The last one kept coming, his face contorted and screaming. Ty lifted his pistol. He didn't remember taking it from the holster or pushing off the safety. It was just there. He didn't aim or blink as he rose up and fired at point-blank range. The NVA's head snapped back and his legs buckled. He hit the ground and fell backwards.

Sergeant Hammonds crawled behind a fallen tree and stopped to catch his breath. He had been sent by the platoon sergeant to find the company commander and learn what the platoon was supposed to do. The first platoon was on the eastern side of the company perimeter and had not been attacked. When the NVA overran the third platoon's western sector, the first platoon had turned around and shot down those who tried to continue the attack through the perimeter. There had been a twenty-minute lull after the assault, and the first platoon had lost radio contact with the captain. The NVA had pulled back but their mortars had continued to pound the perimeter, making it impossible to move about without crawling.

He heard radio static ahead and resumed crawling. Near a large stump he saw the captain lying on his stomach with his fatigue pants pulled down to his knees. The RTO was placing a bandage on the bleeding right cheek of the officer's buttocks. Hammonds felt better on seeing Cat beside the wounded first sergeant, holding a canteen up for him to drink.

The captain turned his head toward Hammonds and spoke with surprising calm. "What's your platoon's status?"

Hammonds hugged the ground as a bullet cracked overhead. "Sir, we don't have anybody hit, but we're running low on ammo and grenades. The platoon sergeant sent me to find out what your orders are for him."

"Where . . . where the hell is Lieutenant Salias?"

"I haven't seen him since the first shots were fired," Hammonds said and frowned. "Sergeant Ramaldo has taken over. He wants to know what we should do."

The captain dug his hands into the dirt to fight back the pain. "Tell . . . tell him to tighten the perimeter and tie in with the platoons to his right and left. Dig in deep. We got hit by a mortar round that got six of us. We got through to battalion and they're sending out medevacs and a resupply of ammo once we get this damn perimeter secured."

A mortar round hit twenty yards away, shaking the ground and sending up a dust cloud. Hammonds raised his head, nodding at the captain, then looked at Ty. "See ya later."

Ty raised his right thumb. "See ya."

The darkness was gone for an instant when another mortar round exploded in an earsplitting, blinding flash. Ty held Saber down as dirt and debris showered them. He shook off the dirt and looked into the blackness, straining to see if anyone was hurt. He couldn't see anything but purple spots from the previous flash of light. A grenade exploded across the perimeter, but he didn't flinch. He was too tired to cringe anymore. The 81-millimeter mortars thunked out two rounds from the crater in a defiant response to the enemy mortar. Then a low drone passed overhead, and suddenly the sky was set ablaze with floating lights. The parachute flares dropped by Spooky immediately brought a tinge of hope. Ty raised up, checking the trees to his front, then knelt back down beside Saber. The flares cast an eerie glow over the crater, the fallen, twisted trees, and the stiff, grotesque bodies. Cordite from the firing mortars floated in a low-hanging cloud and mixed with the odor of blood and freshly plowed earth. The golden glow of the flares deepened then slowly faded into blackness. The shadows danced and swayed tricking the eyes and nerves into believing another attack was coming. Men threw grenades at noises, shadows, and ghosts in the darkness.

Hammonds tapped Ty's shoulder. "You okay, Cat?"

Ty welcomed the nudge. He was glad to be reminded that another living human was beside him. "Yeah, how 'bout you?"

"Yeah, I'm fine . . . naw, I'm spooked half out of my mind but sure glad you decided to join us."

Another series of flares popped overhead, and one of the mortarmen dropped a round in the tube.

Ty leaned back against Hammonds's shoulder. "I gotta tell ya the truth. I was told to join you guys. Otherwise I'd still be in my deep, deep hole thinking about you all."

Hammonds smiled in the golden light. "You're better off with us anyway. We're lucky. Did all the wounded get out?"

"Yeah, the pilots really deserve a big kiss for that one. They were taking fire all the way in. We got all the wounded out, plus we got a resupply of ammo and grenades. I wish they woulda brought in water. Saber has just about had it."

Hammonds lowered his head. "We all have."

Ty looked at his watch; it was almost midnight. The NVA had attacked twice with grenades and rockets, but they had been repulsed each time. If the resupply chopper hadn't come, the enemy would have taken the perimeter. One man, a pilot he didn't know, had saved the company of desperate men with a resupply of ammunition and much needed grenades.

A flash of white-orange light went off down the hill and was followed by a whooshing noise. Ty and Hammonds ducked as the rocket screamed overhead and exploded behind them. Hammonds raised up, throwing a grenade at the spot where the NVA soldier had fired the launcher and flattened himself. The crack and echoing boom were hardly noticeable among the other grenade explosions going on around them.

"AHHHHHH NOOOOOOO!" Surf screamed and rose up from his foxhole, shooting his M-16 blindly at the shadows. Hammonds yelled as he balled up, knowing what was going to happen, "STOP SHOOTING! STOP SHOOTING!"

Within five seconds chicom rifle grenades hit the ground all around them. The explosions ripped through the night air, covering the men in dirt, dust, and splintered wood. Next came the mortar rounds. In the distance was the metallic thunk pop, and then came the wait. In twenty seconds they would know if they were going to live. The rounds impacted first twenty, then thirty feet to their right, just outside the perimeter.

Hammonds spat out dirt and whispered loudly, "Goddamn it! Nobody fire your rifle! The muzzle flash lets 'em know where we are! Book Man, take care of Surf and get him calmed down!"

Ty hugged Saber. Living was now a matter of luck. There was no protection from the mortar rounds and no protection from men who made mistakes. Surf had reached the breaking point, where living or dying didn't make any difference. Sitting in a hole all night waiting to die had gotten to him. It was the worst nightmare come true. Like a frightened child who knows a monster is waiting in the darkness under the bed, each man in Bravo Company waited and cringed in his foxhole. Only there was no mother close by to scream out to or to crawl in bed with. There were no hugs or gentle words of reassurance. There was no light to turn on to feel safe. The men of Bravo Company were living in a nightmare where the monsters were real.

Ty watched the darkness slip away, praying it would hurry its retreat, though as things became more visible, they became more depressing. The night had hidden the awful truth of death. The smell grew worse in the rising, smoky mist. Gunfire cut through the silence, causing Ty to jump, and he accidentally hit Saber with his raised weapon. The southern part of the perimeter seemed to explode and then rattle with M-16 fire. Someone yelled, "Medic!" and another yelled, "Incoming!"

Ty flattened himself and threw his arms around Saber. The incoming mortar rounds landed forty feet away, and someone screamed.

Hammonds yelled for his squad to sound off. Silk and Bugs both hollered from their holes, "Yo!" Book Man barked out a "Here!" and Cowboy and Surf answered up with "Okay."

Hammonds exchanged a relieved look with Ty and raised his head to spot the lieutenant, who was yelling for him. A bullet cracked by his ear, missing him by only an inch. "Shit! Goddamn sonofabitchin' motherfuckers! Shit yeah, shoot at me, you bastards! You couldn't do me last night!"

Ty reached out and put his hand on the seething man's shoulder. "Save it, Sarge. We ain't outta this yet."

Hammonds lowered his chin into the dirt. "I hate this shit, Cat. I hate this fucking hill, this fucking country, and this fucking war. We've been here half a day and all night, and now the lieutenant decides to lead the platoon again. I'll bet the sonofabitch has been lying in a foxhole the whole time shitting his pants. Fuck him!"

The sound of approaching helicopters brought all the men's eyes up. The sight of the gunships was like a shot of hope.

"GIT SOME!" yelled Silk.

Ty hugged Saber to him as the lead gunship lowered its nose and streaked in for a rocket run. Minutes later he raised up. Someone was yelling for him. A captain he didn't recognize made his way over the felled trees. "Nance, I'm the new commander. We're going to begin searching outside the perimeter. You and your dog are going to lead us."

Ty stood in the center of the perimeter with his old squad. Stacked beside him were twenty-two AK-47 rifles, one RPD machine gun, a pile of rocket launchers, and hundreds of chicom grenades. The company had completed the search around the perimeter and down the ridges and had found eighty-one dead NVA and one wounded prisoner.

Hammonds used his foot to turn over the body of an NVA soldier. "These guys are well fed, and they're wearing new uniforms. They have new AKs, and they're carrying the same basic shit we carry. The press ought to see this and quit saying we're fighting farmers. This guy is a hardcore infantryman just as good as we are and just as well equipped."

Ty took the canteen from the dead man's equipment and poured water into his hand for Saber. "Those platforms we found in the trees are something we haven't seen before. If we ever get into anything like this again we better hose all the trees down for snipers."

Silk sat down and took off his helmet. "Again? Man, I seen enough; I'm ready for da fuckin' house. Dis shit is gettin' real fuckin' old, man."

Bugs collapsed to his knees and looked up at Hammonds. "How many we lose?"

Hammonds took out his canteen and drank before answering. "Eight killed and fourteen wounded yesterday, and Platoon Sergeant Cabrera got it this morning. There's a few more wounded that will be medevaced in a little while."

Book Man sat back on his rucksack and shut his eyes. "We started with 102 men . . . that leaves us 79 in the company."

Cowboy looked around him at his friends. "Yeah, but *we* all made it. That's what counts."

"Fuckin' A!" Silk said, holding out his hand for Bugs to slap.

Ty remembered the plan the captain had revealed the day before and closed his eyes. Taking Hill 823 was just the first of many. Alpha and Delta companies had reported two men killed and twenty wounded. The fourth battalion had lost the equivalent of two platoons—half a company in a day and a half of fighting. He wondered how many steps the battalion could afford to make.

* * *

Colonel Thong drummed his fingers on the table as he listened to the report from his operations officer. The Third Battalion was finished. Only one company showed more than fifty percent strength. The Americans' fire support had decimated the ranks. He stopped drumming and stood up. "Have the remaining men form into a reinforced company and report to the Sixth Battalion. The Yankees are building a firebase on 823 and will be searching the entire area."

The operations officer's face showed signs of strain. His eyes were bloodshot and sunken. "Reports from the scouts confirm more Yankee and puppet units are arriving everyday at Dak To. The tall one must be very happy."

The colonel's jaw tightened. "Hold your tongue. The general knows all too well the consequences."

Jason stood outside the operations tent and watched the buildup. The Second Battalion had arrived the day before and had moved to the old Dak To airstrip, just a klick east of new Dak To. Both bases were swarming with activity. Tents were thrown up anywhere the ground was flat. Slicks, gunships, medevacs, and small observation choppers passed over every few minutes on every conceivable type of mission. C-130s landed, unloaded, and took off every few minutes around the clock, bringing in more men, equipment, and ammunition. Fighter planes crisscrossed the skies. The air was tense with excitement.

He took a deep breath and walked back inside the stifling operations tent to thumbtack maps to sheets of plywood. He had to stay busy. The battle reports from the Fourth Batt had shaken him. The NVA were doing exactly what they did to his unit in June—they were attacking the perimeters in waves. He felt better since calling the Thirty-ninth Scout dog detachment that afternoon and finding out no dog handlers attached to the Fourth had been wounded or killed, but he still felt sick inside. He didn't want any man to experience what he had gone through, especially Ty.

The major walked into the tent and tiredly sat on a folding chair. "I guess you've heard all hell is breaking loose south of Ben Het," he said tiredly.

Jason motioned toward the stack of reports. "Yes, sir. The Brigade runner is bringing those over every hour."

The major sighed as he eyed the messages. "Well, I just left the old man, and we've been ordered to plan an assault to join the ruckus. The Fourth Battalion cleared a firebase on Hill 823. They

call it Firebase 15. We are going to air assault in and establish
another firebase, Firebase 16, farther into the mountains to support
a bigger search. Looks like we're going to join the battle.''

Jason looked at the map he had just tacked up. "There's a big
hilltop eight klicks southwest of the firebase that would be perfect.
It commands the whole valley to the east . . . it's Hill 875.''

Hanlon stood and looked at the map and pointed at another spot.
"No, let's plan for this smaller hill, here, that's only six klicks away
from 15. I don't want to take too big a bite. We'll request bomb
strikes on its top just before we go in.''

Jason marked the smaller hilltop with a pencil. "When are we
supposed to go in?''

The major tossed his helmet to a corner of the tent. "Plan it for
the tenth.''

Ty jumped off the Huey with Saber and walked toward the buck-
ets of iced-down soft drinks. Ben Het was nothing more than a
dirty, ugly mound of red dirt, but it was out of the mountains and
represented civilization. Lieutenant Jenkins had Cokes waiting for
the entire company when they got off the choppers. Ty gave Saber
a chunk of ice to lick and opened a can. He brought the drink to
his lips. Nothing in the world could have tasted better. Not only
was it ice cold and delicious but it was a part of home.

Hammonds and the rest of the squad gathered around Ty and
drank in silence. They didn't want to spoil this wonderful moment.
Silk lowered his can at the sight of a familiar soldier approaching.
"Man, you better have a picture of a good-lookin' hole or don't be
comin' back talkin' jive.''

Caddy smiled broadly and tossed a packet of pictures toward the
big black paratrooper. "Caddy messes with only class. Check it
out. She was a model for the Thai magazines.''

Bugs, Cowboy, Book Man, and Surf all grabbed for the pictures
as Ty and Hammonds embraced Caddy. Hammonds patted his
stomach. "You got fat!''

Ty grinned. "Yeah, the good life put some pounds on ya.''

Caddy began to retort when Silk let out a yell and shoved a
picture in front of Bugs's face. "I told you she'd be a queen! Look
at them watermelons, man!''

Bugs pushed the picture away. "That's makeup! They're probably paste-on tits. Dink boobs don't get that big, and you know it.''

Cowboy held up a picture. "Caddy, what was you all doin' in
this one? I can't tell if you was upside down or she was.''

Book Man glanced at the picture and took off his glasses to clean off the dust. "Cowboy, the maiden is performing a form of fellatio in a position unknown to the women of the Western world."

"Say what, man?" Silk asked.

"Fe-lat-shee-o," Bugs said. "It means the broad likes to be feeled up before gettin' it on. It's Eye-Italian."

Caddy laughed and looked at his friends' tired, unshaven faces, knowing they'd been through hell. Their eyes told their own story. He put his arm around Ty. "I heard it was real bad. I wish I'd been with you all."

Ty exchanged glances with Hammonds. "You didn't wanna be there. I just hope someone figures out how to blow the mountains away with B-52s and leave us out of it. The dinks got us by the balls up there."

Caddy tossed his head toward the bunkers. "Come on, I've got some beer for you guys. I heard the Fourth Batt is going to take a break for a while."

Hammonds raised his Coke can. "I'll drink to that."

31

General Duc walked into the busy operations center and all work stopped. The six staff officers he had working around the clock smiled at him. The news from the spies in the south was better than they had expected. The Yankees and puppets had committed over sixteen thousand men to the battle. The entire American Fourth Division was in Dak To, as was the 173d Airborne Brigade. A brigade from the First Cavalry Division was in Kontum screening the southern sector, and six ARVN battalions had been sent from the Saigon area to search north of the Dak To airfield. The diversion was a resounding success.

He stopped in front of the large calendar on the wall and picked up a pencil. The calendar began on the first and ended on the twentieth, representing the second part of the plan—he was to hold the enemy in the highlands for twenty days. He drew an X through the tenth day and faced his officers. "Comrades, we have ten more days to fight the enemy. You have pleased me with your dedicated efforts for the Fatherland. You are all heroes, and you will not be forgotten."

The staff officers hid their smiles and resumed work immediately. Colonel Kinh offered a cup of tea to the general, who sat down and picked up the reports from the regiments. He took the cup from Kinh and motioned for the colonel to sit beside him.

"My friend, the battle is unfolding much more slowly than I had expected. I thought the Americans would attack quickly so that we would not have time to lick our wounds or to reorganize. As it is, they are helping our schedule."

Kinh folded his hands in his lap. "They have no time schedule, my general. We have taught them to be cautious. What I do not understand is why they have not used their silent bombers more, with their bombs that hit without warning. I must admit to you that I fear great losses from those bombs, should they saturate the mountains."

General Duc sipped his tea and looked through the reports. He spoke softly. "I, too, worry about the bombers. Perhaps they are committed elsewhere, or perhaps the Americans want to be able to count our bodies for the statistics they seem enamored by. Whatever the reason, we must hope they continue not using them." He read two reports and stopped at the third. "The 174th Regiment has withdrawn back to their third phase line, correct?"

"Yes, they have fallen back without being detected, just short of Hill 875."

The general looked over his shoulder at the wall map. "They must be prepared to move at a moment's notice, but inform Colonel Huu I am depending on him to remain in the sector until the fifteenth."

Jason was relieved when he heard that his battalion's air assault was delayed another day until he found out the reason why. The Fourth Division's Third Batt, Eighth Infantry had hit an entrenched NVA company, and had sustained eighteen killed and many wounded. One company was down to forty-four men, and another had only fifty-six. Every available asset was being used to help the embattled battalion to disengage and to recover the wounded. Two choppers had been shot down and two more hit so badly they were put out of action.

He walked out of the tent and sat on a nearby sandbagged bunker.

He still had not been able to sleep nights, thinking about the men he had lost, and recent events had only made the nightmares worse. Casualty figures were skyrocketing with no end in sight. The high-ranking brass were committed to finding and destroying the enemy, and the NVA were equally committed to making them pay for their folly. The battle had turned into a war of statistics. Strategy was simply to kill more enemy than they killed Americans and call it winning. Somehow it didn't seem to make any difference anymore. The hospital was full of winners. Killing and counting was not a strategy he had learned at the Infantry School. The 173d was taking ground one day and leaving it the next, only to come back two days later and fight all over again for the same real estate. The war was turning into a mindless maze of rules and regulations that no one understood. Cambodia could not be bombed, although the enemy was staging from base camps there. B-52s couldn't be used because units were too close to the targets, but hell, everything in the mountains was a target. Why didn't the leaders just order their men out and blow the mountains to smithereens?

"Jay, the operation getting you down?"

He turned around and looked into the ruddy face of Major Waters, the Second Battalion's chaplain. The big man had his usual smile, which always seemed to put people at ease. Unlike most of the chaplains Jason had met, Waters knew how to talk to the men and to put them at ease. He was always in the field and shared the hardships of the paratroopers, whom he considered friends. The troopers respected the middle-aged priest and affectionately called him "Father Mike." Every man in the battalion knew that if they had a problem, Father Mike could be counted on to listen, and he would do everything possible to help.

Jason returned a smile. "Hi ya, Father! How was your R and R?"

Waters sat down and looked at the setting sun. "The miniskirts are getting shorter and this old man had a tough time getting on the plane to come back, especially to this. How is your brother doing? Is he still with the Fourth Batt?"

Jason leaned back on the sandbags, amazed that the chaplain had remembered their conversation of a month before. He had mentioned Ty only in passing.

"He's in the Thirty-ninth Scout dog detachment now, but he's attached to the Fourth Batt. He's hangin' tough."

Waters kept his gaze on the mountains. "I know you must be worried about him. This battle is turning out to be a very difficult test for us all."

"It's screwed up, Father, a real mess," Jason said. He shook his head. "The NVA wanted us here. I heard a general say to our commander that we ought to thank God the enemy has decided to fight us so we could show the people back home we could kick ass. Somehow I don't think the general knows what's going on."

Waters eyed Jason with concern. "Are you worried about your brother or angry with the general?"

Jason lowered his head. "I . . . guess the casualty reports have gotten to me. I just hate to think of Ty having to go through what I did. It was . . . was just too much for anyone to take."

"You took it," Waters said softly.

Jason looked toward the mountains. "No, I didn't. My men are still crying out to me. On nights like this I can hear them."

Waters put his arm around Jason's shoulders. "Turn loose, son, let them go. This war can't be borne on the shoulders of a single man. There is no good in bearing the guilt of those who have already gone. Think about those who are living. They are your hope."

Jason kept his distant stare. "I'll try, Father.

Ty was lying in the shade underneath a poncho when he heard the company commander's RTO come running up out of breath. "Ca . . . Cat, man, I've been lookin' everywhere for you. The old man wants you ASAP."

Ty got up slowly. "What's he want, ya know?"

"No, man, he just wants you like five minutes ago. Come on, man."

Ty motioned for Saber to stay. "Caddy, watch him for me. I'm probably gonna get my ass chewed for Saber barkin' all night."

The company commander was somber as he paced back and forth in front of the radio. His jaw tightened at the desperate voices coming over the speaker. He had been told by the battalion commander early that morning to monitor First Batt's frequency and to keep abreast of the situation. First Batt had been searching two klicks west of Hill 823 and had found several well-used trails littered with bloody NVA bandages. The battalion was split into two units, and one of the units had walked into an enemy ambush. The unit was surrounded and had had half their men killed or wounded. They had lost all of their medics and were running out of ammunition. The situation was desperate.

The radio's static stopped and an excited voice filled the bunker. "He's hit! My God, the old man is hit! Paraglide Six, our CO has been hit in the head! They're everywhere. We can't hold them!"

The captain stopped his pacing. "Son of a bitch!" He looked up and saw Ty standing in the bunker entrance. "Nance, we have been alerted to go and help the First Battalion. They're surrounded just west of 823. The battalion commander called me a little while ago. The first company to go in will be Charlie Company. Their dog handler is sick, so you're to take his place. Pack your ruck and draw a basic load. Be prepared to load choppers in fifteen minutes."

Ty turned around without speaking and began jogging to his bunker.

The wind tore at Ty's legs as the chopper streaked over the rain forest at tree-top level. He had his arm around Saber's neck and looked over his shoulder at the commander of Charlie Company. The young officer was yelling into the radio to be heard over the engine noise, "Get ready! We'll be there in a few minutes!"

The other men in the helicopter nervously shifted their rifles as they watched the green ocean below go by in a blur at ninety knots. The captain had told his company just before loading that the LZ was only six hundred to seven hundred meters from the surrounded companies, and they were to run if necessary to get there as quickly as possible.

The Huey began to slow down, and Ty tightened his grip on Saber and on his weapon. Suddenly the bird dropped and settled into a small open area. Ty landed on a small bush and fell head first. The captain pulled him to his feet. "Move it!"

He quickened his pace, letting Saber have all the slack he wanted. The sound of gunfire and artillery was leading them to the battle. The squad leader ran up to him and whispered, "When we get close, the old man says we're to start running and hollering. Yell something American so the First Batt boys don't shoot your ass."

As he topped the crest of a hill, Ty stopped. Strewn in front of him were American rucksacks and equipment. Two NVA were squatting with their backs to him, rummaging through the packs. Ty raised his weapon to fire, but both men turned and threw up their hands. The squad leader ran ahead and pushed the men face down into the red dirt. The squad fanned out and searched the hilltop as the captain kept the rest of the men moving. Only a few hundred meters down the ridge was the sound of gunfire from the embattled unit.

As he jogged along with Saber, Ty could feel the presence of the enemy. The feeling sent cold chills up his back. He could hear Sergeant Winters yelling to him somewhere in his brain, "Take it slow, get in the groove! Never hurry!"

Saber strained at his leash, pulling Ty along in a mindless dash. Shots rang out somewhere behind him and were immediately answered by the men of Charlie Company. The captain kept his voice low but confident. "Keep moving. Keep moving, don't stop now."

Bullets cracked overhead. Leaves and branches began falling like rain. He passed by a crashed helicopter that was still smoldering and covering the trail with smoke. One NVA soldier ran through the smoke only ten feet in front of Saber, then another. Ty didn't get a shot off in time, but he began firing into the bamboo anyway. The men behind Ty began yelling and running faster, overtaking him. More men passed by screaming at the top of their lungs, "AIRBORNE AIRBORNE AIRBORNE!"

Ty joined the commander and the first sergeant as they ran down the trail. They jumped over the bodies of two dead NVA and burst through a small clump of bamboo. Ty tripped over something and fell. Bullets slammed into the ground beside his head, and he heard Saber whine. He rolled and sprang to his feet. Saber was running in circles, whining and nipping at his side. The dog was bleeding profusely and yelped in hysteria at the pain. Ty fell again, trying to grab the leash. He hit on something soft that let out a putrid odor. He gagged and looked down at the body of a dead paratrooper. Black ants were crawling into the corpse's mouth and nose in regimental rows. His stomach was ripped open and his intestines, filled with gas, looked like long, curled pink balloons. Ty yelled to Saber, but the gunfire and screaming drowned out his plea. A rocket whooshed by his shoulder as he jumped for the leash. Saber yelped and bit at him, but he wrapped his arms around the dog's head and pulled him to the bloody ground.

He wrestled with the dog for only a few seconds before the animal quit fighting. Then he slid his hand down to the wound and bit his lower lip. The bullet had passed through Saber's left side and had blown out his right. His insides were ripped apart. The dog jerked with spasms of pain and whined as if being beaten. Ty pulled out his pistol and put it to his friend's head. He looked into the dog's sad eyes. With tears streaming down his face, he whispered, "I'm sorry, buddy. God, I'm so sorry."

Blam!

Dazed, he lowered the smoking pistol and released Saber's body. A paratrooper ran by and stepped on the carcass. Ty raised the pistol in a rage and almost fired at the man, but a sergeant grabbed his shoulder. "Come on, don't stop! The perimeter is just ahead!"

He picked up his rifle and put on the helmet he had lost. Then he wiped his eyes and looked at his dead friend one last time. "Good-bye, buddy."

Ty forgot the loss of his friend with one look at the pathetic sight before him. The perimeter was only fifty meters across, but it was filled with row after row of wounded and dead men. Their bodies were covered in a light dust, making all of them look the same. Dead NVA lay among the paratroopers and were stacked in piles on the edge of the perimeter, which was marked by hastily dug holes clawed out by hand. Two dead machine-gunners lay behind their guns, shot several times in the head. They still cradled their weapons, as if waiting for another attack. A man could have stepped on bodies for the entire fifty meters and never touched the ground.

A wounded soldier looked up at Ty with wide eyes. "Wa . . . water." Another holding a bloody bandage to his jaw stretched out one hand. "Water, please."

Ty took out his canteen, and a sea of broken men seemed to move toward him all at once in an unstoppable wave. He gave all he had and more came begging and crying. Tears came to his eyes. He felt totally helpless. A young soldier who could not have been more than nineteen grabbed at him. "Loosen the bandage on my leg for me. It hurts real bad." Ty bent down to comply and had to wipe his eyes so as not to show the tears. The soldier had no leg.

A medic from the Fourth Battalion yelled and threw him an aid bag full of bandages. "Look around and put a bandage on anybody who needs it, but for God's sake, don't take any off."

Charlie Company finished searching the area and came back to help. In several minutes all the wounded had received water. Ty was covered in blood and had wrapped every conceivable type of wound. He had found that the men on the outside rows were shot seven to ten times, their bodies protecting those on the inside. Most of the injured had more than one wound. They had been hit by gunfire as well as grenade fragments and rocket shrapnel.

The first sergeant knelt beside him. "Keep helping out here. We're going to set up another perimeter on the outskirts of this one until we get an LZ cleared."

A soldier tapped the first sergeant's shoulder. "Top, I counted them like you wanted: twenty-one dead, 154 wounded, and two missing."

The first sergeant grimaced. "Two fuckin' companies chopped up . . . damn, this battalion has had it."

Ty wiped the sticky blood from his hands onto his dirty trousers and opened another first-aid packet. "It ain't over, Top. We'll make 'em pay for this."

"How many more will it take to get revenge, kid?" The sergeant's eyes saddened, and he stood up. "I can tell ya . . . too many, just too damn many."

* * *

Jason stepped off the skid of the Huey and ran to a nearby hole to escape the dust. He just made it in time and turned his back as the helicopter lifted off and blew up a red storm cloud. He waited a few seconds more before lifting his head to get his bearings. The small hill looked as if someone had dropped a giant box of toothpicks all over it. Battered, leafless trees formed an abstract maze a laboratory rat couldn't negotiate. Bomb craters, foxholes, and howitzer firing pits pockmarked the hill. Stacked columns of artillery ammunition crates were the only things that looked orderly. The battle-weary artillerymen were covered with red dust.

Jason saw the antennas to his far left and climbed out of the hole. The day before, the Second Battalion had air assaulted onto the scarred hill without incident. He was to man the forward operations center and relay radio reports back to the main TOC in old Dak To. The battalion had walked out of the new firebase that morning and was to search the mountain ridges to the west.

The operations sergeant held up a canteen cup in greeting as Jason walked toward him. "Well, well, looks like they sent you to purgatory, too, huh? Welcome to Firebase 16."

Jason climbed down the ammo box steps and threw his hand up as if waving the craggy-faced NCO away. "Don't be messin' with me, Harper. I haven't had my coffee yet this morning."

Harper laughed and poured some coffee into an empty C-ration can. "Here ya go, L-tee. This will make ya feel better."

Jason sipped the hot liquid while looking over the bunker fashioned from wooden 105-howitzer ammo boxes. The boxes were stacked head high and covered with tin, then with sandbags. He stepped inside the small confines and nodded approvingly. Three candles burning in C-ration cans gave off a golden radiance that reflected off the wood box walls. More of the ammunition crates were used as tables, chairs, and shelves to hold food, radios, and weapons. "Harper, I gotta hand it to ya, it's real homey. Ya done good for a damn Texan."

The thirty-three-year-old sergeant sat down pointing to the radio speakers.

"I rigged up two squawk boxes so we could hear even if we was outside. I know you officers sleep all the time, so one of the speakers is in the corner where you'll crash."

"Thanks," Jason said sarcastically.

Harper hid his pleasure at seeing the lieutenant's good humor and mood. He had been working with the young officer since he got out of the hospital and had grown to like him. He usually didn't like officers, but the lieutenant's genuine concern for soldiers had broken the ice. Most officers only talked about taking care of enlisted men because it sounded professional. Johnson didn't talk. He did things that made a difference. Johnson was good, but he was guilt-ridden about surviving the massacre in June. At odd times he would cry, and sometimes, when he pulled night duty, he would stare off into space as if in a trance and shake like a leaf. The kid had problems, but he was still a damn good man whose heart was in the right place.

"Sir, you might as well drop that ruck and take a load off your feet. The companies left about an hour ago and should have reached the first series of ridges. I haven't heard from them in the past twenty minutes."

Jason looked at a map spread across two crates. "I'd better mark this and . . ."

The speaker suddenly rushed with static as the Alpha company commander's voice came over. "Eagle, Alpha three, this is White Six. We're in contact at phase line one. Enemy is in bunkers on Hill Yankee. Estimate company-size element with machine guns. I have three KIA and twelve WIA. Need Arty to fire target one zero seven immediately, I will adjust. Have medevac standing by. I have no LZ close by and will have to cut one. How's your copy? Over."

Harper had already picked up the handset as Jason plotted the information on the map and picked up another handset to call the artillery. "Roger, White Six, have solid copy. Artillery will be on the way in two mikes. Charming Six will be overhead in ten mikes. Out."

Jason sat by the radio and stared at the map in front of him. Even now, Charming Six, the battalion commander, and the operations officer were in the command and control helicopter three thousand feet above the firefight issuing orders to the company commanders below. The battalion commander had arrived thirty minutes ago and had taken over the situation. From his chopper, he could talk to the ground commanders, artillery, medevacs, Air Force, and the brigade commander. He could do all this in relative safety, while viewing the terrain and adjusting the artillery and air support. Jason had heard the troops refer to the choppers as the "flying circus" or the "fly high boss." That was the problem: the commanders weren't on the battlefield leading their men. There was no leading by example, no making on-the-spot decisions based on cold facts and intuition. At high altitude, the battalion commander could rely only on information from ground commanders. The flying circus leaders couldn't see the death or smell the cordite. They couldn't hear the crack of bullets or see the pain. They flew above it all, blinded by the rain forest canopy and deafened by the radios blaring in their earphones. The system worked if the commanders were experienced and had been on the ground before, if they could visualize the battle and be there in his head, he was like an angel of God. If they couldn't, they killed unintentionally by making mistakes and doing nothing when something had to be done.

Jason listened to the radio and followed the battle on his map. When the control chopper ran out of fuel he would have to run the operation until the commander returned. Alpha Company had reached a saddle and was on the way up a hill when he was hit. The company commander tried to maneuver forward, but his platoons hit strong resistance. He formed a perimeter but the enemy tried to flank him, and he quickly withdrew so as not to be surrounded. Alpha pulled back to Bravo and Charlie companies on a knoll but was immediately attacked by NVA who had crawled within fifteen meters of the perimeter.

Harper walked into the bunker and set a C-ration can of beef and spice sauces in front of Jason. "Eat up, L-tee, you're gonna need it. Looks like we're gonna be here awhile."

Jason took the spoon the sergeant held out to him. "How come it doesn't bother you? It's just business as usual to you."

Harper sighed and sat down. "It bothers me, believe me, but what can we do? Wishing and praying doesn't do a damn bit of good. I was on radio watch when your platoon was hit. I listened to you talking and pleading for help. I didn't know you from Adam, but it still bothered me. I've just learned not to show it."

Jason put down the spoon. "Alpha Company has paid enough."

Harper scratched under his arm. "They've all paid enough," he said. "Alpha just happened to be the ones that got into it this time."

At sunset the choppers came in. The first of the arriving men crawled out of the Slicks as if they were in slow motion and walked toward the bunkers like zombies. Hammonds had waited most of the afternoon for Charlie Company to return. He stood on top of a bunker and looked at the face of each man as he passed by. None returned his stare or acknowledged his presence. The word throughout camp was that Charlie Company had saved the beleaguered unit with their cavalry-like charge, but very few men of First Batt were left to thank them. Because of its excessive losses, the First was now considered combat ineffective.

Hammonds hopped down. He hadn't seen the man he was looking for. The last chopper landed and seconds later lifted off, hiding itself in a dust cloud. He strained to see through the dust. Five men appeared. None were his man. His stomach knotted then relaxed as a sixth soldier materialized. Hammonds saw a walk he knew.

Ty shuffled with his eyes shut to avoid the powdered dirt. He was too tired to wipe the red dust from his eyes and mouth. He cracked his eyelids only enough to follow the ground in front of him and saw a pair of boots. Opening his eyes further, he discovered his friend. The familiar face made him want to cry and to fall to his knees, babbling. He had been among strangers for too long.

Hammonds didn't need to ask where Saber was, the Cat's eyes told him. The soldier's uniform was stained black with dried blood and sweat, and his right sleeve was ripped open, exposing his bandaged arm. The Cat had aged five years since he saw him two days before. He put his hand out. "We missed you, Cat."

Silk, Cowboy, Bugs, Caddy, and the rest of the men gathered around Ty and took his pack and weapon. Silk held out a warm can of Coke. "I saved it for ya, man."

Ty held the can with tears in his eyes. He had never felt so much love for his friends before. The past two days of not knowing anyone's name and knowing they didn't know him tore him up inside. The wounded in the perimeter hugged each other, not wanting to be separated from their buddies while being medevaced. He couldn't understand it then, but now he did. All they had left was each other. Alone they were nothing. They couldn't survive by themselves. Friends made a team, and a team was hard to kill. Friends took care of you when you were hurt or down. Friends wouldn't leave you, and they would share whatever they had with you. Friends would die for you because they knew you would die for them. Being alone among many was the worst feeling in combat Ty had ever felt. He felt so vulnerable and naked. Fear was intensified, for there was no one to share it with. The fear of dying and being left for the ants like the soldier he had fallen on was always in the back of his mind. When he had been hit by shrapnel that last night, no one asked how he was or helped him. The others were with their friends and were taking care of their own. It wasn't intentional. Charlie Company was a good group of men, but they didn't know him. He was an outsider.

Ty had dreamed of nothing but sleep when he was on the chopper, but now he wanted only to be with his friends.

* * *

Colonel Kinh woke the general with a gentle nudge. The old soldier sat up immediately. "You have news?"

"Yes, the 174th is engaged. The unit that secured the hill south of 875 sent out three companies and hit Colonel Huu's Fourth Battalion defenses. He has asked to pull back now and not wait until the fifteenth."

General Duc lay back down. "Tell him to fall back only to his next defensive positions in the sector and to wait. If the American search continues and his battalions are found, then attack. He must hold them until the fifteenth."

Kinh nodded and left the room.

Jason smelled coffee and tossed back the nylon poncho liner. He got up from his bed on the dirt floor and sat down at the ammo box table.

Harper pushed a full canteen cup of coffee toward him. "You didn't sleep much. Why don't you crash again for a couple of hours? I can handle it."

Jason looked at his watch. It was 3 P.M. He'd lost track of time the past day and a half. He slept only a few hours at a time and constantly got up to monitor the radio. The day before, Alpha Company had suffered three dead and twenty-one wounded. Bravo had one KIA and eleven wounded. They had found only four dead enemy. The two companies had returned to the firebase that evening but went out again today at 1300 hours. Their mission was to search the mountaintops they hadn't reached the day before, but from a different route.

He took a sip of the hot coffee. "Anything so far?"

"Naw, it's quiet." Harper set down his canteen cup. "Look, L-tee, it may not be any of my business, but you'd better talk to a doctor. It ain't right to toss and turn like you do in your sleep. It was hard for me to concentrate on listening to the radios with you moaning and grinding your teeth. You scare the hell out of me. It just ain't natural."

Jason's bloodshot eyes moved slowly toward the sergeant. "You're right, it isn't your business."

The speakers suddenly stopped hissing. "Eagle Alpha three, this is Blue Six. My lead element has found some bunkers just north of checkpoint two. We're checking them out and . . ."

The sound of an explosion and machine-gun fire came over the radio. Jason grabbed up the handset just as the Bravo company commander began shouting over the sound of gunfire. "CONTACT! WE'RE IN CONTACT! FIRE TARGET . . .

TARGET . . . SHIT, I CAN'T REMEMBER IT! . . . No, wait,
target zero four!''

Ty sat down dejectedly. "You don't have a dog for me, and all
you want me to do is sit around and wait? Come on, Top, I could
sit here for weeks.''

The first sergeant leaned back in his chair. "What the hell is it
with you? Haven't you heard the morgue has run out of body bags?
Shit, the brigade has had over a hundred men killed. Don't be tellin'
me you wanna go back, or I'll send your ass to a shrink.''

Ty rolled his eyes. "Naw, Top, just let me go back to Bravo
Company, Fourth Batt. They're the brigade reserve. They won't be
doing anything.''

"You can do nothing here just as well as do nothing with them.''

"Top, it's different with my friends. I don't know anybody here.
I'll go nuts. Just let me go back until you get me a dog.''

The senior sergeant lit a Lucky Strike. "If you ask me, you're
nuts already. . . . Aw hell, go on back. I'll say you're our one-man
recon team assigned to the Fourth. But don't get in any trouble!
Now, get out of here!''

Ten minutes later, Ty stood on the road waiting for a truck headed
for Ben Het. He stepped on a black ant that had crawled over his
boot. "Not me, ya bastard. You're not gonna get me.''

Jason listened to the battalion commander talking to the Bravo
CO. There was nothing the two men could do. Bravo had been hit
on three sides and had tried to pull back, but they couldn't carry
all their wounded. They wouldn't leave their men, so they formed
a perimeter to fight it out. Artillery was coming in within twenty-
five meters of the surrounded unit, but the NVA were staying within
fifteen meters in the thick bamboo, hugging the perimeter.

He could see the battle, he could feel everything the terrified
men were feeling. He shivered, yet he was sweating, knowing exactly what they were going through.

Harper stared at him from the entrance of the bunker. He was
worried that Jason was going to pass out from exhaustion. Harper
had tried to relieve him, but the stubborn Okie just ignored him
and continued to follow the battle on the map. He wasn't writing
in the log book like he was supposed to do. Instead, he seemed to
be fighting alongside the Bravo commander.

Jason couldn't keep his head up any longer, but he didn't want
to shut his eyes. When he did, the men came back to life and

screamed out to him. He had to stay awake and help those who needed him, but some were beyond help. Bravo Company was finished—they'd lost a total of twenty-two men killed and twenty-eight wounded in two days. They had survived the battle only to be put out of action as a company. They would need fifty replacements and time to heal the mental wounds. The dead would join the men of the Second Platoon in Jason's dreams and add to the screams that wouldn't let him sleep. Again he had been powerless to help or to save a single man.

Again . . . again . . . again.

Sergeant Hammonds looked up at the hot sun and tossed down his shovel. Three hours of filling sandbags was enough. He motioned to the squad. "Come on, that's all we need. Let's get a shower."

Silk hung back from the others as they walked across the dirt field. "I don't need no shower, man. I'll wait on you guys in the bunker."

Book Man turned around. "You need it worse than any of us. I had to hold my breath working next to you."

Silk stabbed a finger in the air. "Fuck you, man. I like my stink."

Hammonds and Ty exchanged smiles and suddenly turned around and ran toward Silk. "WE DON'T!"

Silk held his ground only for a second, thinking he could handle the two attackers, but when the rest of the squad began coming for him, he bolted.

Ty easily caught up to him and tackled him at the knees. Both men tumbled into the dust and were quickly joined by the rest of the squad. Silk kicked and clawed for several seconds before giving up. "Come on, dudes, I hate water, man!"

Lieutenant Salias walked out of his bunker and saw Sergeant Hammonds and his squad carrying the struggling, half-naked Silk across the road. He took a few steps into the hot sun. "What do you people think you're doing?"

Hammonds let go of Silk's foot but had the men keep walking. "Sir, we're escorting an individual who has failed to comply with your hygiene standards. We are also conducting a class on how to carry wounded."

Salias fumed at the sarcastic reply. "Stop what you're doing!" He strode out and stood in front of Silk. "Is this a racial incident? Are these men violating your rights?"

Silk nodded. "Yes, sir, these white muthafuckers and Uncle Toms is saying I stink." He stepped within an inch of the officer and held up his arm so that his armpit was almost touching the lieutenant's nose. "It ain't so, is it?"

Salias almost fainted from the odor. He quickly backed up and looked at Hammonds. "Ah . . . carry on with your mission."

Silk threw out his hands in a last plea as the men pushed him over and began carrying him again. "Sir, they gonna take away my stink rights! . . . Sir, you is prejudiced!"

Salias looked around, making sure no one saw the incident and hurried back to his bunker.

Hammonds saw the officer disappear and fell over laughing. Ty busted out and slapped at Silk's head. "Stink rights? Where the hell ya get that one?"

Silk fell into the dirt as the other men grabbed their stomachs in laughter. "Pretty good, huh? I's made it up."

General Duc sat staring at the wall map. His thoughts were of thirteen years ago. Colonel Kinh cleared his throat to gain the officer's attention. "We have made contact with the special units, and they are prepared to carry out your orders."

Duc kept his stare, remembering the sound of the mortars when he gave the signal for the barrage to begin. His eyes slowly shifted to the colonel. "Execute the attack tomorrow."

Kinh smiled. "The South's newspapers are talking of the great victory at Dak To. Perhaps tomorrow the press will become suspicious of the facile stories and begin printing the casualty reports. The 174th reported they wiped out two Yankee companies yesterday."

"The 174th's reports are exaggerated," Duc said slowly. "The Americans estimate the numbers they kill to please their politicians. We exaggerate to lift the morale of our soldiers. We all lie, except for the men who fight in the holes. They know the truth."

He rose from his chair. "It is time I knew the truth as well. Prepare a small unit to accompany me to the battle."

Kinh's eyes opened wide in disbelief. "No, my general, you must remain here and direct the effort."

"What is there for me to do? I sit and listen, I do nothing, and I am feeling like an American politician waiting on lies. It is time for me to join my men. I need their truth."

"But you have paid the price for the Fatherland. You have done enough."

Duc walked toward the door. "Come, inform my deputy he is to take over and to send radio reports to Hill 875, where we will be. I will show you who is paying the price. They are waiting for us in the bunkers.''

32

Corporal Nguyen Ban lowered his binoculars as the third C-130 landed and roared down the runway. He could see the large unit of ARVN troops waiting on the ramp and signaled his men to ready the first round. Two of the big transport planes were already stopped in front of the ARVN battalion, waiting for the men to load. Ban smiled at his gunner, knowing they would be heroes in only a few more minutes. When the third transport stopped by the others, they would have a target they could not miss.

He held up the binoculars again and double-checked the range. He and his men were members of the elite Special Unit assigned to the First NVA Division. They had been reconning the Dak To base camp for five months and had maps depicting every detail to include ranges. He was located only a kilometer south of the airfield. Their mission was to destroy an aircraft on the runway, blocking it from further use. Later that day, the four mortar tubes of the Second Platoon, hidden on the other side of the camp, were going to saturate the ammunition storage area and try to destroy the newly arrived stockpile of howitzer ammunition stacked in the open. The purpose of the mortar missions was to make the Americans fearful of a ground attack so they would keep a large unit of men on hand. The general's plan was to keep the Americans and puppets fighting in every direction and not able to mass their power. They would be forced to use valuable ground units and aircraft for the security of the base.

The C-130 rolled to a stop and lowered its ramp. Ban turned around and nodded. The assistant gunner dropped the 82-millimeter mortar round into the tube. THUNK!

Ban lifted his glasses and waited. The deadly warhead arched high in the air and dropped almost straight down, hitting one hundred meters short of the second parked transport and throwing up a puff of concrete debris. The third transport's crew had just left the plane when the round went off, and they immediately ran back to try and save the aircraft. He could see the South Vietnamese soldiers scattering like rice chaff in the wind, trying to find available cover.

"Add one hundred, fire for effect!"

The gunner quickly made the adjustment and nodded to his assistant, who already had the second round partially lowered into the mouth of the tube. THUNK!

The round exploded only a few feet from the second parked plane and blew holes through the metal skin, rupturing the right wing tanks. Fuel gushed out like blood from a wounded bird. The third round hit behind the tail section, and its searing hot metal caught the fuel on fire. Within seconds the C-130 was engulfed in crackling flames.

"Right two hundred, drop fifty!"

The third C-130 began backing up as the fire-engulfed plane seemed to leap off the ground. Another mortar round had exploded directly in front of the plane's nose, momentarily lifting it into the air.

Ban lifted his glasses and judged the distance and speed of the last target that was trying to escape. "Left, four hundred!"

Both parked planes were now burning fiercely, sending up two black clouds of smoke, as the pilot of the third aircraft gunned the engines. His only hope was speed and distance. He had to get out of range of the ripping shrapnel.

Ban cursed as the round fell behind the bellowing bird. "Left four hundred, add one hundred!"

The pilot kept the throttle forward, forgetting the beeping, danger-warning light. If shrapnel hit his fuel tanks, he would be cooked alive.

Ban smiled at the explosion in the side of the rolling transport. He lowered his glasses to see the plane burst into flames, but the wounded bird was still moving, despite the gaping holes in its fuselage. He looked at the wooden stakes he had placed in the ground earlier and knew that before the mortar crew could adjust the tube again, the plane would be out of range. He got up and jogged down the knoll. "You destroyed two of the planes and damaged another!"

The gunner patted the assistant on his back and hurriedly began disassembling the mortar from the base plate.

* * *

Every man on the perimeter was waiting for an attack or the dreaded mortar rounds. The emergency call twenty minutes before had the Fourth Battalion paratroopers running around in mass confusion, scrambling for cover. Ty had run to three foxholes before finding one he could squeeze into. Unlike previous red alerts, he knew this one was real. The two huge black clouds to the east told their own story, along with the helicopters that filled the air like angry bees looking for the enemy mortar crew.

The sun beat down unmercifully, and the tension gave way to suffering in the crowded holes and bunkers. Finally, the company commander yelled out, "STAND DOWN, YELLOW ALERT!"

Ty crawled out of the hole and joined Hammonds, who emerged from the command bunker. "I heard they hit the airfield and got a bunch of Arvins."

Hammonds scowled. "Don't listen to the rumors. The facts are they hit two C-130s and crippled another. I heard it on the radio."

Ty could see that Hammonds was irritated. "What gives? You look sour as a lemon. The command bunker get to ya?"

"I heard a lot more on the radio than just about the mortar attack," Hammonds said. He walked into the shade beside an engineer road grader. "The Second Batt boys got kicked real good near Firebase 16. They've lost the equivalent of a company of men the past three days. This fucking battle is going all wrong."

Ty hated what he'd just heard, but he felt relief in knowing that his brother was in the rear somewhere, safe. Hammonds sat down in the dust and leaned back on a tire. "This isn't over by a long shot. The brass think the dinks are withdrawing back into Cambodia and want the Herd to pursue them. Can you believe that shit? They want us to 'pursue,' as if it were nothing more than running down a road to catch a thief. How do you *pursue* up in the mountains? Shit, the whole company has to walk single file! We can't spread out like it was a damn open field! And we sure as hell don't run after them!"

Ty stared at the billowing black clouds in the distance. "Relax, Sarge, we're the reserve. Maybe they won't use us."

Hammonds picked up a dirt clod and tossed it toward the perimeter wire. "I don't like this shit. Before it was terrible, but at least it made sense. This whole Dak To thing seems half-assed. So many units are here that the artillery and air can't support us all. If the Fourth Division legs get in trouble, they get all the support and we get the leftovers. They gave us the worst area but the least support. Even the old man says we're not getting what we're supposed to. I'm worried, Cat. I don't like what I'm hearing and feeling. I feel like I'm on the Titanic and the captain has just told us we've had a small problem, but there's nothing to worry about. I don't think the big boys want to admit we've hit an iceberg.''

Ty didn't want to agree. Negative thoughts were destructive. He had seen the effects too many times, when men had thought the worst and it had affected their judgment. He wasn't going to let that happen to him. He had seen the worst the war had to offer, and he could handle it—he and his friends. He had to believe that the high-ranking decision makers were doing all they could.

He sighed. "Sarge, you gotta relax. We're the reserve, and we aren't going anywhere for a while. You can't be upsettin' the squad with all this bad mouthin'.''

Hammonds stared at Ty as if looking through him. "You go on point alone and nothing bothers you. You're lost in another world out there. I've seen you. But me, I'm thinking about my guys and praying that nothing happens and that you don't find anything. I'm getting short, Cat, thirty days and a wake-up. When I first got here, I was into it like you are. I really thought I was good and could keep my guys from getting hurt. Now . . . now, I don't know. I'm finding out that the people who sent me and who are making the decisions don't know what the fuck is going on. And if they don't, who does? What the hell are we doing? They say we're winning, but I don't see it. I only see the numbers of men we're losing. If this is winning, I don't want to play the damn game. It costs too much.''

"Do you have a choice?" Ty asked softly.

Hammonds dropped his stare as if dead tired. "No . . . no I don't, but I'll tell you something: my kids will. If I ever have a son, he's going to know what this war really was—a waste. He's gonna ask the questions that I didn't before he has to go off and fight.''

Ty stood up and pulled Hammonds to his feet. "You're too ugly to have kids. Come on, we've got weapons to clean.''

Corporal Ban looked at his watch. It was almost 5 P.M., time for the Second Special Unit Platoon to begin the attack. He sat down and rested his binoculars on his knees. The planes they had hit this morning were now black jumbles of wreckage, and swarms of engineer units were trying to clear the smoldering metal from the runway. Off to the right were the covered mounds of the ammunition-storage area and the huge stocks of artillery ammunition—the next target. His total concentration was on the ammo dump, and he didn't see the first explosion. The gunner sitting beside him pointed excitedly. "It has begun!''

Ban shifted his field glasses to the row of buildings behind the ammo dump. The first salvos had fallen short and had hit the buildings, starting a fire. "What did they hit?" he asked.

The gunner looked at his camp sketch. "The postal unit and a supply hut. The Yankees will not be getting their mail."

Ban laughed as the second salvo landed in the storage area. He watched the rounds hit for several minutes, thinking they were wasting their time trying to penetrate the earth mounds, when suddenly, from the entrance of an ammunition bunker, a geyser of flame leaped out. The mound of earth shook, then lifted up like a hat and disappeared in a tremendous explosion. The entire dump was covered in flame and smoke.

"What happened?" asked the gunner, grabbing for the binoculars.

Ban stood and stared in disbelief. Their luck had been too good to be true. A mortar round had landed in the entrance of a bunker that held white phosphorous artillery rounds and had caused a fire. The bunker exploded and showered the rest of the storage area with the burning rounds, causing more fires. That single mortar round was going to destroy the entire dump. Already the ground was shaking. Fireballs were arching across the sky. Flare rounds were going off and explosions were throwing fountains of dirt skyward. He looked with wide eyes at his gunner. "We have destroyed a thousand tons of ammunition! We will be honored by the Tall One himself!"

Jason stood on top of the bunker and looked southwest. Toward the mountains was an orange glow that looked like stadium lights. He and most of the men on the firebase had heard about the ammunition dump explosion, but few realized the extent of the damage until the sky to the southwest had lit up. The dump was hit at 1700 hours. Three hours later, it was still burning and exploding.

Chaplain Waters, who had joined Jason in the bunker for the night, called to him from the entrance. "Jay, Sergeant Harper needs you."

Jason hopped down and stepped into the candlelight. "What's up?"

Harper tossed down the radio handset and looked at the message he had just copied. "It's worse than we thought. They got all the ammo for the howitzers, mortars, and small arms. The ammo we have now is all we're gonna have for a while. Corps is going to emergency resupply us, but in the meantime, no more search and destroy ops. We don't have enough backup ammo to get us out of a crunch.''

Jason quickly calculated in his head as he sat down. "It's gonna take a couple of days to get the ammo replaced, even if they fly in C-130s nonstop. Does the ol' man want me to inform the companies to return to the firebase and wait?"

"Nope, they're to stay in place and kick back," Harper said. "We're going to get priority because we're in the pursuit mode, whatever that means.''

Jason was secretly relieved at the chain of events. He knew the men needed the rest. The pursuit mission was a standing joke to all the company commanders.

Harper looked over the message and mumbled absently, "Looks like we're not gonna get any care packages or Dear Johns. They hit the postal building, too.''

Ty sat on top of the bunker, watching the glowing fire still raging in the ammunition dump ten kilometers away. He looked up at the stars. For the first time he felt short. His time in country was dwindling down to the last ninety days. The short-timer's calendar he kept inside his helmet had not been marked in months, but that afternoon he had brought it up to date. Three more months. Ninety days. Two-thousand-one-hundred-and-sixty hours and he would be back on his hill.

He shut his eyes, and the image of his father's picture became crystal clear in his mind. Strange, but he had not dreamed about his father since Jim Deets had been killed a lifetime ago. Instead, his dreams had been of Deets, Teddy Bear, Paddy, Goldie, and the many others he had seen killed or wounded. Their pain tore through his heart nightly as a reminder that it just as easily could have been him. Nothing would erase from his mind their faces and the grief their loved ones must have felt. He knew the Chosen would be cared for by others, like his father, but the mothers and fathers of those taken so young would never understand.

Ty cleared his mind and lay back on the bunker, looking up again at the stars. He closed his eyes and felt an old friend's presence.

Saber placed his head on his buddy's shoulder to comfort him as he had done many times before. They needed each other a little longer.

General Duc gazed at the glowing orange sky. It told him he had made a tactical error. The 174th's commander, Colonel Huu, shrugged his shoulders. "We could not have known that the special unit was going to be so successful. It is not your fault for following the plan.''

The general broke his distant stare. "You are right, my friend. But if I had left you in place a day longer, you could have struck the Americans and finished them off. The tiger's throat was given to us, and I was not ready. You could have attacked tonight and they would not have been able to rearm themselves. The victory we sought would have been ours by the luck of a single mortar crew.''

Colonel Huu brushed away a persistent mosquito. "It is said 'would haves' and 'could haves' would make us all famous men. Our plan has worked beyond our dreams. The Yankees will not be able to do anything until their supply of ammunition is replenished. Our schedule will be met easily.''

"You are right again, my friend," Duc said. He took the colonel's arm and began walking him toward the command tunnel. "Our schedule will be easily attained, but there has been a change. I have been asked by General Giap to hold as long as possible. It seems our success has given our leader more than just a diversion. The general informs me that the newspapers in the United States and in the South are focusing on Dak To. This is the biggest battle yet fought by the Americans. They believe we are trying to take the highlands back, and their political leaders' attention is on this single battle.''

He stopped and looked again at the distant orange glow. "The American people will read tomorrow in their newspapers about the loss of ammunition stockpiles, and their leaders will worry. They will ask how it could have happened." He turned and looked into Huu's eyes. "The American people will ask about casualties and question their military leaders' tactics. They will give us the victory we seek.''

The colonel lowered his head. "Are you telling me to stay beyond the twentieth and hold this hill?''

Duc laid his hand on Huu's shoulder. "The general has asked me. I am sick of this war. Today I lost an opportunity to deal the Americans a devastating blow by wiping out a battalion, but the real victory is still at hand. You and your men, along with the company from the Sixty-sixth, are the instruments of that victory. The longer you hold this hill, the more their people will question the need to take it.''

Colonel Huu raised his head. "I will hold as long as possible and give you your victory.''

"Not for me," Duc said slowly. "It is for the reunification.''

General Duc watched his commander disappear into the darkness and sat down in the place he had sat so many years before. His decision would seal the fate of the hill's beauty. Already the land had been spoiled by the trenches and bunkers, but the trees still remained . . . for now.

He shut his eyes and dug his hands into the soil. "I'm sorry, old friend. I'm sorry."

33

Ty wiped the sweat from his forehead and took a long gulp from his canteen. Bravo Company was on a road-clearing mission again, but it beat the hell out of humping in the mountains. Nobody was complaining about walking up the road toward Dak To and protecting the engineers who were improving the dirt highway. Over the past few days, they had been rotating with Charlie Company in the clearing operation, and everyone was convinced the battle was over.

Hammonds strode up. "Cat, I just got word you're to report back to your first sergeant day after tomorrow. He said he had a dog coming in for you."

"Good. This walking is for grunts. Us special guys don't do this type of dirty work."

"Who do you think is leading this convoy and checking for mines." Hammonds asked. "Yeah, a dog team. Keep talking and I'll have you replacing that fool."

Ty could tell that Hammonds wasn't feeling as down as he had been a few days ago. "Sure good to see you lost that lemon face of yours. Me and the boys were gettin' worried."

Hammonds laughed and took out one of Caddy's pictures. "I've been looking at this and driving on. Just twenty-eight days, and I'll find me a whore and do whatever Caddy is doing in this picture."

Ty glanced at the photo. "Well, Sarge, if you don't know what he's doing, you have definitely been here too long."

Hammonds laughed and threw his arm around Ty. He squeezed Ty's neck roughly and let him go. He walked a few steps and suddenly looked back with a strange, sad expression. "Women. I don't know. I don't even understand the whores."

"Sarge, we're all gonna be happy again when we get outta here," Ty said softly. "You'll find it again."

Hammonds nodded reluctantly and shifted his eyes toward the road. "What I felt only comes around once. I just hope second best is back there somewhere. I couldn't stand to go back and think about this fuckin' place."

Ty put his arm around Hammonds's shoulder. "I know."

Jason sat outside the bunker listening to the Charlie CO brief the other two company commanders on their new mission.

". . . and a Special Forces company was inserted at the bottom of Hill 875, just two kilometers southwest of us. The company moved up the south ridge only five hundred meters and was hit by machine-gun fire that killed their point man. They managed to break contact and pulled back to the valley. We've been ordered to move from here and assault that hill and clear it of all enemy. Charlie Company will lead, followed by Delta, then Alpha. Bravo is still at old Dak To trying to get back on its feet. The colonel has made me the commander for the operation, so I'm gonna need your help. I've never been an acting battalion commander before.

"Any questions?"

He answered several questions, then added, "By the way, the ol' man is giving us his forward operations center for backup radio support. Lieutenant Johnson and Sergeant Harper will be going with us. Chaplain Waters has requested to go, and the ol' man okayed it. You guys keep an eye out for him. That's it. We'll be leaving in an hour, so you'd better brief your people. I'll be up with my company behind the lead platoon. Good hunting."

Jason was shocked to hear that he was going out with the unit. Neither the major nor the colonel had said a word to him. He quickly approached the acting commander. "Sir, is there anything special you want me to do?"

The captain shrugged. "I'll get you two RTOs from headquarters to carry the radios. Just stay back in the rear with Alpha and monitor the radios. Keep the ol' man informed if the companies have communications problems. You're strictly backup."

Jason nodded. "Sure thing, sir. I guess I'd better pack my ruck."

He took several steps, then stopped and glanced back at the hill again. It was odd, but from where he stood, 875 looked like Red Hill. The trees were different, but the hill had that same majestic aura. He couldn't help but think about what would happen if the situation were reversed, if he were home and given a company with a mission to defend Red Hill.

A shiver ran up his spine, and he quickly walked away. Shaking off an ominous feeling, Jason continued on to the bunker. He could only hope and pray the enemy on 875 had withdrawn.

They were moving slowly for a good reason: the trail was covered with recent tracks. The three hundred men of the Second Battalion heading for Hill 875 could feel the enemy's presence. It was there, hanging in the humid air.

Sergeant Harper spat a stream of tobacco juice toward the bamboo. "L-tee, if I find out you volunteered us for this, I'm gonna wring your damn neck. I'm an operations sergeant, not a humping sergeant. I already did this shit my last tour."

Jason couldn't help but smile. "I didn't volunteer us, but hearing you bitch makes me think I should have. You sound like a whining old lady."

Chaplain Waters patted Harper's back. "Sergeant Harper, if it's any consolation, I'm older than you. Us old men need to exercise for our health."

"Sir, don't take this wrong, but you must be drinkin' your communion wine," Harper said. "We're in hostile country and you're talkin' about how a walk is good for our health? Field grade officers are supposed to be smarter than that."

Waters chuckled and was about to respond when the RTO in front of Jason stopped and held out the handset. "Sir, Charlie Company's point man found something ahead."

Colonel Huu peered out of the bunker firing port. "Are you sure they have stopped?"

The young scout sergeant spoke calmly. "Yes, Colonel. They found the hospital tunnel entrance and formed a perimeter just six hundred meters down the ridge in the saddle. I estimate at least three companies, and they are carrying their mortars."

Huu nodded in thought and turned away from the firing port. Bending over, he entered the communications tunnel that angled down for a few meters, then stood erect and looked around. The tunnel ran twenty meters to the trench line and continued again to another bunker system that was twenty meters farther beyond the

trench. This was the most elaborate of all the fortifications he had
seen. The engineers had outdone themselves. The complex had
three major defensive lines all tied in with phone wire and bombproof tunnels. The command center, located directly beneath the
center of the hill, was like the hub of a wheel, with eight tunnels
running out of it toward the defense positions. The control center
was beneath fifteen meters of soil, and was reinforced with ironwood and sayo support beams. Ammunition storage areas were dug
into the side of each tunnel, providing the defenders with enough
supplies to fight day and night for two weeks.

He walked through the tunnel, lighted by an occasional candle,
past the second defensive line then the third. He entered the command center, where General Duc was seated in front of the wall
map. "Comrade," he said "I must insist you leave immediately.
The Yankees have stopped only six hundred meters down the
northern ridge and are preparing for the attack."

The general waved him to a chair. "There is time. You know
they will call in their air and artillery first. You know where the
attack will come. Now, tell me, what is your plan?"

Huu confidently picked up a bamboo pointer. "The northern ridge
is narrow, perhaps only large enough for two companies abreast in
an attack. The Americans will hit our first defensive line of bunkers
and be stopped. They will then do what they always do: pull back
and call for more air and artillery support. When they do this, I will
order my Second Battalion to attack their rear and flank. The battalion commander and his captains have already walked the terrain
around the hill and know the infiltration routes constructed by the
Sixty-sixth Regiment. The attack will cut the Yankee force in two,
and we will wipe out the rear unit. We have mortars and B-40 rocket
launchers located on the next ridge. They will support the infantry
once the attack begins. The Third Battalion has the mission of supporting the Second by maintaining a steady rain of fire on the enemy
and keeping him inside our steel ring. All around the American
perimeter will be squads whose only purpose is to engage helicopters. Other squads will be designated as snipers."

General Duc glanced at the row of field phones along the earthen
wall. "Do you have communications with all your units so that the
attack is coordinated?"

"Yes, both wire and radio communication, and I have runners
if necessary." Huu lowered his voice and stepped closer to the
general. "The defensive plan is as we discussed. Once the Second
Battalion attacks, they will return to Cambodia; I have no room for
them in the bunkers. The company from the Sixty-sixth Regiment

and my two companies from the Fourth Battalion will remain in the complex and hold the hill until ordered to leave.''

The general rose and looked at his operations officer, Colonel Kinh. ''Do you have any suggestions?''

Kinh was still in awe of the complex. He didn't think it possible to take the hill after seeing the extensive tunnels and protected fighting positions. He lowered his head. ''I can only offer my respect to you and your men for what you are about to do.''

General Duc put out his hand toward the confident commander. ''Remember, my friend, plans are only guides. The Americans have their plans as well. Beware: you are facing the tiger.''

''I will not fail you,'' Huu said confidently.

The general patted his shoulder and picked up his small pack. ''We will be back at the base by nightfall and listening for your reports. Good luck, my friend.''

General Duc stopped his small group of men once they had climbed a ridge. He turned and looked at the hill.

''What is it, Comrade General?'' Colonel Kinh asked.

The general took a deep breath and turned around. ''It's nothing. I was just saying farewell to an old friend. Come, we have a long journey ahead of us.''

Jason stepped inside the earth-walled room and gasped. He had heard about the tunnels, but the sight before him was beyond belief. The entrance to the tunnel was very small and the corridor was initially narrow, but the farther he and the others had walked, the larger the corridor became. Now he stood in an empty hospital ward. The beds were made from bamboo and were aligned perfectly, as were the storage shelves. The NVA must have had plenty of time to evacuate, as they left nothing behind but a bag of bloody bandages. The Charlie company commander panned his light back to the tunnel. ''I wanted you to see this so you could report it to the old man. I'm going to start calling in arty and air on the hill.''

Chaplain Waters stepped in front of the senior company commander. ''Harry, the best of luck to you. There isn't a better man I know to lead us up that hill.''

Captain Harry Kaufman shook the major's hand warmly. ''Father, it's a little early. We're going to attack tomorrow morning. But thanks.''

Jason exchanged glances with Sergeant Harper. If the NVA had built this, what could they expect to run into on the hill? Harper shook his head. "I don't think we could build anything like this. We just don't have the patience."

Jason could not imagine the time and number of men it would have taken to dig and haul out all the dirt let alone to construct such a shelter. He was impressed and fearful at the same time. The Vietnamese showed amazing tenacity and dedication. He looked one more time at the line of beds and stepped back into the tunnel corridor.

The fighter came in low and released its five-hundred-pound load. The bomb seemed to glide to earth and disappeared into the tree-tops. Then suddenly the ground shook. Seconds later the shock wave hit, followed by the horrific sound of man-made thunder. Again and again the planes came and dropped their bombs. The hilltop was slowly being turned into a scarred wasteland. The artillery had fired first and had managed to blow holes in the canopy formed by centuries-old trees. Later the Air Force air controller had fired a marking rocket, and the jets streaked in for the kill.

Jason sat beside Waters on the edge of the perimeter and watched the destruction as if it were a Fourth of July fireworks show. Jason felt at ease with the chaplain who always seemed to have time to talk to a passing soldier. The service he had given an hour before had been attended by almost all the men.

Jason glanced at his watch. It was almost 9 P.M. "Father, do you think anyone could live through such a pounding?"

Waters leaned back and closed his eyes. "What I have seen of these people tells me yes. I can't imagine their suffering, but I feel compelled to pray for them."

Jason stood and put on his helmet. "Tomorrow, I hope you don't have to do that for us."

Waters smiled. "I'm praying for that, too."

Dirt cascaded down the far wall and covered the field phones. Colonel Huu kept his balance as the earth beneath his feet shook again. A captain in charge of the first line of bunkers stumbled into the dust-filled control room. "Colonel, bunker three has collapsed and its communications tunnel is blocked. Several connecting tunnels have partially caved in that lead to the trench lines."

Colonel Huu spoke hoarsely through the silk scarf tied around his mouth and nose, "Use the wood in the storage areas to shore up the weak points. This is just the beginning. Keep your men busy and digging."

34

Captain Kaufman sipped coffee from a canteen cup as he pointed at a terrain model he'd made earlier that morning. "The operation will be executed as follows: we will depart the perimeter at zero nine thirty after I lift the artillery fires. The trail that runs up the north ridge is our center boundary. We'll attack with Delta Company on the left and Charlie on the right. Both attacking companies will have two platoons forward and one in reserve, along with the weapons platoon. Alpha Company will follow to secure our rear and be our reserve.

"We'll move almost due south along the ridge, which has a gradual slope and is about one hundred meters wide all the way to the crest of the hill. The ridge drops off sharply to the east and more gradually to the west. The whole thing is vegetated in fairly thick bamboo, scrub bushes, and tall trees. We must keep the movement coordinated and on line. I will be following behind the lead platoon on the right side of the trail, and I want you to keep me informed at all times. Once we reach the top, we'll consolidate by using the clock method. The center of the hilltop facing south will be twelve o'clock. Delta will consolidate from nine to twelve, Charlie will be from twelve to three, and Alpha will occupy from nine through six to three o'clock. Lieutenant Johnson and Sergeant Harper will be with Alpha Company; they'll be monitoring the horns and keeping the old man informed. If there are no questions, inform your people and be prepared to move at 0930."

Jason got up and patted Major Waters's back. "Come on, Harper has some coffee for you."

Waters smiled. "Thank him for me, Jay, but I've got to talk to the point team in Delta Company. I'll be back with you before we move out."

Jason returned to his position in the perimeter and took out a C-ration can of peaches from his ruck. Sergeant Harper sat up with an irritated scowl. "How in the hell can you eat at a time like this? Tell me what the captain said, for Christ's sake."

"He gave the standard Fort Benning operations order," Jason said, opening the can. "Two up and one back in reserve, just like the book teaches. Nothing fancy."

"*Us*, damn it! What are *we* doing? Staying here and watching, I hope."

"Nope, we're going with Alpha. Chaplain Waters will be with us, so don't worry about anything."

Harper shook his head and stared at his battered boots. "'Don't worry,' he says. 'The chaplain will be with us,' he says. Damn it, L-tee, the padre don't even carry a rifle."

Like all the others, Jason had become desensitized by the constant artillery pounding. He put on his pack and checked his rifle before motioning his small CP group forward. The attack had been delayed a few minutes because the last jet strike had been late. The lead elements of Charlie and Delta companies had begun walking up the hill at exactly 0943. Jason waited until the lead companies had gone far enough ahead for Alpha to move before making his way up the ridge. Harper cussed and bitched the first five minutes until Chaplain Waters reminded him of his language. Harper looked to Jason for help. "Tell the padre I don't mean nothin' by it. It's just habit."

Jason smiled at Waters. "It's too late for him, Father. He's beyond anyone's help."

Harper frowned. "Thanks a lot, L-tee."

Private Bui Ngoc Duong, the machine-gunner, and the assistant gunner crawled out of the communications tunnel and into their bunker. Duong anxiously looked out of the firing port and immediately felt like crying. Months before, the general had visited his position and warned him of the destruction, but it was beyond his dreams. The deep tunnel had protected him from the bombs and artillery, but nothing had protected his wonderful trees. They were almost all gone, and those that were left were battered sticks with leafless limbs. The ground was plowed up and covered with small craters and the twisted, shattered bodies of the trees.

The field phone hummed by the gunner. He quickly picked it up, having forgotten his instructions to keep the phone at his ear and report seeing anything that moved. He spoke apologetically to the senior sergeant and held the phone in the crick of his neck as he prepared his machine gun.

Smoke filled their nostrils from the small fire started on the hilltop but it was not a choking smoke. Suddenly, the gunner stood up with the phone to his ear and signalled to the others. ''The second bunker sees them.''

Duong looked out the right firing port and unconciously ducked. Twenty meters down the slope were two Yankees climbing over debris. The gunner motioned Duong to take his position. He was to shoot and kill the first Yankees. When others came to help their comrades, the gunner would open up with the machine gun.

He swallowed a lump in his throat and aimed his AK-47. He was to wait until he couldn't miss. The approaching big, white-skinned American soldier was being very cautious. His uniform was filthy and his helmet seemed too big for him. Duong felt sympathy for him, for his pack was huge and must have been heavy. He aimed at the man's chest and squeezed the trigger.

''CONTACT!'' screamed the second platoon leader to the Delta company commander. The second squad leader heard the shot and looked up in time to see his point man pitch backward, struck in the chest. He raised his head to see if he could spot the sniper as his men yelled for the medic. He couldn't see anything but blown-down trees and smoke. The medic ran past and hopped over a log close to the point man. He began to feel for a pulse when a bullet struck him in the head and knocked off his blood-spattered helmet.

The Delta company commander yelled for his men to get on line and advance. The two lead platoons crawled into a ragged line behind fallen trees and clumps of splintered bamboo. They began moving forward, still not seeing the enemy.

Private Duong moved to the other firing port, making room for the machine-gunner and his assistant. He could hear the 174th's senior sergeant yelling from inside the tunnel for his men to hurry to their positions in the trench. The liberation platoon of the Second Company was taking its place in the trench line just behind his bunker.

Peering out the portal, Duong saw nothing. Then he heard the first of the Second Platoon's grenades and rockets exploding down the ridge.

* * *

Jason and Major Waters ran up the slope toward Captain Kaufman's CP. They had received word to come forward and see the situation firsthand.

Kaufman yelled for them to stay down as they approached his position beside the trail. He waited until they were safely behind a fallen tree before speaking. "We're into something bigger than we expected. Delta's point team got hit, and the company deployed and started up. They made it fifteen yards and were stopped cold by NVA in trenches and machine-gun fire from bunkers. Charlie Company tried to advance on their side and hit the same type of resistance. I lost a medic and Lieutenant Smith from the Third Platoon during the attack. Between Delta and my company, we have twelve wounded and four dead. I'm going to pull the companies back and pound the hell out of the hill again with arty. Chaplain, we'll consolidate the wounded near that lone tree forty meters behind us, and I'd appreciate it if you'd watch out for things there. Jay, I've been talking to the old man on the horn, and he's trying to get me air support. I want you to tell Captain Kaley of Alpha Company that I need some of his men to start clearing an LZ so we can get our wounded out and get a resupply of ammo."

Minutes later, Jason was kneeling beside Captain Kaley and his RTOs. Kaley spoke tiredly. "We've got one platoon strung out behind Charlie Company's rear trying to stay in visual contact, and we're doing the same thing behind Delta Company. First Platoon is my rear security. I'll have the weapons platoon cut the LZ."

One of the RTOs sat up and handed the handset to Kaley. "They're having problems up ahead. One of the platoons didn't get the word to pull back and kept fighting up the hill. They got hit by our artillery and they're pinned-down by the dinks. Captain Kaufman is sending another platoon up to try and get them out."

Kaley looked at Jason and frowned. "This isn't looking good. We're going to need at least another battalion to take this damn hill."

Colonel Huu threw the field phone and yelled for a runner. The operations officer turned from the wall map. "You couldn't make contact?"

Huu was steaming. "No! The phone and radio are out! The infantry are still waiting for orders to attack!" He grabbed the young runner's shirt and pulled him to within inches of his face. "Go to the Second Battalion and tell the commander to attack the enemy's rear and flank immediately. Tell him we will begin the mortar attack at . . . ." He looked at his watch and made a quick

estimate of how long it would take for the battalion to move into
position. "The mortars will begin firing at 1430 hours. Go! And
be quick!"

Captain Kaley took one look at the progress of the weapons
platoon at clearing the bamboo and trees and put the handset to his
mouth. His men were getting nowhere with machetes. He had to
request an LZ kit that had the chain saws and demolition needed
to clear a big enough area.

Hearing the request over the radio, Jason grew worried about the
wounded. He blew dust off his rifle and stood up. "Harp, I'm going
up to that big tree all by itself up the ridge to see if I can help the
chaplain. You just sit tight and keep listening to the radios."

"No sweat, L-tee," Harper said as he dug a foxhole with his
entrenching tool. "You just go on and play hero all you want. I'm
digging myself to China and be halfway there by the time you get
back."

Jason pointed at his radiomen. "You guys should take a lesson
from this vet and start digging."

Chaplain Waters took a poncho from a dropped rucksack and
spread it on the ground. Then he motioned to a wounded soldier.
"Come on, son, pick your legs up and get on the poncho. The ants
are getting bad where you're laying."

Jason stopped at the row of wounded behind the tree and suddenly felt weak. The horrible scene was all too familiar. He fought
through the weakness and stepped closer. The smell hit him. He
halted again. The odor of blood and dried sweat caused him to
shudder uncontrollably. His skin crawled with the memory of
Simpson's blood dripping down his back.

Waters glanced up and saw Jason staring at the wounded. He
spoke softly. "Jay, could you search through some of the rucks
behind you and bring me ponchos?"

Jason stood frozen to the ground, not hearing the artillery or the
chaplain's words. His mind was somewhere else.

Waters walked up to him and put a hand on his shoulder. "Jay?
Jay, we need your help. Will you get me some ponchos from the
rucks behind you?"

Jason's eyes focused and he took a deep breath. "Yes, sir."

The second squad leader and first sergeant of Delta Company
crawled toward the hidden bunker. It was only fifteen meters up
the ridge from where the point man had been shot earlier that morn-

ag. One of the men in the squad had seen a tongue of flame and spotted the small aperture. The squad followed closely behind them. First Sergeant Deebs had volunteered for the attack. He was tired of seeing his men getting hurt. He carried a claymore bag full of grenades and crawled low alongside a downed tree to within a few yards of the firing port without being seen. Taking a grenade from the bag, he pulled the pin and counted to two before raising up and pitching it into the firing port. Seconds later the grenade went off to screams of joy from the pinned-down men. Deebs tossed in two more for good measure and waved his men forward.

Private Duong lay just inside the tunnel trying to clear the ringing in his head. The first grenade had landed at the assistant gunner's feet, and he had kicked it into the grenade sump dug into the floor of the bunker. The device exploded before it fell into the hole, severing the assistant's foot at the ankle and wounding the gunner badly in the legs and waist. The second and third grenades landed next to the two crumpled bodies. Duong had been in the tunnel getting more ammunition when the assistant had yelled a warning.

He shook his head and crawled into the dust-filled bunker. The bodies of his comrades were ripped horribly. They didn't look like people anymore. Blood and pieces of flesh were all about him. The place looked like a slaughter house for pigs. Through the portal he saw the Americans approaching. Backing up, he picked up his rifle and opened the box that held a dozen grenades. Placing them in a row on the firing ledge, he lifted his weapon and fired his AK until it was empty and began tossing grenades out the portal.

Deebs spun around at the sound of the AK fire. Two men fell, shot in the legs before his eyes. "SONOFABITCH!" he yelled, and crawled toward the bunker again, but a grenade fell only a few feet from him. He rolled over into a depression just as the device went off, showering him with dirt.

The squad leader yelled, "Fall back! Fall back!"

Deebs cussed as he jumped to his feet and ran, just making it to a crater before another grenade exploded.

Jason had heard the chopper come in twenty minutes before and had hoped the weapons platoon was making progress with the landing zone. Some of the wounded were in very bad shape. Chaplain Waters had already given one paratrooper last rites. Jason stood. He thought he had heard a mortar firing. He wasn't sure if it was one of theirs or the NVA's. The answer came fifteen seconds later when a thunderous CRACKwhaWHOOM filled his ears. The round had hit down the slope where the chopper had hovered and kicked out the LZ kit. Damn, the dinks had mortars, too! If they were

trying to find the range they were right on target, he thought. An
medevacs trying to come in would be torn apart by shrapnel.

A wounded soldier grabbed Jason's leg. "Sir, are we sur
rounded?"

Jason squatted down. "Of course not, that was just a morta
round to our rear. Take it easy and lay back. We'll get you ou
pretty soon now." He was about to pat the soldier's hand when h
suddenly stood up. The flanks! he thought. My God, the flanks
They'll do exactly what they did to me and the platoon. He bega
running down the ridge to warn Captain Kaley.

Specialist Selly sat alongside the trail with his team, smokin
cigarettes. The machine-gunner next to him backed up from hi
gun and said, "Man, hard-luck Alpha has got skate duty this time
I dig this rear security bit. Poor ol' Charlie and Delta sound lik
they're in a beehive. I dig nobody shootin' at us, man."

Selly blew out a cloud of smoke. "Get back on the gun and b
quiet. You can never tell when . . . what's that?"

The machine gunner listened for a moment and quickly readie
his M-60. "Sounds like a platoon of elephants coming, man."

Selly tossed his cigarette behind him and motioned his men dowr
"Hold your fire until we see who it is," he whispered.

Twenty feet in front of the outpost the trail made a sharp turn t
the right. From around the bend came two columns of NVA wit
blackened faces, jogging up the trail shoulder to shoulder. Th
machine-gunner let them get within fifteen feet before pressing th
trigger.

Jason was blown off his feet by an impacting mortar round as h
ran toward the LZ. He lay looking up at the sun. He could hea
nothing but a dull ringing. The sun seemed exceptionally warm o
his face, making him suddenly uncomfortable. Sitting up, he wipe
the sweat from his eyes and brought his hand away covered i
blood. Still feeling no pain, he touched his face and found the gas
below his eye. The skin was laid back like a slice out of orange.

Another mortar round landed below him, then another. Me
were yelling that the rear outpost was under attack. Jason got u
and saw Captain Kaley with his headquarters group next to a tre
only twenty yards away. Wounded men from the previous morta
rounds were lying in front of them. He began to run to their positio
when a mortar round exploded in the tree above the group, show
ering them with shrapnel. Kaley went down, hit in the back, an
the others screamed out in pain.

Jason began to move toward them when he saw, from the corner of his eye, three men break out of the trees from down the ridge. All three were turning and shooting back into the trees and screaming, "THEY'RE COMING! THEY'RE COMING!"

He knew in an instant that his fears were being realized. The NVA were attacking the rear. He began to turn and face the onslaught when firing broke out from the west. GOD, NO! They were attacking the rear and west flank simultaneously. The only hope was to get the platoon on the other flank into a perimeter and to hold off the wave of attacks long enough to make a break for Charlie and Delta's perimeter. He broke into a dead run toward the platoon following Delta Company, screaming for everyone he saw to form a perimeter.

Sergeant Harper balled up as the bamboo behind him was chopped to pieces by machine-gun fire. His foxhole was only forty yards from the rear OP, and he had laid down protective fire for a soldier who had run up the trail throwing hand grenades behind him. The soldier, Spec-4 Selly, jumped into the hole with Harper. He said the NVA had killed his team and were attacking. Harper had made a decision to move back to the Charlie and Delta perimeter, but the NVA machine-gun fire from the west and rear had them pinned down. He peered over the lip of his hole and felt his stomach shrivel into a twisted knot. NVA were pouring out of the tree line and running up the trail.

Captain Kaley saw the attacking enemy from the west and pushed aside the senior medic, who was working on his back. He raised his rifle and began firing, hitting three of the screaming men before being struck by a stream of bullets. The rest of the headquarters group fired until their weapons were empty. Then they tried to use their M-16s as clubs. The wounded men in front of the dead captain screamed in horror as the NVA ran over the top of them in a human wave, stabbing them with fixed bayonets.

Harper jumped out of his hole, knowing they would be overrun like Alpha Company's headquarters, and yelled for the RTOs to follow him up the ridge. The first enemy wave had passed, rushing toward the flank platoon, while ten to fifteen more NVA were running around shooting those the others had missed. Harper fired at two NVA only several feet away and spun around to cover the backs of his small group of men. More NVA came out of the tree line below him, running and shooting, as Selly and the RTOs dashed out, firing left, then right.

Jason had formed a perimeter with nine men and had to wait only a minute before the NVA appeared in a spread-out line. He lay down and took aim while talking calmly. "Semi only. Take your time and aim."

The first line of enemy were brought down only ten yards in front of the position. "Aim, shoot, and pick another target. Aim and squeeze, don't jerk."

Five more NVA went down, but still more came yelling, "Tien len! Tien len!"

Sergeant Harper saw the perimeter formed by Charlie Company and screamed for them not to shoot. Selly and the RTOs jumped into a crater beside a machine-gun position and yelled for Harper to join them. The sergeant was white-faced from the sprint and could barely move his legs. He jerked and pitched forward into the red dirt. A bullet had torn through the back of his leg, knocking him down in front of the crater. Selly jumped up, grabbed the moaning sergeant, and pulled him into the hole.

Jason turned around and saw that more of the platoon had joined their perimeter, including the platoon leader, who had been wounded badly in the arm. He crawled to the lieutenant and explained what had happened and that they had to back up and join with Delta and Charlie companies' perimeter before being completely cut off. The lieutenant barked at his men, "First squad, you lay down covering fire while the rest of the platoon runs up the ridge. Everybody put in a fresh magazine. You're moving in thirty seconds."

Captain Kaufman ran back and forth between Charlie and Delta companies, tightening the perimeter. The situation was looking bleak, and he called the battalion commander to tell him that they were surrounded and needed an emergency resupply of ammunition. He could barely hear the colonel's reply over the mortar explosions. Rockets were swooshing into the perimeter, and shrapnel whistled and whizzed overhead.

Kaufman was grabbed by his first sergeant. "Sir, Alpha Company has had it! There are only a few of them left, and they say there are lots of wounded down the hill. Kaley and his headquarters group all bought it!"

Kaufman looked around a battered stump toward the sound of

his men's yelling. A few survivors from Alpha were running up the slope, led by Lieutenant Johnson. "Get those men on the perimeter as soon as they come in and do the best you can, Top. Make sure our men look before they shoot, so we don't hit any of Alpha's men trying to make it in."

Jason fell heaving into a small crater. He felt as if his chest were crushed. A Delta soldier crawled over to him and lifted his chin. "Better let me bandage that wound, L-tee; it's gettin' full of dirt."

Jason fell back against the plowed earth breathing in gasps as the soldier wrapped a piece of towel around his face. "Sir, it ain't much, but it'll keep the dirt out."

Jason sat up and inserted another magazine in his rifle. The soldier looked at him in disbelief as he began climbing out of the crater. "Where you going, sir? Jesus, stay in the hole."

Jason shouted over his shoulder, "We've got men down there!" He ran down the ridge for twenty meters and fell into another mortar crater. He heard something behind him and spun around ready to fire but stopped himself. The young soldier plus three men from Alpha Company had decided to join him. Mortar rounds were impacting farther down the ridge, and no NVA were in sight. He raised up and could see bodies scattered everywhere. Off to his left were four wounded paratroopers trying to make it up the hill during the lull. To his right, the squad and lieutenant that had remained to cover the rest of the platoon were making a break without receiving fire. Jason jumped to his feet and ran toward the wounded men.

One of the men saw him approaching and fell to his knees crying. Jason yanked him to his feet and pushed him along, but the soldier turned around. "They're down there. I heard them. They're going to attack again!"

Jason got down to protect their backs as the others helped the wounded up the slope. He heard them, too. Commands were being shouted. He had heard almost identical commands once before.

Two more men from Alpha Company broke out of the trees just to his left and ran toward him. "Where is everybody?" they shouted hoarsely. "We were on flank OP and seen what must a been a battalion of dinks go by but couldn't do anything but keep quiet. They was all around us!"

"You see anybody else from your platoon?" Jason yelled, still watching down the hill.

"The only ones we saw were dead. Where is everybody, L-tee?"

Jason decided to check just a little farther down the ridge for other wounded. He couldn't stand the thought of leaving anyone behind, knowing what had happened last time. "Come on, you two, stay with me. We're gonna check for wounded."

He came up to the partially cleared LZ. The ground was covered with paratrooper and NVA bodies in every conceivable position of death. Some were open-eyed, staring at eternity. Others were grimacing in frozen horror. A low moan nearly caused him to urinate in his pants.

He approached the noise, praying it was an Alpha survivor and not a wounded NVA. A black soldier raised up and looked up at him with tears running down his face. "We made it, Bill . . . Bill, they've saved us." He patted the man lying beside him. "Bill . . . we're gonna make it."

Jason knelt and turned over the soldier's white friend to check his wound. The stocky man smiled strangely at Jason and raised his hands from his stomach, releasing his intestines, which began oozing out from the wide gash in his abdomen. Jason put his hand over the wound and began to yell for help when he heard the NVA commands again. The voices were very close.

One of the men standing behind Jason saw the first enemy assault line step out of the trees forty meters away and threw himself to the ground. "WE GOTTA GET OUTTA HERE!"

Jason tried to lift the stocky soldier, but he was too heavy. The black paratrooper became hysterical. "His guts! His guts are coming out!"

Two other men grabbed the wounded man's hands to drag him up the slope but it was too late. The stocky soldier's eyes became fixed. Jason yanked the corporal to his feet and pushed him ahead. "Leave him! GO, GO!"

Bullets began cracking overhead. Then suddenly the air seemed filled with whizzing lead. The corporal screamed and fell, shot in the arm, and another of the men went down hit in the back of the shoulder. Jason pulled the corporal to his feet as the other soldier helped his wounded friend up. Grabbing the corporal, he began running and yelling for the others to follow. They kept low and ran up the slope, staying in the thicker vegetation, with the NVA close on their heels. The paratrooper who had been hit in the back kept falling down despite his friend's help. Jason released the corporal and helped lift the bleeding man. They continued running and hollering toward the perimeter.

Delta Company laid down covering for the four approaching men. Jason pitched forward and fell into a warm, smoking crater created by a recent mortar round. Behind him the NVA attacked in a wave assault. He vomited and tried to breathe, but no air would come as the sky overhead cracked and popped with bullets.

Captain Kaufman watched the copter circle and suddenly drop to make its attempt. It barreled in and began its flare but was hit immediately by deadly crossfire. The Huey shuddered and dipped its nose to gain airspeed as the crew kicked out the ammunition pallet to lighten the load. It wasn't enough. The aircraft groaned and slipped backward as if being pushed by an invisible hand. Kaufman turned his head just as the olive-drab bird crashed into the trees.

The first sergeant slapped his rifle stock. "That's the third bird we've lost! They're blowing them out of the sky!"

Kaufman motioned to lieutenants Lantz and McDonough. "We need that ammo. Organize retrieval parties and crawl down to where that last bird dropped the pallet and see if you can get it for us."

Minutes later, the officers began making their way down the steep eastern slope followed by two squads. Lantz took six steps and was shot in the head; he was killed instantly. The ground around the remaining men was riddled by machine-gun fire from down the slope, and they scurried back toward safety.

Kaufman exchanged looks with the first sergeant, who slapped his weapon again. "We've got thirty to forty dead and at least a hundred wounded," he said, trying to hold back his tears. "Sir, we've got to get some ammo or none of us are gonna make it."

Jason crawled down the defensive line and instructed the men to pair up and dig in as deep as they could. He had been hit in the shoulder by shrapnel, but the wound was not deep. The jagged piece of metal was embedded just under the skin, and his arm ached with every movement. Several men asked if they could help him, but each time he shook his head and kept crawling. He had to keep moving or he would start thinking about his pain and the pain of so many others. He had found positions where every man was wounded and others where all were dead. He ordered the more seriously injured moved back to the lone tree for medical attention, but he stopped the slightly wounded from going. It was like playing God, deciding who would stay and fight and who would be able to lie and wait for evacuation from the battlefield, but for Jason the role wasn't difficult. He knew what the outcome would be if most didn't stay on the front line.

He stopped at a position to give the men instructions and was shocked when Harper raised his head and looked at him. The sergeant was barely able to keep his chin up, but he still broke into a smile. Jason unashamedly hugged him. "God, am I glad to see you. I thought for sure you were . . ."

"I thought the same about you," Harper said, lowering his head to hide his tears of relief.

Jason examined Harper's leg wound, then slapped his behind. "You're out of this. That's an order. Come on, I'll help you get back to the casualty tree."

Harper clutched his weapon tightly. "I don't wanna go. I saw what happened to the wounded by Captain Kaley. I'd rather stay here and take my chances."

Jason gestured for one of the other men in the position to help him, and they began dragging Harper toward the tree. "Harper, my friend, you're as mean as a snake. I want you to keep an eye on Chaplain Waters for me and make sure he doesn't try and convert all those boys into mackerel snappers."

"God, it hurts," Harper said through clenched teeth. "I hope they get us out pretty soon. I've never felt so shitty."

Jason quit talking and bit his lip. His arm was sending tremors through his whole body, but as he got closer to the tree, he forgot his own wound. The injured were lying in rows around it with only a few medics to help them. Chaplain Waters looked exhausted as he moved from one man to the next and forced a cheery smile.

Jason called a medic over as he laid Harper down on the end of a long row. "Have you got anything you can give him?"

"We're out of everything," the medic said tiredly. "The only thing we can do is get them out of here. Do you have any water you can spare for them?"

Jason felt his canteens. "Sorry, I'm out, too."

Chaplain Waters saw Jason and walked over. "Jay, good to see you. Have you got any water? We need it desperately for . . ."

"Sorry, Father, the medic already hit me up. I'm all out."

Waters showed the first sad expression Jason had ever seen from the man. "It doesn't look good for a lot of them unless we get them some fluids."

Jason began to speak but the chaplain noticed his discomfort. "I'm sorry. I'm rambling and here you are hurt. Let me take a look at that shoulder."

Jason backed up, feeling ridiculous. His wound was so minor, compared with those of the others. "It's nothing, Father, really, you've got more to do than . . ."

"Stand still, and that's an order from God's disciple!" Waters said sharply. He checked the wound and spoke over his shoulder.

"Sam, we need you here just a sec. This big, stubborn lieutenant has a shrapnel splinter that needs to come out."

A medic approached and had Jason sit down. "This is gonna hurt like hell," he said as he pulled out a scalpel from his aid bag. "I'm gonna make an incision, then take that sucker out. It will hurt now, but it won't be near as bad later on when you try and move your arm. Bite on something and hold still."

Jason saw the soldier pick up the blood-covered scalpel from the top of his medic bag. He knew better than to complain. It was probably all he had left. The medic had been right. It did hurt like hell. Minutes later, he was bandaged and on his feet. The medic had also checked his facial wound but said it was clotted and that was good enough for the time being.

Waters was talking to Harper when Jason came over and knelt beside his friend. "Father, I've got to talk to Captain Kaufman and see what he wants me to do. You watch out for this old trooper for me."

"Sure. I'm going to wash his mouth out with soap first. I'll see that he stays still for awhile."

Harper stuck his hand up toward Jason. "Thanks, L-tee . . . don't be playin' hero. Come back and see me later, will ya?"

Jason took his hand. "Sure will. Just take it easy, old-timer."

Captain Kaufman looked at the crest of the hill as a bomb exploded on the other side. "Joe, move it closer to the top. How's the artillery holding up?"

The forward observer lowered his handset from his ear. "We have plenty of rounds for the night. We're keeping the eastern and western flanks peppered."

Kaufman sat down tiredly and glanced at the rows of wounded only a few paces away. "We need to get those men outta here." He looked at Jason, who was sitting nearby. "Jay, thanks for walking the line for me. Now I have something else I want you to do. We've got another chopper coming in a few minutes, and it's going to drop in a couple of pallets of ammo. I want you to get some flashlights and make a spot for him. If he makes it in, get the ammo distributed to the platoon sergeants. I'll send Reddy with you with his radio so you can talk to the bird and guide him. We've lost six helicopters so far, so the birds are going to be coming in fast."

Jason nodded and stood up. "Yes, sir . . . Sir, we're going to need water and medical supplies, too, if we can get them. Chaplain Waters told me they're out of everything."

Kaufman pointed at his RTO. "Call it in." Then he pointed at another radioman who looked all of twelve years old. "Reddy, you go with the L-tee and get that bird in here."

Jason saw the approaching helicopter in the fading light and turned on the three flashlights he had placed in a large crater just twenty paces from the edge of the perimeter. He climbed out of the hole and stepped back, ready to run if the pallets missed their mark. Reddy gave the pilot a course direction and stood on the lip of the crater. Jason yelled for him to get down, but the small soldier's total concentration was on the fast-approaching chopper. The Huey began to flare as green tracers arched across the sky in front of its nose. Jason threw himself to the ground knowing the flying bomb was going to explode any second. Reddy screamed into the radio, "Not yet, not yet . . . NOW!"

Out of the shaking machine came large boxes plummeting toward earth. Jason looked up just as the pallets hit, with a thud, dead center in the crater. The Huey banked hard right, almost turning on its side, as angry green tracers shot past.

"Hot damn!" Jason yelled as he ran for the crater.

Reddy and Jason handed out ammo bandoliers to the gathered platoon sergeants, who slung them over their shoulders until they could hardly walk. Several of the NCOs had already made one trip and had come back for more.

Jason felt renewed hope every time he opened an ammo can and pulled out bandoliers. But when an Air Force jet flew over at low level from the northeast, shaking the ground and hurting their ears with its thunderous roar, one of the sergeants looked up and gasped, "God, no!"

Jason spun around and saw the distant casualty tree in the twilight. Then, suddenly, evening turned to day in an instant flash of brilliant white light, followed a millisecond later by an ear-shattering explosion that knocked them off their feet.

He lay in a fog, not feeling or seeing anything. Suddenly, his head and eyes felt as if they were going to explode. The terrific pain slowly subsided and he tried to sit up, but his body was numb and he couldn't move. Blinking his burning eyes he tried to lift his head, but a weird tingling sensation began at his toes and crawled up his spine. He felt as if he'd been run over by a truck and left semiconscious. Digging his hands into the soil, he turned himself over and focused his eyes. Everything seemed darker and hazy. He felt something touching his arm and forced himself to sit up. Reddy lay a few feet away. "Sir, I can't feel my legs," Reddy said thickly.

Still groggy, Jason crawled over and began to check him for wounds. "Your . . . your legs are fine. You probably just . . ." He stopped in midsentence as he felt past Reddy's boot tops. Reddy had no feet, and warm blood was gushing into Jason's hands. Jason applied pressure to the young soldier's thin legs and yelled toward a sergeant who was just picking himself off the ground. The sergeant crawled over and Jason whispered quickly, "Give me your belt and something else to tie a tourniquet!"

Reddy began writhing on the ground. "My feet hurt real bad, sir."

Jason used the sergeant's belt to tie off one leg, and, with the strap of a bandolier, repeated the process on the other leg. Only after he had finished and wiped his hands in the dirt did he turn around to see what had happened. It was then that it all hit him. A bomb had struck a limb of the casualty tree and exploded in an airburst, showering the perimeter with shrapnel. Reddy had been hit by a big piece of the hot iron, which cut his feet off like a giant razor blade just above the ankles. His boot tops were still laced. Jason could make out two other men lying nearby, frozen in death, and jerked his head up. My God, Harper!

He broke into a run, fell down, and tried running again. His body didn't seem to want to respond. Staggering toward the tree in the darkness, tripping and falling several more times, he passed bodies and men standing in silent shock. He heard hysterical screaming behind him for "Mediiiiic!" He kept moving toward the tree, passing small fires started by the explosion. He tripped again, falling over a body, and got up just as a flare popped high overhead. The tree was just ahead, but it was a quarter of its former size. Its top looked like a splintered willow. The rows of wounded men were gone. Jason walked ahead in a stupor as the parachute flare swayed in the wind and cast its eerie light over the destruction. Mutilated forms lay stacked everywhere, covered in a fine coating of dirt and wood particles that somehow made them look unreal, as if they had been there a long time and had been partially absorbed by the hill. Suddenly, there was complete silence. Jason swayed and caught himself. There was no movement except for the dancing shadows. He walked over the plowed ground, avoiding the arms, legs, and torsos of those whom he had sent back from the line for evacuation. They weren't just dead. They had completely ceased to exist in a flash of light. A radio with the bottom third sliced off was all that was left of the command post. Captain Kaufman, his officers, the first sergeant, the forward observers, the RTOs, the medics, all of the wounded, Harper, and Chaplain Waters were all gone. He had been walking over what was left of them.

The flare faded, like Jason's heart, then went out, leaving the grieving officer alone in the darkness.

35

Sergeant Hammonds gathered his men in an engineer bunker and took out his notes from the hour-long meeting he had just attended. He looked over his scribbles, obviously upset, and tossed down the pad. He already knew what needed to be said. "Guys, the Second Batt is in big-time trouble, and the Fourth Batt is going in to get them out. Everybody pack your rucks tonight with all the ammo and water you can carry. We're the first company to go in. We'll be picked up at first light tomorrow and flown to Firebase 16. Once our company is ready, we're humping two and a half klicks to the southwest to a hill called eight hundred-seventy-five. We're going to link up with the Second Batt in a perimeter just a couple a hundred meters from the hilltop. They got waxed by a rear-and-flank attack this afternoon, and supposedly one company got wasted. The dinks are thick around the hill and have already knocked down six choppers and shot up a couple of others. We're going to be the lead platoon and, yeah, we're gonna be the lead squad. Bugs, you'll be on point and . . ."

Ty stood. "I'll walk point."

Hammonds waved him down. "You're out of this, Cat; you report to the Thirty-ninth tomorrow. Like I was saying, Bugs, you take point; Cowboy, you'll be slack, and . . ."

Ty leaned back against the sandbags, listening but not really paying attention. He wanted to be with his friends when they went in. He knew that when he reported to his first sergeant tomorrow he would still be thinking and worrying about his old squad. It would have been different if they were on a road-clearing mission or just filling sandbags, but they weren't. It was a big mission, they needed him. He looked around at their solemn faces and lowered his eyes, knowing the real truth. He was the one who needed them.

General Duc listened to the radio report from Hill eight hundred-seventy-five and stared blankly at the wall. Again victory had been lost by his improper planning. The battle today had gone badly. The Second Battalion of the 174th was unable to split the attacking force. Their efforts had been heroic, but the Americans showed they were fighters. The effort was not followed up quickly enough by a second attack, for the battalion commander and his staff were killed by artillery. It had taken too long for the senior company commander to reorganize the battalion, and they had lost the element of surprise. The American artillery and bombs had decimated the remaining men before they could mount another full-scale attack, but then the impossible had happened. It was fate. An American bomb had fallen inside their own perimeter. The report he had just received from Colonel Huu confirmed his suspicions. The bomb had done considerable damage to the Americans, who had no overhead cover. The air strikes and artillery had ceased pounding Huu's fortifications for thirty minutes, meaning the American communications and command element must have been temporarily knocked out of action. It was then that he should have attacked with a reserve force . . . but he had no reserve. The remaining men of the Second Battalion were en route to the base. The Third Battalion was broken into platoon- and squad-size elements with no means to contact them and coordinate an immediate attack. He had let the plan run him again. He should have left Colonel Huu a battalion from the Sixty-sixty for exploitation. If they had been hidden a kilometer away, they could have . . .

He put the thoughts out of his mind and faced his operations officer, who was seated at the table. "Inform Colonel Huu that his message was received and that he is to be congratulated for stopping the American attack. Tell him I am sending two more mortar platoons to assist him in pounding the American perimeter. The plan he and I discussed is to stay in effect. Hold as long as possible but do not remain until overrun."

Colonel Kinh knew what the general was really thinking and pointed at the map. "We have a battalion from the Thirty-second within five kilometers of Hill eight hundred-seventy-five. We could have them move tonight and attack at first light and . . ."

General Duc smiled sadly and raised his hand. "No, my friend, the chance of exploiting the freak accident is over. The tiger is wounded and more dangerous than before. The smell of his own blood makes him fierce. Surprise is gone, and he knows his enemy is worthy. He will not underestimate us and will give as much as he takes.''

Kinh sighed and leaned back in his chair. "We had him, we had the bastard.''

"Perhaps,'' the general said softly as he walked to the door.

It had been the cries for help that had made Jason leave the tree. He didn't know how long he had stood praying that it would all turn out to be a nightmare, that he would wake up and talk to Harper and Father Mike again. But the screams assured him it wasn't a dream. He had tried to ignore them. He had even covered his ears. But they wouldn't go away. Young men needed him. Again.

He walked to the perimeter's front line and spoke calmly to the panicked soldiers, who had thought everyone had been killed or that they were about to be overrun. One soldier killed himself with a pistol just as Jason approached his hole. The trooper's legs were both gone and he hadn't been able to take the pain. Jason moved from position to position calming the scared and hurt. He did so simply by telling them the truth. He admitted to them that it wasn't going to get any better and that they would have to fight to stay alive. They would have to forget their own fears and help each other, because only together could they survive awhile longer.

A flare popped overhead, exposing a standing soldier who made no move to take cover. A young, wounded paratrooper pleaded for him to get down, but Jason just walked to the next foxhole. "You men dig in deeper and oil your weapons,'' he commanded softly.

A sergeant looked up at the officer, who looked huge in the golden light. "Is . . . is there enough of us left to hold the fuckers off?''

"There's at least you and me,'' Jason said and kept walking. "And that's by God enough.''

The sergeant's eyes flickered in the swaying light, and he woke the specialist next to him. "Wake up, damn it. Clean that weapon and oil it.''

A soldier ran up to Jason just as the flare went out. "Sir, they need you up at the new CP. They found out you were still alive and told me to find you.

"Who's 'they'?'' Jason asked.

"Sir, Lieutenants Shiler and McDonald. They're the only officers left who aren't dead or hurt real bad. They've taken command of the perimeter and need your help.''

* * *

Jason stepped down into the crater and lifted the poncho. Lieutenant McDonald from Delta Company and Lieutenant Shiler from Alpha were sitting under the poncho, using a red-filtered lens flashlight to look at a map. Until now, the two officers had been platoon leaders, but the circumstances of their present situation left them commanding their respective companies and in charge of the perimeter.

Shiler swung the flashlight into Jason's face. "Damn, are we glad to see you. How you doin', Jay?"

Jason pushed the light away. "All right. Good to see you guys, too. What's the status?"

"Not good," McDonald said tiredly. "The only communication we have with the battalion commander is over Lieutenant O'Cary's radio. He's wounded real bad, but he's staying in contact with them. As far as artillery, we've got one forward observer RTO in Alpha Company.

"And the casualties?"

McDonald lowered his head. "Of the sixteen officers, eight are dead and the rest of us are wounded. A couple are bad, like O'Cary and Remington. I couldn't get a good count, but I'd estimate at least forty killed by the bomb and another forty from the earlier attacks. We've got about another hundred wounded. In other words, two-thirds of the battalion is dead or hurt. There aren't any officers left in Charlie Company, so Platoon Sergeant Krawtzow has taken charge. The men were real shaken up and a few panicked after the shock over the accidental bombing wore off, but it looks like most have calmed down."

Shiler folded his map. "We've formed this command post and are consolidating the radios. We need to know what the hell is happening and to keep the old man informed. I've got a casualty point being established, but we need to get the perimeter tightened up. Jay, I want you to get this command post organized for us, while me and Mac make the rounds and start getting the perimeter ready for an attack. I need to see what we look like and plug the necessary holes."

Jason set his rifle down and took off his helmet. "You guys go on. I've got it."

Ty awoke to a tap on his shoulder and rolled over. "I've got radio watch already?"

Hammonds sat down beside him. "No, I just got off pulling the duty in the TOC. Pack your shit, Cat; you're going with us. I talked to Salias and he gave the okay.''

Ty sat up. "Why the change of heart?"

Hammonds stared at the ground. "In the TOC they've got a radio on the Second Batt's frequency. It's worse than was reported. An Air Force jet accidentally dropped a bomb in their perimeter, and it hit in the middle of the CP and medical evacuation point. They lost all the company commanders except one, who is seriously injured, and most of the other officers and senior NCOs are KIA'd or WIA. Just a few lieutenants are running things, and it looks like the battalion is holding on by its fingernails. One of the officers was on the radio and was giving the report to their battalion commander. The colonel got real emotional and wanted to know who he was talking to.'' Hammonds shifted his eyes to Ty. "It was your brother.''

36

Jason shivered and pulled the poncho tighter around his shoulders. The sounds of crunching artillery and the thunderclaps of impacting bombs weren't registering in his brain anymore. He had stayed awake all night to take turns with Lieutenant O'Cary giving situation reports to the battalion commander and adjusting artillery and air support. O'Cary had lost a lot of blood but had refused to leave the radios. He said it was the only way he could keep fighting. The wounded officer had finally drifted off to sleep a few hours ago.

Jason's jaw was sore and his teeth were chattering. The early morning cold had crept into his bones, and he didn't think he could move unless someone helped him to stand.

The cold was bad, but he didn't want the darkness to go away. Within the blackness he didn't have to see the death and destruction. He wanted the sun's warmth, but he dreaded its light.

"Jay? Is that you?"

Jason recognized Lieutenant Shiler's voice and could see his faint outline above on the lip of the crater. "Yeah, Joe, come on down."

Shiler climbed into the hole and lay back in the soft earth. "Any news?"

"Yeah, the old man says the brigade commander is sending in the Fourth Batt to relieve us. He's also sending in resupply birds at first light and wants us to try and clear an LZ the best we can. . . . How are the men doing?"

Shiler closed his eyes. "What's left of them are freezing to death and thirsty as hell, but I think we can hold the perimeter with what we've got. If the dinks had a big force they would have attacked during the night. If we can hold out till the Fourth gets here, we'll make it. The dinks have got to be hurting as bad as we are with all the arty we've hit them with."

He sat up tiredly. "Jay, when it gets light I want you to check on the wounded and give me a report. We'll let O'Cary run the radios. Our first priority is going to be getting them out of all this; they've had to wait too long as it is . . . Jay? Jay, did you hear me?"

Jason lowered his head in the darkness. "Yeah."

Two B-40 rockets swooshed across the perimeter and impacted into the trees. The explosions startled Jason, and he threw back his poncho and readied his rifle. He shivered as he looked at the gray sky above him. He knew he had a duty to perform, but he felt too weak. His arm ached and his face was throbbing. All the excuses passed through his mind, but he forced himself to stand and peered over the crater rim. It was worse than he had imagined. The landscape looked as if an atom bomb had been dropped. Scattered among the leafless, battered trees that remained were equipment, bodies, parts of bodies, and trunks and branches, blown down and splintered as if they had been dropped from a thousand feet. Steeling himself, he crawled out of the crater toward the rows of wounded.

He checked each man. Three had bled to death during the night, including the young RTO, Reddy, who had helped him pass out ammunition. There were over sixty men lying in rows, but twenty-three were very seriously wounded. They had glazed, vacant eyes and were still shivering from the night's cold. Some had been bandaged, but most had their wounds covered with towels, T-shirts, or ponchos.

Jason wanted to go back to the crater and put their misery out of his mind, but their sunken eyes stopped him. Their pain tore through his heart, telling of their untold suffering and despair. There was nobody left to help them. There had been thirteen medics in the battalion; eleven were dead and the remaining two were wounded. Someone had to take charge of the wounded and give them hope.

Jason's face turned to stone, and he began searching the nearby dead for their first-aid packets and anything else he could use as bandages.

"Delay! What the hell you mean delay?" the irate company commander blurted into the radio handset. He listened intently and pushed the side bar. "Yes, I understand we're short of aircraft, but goddamn, this is an emergency. Can't we get some help from other units?"

Hammonds backed out of the bunker on hearing the response and shook his head at the absurdity. He walked over to his squad and sat down dejectedly. Ty sat up with the rest of the men wanting to know what was holding them up.

The sergeant spit into the dust. "It's all fucked up. We can't get enough aircraft to carry us in. The aviation unit that supports us has had six birds shot down and five more shot up so bad they can't fly. The damn brigade staff won't ask the Fourth Division for help because us Airborne prima donnas take care of our own. It's the biggest bunch of bullshit I've ever heard of."

Ty got up and walked to the command bunker's entrance just as the captain tossed down the handset and picked up another one. "Papa Victor Six, this is Yankee Bravo Six. We have a problem with aviation and have been delayed at this location for at least two more hours. I need your support in calling higher and finding out about getting us some birds, over."

The battalion commander's voice came over the speaker. "Bravo Six, this is Victor Six. I don't accept what I just heard and will investigate now. Be prepared to move immediately. Out."

Ty knew that the old man was as perturbed as his captain and would make things happen. The sky had been full of helicopters all morning. Surely it was just a minor snafu that the brass could fix.

Hammonds looked up as Ty approached. "Well?"

Ty sat down and leaned back on the sandbags. "The battalion commander is fixin' it."

Colonel Huu shifted his bloodshot eyes to the operations officer. "What is our status?"

Major Vuc ignored the rumbling of the artillery impacting above them. "The first bunker line is so close to the Yankees the artillery has barely touched them, and they have reported light casualties. The second bunker line has damaged bunkers on both ridges but reports they are clearing the damage and will be operational in six hours. The trench line is partially caved in, but work parties are clearing the dirt and making them passable. The third defensive line has had the most damage, and we will not be able to rebuild the bunkers. All tunnels are cleared, and the casualties overall have been light.''

Huu let the information sink in and prepared himself for the next report. "And what about the Third Battalion?"

Vuc knew the colonel was concerned about the men who were surrounding the Americans. They had no tunnels to protect them from the bombs and artillery. He allowed himself a weak smile. "The Third is doing much better than we had expected. They report their observers can clearly see the Yankee perimeter from their tree platforms and have been able to adjust our mortar fire very effectively. They also report they have dug in their machine guns and can accomplish their assigned mission of keeping the helicopters away. The infantry squads have not fared so well. They have taken heavy casualties from the bombs and have had to reorganize several times.''

Huu sipped water from a metal canteen. "What are the casualties of the Third?''

"Forty percent," Vuc said, erasing his smile.

Huu screwed the cap back on the canteen and stared blankly at the earth wall. His Second Battalion had lost eighty percent of their men to the American gunfire and artillery during their courageous attack, and now his Third Battalion was being slowly eaten away by the artillery. How long could they keep the ring closed around the Yankees?

He raised his head. "Contact the Third's commander and tell him to concentrate on using the mortars and snipers. Have the infantry fall back to safe locations and consolidate to await further instructions." He shifted his eyes to the major. "The Yankee perimeter is small and is an easy target for our mortars and rockets. Have our mortar crews dig three deep firing positions and then begin pounding the Yankee perimeter. They should fire for only a short time and move to the alternate positions to confuse the Americans as to their exact location. The infantry will be safe and will be my reserve to use when the time is right.''

Vuc stepped to the table and took the colonel's arm. "I will tell them, but now you must rest. Lie down and sleep; I will awaken you when something changes.''

Huu let himself be guided to the side tunnel, where hammocks were strung on sayo wood posts. He lay back in a hammock and looked up at his friend of many years. "How much longer do you think we can hold the hill?"

Vuc ran his fingers through his short black hair. "We have taken the worst of their bombing, and they haven't hurt us. With the supplies and good men we have . . . I believe a week. Perhaps longer."

The colonel shut his eyes. "The Tall One will be pleased."

The gunships streaked in, firing their rockets. A Huey followed, flying at ninety knots just above the treetops. Jason held his breath, praying the bird had medical supplies and an LZ kit on board. The chopper began to flare when green tracers from the hidden NVA machine guns crisscrossed the sky searching for their prey. The Huey pulled up to escape but still had to fly through the green streaks that formed a wall of lead. Jason tensed as the bird took the hits and began to shudder. Dipping its nose, the chopper picked up speed and banked away in a hard turn, barely escaping destruction. He watched the helicopter until it disappeared, then turned to face the men to whom he had promised new bandages and morphine. Their stares were not from frustration or anger, but from acceptance. He spun around and strode toward the perimeter line to search more of the dead for water and first-aid packets.

A lone Huey landed and kicked up a cloud of dust beside the command bunker. Ty and the rest of the squad got on and in seconds were over the Poko River. He knew that when he got to Firebase 16 they would have to wait for the entire company before they could begin the hump, but right now it didn't matter. At least he was getting closer.

Hammonds looked over at Ty and wondered how he could keep from screaming. Despite the efforts of the commander, the lone Slick was all they had to move out the entire battalion. A C-47 Chinook was supposed to help transport them beginning at one thousand hours, but it was clear that it was going to take all day for the battalion to be moved. The Huey could carry eight men and the Chinook thirty. The battalion was going in with three companies with a total strength of two hundred-seventy men. The plan was to assemble one company at a time and begin the march. Because the Airborne troops were too proud to accept help from legs, the Second Battalion of the 503d would have to hold another eight hours before being relieved.

* * *

Lieutenant McDonald gathered six men from Delta Company behind a fallen tree. "Men, I'm sending you out on a patrol up the hill to knock out the snipers. They must be the ones that are calling the mortars on the perimeter and keeping the choppers from coming in. Take two grenade launchers and knock their dicks in the dirt."

The sergeant in charge of the patrol inspected each of the men and their weapons. He drew a sketch of their route in the red clay and then told them how they would accomplish the mission. Five minutes later, the patrol began crawling forward. They had made it only twenty yards from the fallen tree when an NVA machine gun opened up, catching two of the men in the open and killing both instantly. A third soldier tried to drag one of the men back and was stitched across the shoulders. His screams were drowned out by the impact of three mortar rounds that hit by the fallen tree.

Stunned, McDonald stood up and yelled to the survivors, "GET BACK! GET BACK!"

Jason's hands were trembling as he ignored the yelling and shooting and concentrated on finding the bleeding artery in a soldier's groin wound. The paratrooper had been blown out of his foxhole by a mortar round. The skin on his right arm had been peeled back, exposing muscle, but the groin wound was worse. Jason was using a paper clip he had found on his sweat-soaked notepad. His hands were covered with blood as he pushed aside damaged tissue and slipped the clip over the cut, bluish-purple artery. The middle-aged sergeant writhed on the ground held by a curly blond soldier who had lost his helmet. Jason used black sewing thread and a needle he had gotten from a dead soldier's rucksack to try and sew the artery closed. Sweat stung his eyes as he slipped the needle into the slippery artery and pulled, but the knot slipped through. He quickly wiped his hands on his fatigue pants, then tied two knots on top of each other and tried again. The knot held. He inserted the needle again but felt a tap on his shoulder. The curly blond shook his head. The sergeant was dead. Jason leaned over without thinking and bit the thread in two, saving as much as possible. Then he moved across the bloody ground to the next soldier, who had lost three fingers from rocket shrapnel.

Private Bui Ngoc Duong placed a belt of ammunition into his machine gun and ordered the new replacement to sweep up the expended casings. Duong had been waiting all morning for an attack and was relieved when only six Yankees crawled out of their

perimeter. The men who had attacked his bunker the day before
and killed his two comrades must have died during the night and
not told anyone the location of his bunker. The small patrol had
snuck out of its position and crawled directly in front of his firing
port. They had been easy targets.

He looked at the scared replacement and patted his shoulder. "If
they come again we will do the same thing. I built this bunker and
it is very strong."

The soldier glanced at the dried blood on the wall. "The senior
sergeant said the Americans threw in grenades. How did you survive?"

Duong pointed at the grenade sump. "Kicked the grenade into
the hole. But it will be different next time. I have added wood and
made the firing ports smaller. They will have to throw their grenades from in front of the ports. If they attack in force and come
within close range, just keep shooting, even if you do not see a
target."

An artillery round exploded just behind the bunker, knocking
both men to the clay floor. Duong grabbed the confused replacement and pulled him toward the tunnel. Another round exploded
almost in the same spot. Duong spit dust from his mouth. "Follow
me. We are going to the shelter dug into the side of the tunnel."

Ty saw a body and froze. He stepped forward cautiously and saw
four more lined up in a neat row. Gauze bandages covered with
dried blood and NVA equipment were strewn all around the day-
old corpses. He studied the footprints next to the bodies and continued moving. He had moved ahead only fifteen steps when a voice
rang out from behind him. "Hold up!"

Lieutenant Salias walked forward sweating profusely. "What the
hell do you think you're doing?"

Ty pointed at the footprints on the trail. "Sir, these prints are at
least six hours old. The dead dinks are just like the others we've
found. They were left to be picked up later. We're not going to be
ambushed here."

Salias pointed his finger at Ty's face. "I told you before, we're
following orders. We've found thirty-five bodies so far, confirming
the NVA are massed in this area. We *will* stop and send out screening patrols to check our flanks!"

Hammonds walked up and spoke over the officer's shoulder.
"Lieutenant, we've fucked around long enough with these stupid
screening patrols. The Second Batt needs us now!"

Salias shifted his anger to Hammonds. "Shut up, Hammonds!

You know nothing about NVA tactics. Any fool could see we are being set up for an ambush.''

Hammonds glared back. ''Any *fool* wouldn't have sent the Second Batt against an entrenched enemy on a fucking hill. Since when did you officers get so damn smart on NVA tactics? You been reading the casualty lists?''

''Enough! When this is over I'm pressing charges for insubordination.''

Hammonds smiled cruelly. ''And I'm pressing charges for stupidity.''

Salias turned around. ''Get the screening patrols out!''

Ty could hear the artillery making impact on the hill ahead. He slowed only a moment to check his bearings and began walking up the slope. He felt strange. The hill's slope was just like Red Hill's. He took three steps and knew he was close. A GI jungle boot was lying on the trail. He moved closer and bit his lip. The boot still had a foot inside, which was covered with ants. He pointed toward the boot without taking his eyes from the trail and kept walking, still with the strange feeling he had been there before. Hammonds kicked the boot off the trail with his foot and followed.

Ty had seen bodies before, but this time it was different. This time he looked over the dead soldiers lying alongside the trail to see if one of them was his brother.

Ty had not counted the dead men he had passed but he could envision what had happened by the way they lay. The NVA had overrun their positions and had shot them as they passed by. One machine-gunner was still clutching his gun as if protecting it from harm. Ty stopped, seeing the first NVA body among the paratroopers. This corpse was unlike the others; it still had color and wasn't ashen. He was a fresh kill.

Ty yelled ahead, ''FOURTH BATT COMING IN . . . DON'T SHOOT!'' He took several steps and broke out of the thick vegetation into a semiwasteland. A shiver ran up his back. Four men stood up from a foxhole only twenty meters away and waved him forward. Ty couldn't believe their faces—they looked dead. They were the same gray color as the bodies he had passed. The closer he came, the more his insides churned. The filthy men stood with no expression or words. Their eyes were sunken back and lifeless except for a slight, dull glimmer that Ty knew was all the joy they were capable of showing.

* * *

Jason tried to tear the end of a towel with his hands, but he didn't have any strength left. He lowered his head. The sun's glare was suddenly blocked by a soldier standing on the crater rim. Jason looked up but couldn't make out who the man was and put his hand to his forehead to block the glare. His eyes adjusted and he saw a smile. He hadn't seen a smile in twenty-four hours. Jason stood and stepped closer. God, no! His eyes watered and he tried to speak, but his parched tongue was mired in sticky white cottonmouth.

Ty forced himself to keep the smile despite what he saw. Jason was like the others. He had a gray pallor and his eyes were sunken. Below the right eye his cheek was slashed and swollen to almost twice its normal size. The gash was filled with dirt and was seeping yellow liquid. His brother was trying to talk but snow-white dribble was drooling over his cracked lips.

He stepped down into the crater and hugged Jason, wanting to take away his misery. "I'm gonna get you outta this."

Jason held the water in his mouth, savoring it. The liquid was warm but worked like a miracle drug. He let a little seep down his sandpapered throat and rolled his eyes back, feeling the relief, as Ty and the others in his squad gave drinks to the wounded from their spare canteens.

Ty sat down and handed him another canteen. "Drink it slow, but drink it all. You need it."

Jason took another swallow, feeling hope for the wounded for the first time. The water, Bravo's medics, and the additional soldiers lifted his spirits, but the sight of Ty had sickened him. He didn't want him there.

Ty could see the worry in Jason's eyes. "You look like you've been through hell. The other companies will be here in a little while, and we'll get the perimeter expanded. We should be able to get the medevacs in this evening."

Jason took one more swallow before trying to speak. "Sta . . . stay in this hole and don't get out for anything. There are more of them than . . ."

The sound of an approaching helicopter stopped him in midsentence. Jason's eyes shifted skyward just as a Huey popped up over the ridge and began its flare. Immediately NVA machine guns began firing, filling the air with tracers. The chopper dropped like a rock below the bullets, and four men jumped from the aircraft from fifteen feet into the debris. The bird seemed to hang for a moment then suddenly dropped lower.

Jason jumped to his feet and pointed at the five men in the first row who were the most seriously wounded. "HELP ME GET 'EM TO THE SLICK!"

Ty, Hammonds, and the others picked up the wounded in ponchos and ran toward the whining machine. The crew chief frantically grabbed the men like slabs of meat and tossed them to the vibrating floor. The Huey rose and the NVA machine guns opened up again. Banking left, the bird picked up speed and streaked down the slope.

Hammonds stayed low as he ran back to the crater with Ty and Jason. "Sonofabitch, there's at least ten machine guns out there!"

Ty heard from a surprisingly short distance away the metallic thunk of a mortar firing. "Ooooh shit." The men ran harder and threw themselves into the crater. The mortar rounds hit where the chopper had landed, throwing up clouds of dirt and whizzing shrapnel that sliced through the air. Ty tried to get up but couldn't. Jason had thrown himself on top of him for protection.

Jason rolled off and lay in the dirt, exhausted from the run. Ty sat up with a grin. "You're still pretty fast in a crunch."

Jason rolled his head to the side and looked at Ty with cold, lifeless eyes. "You shouldn't have come."

Ty patted his brother's hand. "Somebody has to take care of you."

A runner crawled to the edge of the crater. "Lieutenant Johnson, the battalion XO came in on the chopper and wants all the officers to see him at the CP."

Jason got to his knees, feeling faint, and glanced at Ty. "You stay put."

Ty could see that he was about to fall over from exhaustion and grabbed his arm. "I'll go with you."

Jason pushed his arm away and motioned toward the wounded with his rifle. "Stay and watch out for my men; they need you more." He stood and climbed out of the crater without looking back.

Ty exchanged worried looks with Hammonds, who shook his head. "He's had it, Cat. When he gets back, make him get some sleep. I'm going to have the guys dig in around the wounded; you stay in this hole with your brother."

Major Shelly looked at the exhausted, filthy officers before him and passed around his canteen. He was still shaking. What he had seen had sickened him. He had never seen men in such horrible condition. The dead lay in holes with the living, and he hadn't been able to tell them apart, except when the living moved. They moved and spoke, but they all seemed like they were in a trance. Their blank eyes had told him the battalion was finished. They weren't capable of doing what the colonel wanted. Neither the colonel nor anyone else could understand unless they saw them.

He glanced at the remaining officers, wanting to cry. He had been in the battalion for several months and still couldn't believe so many of his friends and fellow officers had died. He shook his head and stiffened his back. He had to be strong and tell these remaining young leaders what the colonel had told him: they still had to think and act like soldiers.

Shelly cleared his throat before speaking. "You men have done the impossible for long enough. I'm just sorry I couldn't get in here earlier. The old man wanted me to tell you you've done a magnificent job and . . ."

"Why didn't *he* come in?" one of the RTOs whispered.

Shelly continued, ". . . proud of your actions. I am now assuming command of the operation, and our first priority is to clear an LZ. We'll get the wounded out, get resupplied, and then concentrate on taking the hill. The other two companies from Fourth Battalion are coming in this evening and will expand the perimeter. Tomorrow morning at first light, we'll begin an even bigger expansion and clear the LZ. When the two companies arrive, I want our Second Battalion men to get some sleep. That's it for now. When they arrive, we'll have another meeting. Stay close to a radio so I can call for you."

Colonel Huu listened to the radio report as he studied the wall map. The first American company from a relief battalion had joined the perimeter. Observers located in trees had seen the men arrive, and scouts had reported two more companies en route.

Major Vuc looked over the colonel's shoulder at the map. "We could send another company to stop the other two."

Huu shook his head as he sat down. "No. If we did that, the helicopters could land. We need every man in position to stop the helicopters. The three additional Yankee companies will not change anything. They can only attack up the narrow ridge and haven't room to maneuver additional men. Contact the mortar sections and have them ready to fire a concentration at first light tomorrow morning. I want the snipers to notify us as soon as they see the Yankees preparing to attack. I will radio the general myself and tell him of the situation."

"Will you tell him we will be able to hold?" Vuc asked.

Huu smiled, feeling confident. "Yes."

* * *

Ty turned around in the darkness and pulled the poncho up around Jason, who was still sleeping despite the constant pounding of artillery and the popping of flares overhead. Jason had come back from the meeting and had told the wounded that tomorrow an LZ would be cleared and they would be going home. Afterward he had argued, but Ty had made him lie down and sleep.

Hammonds crawled into the crater after checking the rest of the squad. "Cat, how's your brother doing?"

"He's still crashed."

"Good, he looked like he was about to drop. Shit, they all did. The wounded are the worst I've ever seen. Jesus, some of them have already got gangrene setting in. I don't know how they've made it this long."

Ty nodded, still sickened by the sight of American soldiers using T-shirts and underwear as bandages and having to use safety pins to close wounds. Their silence was the toughest thing to take. They didn't make a sound, as if it didn't matter or no one cared.

Hammonds scooted closer to Ty for the warmth. "What do you think our chances are in taking the hill tomorrow?"

Ty rested his cheek on the rifle stock. "I'm gettin' my brother out of here tomorrow . . . screw the hill."

General Binh Ty Duc rose from his bed unable to sleep and lit the kerosene lamp. He picked up the opened letter from General Giap that had arrived by courier and reread the penned lines one more time. Giap praised his efforts and those of the regimental commanders. The letter reported that the infiltration into the cities and the caching of ammunition was going on undetected. The success of the Tet offensive would be a direct result of the diversions in the highlands.

He tossed the letter to the floor and walked outside into the darkness. He could hear the rumble of artillery only ten kilometers from where he stood. His men were holding a red clay hill that had no value, and yet the Americans were dying trying to take it. The battle was an aberration of logic. He was no longer a military leader concerned about strategy or tactics, but rather a politician using his men to send a political message. The American military leaders were doing the same. They had ordered the hill to be taken only to prove they could.

Jason awoke to the sound of a mortar round exploding close by. He was drenched in sweat although he was shivering from the cool night air. The screams in his dreams wouldn't go away even when he awoke. Then he realized that he wasn't dreaming, that someone was crying out hysterically. He sat up and felt in the darkness for his brother, but Ty was gone. His stomach shriveled into a knot and his heart pounded in fear. The screaming stopped, and he could hear heavy breathing and the noise of men running. They were coming toward him. The ground shook with the impact of another mortar round, and dirt clods fell like hailstones. The sound of breathing was louder, as if the approaching men were almost on top of him. He raised his rifle, pushing off the safety.

"Take it easy, we're almost there," said a familiar voice. Jason lowered his weapon, shaking so badly he dropped the M-16 in the dirt.

Ty and Hammonds dragged an injured man into the hole and Ty yelled out, "Mediiiiic!"

Hammonds flipped on his red-filtered flashlight as other men came over the lip of the crater carrying two more wounded. Ty pulled out his knife and cut the right pant leg of the soldier he had carried as Hammonds panned the light on the man's thigh. A six-inch gash in the flesh was spouting a thick stream of blood.

Jason reached down and pushed the light closer. He put his fingers into the wound, feeling for the artery, and pinched it closed. Then he looked at Ty with detachment and in a strange voice said, "Tie a tourniquet just above the wound."

Ty looked into his brother's face, not knowing him, and quickly took off his belt. Jason showed no expression or emotion, although his fingers were inside a human being, keeping him from bleeding to death. It was as if he were in a trance.

A medic knelt beside Jason and slipped a clamp down on the artery. "Got it."

Jason wiped his hand in the dirt and looked around at the other wounded. Speaking with the same air of detachment, he said, "Whose are they?"

Hammonds kept his light on the wound for the medic to work. "They're from our company, sir. The round hit beside the company CP. The captain and first sergeant have light wounds, but these three got it pretty good. Hayes here is the worst."

Jason put on his helmet and stood up. "I'm going to the major and check on the status of the other companies."

"Jay, hold up; I'll go with you," Ty said.

Jason spun around. "No! And don't be running off again. Stay in that hole and dig in deeper . . . I can't lose you, too." He turned and melted into the darkness.

Ty began to follow him, but Hammonds grabbed his leg. "Stay here and do what he says."

Ty broke the grip with a jerk. "He's sick. He's got battle fatigue or something."

Hammonds grabbed him again. "Get your ass down. He knows what he's doing. He's worried about you, that's all."

Ty stared into the darkness. "You saw him. He acts like it . . . like it doesn't bother him."

"It bothers him," Hammonds said softly. "He's just found a way to keep it inside. He's like you when you're on point . . . but he's in a different groove."

37

Hammonds awoke to a gentle nudge from Ty. He sat up and looked around the crater. "Where's your brother?"

Ty nodded toward the rows of wounded lying in a depression beside their position. "He came back late last night from the CP and was worried about a sergeant named Ferguson. Jason stayed with him 'cause he wasn't doing very well and he wanted to keep him warm."

Hammonds was about to speak when Lieutenant Salias crawled into their hole. "Hammonds, get your squad ready to help carry the wounded. Medevacs will be coming in a few minutes."

Hammonds peered over the rim. "Who's going to clear the LZ?"

"Alpha Company's First Platoon is on its way right now," Salias said. "Once you're done loading the wounded, get your weapons cleaned. We're going to attack the hill at eleven hundred hours."

Hammonds heard a distant, familiar noise and tapped Ty's arm. "You'd better get your brother up. I hear the birds."

Ty crawled out of the crater toward the wounded but saw that Jason was already awake and had litter teams positioned. He went up beside Jason, who was staring down the ridge in total concen-

tration, waiting for the bird. ''Jay, you want me to help you carry
Ferguson?''

Jason kept his distant stare and spoke without emotion. ''He died
an hour ago.'' He lifted his head on hearing the Huey approach and
yelled toward the litter teams, ''Get ready!''

The first chopper made it in without a shot being fired and picked
up eight of the badly injured men who had been waiting for nearly
fifty hours. Jason ran back toward the rest of the waiting wounded,
feeling elated. The NVA must have pulled out during the night, and
he could finally get his men home.

The chopper lifted off as another one made its approach. Jason
yelled for Ty and his squad to hurry, when, without warning, incoming mortar rounds exploded in the perimeter. He was knocked
to the shaking ground and screamed in horror, ''NOOOOO!''

The promise of hope he had given to the wounded turned to
smoke as the medevac pulled up to avoid the deadly shrapnel only
to be hit by green tracers from the NVA's chattering machine guns.
The helicopter shuddered but kept gaining altitude. Trailing a thick
cloud of smoke, the bird banked for the valley.

Ty had seen his brother fall. He grabbed Jason's collar and
dragged him into the crater just as more mortar rounds landed in a
succession of quaking, ear-shattering explosions.

Jason fought Ty's grip and turned over to see where the rounds
were landing, praying the wounded would be spared. They were,
but the men who had been sent to clear the LZ were not. The
distinctive warning sounds of the mortars had been drowned out by
the noise of the choppers. First Platoon of Alpha Company had
been caught in the open with no holes to take cover in and were
being cut to pieces. The trapped men couldn't run or they would
be cut down by steel splinters, but they couldn't stay in the open
either. It was like watching a group of drowning men being circled
by sharks. No one could do anything for them but pray.

The mortar shells rained down steadily for several minutes, sending up geysers of dirt and cutting jagged iron. One hysterical soldier
lying in the impact area jumped to his feet to escape but was torn
almost in two by shrapnel. Others lay motionless, while some dug
frantically into the clay.

The explosions suddenly stopped, leaving only fading echoes.
The absence of sound was as unnerving as the barrage. The first
noise to break the silence was a lone whimper, which steadily grew
into a cry as it was joined by many others. ''Medic! MEDIIIIIIC!''

Jason couldn't stand it any longer. He had evacuated eight men only to have more join the green poncho rows. He got up and walked toward the newly wounded to see what he could do.

Silk and Cowboy laid the last of the wounded on ponchos and crawled into the crater with the rest of the squad. Hammonds looked up tiredly from the bottom of the hole. "What was the count?"

Book Man wiped dirt from his rifle. "Three bought it and seventeen were wounded."

Hammonds's jaw tightened. "So much for us being a relief force . . . looks like we're just more meat. Salias briefed me while you guys were carrying the wounded. We're attacking the hill at eleven. Alpha Company is going to be to our left and Charlie to our right. Bravo Company is going to be in the center, and we're going to be the base squad."

Silk shook his head dejectedly. "Man, here we go again. Dis shit is gettin' old. Why they puttin' us in the middle? We gonna have our asses hangin' in the wind."

Bugs snickered. "I hope they have a truck full of Purple Hearts."

"Shut up and quit sniveling; I don't like it any better than you do," Hammonds said impatiently. "We don't get a vote, so just suck it up and get your weapons clean. At ten-thirty we start moving up to get on line."

Ty heard the plan and crawled out of the crater to look for Jason. He found him sitting beside an ashen-faced soldier who was staring blankly at the sky. The young paratrooper's blackened torso looked as if animals had ripped out hunks of meat from his side and rib-cage.

Jason checked for a pulse and sat back tiredly. The soldier was alive but wouldn't last long if he didn't receive whole blood.

Ty crawled up beside him. "Jay, come on back to the crater; it's safer than out here."

Jason kept staring at the wounded soldier. "You go back and stay put. This is where I belong."

"But Jay!"

"Get back to the hole and stay there!"

Ty's face hardened. "I'm going with my squad on the attack. It's the only way we can get you and these men off this hill. I came up here to tell you. You just said it for both of us: You belong here . . . and I belong with my friends."

Jason's looked up at Ty as if seeing him for the first time. The distant coldness evaporated, and his eyes watered. He lifted his dog tag chain from his neck and held it out. "Take the wings back to your hill, Ty."

Ty pushed his hand away. "You keep 'em; they've been good luck for ya."

But Jason kept his trembling hand extended. Then he lowered his head and started to cry. He couldn't help himself. His tears began flowing and he couldn't stop them. Frustration, guilt, and grief poured from his soul. Death and misery had finally overcome him. He slumped over, unable to sit erect, his entire body shaking with bone-weary sadness and emptiness. He was tired of the blood, dirt, and pathetic stares; tired of the smell of burnt and infected flesh; tired of the despair. It all seemed so hopeless. Living was a nightmare . . . until he had looked into his brother's face.

Ty crawled over and hugged him tightly. "I love you, Jay. You're gonna be fine. We're gettin' off this hill and goin' home. Ya hear me? We're goin' home. That's a promise."

Jason hugged Ty, not wanting to let him go, and spoke in a whisper. "You can't do it, Ty."

"I'll be back," Ty said softly. "The sooner we take the sonofabitch, the sooner we'll both be going home."

Jason let his hands fall and forced a pained smile through his tears. "I'll see ya, brother."

Hammonds crawled down the line of waiting men and shouted over the crunching artillery, "We're not attacking till fourteen hundred hours. The Air Force is going to soften it up more for us."

Silk took out his entrenching tool and began digging. "Man, I ain't layin' here behind this tree and let no gook mortar git me."

Bugs shook his head and leaned back on a fallen tree. "Man, if they're gonna get you, they're gonna get you. Why bother?"

Cowboy slapped at Bugs's helmet. "Dig, fool. I'm beside ya and I don't wanna get splattered."

Ty had already dug under the tree to protect himself from the indirect mortar rounds and had widened the hole to make room for Hammonds. Caddy crawled into Ty's hole. "Cat, help me with Surf. He's scared to death and just shit his pants. The dude is locked up stiff."

Caddy backed out of the hole, and Ty began to follow him when mortar rounds impacted close by, shaking the ground. Caddy screamed and raised up, frantically, clawing at his back as if he were on fire. Ty grabbed him and threw him on his stomach. An ugly iron splinter was lodged in the middle of his back, smoking like a red-hot coal. Ty grabbed the jagged piece of iron, but it burned his fingers. Taking the towel from Caddy's neck, he put it

over the hot metal and pulled it out. Caddy collapsed like a limp
doll.

"MEDIC!"

Lieutenant Salias crouched behind Hammonds and looked at his
watch. "It's time, move out."

Hammonds turned around and grabbed the lieutenant's collar.
"YOU lead us, SIR! It's time you earned your pay!"

Salias's eyes grew wide. "I'm supposed to stay back and make
sure the platoon stays on line."

Hammonds jerked the lieutenant to his feet and shoved him forward. "It's time an officer led instead of followed. Lead us, goddamnit!"

Salias surprised Hammonds by smiling cruelly. "This time you're
right. FIRST PLATOON, ON YOUR FEET! MOVE OUT!" He
waved his men forward. "FOLLOW ME!"

Private Duong and the replacement pushed with all their might
and moved the limb only a few meters, but it was enough. They'd
used a bamboo pole and extended it through the firing port to push
a blown-down tree limb that blocked their field of fire out of the
way. The replacement quickly pulled the pole in as Duong readied
his machine gun. The attackers were silhouetted as they climbed
toward the bunker over the logs and debris. He held his breath,
aimed, and squeezed the trigger. The recoiling weapon felt good
as he began sweeping the barrel back and forth, raking the assault
line.

Colonel Huu yelled into the field phone, "They are attacking!
Every available man to the trenches!" He hung up and grabbed the
next phone handset. "They are attacking. Fire your mortars just to
the front of our first defensive line."

He tossed down the handset and spun around, facing his staff
with a smile. "At last!"

Bravo Company had advanced only fifteen meters before being
pinned down by withering fire. The company commander screamed
for the First Platoon to advance while the Second Platoon laid down
a base of fire.

Salias rose from the ground. His left shoulder was bleeding from
a bullet graze. "MOVE OUT, FIRST! DON'T STOP!" He took
two steps and was hit in the chest. He spun around, spitting up
blood, and dropped to his knees. "Don't . . . don't stop."

Hammonds saw the lieutenant fall and stepped over his body as he fired at the hilltop. The second squad rushed forward but was mowed down like wheat stalks. Ty saw the muzzle flash of the machine gun that had decimated the second squad. He pulled Hammonds to the ground. "Bunker to our right twenty meters!"

Hammonds motioned his squad down. "Cowboy, Silk, Surf, cover us! Bugs, come with Cat and me."

Ty tossed a smoke grenade in front of the bunker's firing port and threw himself behind a stump. Hammonds waited until the white smoke spread and yelled, "NOW!"

Hammonds, Ty, and Bugs ran toward the bunker as the rest of the squad laid down a base of fire. The three men ran through the smoke and fell to the ground behind the firing port. Hammonds gagged on the choking smoke but took out a grenade and pulled the pin. He let the lever fly, counted to two, and tossed the grenade toward the slit. The device hit the side of the small opening and bounced back. Hammonds cursed and flattened himself against the ground just as the grenade went off only six feet away. The vicious blast blew off his helmet, and fragments tore into his face and shoulders. Another NVA machine gun from the supporting bunker swung toward the three exposed men and stitched the ground in front of them. Cowboy saw the muzzle flash and ran up the slope, shooting to draw the gunner's attention, as Silk and Surf fired at the gun port.

Ty dragged Hammonds back and pulled out his pistol. He crawled to the side of the firing port and rolled, shooting, in front of the portal. The Vietnamese gunner's eyes widened as a bullet grazed his cheekbone and blew a hole through his earlobe. Ty's first target fell with the shot, but another soldier stood inside the bunker staring at him. Ty jammed the pistol into the opening and fired two rounds into the man's face.

Duong felt as if he had been hit in the face with a burning club as he frantically clawed the bloody dirt floor, trying to drag himself toward the tunnel. Only a second before, the replacement had been lifted off his feet and thrown back against the far bunker wall, splattering Duong with blood and brains. Duong knew a grenade would be coming next. He crawled to the tunnel and just made it inside when a blast shook the bunker and filled the tunnel with dust.

Ty threw another grenade into the slit and joined Bugs, who was lying in a bomb crater behind the bunker tending to Hammonds's head wound. He raised up and saw Cowboy lying beside the other bunker portal about to pull a grenade pin. Suddenly, just behind the Texan, two NVA popped up from a trench. One fired a rocket launcher, but the other saw Cowboy and fired his AK-47. The burst hit the thin soldier in the back. He jerked with the impact, dropping the primed grenade, and rolled over. Ty raised his submachine gun, but it was too late. Cowboy was lifted off the ground by the deadly blast.

Bugs grabbed Ty's leg and frantically pointed behind him. NVA were popping out of the trench line only fifteen meters behind them, firing rockets and throwing grenades at the remaining men of Bravo Company. The attack was halted. Dead and wounded paratroopers were raked with gunfire as they lay exposed in the bomb rubble, while the rest of the men sought cover behind fallen trees and in craters. No one was able to move forward. The other bunker's machine gun and the guns in the bunkers farther up the slope were shooting anyone who exposed himself. Rockets swooshed down the slope, and mortar rounds rained down death.

Ty crawled into the crater and looked at his unconscious sergeant. Hammonds's face was ripped open, exposing the gums and teeth of his lower jaw. Bugs had placed a shell casing in his mouth to prop it open so that he could breathe, and not choke on his own blood. His shoulder wounds were bad, but none of the wounds were bad enough to kill him if he got medical attention.

Ty took the safety pin from his bandolier and pinned back the flap of dangling skin from Hammonds's chin to just under his lip.

Bugs cringed and turned his head. "Jesus, Cat. What are we gonna do?"

Ty took off his towel and wrapped it around the sergeant's face, then laid him on his stomach so the wound would drain. "You're going to start digging while I keep us covered."

Major Shelly listened to the situation reports from the company commanders and abruptly stood up. "Get the Second Battalion officers up here, NOW!"

Minutes later, he sat looking into the gaunt faces of Shiler, McDonald, and Johnson. "Men, Fourth Batt is getting waxed. Alpha Company has been chopped to half strength and Bravo has already got over thirty wounded or dead. Bravo is pinned down in front of the first bunker line. Charlie Company has taken moderate casualties and advanced to the trench line, but the poor bastards are being ground up on the flanks. In short, Fourth has been chewed up and spit out. Get the able-bodied from our companies and move them up immediately to help evacuate the Fourth Batt's wounded."

Lieutenant McDonald raised his head in exasperation. "Sir, we only have maybe forty troops who can walk. Who's gonna man the perimeter?''

Shelly realized he'd made a rash decision and softened his voice. "You're right . . . okay, send ten men to help get the wounded."

Jason raised a dirty hand. "I'll take the ten men out."

"No, you stay with the wounded. You know the priorities for evacuation if a bird makes it in."

Jason's eyes focused on the major in a rigid stare. "My brother is in Bravo Company."

Shelly returned the stare for only a second, then cut his eyes to McDonald. "You take charge of the wounded. Have the ten men report to Johnson in this crater in five minutes."

Ty peered over the crater toward the trench where the NVA were periodically popping up and firing B-40 rockets. He didn't see anyone. He shifted his eyes slowly toward the bunker to his left and bit his lip. Cowboy was still alive. The Texan was clawing the dirt, trying to pull himself toward a stump.

"What's a matter?" Bugs whispered, seeing Ty's eyes.

Ty pushed the magazine release and inserted a new magazine. "Cowboy is still hangin' in. I'm gonna crawl to the next bunker and knock it out."

Bugs' eyes widened in disbelief. "Shit, man, it's suicide!"

Ty raised up and looked for a route. "The gunner is lookin' down the hill. If I stay high on the ridge, he won't see me." He could see that Bugs was not convinced and didn't want to be left alone. "Look, it's the only chance we've got to get Sarge and Cowboy back alive. The company is pinned down by that damn gun. We're the only ones that can do it. Just cover me and make sure no dink raises up from the trench and takes a shot."

Bugs looked at Hammonds's still form. "What happens to us if you don't make it?"

Ty checked to see if he had two grenades and patted the buck-toothed soldier's shoulder. "Stay here and hope the company makes it this far. Cover me."

He slid out of the crater and crawled along the side of a shattered tree as Bugs positioned himself to watch the trench line. Ty moved slowly and kept his eyes on the bunker. He quickened his crawl every time the gun fired a burst down the hill, knowing the gunner wasn't looking to his left. Ten minutes passed, adding ten years to Ty's life, before he reached Cowboy, who was lying in a slight depression just behind the bunker. Ty rolled Cowboy over and gagged. The soldier had bled to death. His face was grayish white and his uniform was soaked with blood. Ty gently rolled the body back into the depression and pulled out a grenade. He crawled to the side of the gun port and was about to pull the pin when two NVA rose up from the trench behind him. Bugs fired, hitting one of the men, but missed the other, who ducked down.

Ty yanked the pin, let the lever fly, and counted to two before rolling the grenade into the aperture.

Neither the gunner nor the assistant gunner saw where the grenade came from. The small green bomb fell at their feet, and both men frantically kicked at it to knock it into the sump. It exploded as the gunner's foot struck its side.

Ty tossed in the second grenade and ran toward Bugs.

The Bravo commander rose to his feet as the second device went off and screamed for his men to move forward.

Ty dived into the crater with Bugs and frantically crawled toward Hammonds, who was lying in the bottom of the hole. Out of breath, he lifted the sergeant's head and grabbed his fatigue collar.

"Ty?" Bugs said. "Ty, was he . . ."

Ty struggled to pull Hammonds up the crater wall and screamed in anguish, "He was dead, goddamnit! Help me before it's too late for him, too!"

Bugs glanced over his shoulder and saw the company advancing. He reached out for Ty's arm. "They're gonna take this fucking hill. Nothing can stop th . . ."

From the trenches a platoon of NVA rose up firing B-40 rockets and AK-47s, catching the exposed assault line. Bugs was knocked backward by a bullet blowing through his shoulder. He grunted and tried to sit up but was hit again in the hand. Ty grabbed Bugs's foot and pulled him down into the crater just as incoming mortar shells exploded in front of the bunker.

Major Shelly shook his head, knowing the attack had failed. Lieutenant Shiler lowered the handset. "Sir, the company commanders from Fourth Batt are withdrawing. Alpha and Bravo companies report heavy casualties."

Shelly peered over the crater. "Better get ready to shift artillery to cover their withdrawal."

Shiler spoke loudly to be heard over the incoming mortar rounds. "Not yet, sir. We've got to get the wounded off the ridge."

Jason helped a blinded soldier over a fallen tree and had him sit down with the other walking wounded he had collected over the past few hours. At fifty wounded men, Jason had stopped counting.

It simply didn't matter anymore. It would be easier to count those who weren't hit. Out of the ten men he had brought to recover the wounded, four had themselves become casualties and one had been killed. The dead were left where they fell.

A medic stopped Jason from going outside the perimeter again. "Sir, that's it. They're going to start bringing in the artillery and bombers again in just a few minutes."

Jason turned toward the hill. "What about those who are still out there?"

"Sir, you've done all you could."

Jason quickly turned around. "Where is Bravo Company reorganizing?"

The medic pointed to his right. "I saw the company commander over there by that crater."

"What's the count, Top?" the Bravo commander asked. He wiped his face with a towel.

The first sergeant sighed and let his rifle fall to his side. "We got eleven or twelve killed and about thirty wounded. I can't account for five men, so right now they're missing."

Jason crawled over and knelt down by the exhausted commander. "Sir, I'm looking for Spec-4 Ty Nance. Have you seen him?"

The captain exchanged glances with the first sergeant. "Yeah, I saw him. He took out Bunker 2 and jumped into a crater behind the first bunker. He's dead."

Jason heard the words, but they didn't register. "Sir?"

"Well, I think he bought it," the captain said tiredly. "We lay out there pinned down for hours, and I never saw anybody raise up from the crater. It's not far from the trenches, and the dinks were tossing grenades. I know a few of them exploded in the crater. . . . Top, put Nance in for a Silver Star. He was the one that knocked out the machine gun."

Jason stood up. "Sir, please show me where you saw him last."

The captain frowned. "Goddamn, L-tee, what the hell you wanna know about one man for? Jesus, I had eighty damn good ones and now I've got thirty."

Tears streamed down Jason's face as he looked at the darkening battlefield.

38

Major Shelly turned on his flashlight as soon as he crawled under Lieutenant Shiler's poncho. "McDonald is going to find Johnson. I'm going ahead and briefing you. I'll brief them when they get here. As you already know, the Fourth Batt got stopped cold. They had twenty-two killed and over a hundred wounded. Tomorrow the brigade is gonna blow the shit out of the hill with everything the Air Force has got, and the Fourth Batt will attack again. The good news is we've knocked out most of the NVA machine guns that were shooting down the choppers. Most of the wounded from our battalion got out this evening, and we'll get Fourth's out tonight or tomorrow morning. The birds have brought in all the ammo we'll need."

Shiler lowered his eyes, thanking God the wounded had finally made it to safety. "Sir, why didn't brigade bring in another battalion? Hell, we've had it and so has the Fourth. It's simple math. We had almost six hundred men between us, and we've lost almost four hundred men killed or wounded."

"I don't know," Shelly said and shook his head dejectedly. "The decisions have been made at the highest levels. The battalion commander is coming in tomorrow; maybe he can tell us what is . . ."

"SIR!"

Shelly turned off the flashlight and tossed back the poncho on hearing the loud voice. He looked up at Lieutenant McDonald.

McDonald squatted down. "Sir, Jason has gone outside the perimeter to recover some bodies. We gotta shift the artillery back to the hilltop."

"Johnson did what?" Shelly blurted, sitting up.

Jason stopped crawling and checked the luminous compass dial. He had taken an azimuth from the perimeter to where the Bravo

325

commander had pointed out the first bunker. Darkness had set in, and the compass was the only way he would be able to find the crater.

Silk crawled up beside him and whispered, "We gonna stay on yo' ass. We can't see shit."

Jason closed the compass. "Remind Book Man not to shoot his 16."

Silk backed up and passed the warning to the soldier. The Bravo commander had allowed Jason to ask for volunteers from the company to check the crater for wounded. Six men had volunteered, but Jason took only two from Ty's old squad. Those two had insisted. He couldn't afford a larger patrol because of control problems in the darkness and noise.

He closed the compass and began crawling again. He knew the bunker couldn't be much farther away. Ty was alive, he knew it. He couldn't have died . . . he had promised.

"And you let him go out there?" Major Shelly snarled.

The Bravo Company commander sat up tiredly. "Look, it was his brother. He had to know if he was dead or lying wounded in that crater. Besides, it looks like it's not just Specialist Nance. Top tells me my squad leader and another man aren't accounted for. I bet they're all together in that crater, and the chances are one of them might be alive."

Shelly looked at his watch. "They've got thirty minutes to get back before the jets come in. The mission is planned, and brigade won't cancel it because of a couple of wounded."

The company commander shook his head and leaned back against a stump. "No way can they get back in that time. You might as well add them to the list right now . . . poor bastards."

Jason held his breath as the flare swayed high overhead. It had popped only seconds ago, revealing the bunker firing port three feet in front of him. An artillery round exploded a hundred meters up the hill, shaking the ground, but he was already shaking. In less than a minute he would know if Ty was going to see his hill again. The flare sputtered, then went out. Jason crept forward, praying. He crawled to the side of the bunker and put his hand out to feel for the ground. His fingers touched soil and he scooted forward. He reached out again, but his fingers didn't touch anything—he was on the edge of the crater. Another flare popped, but he didn't duck. Instead, he raised his head and looked into the large shell hole. His stomach knotted and futility swept through his body. The crater was empty.

The flare went out and Jason slid into the crater. He was going to let the others crawl in and turn around before starting back when a whisper came from a small hole to his right. "You move, you die!"

Jason couldn't speak. He was startled, scared, elated, and relieved all at the same time. The whisper was wonderfully familiar. "Ta . . . Ty? It's me."

Ty rose from the dirt like a ghoul and stared at the dark figure in disbelief. "Jay?"

Jason grabbed his brother and hugged him. He had never been so happy in all his life. "I knew you were alive. I knew it!"

Silk crawled in and grabbed Ty. "Man, are we glad to see yo' ass. Where is the rest of the dudes?"

Ty began digging out the hole. "They're in the tunnel. We dug into the crater to protect ourselves and hit the top of the tunnel that leads to the bunker. Come on in and help me get 'em."

Private Duong, with a bandage taped over his cheek and ear, followed two new replacements down the tunnel corridor toward his bunker. The lead soldier held a candle and lit others that were dug into the side of the walls as they made their way through the tunnel. Duong had mixed feelings about going back to his bunker. Three men had died horribly within the small confines, and the other replacement's body was still there. He shivered, thinking about having to pick up the stiff man and clean his brains from the walls.

The lead soldier stopped as he approached the entrance to the trench. "Bui, do we go straight?"

Duong waved the two men forward. "Blow out the candle before entering the trench. The tunnel continues on the other side. It goes down, so watch your step."

The soldier in front of Duong paused. "My squad was responsible for defending this part of the trench. I'm the only one who still lives. The others were buried by the bombs."

"My bunker will protect you from the bombs," Duong said as he gently pushed the soldier forward. "Catch up and help hold the candle so Nguyen can light it once we're in the tunnel again."

Book Man tensed and turned around. "Somebody is coming!" he whispered.

Silk and Jason quickly lowered Hammonds to the floor of the small room dug into the side of the tunnel. The room had been the ammo storage area for the bunker and still had several wooden boxes stacked against the near wall. Ty had placed Bugs and Hammonds in the storage room instead of the bunker because of the stink of the corpse. He pulled Book Man back and raised his pistol.

Nguyen stopped and lit another candle. "The smell is horrible . . . look, the tunnel has partially caved in ahead."

Duong halted to wrap a scarf around his mouth and nose as the two replacements continued ahead.

Ty let the first NVA soldier get within a foot of the storage room before stepping out and shooting him in the face. The second soldier, dropping his weapon, stared frozen in fear at Ty. Ty fired, hitting the man just below the nose. The soldier fell to the dirt floor, revealing a third soldier kneeling five meters back with his rifle raised. Ty didn't have time to pull the trigger.

Duong fired. The bullet struck the dark figure and knocked him backward. He pushed the lever from semi to automatic and pressed the trigger just as a huge man stepped into the tunnel, replacing the first. The soldier jerked with the impact of the AK bullets but didn't fall. Duong emptied half the magazine before the man toppled over, only to have another jump out shooting. Bullets tore into Duong's wrist, forearm, and shoulder. He screamed in pain, backing up and shooting with one hand. Another bullet glanced off the wall and hit him in the head, knocking him to the floor. He rolled over and tried to get up, but he had no more strength. The yellow candlelight above him seemed to be fading. He closed his heavy eyelids. He felt no more pain.

Jason lowered his smoking M-16 and rolled Silk's bullet-riddled body off Ty. He lifted his brother's head. "Ty!" Ty grimaced and clenched his teeth. Jason pulled Ty's hands away and tore open Ty's fatigue shirt. The small bullet hole was four inches below the left nipple. He quickly checked for an exit wound and felt sick when he realized there was none. The bullet had tumbled once on entering the flesh and had done untold damage.

Ty's eyes rolled up. "I . . . I'll make it, get me . . . on my feet."

Jason laid him back gently. "Lie still till I get a bandage on you."

Ty could feel Silk's body weighing on his legs and raised his head to see if the man had made it. One look and he knew. "He . . . he didn't have a chance, the poor . . . Jay, you're hit!"

Jason continued biting the wrapper off the field dressing. Blood was pooling on the floor from a painful leg wound he didn't want to think about.

Book Man squatted in the tunnel and kept his eyes on the corridor ahead. "Lieutenant, the tunnel is clear."

Jason placed the bandage on Ty's wound and began to tie it off. "It won't be for long. Someone was bound to have heard the shots. Get your grenades out."

Bugs dragged himself to the tunnel. "Aw, man, not Silk."

Jason tied the knot on the bandage and stood up, but the stabbing pain in his leg was too much and he went down.

Bugs sat up and faced down into the tunnel. "Get that wound bandaged, L-tee, or you're gonna bleed to death."

Jason lifted his pant leg as he spoke. "Bugs, you can walk and crawl, can't you?"

"Yeah, I can make it."

Jason looked at the bullet hole through his calf and began tearing his pant leg. "Book, you're gonna take the sergeant, and Bugs, you help Ty. I'm gonna stay here a little while and make sure they don't pop us from behind."

Ty slapped the ground, trying to reach his rifle. "I'm . . . I'm staying here with you."

Jason spun around. "You're out of here, and that's an order. Book, Bugs, move it."

Ty picked up his submachine gun and sat up. "Book can't drag Hammonds by himself. Bugs has got to help him."

Bugs looked at Jason and lowered his head. "He's right, L-tee."

"Shit! . . . Okay, but damnit, hurry, get out of here."

Book Man and Bugs grasped Hammonds under the arms and dragged him to the crater. Jason handed his compass to Book Man. "Stay low and stay on a one hundred seventy-five-degree azimuth. We'll give you ten minutes, then start behind you. Good luck."

He crawled back into the tunnel and limped into the storage room. He emptied two of the large wooden ammo boxes and pushed them into the tunnel. Scooping up dirt, he began filling the boxes. "This isn't much, but it ought to stop a few rounds if they come."

Ty looked at his brother's leg and spoke with difficulty. "Plug the hole in . . . that calf."

Jason ripped his pant leg back further and tore off a piece of material. "Brother, looks like we're both going home. I'll be limping down the aisle and probably pushing you in a wheelchair. Cover me. I'm gonna move the bodies into the bunker and blow out the nearest candle. They won't be able to see us, but we'll see them."

The senior sergeant rang the handle of the field phone again and waited for only a second before tossing the phone to the corporal. "They still have not hooked up the phone. I will ring Duong's neck instead of the phone."

The corporal put the receiver back in place. "It may have something to do with the shots reported by Sergeant Ninh."

The senior noncom rolled his eyes. "They heard the Yankees shooting at ghosts. Send a signal repair team to check the wires. If they find Duong has been lazy, I will break his head."

"But the sergeant said the shots sounded like they were in the tunnel."

"You go with the signal team then. You will see that I am right."

The corporal picked up his assault rifle and woke the two communications men behind him. "Come, we have work to do."

Jason looked at his watch. "Those last bombs hit almost on the hilltop. I hope they made it all right. In two more minutes we're going to be out there."

Ty began to speak but heard what he had hoped he wouldn't. He whispered almost inaudibly, "They're coming."

Jason lowered himself behind the boxes. "Hope they don't see the blood on the floor. I didn't have time to cover it very good."

Ty didn't answer as he gently pushed off the safety.

Waving a small flashlight, the corporal led the two sleepy signal repairmen down the corridor. One of the men was checking for breaks in the wire.

He shined his light ahead. He saw a pile of dirt and a hole in the roof of the tunnel. "The tunnel has caved in. Duong? Duong, are you . . ."

Ty fired first, aiming low, hoping to knock them all down. Jason joined in a split second later, able to see his targets easily in the candlelight.

It was over in five seconds. The NVA did not return a single shot. Jason quickly changed magazines. "Come on, we're gettin' out of here.

The marine fighter-bomber swept in low and released its bomb. The 500-pounder whistled toward the dark earth. Jason lifted Ty toward the hole when suddenly the ground shook beneath them. Ty fell backward and immediately both men were covered in dirt.

"What?" the senior sergeant yelled into the phone, unable to hear over the bomb explosions. "Yes, yes, I can hear you now. What did you say before?" He listened for a few seconds and stiffened. "Are you sure it was the sound of Yankee rifles? . . . Yes, yes I believe you; my corporal should have called by now. Send a squad into the trenches above the bunker and fire several flares. Yes, I know it is dangerous, but you must be sure the Yankees are not infiltrating. Place guards at the entrance to the tunnel and stop those who have taken the bunker from going any farther. . . . NO, don't send anybody else in. I will report this to the colonel and see what his orders are.''

Ty dug dirt from his nose and mouth and took in a frantic breath. Jason sat up beside him gagging and spitting. Artillery rounds were raining in above them, shaking the ground. Ty lay back in the sweet-smelling soil and felt incredibly weak. He felt as if a giant were squeezing and twisting his insides. Jason brushed off his rifle and lay down beside him. ''We can't go anywhere for a while. Hang with me, Ty, we're gonna make it.''

Ty dropped his submachine gun and grabbed Jason's arm as another tremor tore through him.

Book Man couldn't move another inch and screamed toward the perimeter, ''Help us!''

A voice only a few feet away responded, causing the slight soldier to jump. ''Good thing you yelled or you'd be history, Mac. We thought you was gooks sneakin' up on us.''

Ten minutes later, Book Man was looking up into the face of Major Shelly. ''Soldier, bringing two wounded back was a heroic action,'' Shelly was saying. ''But I can't let you or anybody else go back for the others. Lieutenant Johnson knew when he went out what his odds were. I'm sorry.''

Book Man got up slowly and looked at the dark outline of the hill that was being pounded by artillery. ''Why, sir? Why is that hill so damn important?''

Shelly lowered his head, feeling sick. He didn't have an answer.

39

Jason bit his lip and repositioned his throbbing leg. His calf felt as if it were on fire. He glanced at Ty, who was lying just inside the storeroom. Ty's face was ash gray. The artillery made impact with thunderous cracks, but the vibrating of the ground seemed to have no effect on him. Jason took a drink from an NVA canteen, then offered the tin bottle to Ty. "Drink the rest of it, you need the fluids."

Ty weakly took the canteen with shaking hands. "We . . . we aren't going . . . going to make it."

Jason shifted his eyes back to the tunnel. "The battalion will be attacking soon. They'll find us. Don't worry. Close your eyes and rest. We're going to need our energy to yell like hell when they get close. We don't want them to toss in a couple of grenades on us."

Ty shut his eyes, but the sharp pain caused him to grind his teeth.

Major Shelly fought the dryness in his mouth and forced himself to speak. "The attack has been called off until tomorrow. Brigade has decided to blow the hill apart for the whole day before the Fourth Batt tries to take it again."

Lieutenant Shiler exchanged glances with McDonald. "Wonder why they didn't think of that two days ago," he muttered. "Are they going to bring some more water in? The little they brought in yesterday wasn't nearly enough. The men have had it."

Shelly ignored the first comment, knowing the officer was exhausted. "Brigade lost ten choppers around this damn hill. The priority is on ammo and getting the wounded out. They'll probably bring the water later."

McDonald shook his head and looked up at sky, trying to hold back his emotions. "Two more of the wounded from the Fourth

332

Batt bled to death this morning. I can't stand this anymore." He broke into tears. "I . . . I can't stand it."

Colonel Huu brushed the dust from his uniform and walked into the briefing room. None of the tired men seated at the small table stood. It was no time for ceremony.

He glanced at their gaunt faces and cleared his throat. "General Duc has ordered our withdrawal. We are not to leave anything for the Americans. All our comrades' bodies will be taken to the storage areas and the tunnels destroyed. The Americans must not find a single body. Nothing can allow them to claim victory. The withdrawal will begin immediately through the east tunnel. The outer ring will pull back now, the middle ring in thirty minutes, and the command and center ring will withdraw at fifteen hundred hours. Comrades, leave nothing and ensure the tunnels' entrances are destroyed. That is all, except to say I am proud of every one of you."

As the weary men rose and hurried toward the tunnel corridors, Sergeant Ninh approached the colonel. "Comrade, the infiltrators are still cornered in the access tunnel to Bunker 1. Should I attack now and destroy them?"

Huu stared blankly at the earthen wall. "What would be the cost?"

Ninh's eyes slowly lowered. "Four, maybe six men before we could overcome them."

Huu motioned for his operations officer and spoke softly to the young sergeant. "No. If they still live, so be it. Enough of our men have died. Withdraw immediately." Huu placed his hand on the operations officer's shoulder. "Everyone is to withdraw except the mortar crews on the ridge behind the complex. They only are to remain and fire when the Yankees attack. That will be the last of the killing. The men who held this hill have done enough."

Jason's head snapped up and he looked at his watch. Damn it, he'd been out for forty-five minutes. He could hardly focus his eyes anymore, he was so tired. He leaned over and wiped sweat from Ty's forehead. "You still hangin' tough?"

Ty slowly opened his eyes. "Ja . . . Jay, I'm not gonna make it." Tears welled up and trickled down the sides of his face. "I . . . I can't move anymore."

Jason's chin quivered and he took the chain from around his neck. He lifted Ty's head and put the chain around his neck. He held up the wings. "Look here, brother, the wings; they're lucky, remember? Ten jumps between us and not a scratch. You hang tough. We're Red Hill Paratroopers, remember?''

Ty smiled weakly and lifted his hand to touch the silver badge. He looked at Jason and spoke thickly. "Take care of mom, Jay. I'm the third one she's lost this way, ya know. . . .'' His eyelids fluttered. "Take care . . . care of my hill.''

Jason clenched his teeth and fought back the tears. "You'll take care of it yourself. Don't give up on me now. Ty . . . Ty, you can't give up now.''

Ty's eyes slowly closed. "I . . . I love you . . . Jay.''

Jason shook as tears streamed down his face. "NO! YOU'RE NOT DYING ON ME, YOU PROMISED! YOU'RE GOING HOME . . . YOU HEAR ME? YOU'RE GOING HOME!'' Jason tossed his rifle away and picked Ty up in his arms. He stood, pitched over, and got to his feet again. "You're going home, brother.''

The forward observer looked through his binoculars at the hill and watched the impact of his adjusted artillery rounds. He raised the radio handset without lowering the glasses. "Right five zero, drop five . . . what the hell?''

He leaned forward with the handset bar still depressed. "Holy shit! CEASE FIRE, CEASE FIRE!''

The young artillery officer spun around and yelled toward the command post, "WE GOT FRIENDLIES COMING IN!''

Jason stumbled to his knees and talked aloud as he forced himself up. "We love it. It ain't gonna get better. Fuck 'em; we can hang, no matter what. We're crazy, Ty. We're Red Hill Paratroopers. . . . We're gonna make it.''

Major Shelly stood and saw a big blond soldier limping over the debris-covered ridge, carrying a man in his arms. "Goddamn it, put covering fire out for them! SHOOT DAMN IT!''

Jason didn't flinch as rifle and machine-gun bullets cracked past on both sides of him. He kept moving, ignoring the pain in his leg, and set his eyes to the front. "We bad, Ty, real bad. We can take anything; they can't kill us. You're going home.''

A medic ran forward and met Jason as he limped into the perimeter. "I'll take him, sir . . . sir! . . . sir, put him down and let me see him!''

Jason brushed by the medic and kept moving down the slope to where a resupply bird was coming in.

Major Shelly ran up to Jason. "You crazy bastard, you made it! The old man will want to see you and . . . Jason? Jason, stop walking and put him down for the medics . . . Jason, stop!''

Jason ignored the officer. "They have a bird for you, Ty, they're gonna take you back and fix you up and then fly ya home. Mom will fix you sausage and gravy."

He limped up to the whining helicopter that was being loaded with wounded and set Ty on the vibrating floor. Shelly grabbed Jason's arm and spun him around. "Snap out of it, Lieutenant! I need a report on what you saw in the tunnel."

The crew chief leaned over the put his fingers on Ty's neck.

Jason stared through the major and spoke in a snarl.

The crew chief frowned and grabbed Ty's fatigue sleeve, pulling him toward the door. Jason turned around just as the chief spoke to an approaching litter team.

"This one's dead. Give me a live one—we don't haul stiffs!"

Jason grabbed the crew chief's hands, stopping him from tossing out his brother's body. "He's alive and he's going home; he promised!"

Major Shelley waved the crew captain back and nodded to the pilot to take off. He pushed Jason toward the bird. "Get on!"

Shelley stepped back as the chopper shook and began to lift off. He lowered his head and turned to avoid the biting dust. "Take him home, Lieutenant. At least someone knows what they're doing!"

The triage doctor walked past a row of waiting wounded and knelt beside the soldier a litter team had just set down. He felt for a pulse. "This one didn't make . . . wait a sec!" He lifted his stethoscope and pushed back the paratrooper's fatigue shirt. He listened for a few seconds and spoke over his shoulder to his assisting male nurse. "Get me ringers started here stat! He goes in now!"

The doctor didn't notice the large officer lying on the ground beside the wounded man, holding his hand.

Book Man walked down the rows of wounded and stopped beside the eleventh cot. Bugs's eyes shifted to the visitor. "Book! God, I didn't think I'd see anybody before they shipped me out. You ain't hurt, are you?"

Book Man tiredly sat down on the end of the cot and pushed his glasses back on his nose. "No, I'm fine. I just wanted to see if everybody made it okay. Hammonds was shipped to Japan, and they say you're going, too."

Bugs lifted his head toward the opening of the tent. "Where's Surf? And what about Cat?"

Book Man lowered his head. "Surf didn't make it. Yesterday the

Fourth Batt attacked the hill, and us guys in the Second Batt evacuated the wounded. Surf was hit by a mortar round.''

Bugs closed his eyes, fighting the queasy emptiness he felt in the pit of his stomach. ''And Cat?''

Book Man stared at his filthy hands. ''It doesn't look good. They shipped him to Japan the same day he came in. He was tore up real bad inside.''

Bugs clenched his fists tightly. ''How many fuckers did we kill on that stinkin' hill?''

Book Man stood up, knowing that only a few bodies had been found. An accountability formation had determined that of the 540 men who went up the hill from the two battalions, less than 200 were able to walk back down the ridge, and many of those were walking wounded. He extended his hand. ''It doesn't matter. They say in *Stars and Stripes* we won. Take care, Bugs. I was proud to be in the family . . . you're going to be one helluva postman.''

The staff officers let the solemn General Duc walk ahead. He would want to be alone. The old soldier stepped through the powdery dust and stopped at the hill's crest. The tree he used to sit beside was gone, obliterated like the others. The hilltop was nothing but a desolate, barren scar. The leafless, battered trees farther down the slope were the only signs that life had once existed.

This battlefield would never have a monument erected on it, he knew. Years from now, no visitors would want to come back for the memories. To the politicians, Hill eight hundred seventy-five was already forgotten. It had no more value, no special significance that made it different from other countless hills in his country; it was just another hill. The blood spilled meant nothing, nothing except to him and the men who had fought here.

He sat down on a fallen tree and listened to the silence. He listened as if he could still faintly hear the rumble of artillery, the chatter of machine guns, the screaming men. Only the survivors would understand and remember. Only those who fought on the hill would be able to hear the sounds in the wind.

The general lowered his head, knowing time would allow his heart to mend, but like this hill, he, too, would never be the same. He would never forget his old friend or his fallen men. The sounds in the wind would be with him forever.

40

Jason moaned as he writhed on the wet sheets. The screams were getting louder. Mediiiiic . . . MEDIIIIIC! They're attacking! Bring those guns up! He's dead, sir! INCOMING! Wa . . . water, please, sir. THE FLANKS! Oh, God! His guts are falling out! Help meeeee! Please help me, L-tee. I . . . I can't feel my feet.

He groaned and bolted upright, covering his ears to stop the pathetic cries.

Mea wiped his forehead with a cool washcloth and gently pushed him down. "Lay back, honey," she said softly. "Everything is all right. We're here."

Jason's eyes focused. "I'm sorry, Mom."

Duane leaned over. "Don't worry about a thing, son. You're home now."

Jason took his mother's hand and sat up again. "I didn't mean to wake the whole house." He patted the cast on his lower leg. "I guess I shoulda stayed a little longer in the hospital. This thing still hurts like hell."

Duane sat down on the bed and put his arms around his son's shoulders. "You had to be home for Christmas. We're a family."

Jason patted his dad's back and got out of bed. "Go on. Everybody get back in bed. I'm fine. The pain just got to me. I'm gonna take a couple a painkillers and watch TV until I get tired."

Duane left, knowing he wanted to be alone, but Jason noticed his mother's searching stare as she continued to stand there. He waved her away. "Go on, I'm fine. Really."

Mea nodded in silence and handed him the crutches. Jason absently tossed them to the bed. The cast had a rubber pad on the bottom and he preferred to walk. "Thanks, they just get in the way. Go to bed, Mom."

337

Mea let him pass her before remarking uncertainly, ''I thought your leg hurt.''

Jason looked guiltily over his shoulder. ''Please, Mom, go to bed.''

In the darkness, Jason sat in his brother's chair and began rocking. The blinking cedar tree's lights reminded him that Ty wouldn't be home in time for Christmas.

Jason set his shoulders. He had to try. He hadn't been able to look at Red Hill without thinking of eight hundred seventy-five. The sight of the cabin made him think there was hope. It brought back warm memories. Walking up the path, he tried to keep his thoughts on those days when he and Ty were building the cabin, but the barren trees ahead brought him other, more powerful memories. He broke into a sweat despite the cold wind whipping his face. Unconsciously, he looked left, then right, checking the sides of the trail for a place to take cover if . . .

He reached the huge trees and halted. Beneath their gnarled branches the wounded lay in ragged rows. They were all looking at him with pleading ashen faces. ''Help us . . . help us, pleeease.''

He shook uncontrollably. There were Bagley, Reddy, Ferguson, Sawyer. Chaplain Waters looked up and smiled sadly. ''Jay, you have any water to spare?''

Sergeant Harper stood holding a canteen cup. ''Got any coffee, L-tee?''

Jason clamped his eyes shut, but then he heard the mortars landing with their sickening, ear-shattering WHABOOM! . . . WHABOOM! . . . ''Medic! Mediiiic!''

A fighter streaked overhead and artillery rumbled in the distance. ''THEY'RE COMING! COME ON, MOTHERFUCK-ERRRRRS!''

He turned around and walked quickly down the trail, avoiding the bodies littering the path. He didn't want to touch the ghosts of the past.

Sheriff Hamby got out of his cruiser and walked up the back steps. He knocked and smiled when Mea opened the door. ''Howdy, Mea, is Jason home?''

Minutes later, Jason sat in the front seat of the sheriff's car. ''Cliff, now explain to me again why you want me to talk to this drunken soldier you picked up.''

Hamby pulled out of the driveway. ''There ain't no drunk GI.

That was just a story to get ya out of the house so your mom wouldn't ask questions. I picked you up as a favor for somebody.''

Jason looked at him questioningly. "What the heck you talkin' about? . . . Why we goin' this way? Town is back there. Cliff, what's going on?"

Hamby kept his eyes straight ahead. "You'll see. Just sit back and relax. In just a few minutes, you'll know."

Hamby pulled off the highway onto the dirt road and a minute later rolled the car to a stop in front of the cabin. He motioned toward the hilltop. "He's waiting for you up there. I don't know why he wanted it this way, but it's important to him. He wanted to see you before he saw the rest of the family. Go on. He's waiting."

Jason began trembling. "Ty? Ty is here?" He threw open the door. "He wasn't supposed to be home until the fifth. Cliff, this isn't a joke of some . . .''

Hamby shifted into reverse. "He's waitin', son."

Still wearing the cast, Jason walked as fast as he could. He didn't think about the past or hear anything but the wind as he strode up the hill.

He broke out of the woodline and saw a figure in a sergeant's uniform standing on the hilltop, looking over the valley. His spit-shined jump boots glistened in the sunlight as he turned around. The Class A Army greens fit him perfectly, and his silver parachute wings caught the glint of the sun.

Jason heard himself whisper, "Cat." The man standing ahead of him was horribly thin, and on his face was the same strange smile Jason had noticed the first time he had seen him in Nam. All that was missing was the low-riding pistol.

The sergeant raised his hand in a salute. "This ol' coon dog is back."

Tears rolled down Jason's cheeks as he tried to run up the hill. The two men met at the crest, embracing each other in a bear hug. Ty squeezed his brother tightly, ignoring the pain in his chest. "I missed ya, brother. I thought about you every day and night. You got me home."

Jason returned the hug. "God, it's good to see you! I've missed your ugly face." Grabbing his shoulders, he gently pushed Ty back. "Jesus, Mom is going to be pissed that you didn't call. We were all going to pick you up at the airport."

He grasped Ty's arm to lead him down the path, but Ty stopped him and looked into his eyes. "It's truth time," he said softly.

Jason smiled to cover the discomfort his brother's strange look caused him. "Whatta ya talkin' about? You have people to see and . . ."

"We'll go home when it's over," Ty said. "The hunt needs to end . . . it's time."

Jason kept his weak smile. "Ty, I loved George, but I don't believe in all that stuff he told you. If you have to go, I'll understand, but it's not for me. I'll try and explain to Mom but . . ."

Ty walked to the log bench and picked up his old pack. "I got the stuff we need from the cabin. I won't go without you, and I know you wouldn't do that to me. You care for me too much. Come on."

Jason's shoulders sagged. "That's not fair, Ty."

The sergeant nodded in silence and began walking down the path. He passed the old oaks without looking back. He knew his brother was following him.

Jason tossed and turned on the wool blanket and suddenly sat up, looking into the darkness. The sounds of pleading men were replaced by the soft crackling of the fire. Ty was sitting across from him, his face golden in the fire's glow.

He wiped the sweat from his forehead, yet he shivered from the cold and scooted closer to the fire. He looked at Ty again and could see that he was worried. He shut his eyes, knowing he couldn't lie to him. "They're so DAMN real. I can see and hear them like it was . . . like . . ." He lowered his head. The explanation was locked somewhere inside him.

Ty looked past him into the darkness. "Like it was happening all over again? You're there seeing and feeling it but can't seem to say or do anything to change what happened . . . they die anyway?"

Jason lifted his head. "How did you know?"

Ty kept his distant stare. "I've had a lot of practice. I used to dream about my dad. I would even come here and . . ."

Jason felt his heart breaking as he listened to Ty. He had lived with him for years and had never known. His eyes began to pool and he felt guilty for not loving his brother more and understanding. And yet in his heart he knew there would have been nothing he could have said or done. Nothing would have stopped Ty from praying, hoping, and dreaming his dad would return.

He closed his eyes to stem the tears. Like his brother, there was nothing he could have done to save his men.

Ty shifted his legs. ". . . the dreams of Dad went away in Nam.

They were replaced by the guys who were in my squad. We called the squad a family. Funny how close you get, but it was a family. The first one in the family to get hit was Teddy Bear. We were walking on this paddy dike and . . .''

Hours later, Jason huddled against Ty for warmth. ''. . . when I looked at my RTO lying there after they hit our flank, I wanted to lay down and cry. Bagley was from Vermont and always talked about home and going skiing. I thought he was nuttier than a fruit-cake, loving the cold the way he did. Now I know he was . . . I'm freezing my ass off.'' Jason chuckled and felt strange hearing him-self laugh. ''Damn, that cedar smells good, doesn't it?'' he said.

Ty quietly stood and placed his blanket over Jason's still form lying by the fire. He had known the second he looked into Jason's eyes that his spirit had been taken. The men in his old platoon and the wounded and dead on eight hundred seventy-five had taken it.

He moved closer to the fire and stared at the red embers. The glowing coals crackled as he lifted his head. Today he had discov-ered a new truth: Jason's spirit hadn't been taken. His brother had given it, willingly. He had given all of himself, but it had not been enough . . . it would never have been enough. The men he had loved had been Chosen.

The past days together, sharing tears and laughter, the Chosen had restored most of Jason's spirit but, as always, they had kept a small part. It was their way of never being forgotten. The Chosen would never leave his dreams, but their pain and pleas had been stored away for only the sad days. Their suffering had been replaced by their smiles, laughter and the memories of the better times.

Ty lay down and looked up at the stars. It was time to go home. The hunt was over.

About the Author

Lt. Col. Leonard B. Scott served in Vietnam with the 173rd Airborne and 75th Rangers. His combat decorations include the Silver Star, Purple Heart, and Combat Infantryman badge. Born in Minco, Oklahoma, Scott has returned to stateside duty from his previous post in Berlin.